FOR NO MORTAL CREATURE

By Keshe Chow

The Girl with No Reflection

For No Mortal Creature

FOR NO MORTAL CREATURE

KESHE CHOW

Delacorte Press

Delacorte Press
An imprint of Random House Children's Books
A division of Penguin Random House LLC
1745 Broadway, New York, NY 10019
penguinrandomhouse.com
GetUnderlined.com

Editor: Lydia Gregovic
Cover Designer: Casey Moses
Interior Designer: Michelle Canoni
Production Editor: Colleen Fellingham
Managing Editor: Tamar Schwartz
Production Manager: Shameiza Ally

Library of Congress Cataloging-in-Publication Data is available upon request.
ISBN 978-0-593-89847-5 (trade) — ISBN 978-0-593-89849-9 (ebook) —
ISBN 979-8-217-12262-2 (int'l edition)

The text of this book is set in 11.5-point Baskerville.

Manufactured in the United States of America
1st Printing

For those who have lost a loved one,
and then had to find themselves

Level One

Level Two

Level Three

Level Four

Level Five

The Death Realm

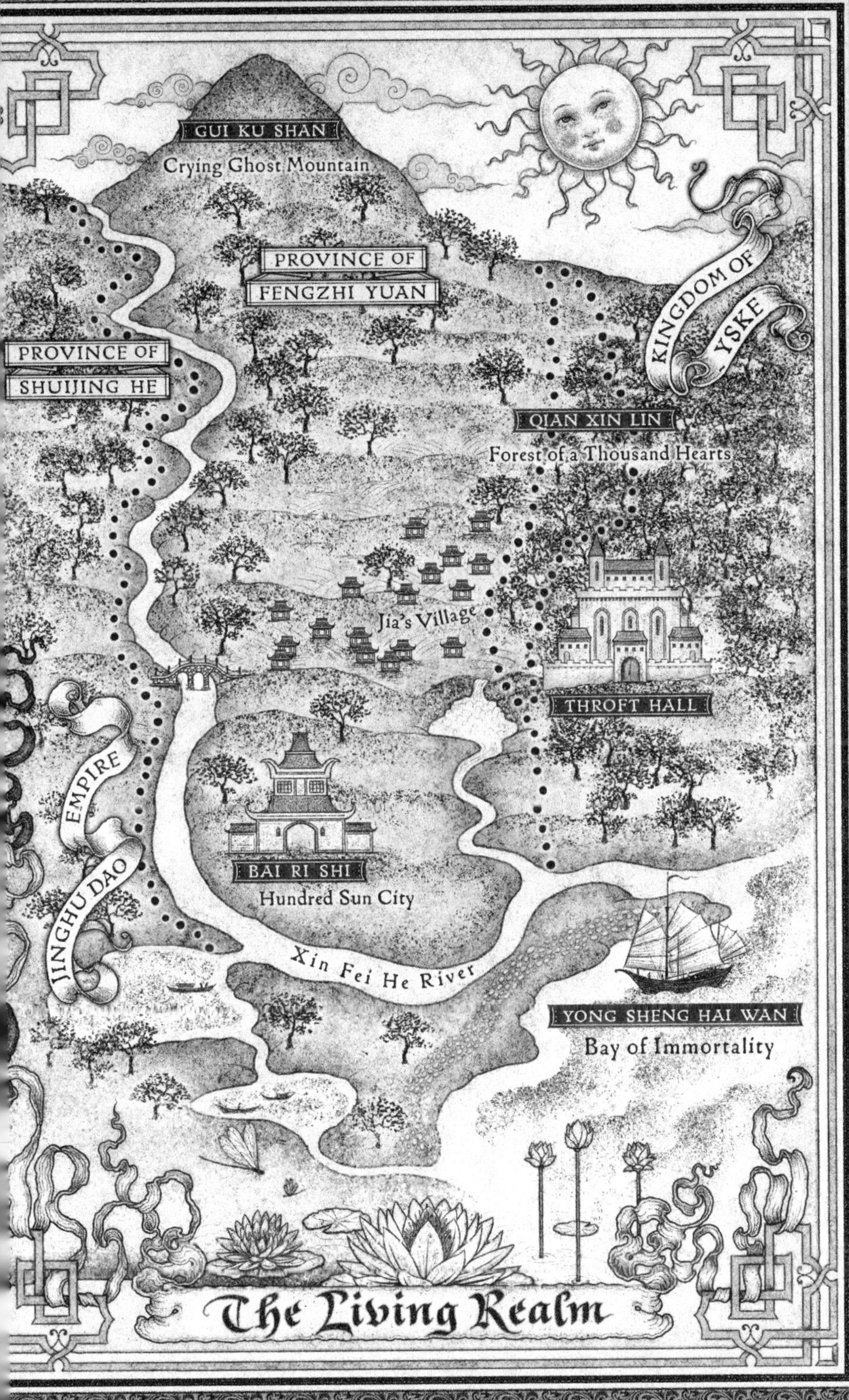

GUI KU SHAN
Crying Ghost Mountain
PROVINCE OF FENGZHI YUAN
KINGDOM OF YSKE
PROVINCE OF SHUIJING HE
QIAN XIN LIN
Forest of a Thousand Hearts
Jia's Village
THROFT HALL
EMPIRE JINGHU DAO
BAI RI SHI
Hundred Sun City
Xin Fei He River
YONG SHENG HAI WAN
Bay of Immortality

The Living Realm

If all else perished, and *he* remained, I should still
continue to be;
and if all else remained, and he were annihilated,
the universe would turn to a mighty stranger:
I should not seem a part of it.

—Emily Brontë, *Wuthering Heights*

人死为鬼
鬼死为聻
When people die, they become ghosts,
when ghosts die, they become jiàn.

—Pu Songling, *Strange Tales from a Chinese Studio*

One

Present day

In the low light of the falling dusk, I found myself thus: half bent over, hands full of Shadowside, the point of a longsword against my neck.

A voice spoke from behind me. "Rise, trespasser," it said, "and drop your loot."

For a frozen, empty moment, I stayed still, weighing my chance of escape. Everything around me—every sensation—distilled into sharp focus. The forest, silent with the promise of unfallen snow. Dewdrops that sparkled on dried leaves beneath my feet. My heartbeat pounding in my ears.

Could I make a run for it? I was alone, and a good way off the open road, meaning I could potentially lose a pursuer in the dark, dense forest. But making even a single movement might prompt my attacker to drive in their blade. And foolishly, I was unarmed, having stowed my dagger in my boot.

No. There was no way to escape this mess.

Inwardly, I cursed my poor decision-making and begrudgingly dropped the herbs.

As soon as they hit the forest floor, the delicate purple flowers began to wilt, disintegrating into the smattering of frost atop the soil. It was shuāngjiàng, late October, season of the Frost's Descent, and even this far south the ground was laced with ice.

I clenched both fists, nails digging into palms, and willed myself not to scream.

Seeing the flowers dying was like a knife twist to the gut. I'd spent days traveling here on foot, with nothing more than a dagger and my wits, making camps up trees to keep safe overnight. And just before I was accosted, I'd spent upward of half an hour sawing through the woody stems with an increasingly blunt blade, cursing as my hands stung, cramped, and blistered. There was a narrow time window to gather Shadowside, and that was now—at the confluence of day and night. At this precise moment, its effects were most potent. Any delays in harvesting it meant the power would wane, rendering it useless, and *damnit* I needed those herbs.

Without them, my grandmother would die.

My heart hammering, I rose slowly, raising my hands to show I was weaponless. Well, my hands were, at least. I didn't volunteer any information about what was in my boot.

"Turn around," the voice said, gruff.

"Remove your blade, then, so I may do so without slicing my neck." I managed to keep my voice even. Internally, though, I wanted to scream. While I wasn't *technically* doing anything wrong by hunting—or gathering plants—this interruption was wasting valuable time.

The sword's pressure relented, just slightly, and I spun to face my attacker.

Typical, I thought, suppressing the urge to roll my eyes. A Lancaster soldier. They were always crawling around the forest like cockroaches: ugly, armored, and almost impossible to kill.

Like most of them, this one was pale, his shadowed eyes gray in the crepuscular light. If it was daytime, they would probably be blue. His helmet hid the color of his hair, but not the thin rivulets of sweat coursing down his face. Clad in iron, he bore the Lancaster sigil—a blue-and-white shield with the silhouette of a tree—upon his chest. Compared to the thin cotton of the hànfú I was wearing, and my feigned indifference, he looked positively overdressed.

"To what do I owe this honor, My Lord?" I said, masking the subtle sneer in my voice. I'd used the Trader's Tongue, the mashed-up dialect that had evolved along the towns and ports that lined the Stone Road, the primary route for trade. With its innumerable clashing cultures, the road's dialect obscured some of the more expository accents of each region, though my black hair, brown eyes, high cheekbones, and pearlescent skin would no doubt mark me as being from west of the border.

"Declare yourself, woman," he demanded, his voice cracking on the last word.

"Liu Jia Yi." I gave my name promptly. No point lying.

The Lancaster soldier pushed on his sword again, the tip indenting the flesh of my neck. "Tell me," he said, and I felt the tremor in his hands. "What are you doing hunting in the Forest of Seld?" His eyes flicked to the dead hare tied to my belt. Earlier that day I'd found it caught in one of my trusty snares.

The last vestiges of daylight slanted through the trees, their skeletal shadows gradually being swallowed by the slowly creeping dark. The boy's breaths had grown uneven; his shoulders had gone rigid; the black of his pupils had flared wide. And it struck me, what he must be feeling, facing me:

Fear.

Great, I thought. *A new one.*

The Lancaster family, who ruled the neighboring country of Yske, had a habit of rotating their roving guard on a reasonably regular basis. The official explanation was that they wanted to ensure their ranks were trained evenly. In truth, I suspected the royal family just had little regard for human lives, even those who were born, lived, and died to serve them. Even those sent out here to patrol the trader routes. *Especially* those sent out here to patrol the trader routes.

The royals, safely ensconced in the Yskian capital, cared little for the fortunes of people stationed at such a far-flung outpost. To them it didn't matter if they sent unblooded youths into such a violent area. If the soldiers survived, they'd be subsequently drafted elsewhere. If they didn't, well . . . There were always more.

"It is only named the Forest of Seld to you," I bit back. My courage was bolstered by the knowledge my attacker was more afraid of me than I of him. "To us, it is Qian Xin Lin."

The Forest of a Thousand Hearts. In the greater scheme of things, it was nothing but a sliver of woodland between the two territories. On one side, the kingdom of Yske. And on our side, its oldest enemy, the Jinghu Dao Empire.

Battles between the two were constant, but the last war between Jinghu Dao and Yske, around three hundred years ago, had been particularly bloody. It had raged for years, neither side gaining dominance over the other. That is, until my empire had revealed its secret weapon: magic.

My ancestors, a clandestine group of sorcerers and sorceresses, had been approached by the army general of the time. He'd recruited them, unleashing their powers at the last moment in order to defeat the rival army. The Yskian's front line, taken by surprise, had been flattened. The remainder were forced to retreat.

Now the forest was all that separated our two territories. Supposedly neutral, this thin sliver of land was the only place along the Stone Road that belonged to no one, that had no rule.

Qian Xin Lin was known to be cruel, vicious, unforgiving—rife with thievery and banditry and all manner of unspeakable things. But to my community it was life-giving. It was the only patch of forest in this Mothers-forsaken region that had anything approaching sufficient game, our main source of protein. The forests in our own province had been stripped bare; hunted to the ground.

Judging by the pattern of the growing moss and the loose formation of the trees, I *had* strayed quite close to the Yskian border. But I couldn't help it. These conditions were favorable for growing the Shadowside that I needed. For the *medicine* I needed.

This soldier was shaking, the sword trembling in his obviously sweaty hands. He couldn't be more than seventeen. My own age. Just a boy. A boy holding a girl at swordpoint in a forest.

"It is . . ." He swallowed visibly. "It is dangerously close to Lancaster territory, my lady. I would suggest you—"

I never got to hear what he suggested, because his words were cut off by the boom of a deep, coarse voice.

"What is this, boy?" the voice demanded. Its bearer, a brawny man with a trimmed black beard and closely cropped hair, strode into view. He looked down at me, a leer twisting his features, his face cracked in a grin. "What are you doing with this rat? *Romancing* her?"

The boy's sword trembled even more, and I almost felt sorry for him. Almost, but not quite. The sword he'd pushed against my neck had a rather negative effect on my sympathies, quite frankly.

Anyhow, I had more pressing matters to attend to than the Lancaster boy's comfort. When it had been him and him alone, I could probably have acted contrite, uttered some pretty niceties, and been sent on my merry way. This new man, though, I'd seen before. He was Andres Brisson, the lieutenant general, one of the prince's right-hand men. He had a reputation for being ruthless, for living by the book. And he was currently regarding me like I was an insect he would sooner squash beneath his boot.

"N-no, sir," the boy stammered, and he pushed on the sword a little harder, as if for emphasis. A sharp sting made me wince. The metallic tang of blood—my blood—permeated the air, and Brisson's grin spread even wider. "I was interrogating her, sir."

Brisson leaned forward, his sour breath fanning my face. "No need to interrogate, boy," he said. "I've seen this one before. She's one of *them*. One of the hidden ones. A filthy"—he spat on the ground—"*witch*."

The boy's eyes widened incrementally and his voice wavered, but valiantly, he held his ground. "A w-witch?"

I almost snorted, but suppressed it, just. My family and I, we weren't witches. Not really. But the Yskian's uncreative use of language meant they didn't *have* a name for what we were.

"Aye." Brisson sneered. "And neutral territory or no, witchcraft is illegal. Will you skewer her, or shall I?" Brisson spoke with bravado, but all three of us knew it was just a front. Prince Essien Lancaster, the sixth son of Yske and the emissary for the region, was the only person in their territory who could condemn, or pardon, a prisoner.

No. Brisson could not kill me without angering his superiors. The most he could do was haul me to the fort, where, as usual, the prince would interrogate me, give me a scare, and then begrudgingly release me. Normally, this was nothing more than a mildly irritating waste of time.

But today? Today it was inconceivable. My Pópo, my grandmother—the person I loved most in the world—was dying. The very thought was enough to stop me breathing; a vise around my throat. *Time* was not something we had to spare.

I suppose that was why I did it.

Andres Brisson took a single step forward, crushing the Shadowside beneath his heel. Anger flared to life in my veins. All I could hear was the roar of my pulse pounding in my ears.

Twisting away from the boy's sword, I unsheathed the dagger in my boot. My arm drew back, ready to slash, stab, or throw the blade, whatever tactic might allow me to get away and *run*.

The boy made no move. He just stood there, his mouth forming a comical O. It was Brisson who lunged forward, grabbing my arm and twisting it in the wrong direction until I screamed. The dagger dropped to the ground, and I thrashed, trying to claw and bite my way to freedom. But Brisson just held me facing away, my back pressed up against him. In my peripheral vision, I saw him palm the pommel of his sword.

He leaned over my shoulder, reeking of sweat and ale and blood, and spoke low into my ear.

"A gift, from Prince Essien," he said, and drove the sword right through my back.

Two

THE FIRST LEVEL
Present day

When I used to picture dying, I thought it would be like one of two things. Either everything would suddenly go black, empty, void-like, eternal. Or else there would be a rush of memories—ones that had been buried deep—that would float to the surface of my mind like detritus from the sea.

My actual death was like neither of those things. It was not painful, nor peaceful, nor tinged with gentle nostalgia. Instead, it was like being plunged into a murky world that, while looking very much like my own, was not.

It was like holding my breath. Like waiting. Like existing in the space between unspoken words.

I squinted, attempting to adjust my eyesight to the gloom. Everything looked the same, except blurrier. The same trees that stood tall, like ghostly apparitions. The same moss-covered forest floor underfoot. The same arching sky, the first lone stars winking into existence.

Dark figures moved around me, weaving between shadowy trunks. My body felt strange; not quite tangible, and certainly out of step with reality. *I should be afraid*, I thought, pressing a hand against my hollow chest, alarmed at the absence of a heartbeat.

Of course my heart was silent—I was dead. And this was the afterlife. Wasn't it? There was no way I could have lived, no way I could have survived such a brutal blow. My fingers strayed to the jagged hole in my gown, prodding the wound beneath. It was present, a puckered mess, but surprisingly it wasn't painful.

A shiver of dread trickled down my spine. Brisson's sword must have run right through me. In our community, we learned about the afterlife as soon as we could walk. Not to fear it, necessarily—but to respect it. And for me, death had been ever-present since the day that I was born.

It was . . . unbelievable, but I'd died. Before my grandmother did.

Just as a shaman had once predicted.

Trying to touch something solid, something real, I stretched my arm out into the darkness. Initially I felt nothing. I could see very little. But then a large, ice-cold hand closed across my wrist. Gasping, I jerked back. The hand gripped tighter and drew me toward it.

"Jia Yi," a voice said, out of the blackness. And the voice that spoke, its honeyed timbre, was as familiar to me as my own.

I screamed, trying to wrench away but failing to release the creature's grip. And then a face, *his* face, materialized into view, looking so much like a suspended moon.

Lin. My childhood friend. Once, he'd been the most important person in my life, equal only to my grandmother. Until he'd betrayed me. Badly.

Then he'd died.

And now, here in the afterlife, my dying brain was invoking visions of him. Why? What had I done to deserve this? Shouldn't my mind be helping me to relive my most pleasant memories?

Not this. Please. Why was it showing me *Lin*?

"No," I croaked out. "You're dead." It took only a fractional second for me to take in his familiar features. He looked identical to when he'd been alive. He had the same hair, one dark lock escaping across his brow. The same bronze skin, the same square jaw. Heavy brows, knitted in fury, drawn down over glittering eyes. He had the look of a boy on the cusp of manhood, his smooth face incongruous with his height and the broadness of his chest.

He hadn't changed one bit since the day he'd died. Except, perhaps, for the shadowy suggestion of a bruise upon his forehead, he had not a single mark on him.

"You are dead too," he said. The slash of his smile was more a grimace. "What did you *do*, Jia? You shouldn't be here. You are not supposed to be *here*." His eyes burned into mine, black pupils dilated into two hollow voids.

He brought his free hand to my décolletage. My skin froze beneath his fingertips, and everything within me tightened. His features twisted into something savage as he traced a slow path down my chest, stopping just above my wound. "What happened?"

I slapped him away from my chest. "Why do you care?"

Seemingly by reflex, he grabbed my arm and pulled me closer. Casting a dark look at our surroundings, as though watching for predators, he snarled, "You shouldn't be here. Tell me: What. Happened?"

My chest heaved, as though trying to draw breath, but no such breath came. "Andres Brisson happened," I snapped. "He stabbed me."

"Brisson?" He spat out the name, then shook his head. "I leave you alone for mere minutes, and . . ." His fingers flexed, digging into my skin. "I'll kill him."

This time, I looked up at him. Properly. Those granite-hewn features, the glower twisting his otherwise handsome face. And his irises, which were a rich amber, shifting, enigmatic, as unfathomable as deep water.

What did he mean, mere minutes? It had been *a year.* A year since he'd died. A year since he'd abandoned me. A year since he'd done something . . . unforgivable.

We were different people back then. We weren't ghosts, for one.

And now he was acting like none of that had happened? As though he hadn't moved on and forgotten me, and I hadn't spent all that time seething with bitter resentment.

I squinted at his face, trying to read him like I used to. But I'd lost the ability.

Which meant I had only one option: escape.

I brought my knee up and shoved it—hard—into his groin. He grunted, staggered backward, and let me go. I took the opportunity. I turned my back on him and *ran.*

I'd always been a fast runner. But not fast enough. His footsteps drew closer, gaining quickly. Before long, he would tackle me to the ground. Or I'd trip over a tree root, or get snagged by a branch, or stumble over the soiled, trailing hem of my skirt.

So I did the only thing I could think of. When I reached the nearest tree, I turned. Taking all the fury I had in my body, I channeled it into my arm, then punched him square in the face.

Pain exploded across my knuckles. I screamed. Blood welled from the wound—I'd split my hand on Lin's annoyingly angular jaw.

For a loaded moment he did nothing, just stared at me, clasping his cheek.

But then he sighed and used the back of his hand to swipe away the trickle of black blood on his chin. *Good*, I thought. *I made* him *bleed, too*. In this realm, in the afterlife, blood was so dark it was almost black, apparently.

Lin's lips pressed together like he was trying to suppress a smile. He reached out and cupped my own jaw with his hand. Almost tenderly. Almost lovingly. It evoked such . . . nostalgia . . . it made me sick. His touch burned, despite the fact that he was cold and dead—as was I.

I jerked away. Immediately, the humor in Lin's face evaporated, and he shoved me against the tree, pinning me by the shoulder.

My entire body went numb as I watched him slowly draw out a long, curved knife. It glowed blue in a strange, unearthly way. He pressed the knife against my throat, forcing me to tip my chin up, the bark of the tree trunk rough against my back.

Could he kill me with that knife? I was already dead. But . . .

Could I die *again*?

I glared at him. For a moment the space between us shivered, as though trying to dispel the tension. His eyes flicked down to the knife for a second, to the bared curve of my throat, then back up. Our eyes locked.

"Oh, Jia." His voice had grown unnaturally hoarse. "I have missed you."

I braced myself as he drew his arm back, as though he meant to slash my neck.

But . . . he didn't. He just froze.

Instead, pain erupted of its own accord. Starting in my core and exploding outward. It was as if I was being stabbed—again—by something *other* than Lin's blue knife.

Lin's image dissolved before me, like dirt washed away by rain.

And I screamed.

I came to, gasping and drawing great ragged breaths, lying upon the floor. All around me was a dense, pervasive chill.

The floor was cold—stone, I presumed, from the roughness of it against my cheek. My fingers flexed against its irregularity, against the porous rock. I pushed my torso up slightly, stopping as the movement triggered a spasm of coughing, shooting waves of pain right through my chest.

I crumpled back onto the floor, then curled inward to quell the pain. And as I clutched my chest, liquid—hot, sticky, viscous—dribbled through my fingers.

Blood.

My heart pounded. Wait. My heart *pounded*? Each faint thump elicited another trickle of blood. Thump. Trickle. Thump. Trickle. My chest rose and fell with each breath that rasped across my sore, parched throat. Lin hadn't killed me, the hole in my chest was bleeding again, and . . .

I . . . I was alive.

But only just, judging from the way I was bleeding.

Instinctively, my hand clamped over my torso, putting pressure on the wound. Pain shot through me. I retched. In the death realm, the wound had been a mere indentation, surrounded by a rough raised scar. Now it was open, the flesh spongy and swollen. My back was bleeding, too—congealed blood slicking my dress against my skin.

Biting my lip to suppress the agony, I forced myself to think. *What the hells just happened?*

As I strained my brain, the memories came rushing back. Lin trying—and failing—to cut my throat. Then a jerk, almost like a hook had sunk into my belly. The misty realm of death receding as my heart spluttered back to life, haphazardly at first before becoming stronger, faster, more regular. Saliva flooding my mouth, coating my tongue, which was thick with disuse. And deep within, my cells kicking into gear as I was ripped through time, through space, through eternity. Back to the surface, to the land of the living.

It must have been a near-death hallucination. A trick my mind had played to deal with the shock of being stabbed. Lin had seemed so real, so visceral, so corporeal, so *there* . . . I could still feel his fingers curled around my wrist. His cold, dead hand pinning me to the tree.

Could my brain have conjured something so hauntingly real? And if I was that close to death, so as to have a near-death experience, how in the ten hells had I suddenly come back alive?

Why hadn't I just died?

I didn't know where I was, or how I was still here; all I knew was that I needed to get help—and fast—if I was to have any hope of surviving.

Rolling onto my stomach, and clutching my wound with one hand, I pushed myself onto my knees. Everything hurt. Even the knuckles of my right hand were raw, abraded.

I stared, cold, clammy sweat springing out upon my brow. I had wounds from punching Lin. Did that mean our interaction had been . . . *real*?

My heart gave a pitiful stutter. Gritting my teeth, I scrunched my eyes closed. There was no time to ponder that now. Summoning every ounce of residual strength, I began struggling to my feet.

"Get down, scum!" Something hard connected with my ribs. The pain exploded again, and I collapsed, my feeble heart speeding up in an attempt to compensate for the shock.

I could barely raise my head. The pain was torturous. The effort required to move, to even look up, seemed insurmountable. But I had to know where I was. What situation I had found myself in. Who had kicked me, a dying girl, while I was bleeding on the ground?

Finally, I drew back my head. A circle of Lancaster men surrounded me. They must have been there all along, but in my foggy, injured state I hadn't noticed.

All were armed, their weapons jostling for space as they pointed at my face. Not just swords but bows. Spears. The men holding them were tense, their brows shining with sweat, their legs braced for quick action. If Yskians hated magic, they feared it even more.

Brisson was the only one who did not look afraid. His mouth

twisted into a smirk, and in the gloomy light his face was bloodless: a mask of death.

"What are you—" I started, but then could not speak any further, for bubbles of fluid choked my chest. A metallic tang hit the back of my throat. Blood. I gagged and then coughed, flecks of red splattering the floor.

"Sir," ventured one of the soldiers, his eyes flicking between Brisson and me. "Didn't you . . . kill her? Sir?"

"Aye," Brisson growled. "But she came alive again, did she not? It is as I suspected." His smirk spread wider. "She is a witch. This proves it."

I shook my head, trying to protest, but all that came up was another mouthful of blood. I understood now. It had been a shock that Brisson had been brave enough to kill me. This would be considered a serious breach of his authority. But he'd been so sure—so *convinced*—of my witchcraft that he'd taken the chance. He'd thought, for some reason, that I possessed resurrection magic.

But why? Resurrection wasn't a known power in our community. None of us had this power . . .

Except for me. The words echoed in my mind. Could it be true? Could I have died and come back to life, with magic I never knew I had?

The young soldier spoke again, jolting me out of my thoughts. "What will happen to her, sir?" he said to his general.

Brisson's smile dropped away. But the sinister gleam in his eyes remained. "We'll let the Spyrre decide."

Mā de, I thought. This was bad. Very bad.

They were going to test me for illegal magic.

Three

Present day

Two of the men closed in and dragged me to a standing position. Pain tore right through me. Clenching my teeth, I held my breath, not wanting to give them the satisfaction of hearing me scream.

I could barely walk, so the group shuffled along, my escorts mostly dragging me as my feet tripped across the flagstone floor. They hauled me through a set of carved mahogany doors and into a circular room, at the center of which was a sunken pit.

I recognized this room. I had been in this room—Essien Lancaster's throne room—many times. Too many times.

So I must have been passed out—or dead—long enough for Brisson's men to bring me here: Throft Hall, the most remote of the Lancaster outposts. The fortress they positioned near their side of the border, to keep out people like me.

If I'd made it as far as Throft Hall, then that must have meant more time had passed in the living realm compared with what I'd experienced during death. How much time had it been? I hacked a cough; my mind churned, trying to calculate how long it would have taken us to make the journey by carriage.

But someone seized me, disrupting my thoughts, and flung me into the pit. I landed in a crumpled heap. The pain crested so high that I could no longer remain quiet; I gave an involuntary shriek. Laughter swelled around me from crowds of soldiers. They stood in clusters on the raised platform around the perimeter of the room.

"Silence, everybody." The voice that cut over the rabble of noise was not commanding, nor loud. Instead, it was cold, decisive. The voice of someone accustomed to privilege, and used to getting his way.

The noise immediately died down. I rose unsteadily, my feet slipping as I struggled to gain purchase in the expanding pool of my own blood. With my hand still pressed over the hole in my chest, I stood to face Prince Essien Lancaster, sixth son of the king of Yske.

Essien was the youngest of the Yskian royals and ostensibly the lowest rank. I presumed that was why he'd been assigned to this Mothers-forsaken place. Throft Hall sat just on the Yskian side of the border, abutting what they called the Forest of Seld—as far as one could conceivably go from the Yskian capital while still remaining in the same kingdom.

Despite having governed the region for years, the prince seemed particularly disinclined to enjoy the charms of the local countryside. Instead, he spent his time shut up within the stone walls of his fortress, waiting for his soldiers to haul in scammers, thieves, and people like me—suspected sorceresses.

Swaying a little, I planted my feet more firmly on the floor, determined to remain upright. I could do this. I had died and come back to life, and probably for a reason: to save my grandmother.

I'd never known my parents—it had been my grandmother, my Pópo, who had raised me. It was she who used to tell me bedtime stories, who used to tuck me into bed as a child. And no matter what I did, no matter how much of a disappointment I turned out to be, she'd never once made me question her love for me.

This time, I had to succeed. I had to get back and save her. Miraculously, I'd been given a second chance.

Straightening my spine, I raised my head, looking the Yskian prince square in the eye. This was the first time I'd ever been brought in injured, but still . . . I would *not* face my enemy lying down.

"Lady Liu," Prince Essien called down to me, addressing me from his elevated throne. "Back again? It has been a while. You must have missed me." The crowd guffawed.

Anger knifed through me. Lady? I was no lady. But every time I came to this vile place, the prince would address me as such. Always sure he was mocking me, I refused to rise to the bait. I just treated him with the same level of condescension as he did me.

My head was light, probably from loss of blood, which by now had slowed to a measurable drip. I glared at him through the dark, tangled curtain of my hair. In contrast, he looked irritatingly perfect, his copper-tinged blond tresses parted neatly to one side and combed back from his face, a circlet of gold placed precisely on top. His eyes, so pale, so blue, fixed on me in what could only be read as disdain.

"Your Highness." I tried to keep my voice even, but it ended in a wheeze. "The only thing I have missed is the opportunity to kill you." Straining with the effort, I gave him a saccharine smile. "I retain some hope that I can remedy that."

I spoke with false courage, anxiety tearing up my insides. Now that I was alive again, this pointless exchange was wasting valuable time. Time to save my life. Time to get home to save my Pópo's life. Or, if I couldn't save her—time to see her again, even just once.

Time was something she did not have. Her time was running out. My eyes flicked down to the puddle of blood pooling at my feet.

Mine was, too.

The seconds dribbled by, and the prince's face did not change. Instead, he fixed his eyes on me, their fringe of long lashes casting his irises in shadow.

"You are hardly in a position to be threatening my life, Lady Liu," he drawled, gesturing to my bloodied chest. "When you *should* instead be bargaining for yours."

"Fuck you," I spat, using the commonest curse of the Trader's Tongue. Immediately, I dissolved into another coughing fit.

The prince waited, impassive, until my histrionics died down. Then he simply continued as though nothing had even happened. "General Brisson tells me that you were accidentally killed, but that you came back to life." He slid a narrowed gaze toward his general, who stood up a little straighter. "He claims this is irrefutable proof that you are, indeed, a witch."

"Accidentally?" I ground out. "He lies."

Prince Essien gave a dismissive wave. His hands were pale, like the rest of him, with elegantly tapered fingers. "You say one thing, he says another. Who am I to believe?" He rubbed his chin, making a false show of deliberation.

He slapped both hands down on his thighs, disrupting the quiet. "I know! We shall ask the Spyrre."

My stomach gave a lurch. This was always going to be the outcome. I knew it; so did Essien Lancaster and everyone else in this room. That knowledge, though, didn't stop the prince from performing the farce of pretending to consider my fate. And it didn't stop the soldiers from shuffling their feet and jostling backward, away from the pit.

The Spyrre were creatures that the Yskians used to detect illegal magic. We did not have them in Fengzhi Yuan. In my limited knowledge of other places, they didn't exist anywhere else, either.

After the last Jinghu Dao–Yskian war three centuries ago, Yskian rulers vowed that they would not be defeated by magic again—ever. They worked hard to develop methods of defense against what they deemed "dark magic." Thus the Spyrre were created.

It was said that the Spyrre were once people who had been tortured with magic until it broke their minds, that this torture had given them such a hatred for sorcery that they were able to detect mere traces of it upon any human.

I had faced the Spyrre before, of course. In my journeys through Qian Xin Lin—what the Yskians called the Forest of Seld—I'd been hauled before Prince Essien more times than I could count.

But this time was *different*.

The rabble of conversation in the room died to a dull murmur as a second set of double doors swung open with a squeal.

These doors led to the dungeons where the Spyrre dwelled, and from somewhere beyond them I could hear clicks and growls that were unlike anything that should exist within the human realm.

I shivered, though whether that was due to the chill in the room, my ongoing blood loss, or fear I did not know. The sickening sounds that emanated from the darkness were gradually superseded by something else: the scraping of creatures dragging their feet along the floor.

And then they came into view.

Drawn by the scent of life, of vitality, they came shuffling through the gaping entrance. There were three of them this time, emaciated, desiccated, each clad in torn, filthy rags. Their skin was dulled to a grimy gray, as coarse and pockmarked as low-grade leather. None of them had any hair.

It was their faces, though, that would strike fear into the heart of even the most stalwart soldier. In the sockets that were once their eyes, a blackness existed, so all-encompassing that it swallowed all the light. Their mouths hung open, full of broken, blackened teeth. And their noses—O Mothers!—the noses were mostly holes, a sorry excuse for skin stretched over a vestigial, cartilaginous rim.

As the Spyrre lurched toward me, the soldiers standing above fell silent. These creatures tended to have that effect on people. Clearly, they were desecrations of life itself. So *wrong*, one could immediately feel they should not exist. They were creatures who existed beyond the laws of time and space.

Even the Yskians, who created them, reviled them. Hatred for the Spyrre was gut level. Instinctual.

The creatures were now close enough that I could smell

their odor—rotted meat and old, dried blood. A hush, leaden and heavy, descended over the room. There were no more murmurs, no whispers against the walls. The soldiers seemed to be holding a single collective breath.

I hadn't thought my heart could get any faster, or weaker, but it did, fluttering feebly against the bony prison of my chest. This test had been one I had participated in many, *many* times . . . and passed. But I didn't know if I would pass this time. And if I didn't, one of them would suck my life force, my qì, right out through my mouth, until I was nothing more than empty flesh.

The closest Spyrre turned its black, soulless eyes on me. And in my direction, with quivering cartilage, the gaping hole that was once a nose drew in a deep, rattling breath. It seemed to tug at the corners of my soul, pinching off bits of my consciousness like they were mere morsels of food.

Stiffening, I held my head high, refusing to look at the cursed creatures, as blood from my wound continued to drip.

The three Spyrre circled me, each of them sniffing with those deathlike inhales. *Please*, I thought. *Please let me not have magic. Not after what happened in the death realm, with—*

I cut my thoughts off. Not even here, with the rabid fear of the Spyrre running through my depleted veins, would I think about that. About *him*.

But as much as I did not want to think of Lin, my mind refused to cooperate. What had happened in the death realm, in that singular moment when he'd pressed his knife to my neck? What had caused me to resurrect, if indeed I had truly died? Had he done something to me with his unearthly blue knife?

He and I both knew I was not supposed to have any magical

abilities: In my community I was what was known as an Empty. That is, empty of magic—I always had been, and had thought I always would be.

I was six years old when it had become apparent. By that age, when I hadn't so much as accidentally lit any of my playthings on fire, or levitated, or unwittingly disappeared, the suspicions started. And when these suspicions were confirmed, well . . . there was a lot of disappointment. The granddaughter of the High Priestess should have deep, strong magic. Not be like me. Not be magicless. Not be a burden.

So, I contributed in other ways. Being magicless meant the Spyrre wouldn't trouble me. I couldn't be identified, tried, or charged as a witch. So my mission became to be a provider. Along with Lin, who also lacked magic, I spent much of my childhood foraging in forests, learning how to set traps and hunt game. And over the years, we became good at it. He and I became the main source of food for the rest of the community, freeing them to focus on the higher pursuits of practicing magic and honing powers.

If either of us were caught by the Yskian soldiers and hauled to Throft Hall, it was no big deal. Detecting no magic on us, the Spyrre would let us go. Every single time. So while the assessment process was downright repulsive, I wasn't *afraid* of it, as such.

But this time? This time I had, very possibly, resurrected myself from the dead. And despite a fatal wound, I was still standing—just.

Maybe Brisson was right. Maybe I *did* have magic: resurrection magic. And it had just never manifested itself before because it never had to.

What superbly shitty timing.

One of the Spyrre circled closer, the smell of decay overpowering my senses. It leaned toward me, and I arched away, pain spearing through my chest. I willed myself not to cry. Any moment now. It would detect the magic I'd suddenly manifested and lunge at me, tearing into my flesh with those blackened, broken teeth.

It sniffed again, right along my collarbone, then down to my leaking wound, so close I could trace the texture of its mottled, husk-like scalp. So close I could feel the cold wash of fetid breath across my skin. One of its hands began to creep toward me, bony fingers closing over my shoulder. Then its head snapped up, and it turned its hollow gaze upon me.

Involuntarily, I whimpered. I was going to die. All I could hope for was that it would be quick. That the Spyrre would tear me apart and end this suffering. The pain of my wound hit me again, and my knees almost buckled. But terror froze me in place, and I squeezed my eyes shut, waiting for the attack.

But the attack never came. The Spyrre, still sniffing, began to let me go, finger by finger, like a spider making a slow retreat from a threat. The smell receded, and the shuffling started again. Steeling myself, I opened my eyes a crack. The three creatures were withdrawing to their dungeon, their tattered robes fluttering behind them.

My breath, which had been lodged in my chest, loosed in a sigh, and I crumpled to the floor. Only then did the sound hit me: protests, shouts, thumps of wooden weapons upon the stone. And the Yskian soldiers, chanting: "Drown her! Burn her! She's a witch! Drown her! Burn her! She's a—"

"SILENCE!" This time, the prince's voice *was* loud. It

boomed across the room, echoing around it, and the noise died down again. "Brisson, see me in my chambers later."

Brisson was sullen. "Aye, Your Highness."

And to me: "Lady Liu. You are free to go."

"Thank you," I whispered from the ground, barely able to draw breath. My head spun; I had lost so much blood, was so dizzy . . .

Maybe this time I would die for good.

The sound of jeering and bellowed insults accompanied me as I slid into unconsciousness. But I registered something else, something strange, just before I passed out.

Prince Essien, squatting next to me, then lifting me into his arms.

Four

Seven years ago

The others had found something, and I wanted to know what.

Quietly, quietly, I crept forward. Then, reaching the edge of the group, I stood on my tiptoes. I didn't want to miss out. Missing out would be *unfair.* I wanted to *see.*

Whatever it was, it was small, because I couldn't see it, not even a bit.

Luckily, my favorite climbing tree was nearby. Its branches were low and covered with snow. I pulled myself up, shivering as a cold droplet dripped down my back. At ten years old, I was still young enough to climb trees. To hide in the leaves. To watch and listen, to hear secrets I could keep for later.

I shuffled along a branch, then clamped it between my legs. The bark was scratchy, but at least now I could see better.

A child. Just a child. Different from us: This child was scruffy, with tan skin and curly dark-brown hair that was *really* messy. Not like me, with my pale skin and hair that was black and shiny-smooth.

I frowned. Having a visitor was strange. Our village was hidden, protected by magic that kept away mean people who wanted to hurt us. Sometimes we even moved so we would stay super super secret. Moving day was exciting. But also it was annoying, because moving was why we had to live in flimsy huts and not real, proper houses. Houses like the ones I sometimes saw on my trips to the big city.

I was staring so hard at the stranger that I didn't notice my branch breaking. It swayed, and I tried to hold on, but it was no use; it cracked. I fell, landing on the ground on top of leaves, dirt, and snow. For a second, I couldn't breathe.

The other children all turned to look.

"What are you doing?" Dai Yu, my eldest sister, said. She had her hands on her hips and her eyebrows looked all angry. "Nosing around where you aren't wanted? Again!"

I shrunk away from Dai Yu's stare, not saying anything.

"Go on then, get out of here." Dai Yu took a step toward me. I struggled to my feet, brushing snow from my knees. Her eyes narrowed to slits and she stamped a foot. *"Empty."*

I gave a sniffle, and blinked hard. I didn't want to cry.

Empty. A useless, magicless Empty. The other children teased me by calling me that name. I could live with it, usually. But when my own sister said it . . .

A tear rolled down my cheek. Then another. And another.

"Oh, don't make her cry." My second sibling, thirteen-year-old Hui Fen, gave Dai Yu a judgy look.

Dai Yu rolled her eyes and, with a flick of her hand, used her water magic to disappear my tears. She always listened to Hui more than anyone—we all did—and I guess this was her trying to fix things.

But it didn't help, not really. It just made me sadder.

Hui Fen was already bending over me. "Come, mèimei. Are you hurt? Shall we fetch one of the aunties?"

Clamping my mouth shut, I shook my head and scrubbed at my tears with my hand. The truth was, I did hurt—I hurt all over. Not only on the outside, but on the inside, too—inside my heart. But I didn't want to miss anything. So I did what my grandmother always told me to do: pretended to be brave, even if I wasn't brave, not really.

Hui Fen—the kind one, the protective one—drew me into the middle of the group.

I blinked. Now I had the *best* spot, right in front of the stranger.

We almost never saw new people. And if new people came, they were usually old: Other sorceresses. Shamans and healers. Sometimes spiritual guides. But never someone so young. And never someone so . . . dirty.

So I stared and stared, Hui's hand resting on my shoulder. And the child did nothing except stare back, with strange eyes the color of weak tea. I'd never seen eyes this color.

It wasn't just their eyes that were odd. They also had a weird face. Normally I could guess where people came from, but this time I couldn't. Were they from up north, from the mountains? Were they from one of the provinces to the west? Or were they a rare dark-headed person who came from over the border—from Yske?

"Hui?" I twisted around, looking up at my sibling's face. "What's going on? Why is everyone staring at this one?"

Hui Fen let out a little puff of air, then bowed their head. With eyes closed, they placed their hands on both my temples.

My mind went foggy, and I went cold all over. My thoughts, which until now had been racing, slowed and slowed. Then an image filled my mind. A memory, seen through Hui Fen's eyes.

The gaggle of children crowd in. The child at the center has a dirty, tear-streaked face, but their lower lip sticks out stubbornly.

One of the onlookers, a ten-year-old boy from the village, reaches out and shoves the newcomer. It isn't hard—more experimental than anything—but the stranger still stumbles a little. The child manages to right themself, and although they are glaring, their tears flow even faster.

"Stop," I try to say. But no one is listening. Instead, they're tittering and elbowing one another.

As is always the case with memory magic, Hui's voice sounds like it is coming from my mouth.

But then all of a sudden, the laughter stops, abruptly; the crowd starts whispering. Pópo is coming.

She ignores the reverential bows and kowtows, and murmurs of "Priestess" uttered in childish voices. Instead, my grandmother just fixes us all with a keen stare. "There now," she says, her voice—as usual—deep and melodious. She gestures at the stranger. "This boy is our new friend. And we are kind to friends, are we not?" She raises one eyebrow.

The meaning of her expression is clear: If anyone mistreats the new boy, Pópo will confiscate the offender's power, albeit temporarily.

We all shuffle our feet, eyes downcast, and murmur our agreement.

All of us except Dai Yu, my sister, who pipes up and says, "But, Pópo . . . Where did he come from?"

"I brought him here. He is to live with us." Pópo smiles and spreads her hands. "He is my guest."

The memory faded, and I was back as myself. I understood now. This must have happened just before I got here. Pópo, who was both my grandmother and the High Priestess, had already left. But everyone else had stayed, wanting to know more about this boy, this "guest." He was the first outsider since I could remember who had ever been welcomed into our secret village.

"Lái, children!" An aunty's shrill voice cut through the babble. She clapped her hands, twice. "Come! Meditation in two minutes. Quickly, now, kuài kuài!"

We all jumped. Children ran off, hurrying to meet the next lesson. Meditation was important—for others, anyway. To me it was boring. I spent most sessions fidgeting, daydreaming, and thinking really hard about how to *not* think.

I *hated* meditation.

One by one, the others left, until only the stranger and me remained. We stood, arms by our sides, just . . . staring.

"I'm Jia Yi," I said, after a while. Then I paused to wait for him to say his name, like I had been taught.

He said nothing. Instead, he looked round the clearing, as if he could *see* something. But when I turned, there was nothing.

"Jia Yi," I repeated, facing him again. I pointed to myself, jabbing my finger against my chest.

Finally, the boy's wide eyes landed on me. He scrubbed at his face roughly, like he was suddenly ashamed of how dirty it was.

I felt sorry for him then. "Don't worry about it. It's hard to stay clean in the forest." Then I smiled, pleased when his mouth finally cracked in a grin. "Wanna see my hiding spot?"

I didn't wait for a response. Instead I turned and ran, bare feet skimming the ground, my skirt swishing around my legs. Cold wind stung my face. I puffed out a misty breath, pretending I was a dragon.

It didn't matter if I missed meditation. Not to *me*. Meditation was supposed to clear your mind for magic, and I had no magic anyway.

I'd barely made it past the tree line before a hand whipped out and grabbed my arm.

I shrieked. Whirling around, I found myself staring up into my grandmother's lined face.

"Little one," she said, her voice stern. "Where are you going? You are supposed to be at meditation."

"I . . . I was just making friends with the new boy." I swallowed, then straightened, then added, in an attempt to soften Pópo's heart, "Your 'guest.' Remember?"

"Ah." My grandmother gave me a knowing look.

Out of the corner of my eye, I saw the boy shift a little, leaning forward on his toes, as though keen to get going. Like a bird about to take flight. The inside of my chest squeezed; I didn't want to get in trouble in front of him. Not when we'd just met. Not when he might become my first-ever real friend.

"I mean, I don't need to do meditation anyway, Pópo, because I don't have magic and meditation is supposed to help with magic and since I'm not magical yet I don't need to do it, right?" I was rambling. "Right?"

Pópo's lips pressed into a firm line, and her eyebrows drew

down. My heart started beating faster. I was losing her. So I did the only thing I could think of: looked up her with my most winsome expression, shamelessly pleading my case. "Please, Pópo? Let me show him around. He'll need a guide if he is to live here. Please? Pleeeeeaaaaaase?"

My grandmother was silent for a few seconds, before one corner of her mouth twitched. "Very well. I suppose you've won me over." She let me go and took a step back. "Be sure to be back by nightfall. And . . ."

Pópo cast a secretive look over her shoulder before leaning even closer.

"Whatever you do, Jia Yi," she said, her voice dropping low. The familiar twinkle in her dark eyes sparked. "Do not tell the others."

Five

Present day

When I woke, nestled in a downy bed, I could not tell how much time had passed. I'd been dreaming: shifting visions of dew-dripped forests and childish laughter. At one point I'd even dreamed of Essien Lancaster, his shadowy form leaning over me. I shivered as I edged toward wakefulness, my mind still half mired in the feverish haze of sleep.

Blearily, I rubbed my eyes. Moonlight spilled through a narrow window fitted with colored glass. A sure sign of Yskian wealth, since glass was rare and expensive and could only be afforded by the rich.

Trying to shake off the fogginess in my head, I pushed myself upright, wincing as my wound jolted with fresh pain. The bed I sat upon was an enormous carved four-poster, heaped with feather pillows, comforters, furs, and silk sheets—the bedding rumpled from my repose.

Going slowly, I swung my legs around in an awkward

attempt to rise. As I struggled to my feet, I drew in a sharp breath, pain lancing through my chest.

I grabbed the bedpost for support, my gaze catching on my right hand. A neat dressing of gauze had been wound around my fingers. My torso, too, was bandaged. My *naked* torso. Someone had undressed me, bound my wounds, and put me to bed in what I assumed was one of the Lancaster bedrooms. But who?

I winced. The fact that a stranger—and an Yskian, no less—had seen me undressed and unconscious was disturbing.

Feeling tremendously exposed, I dragged a sheet off the bed and wrapped it around me, tucking the corners in like a makeshift dress.

Beneath my feet, a plush golden rug adorned the stone floors. The walls, too, were stone, but everything else—the bed, the door, the window frames, the other furniture—was dark-stained wood.

Going to the door, I jiggled the handle, supporting myself against the doorframe. Locked. Next, I tried the window—since it was at ground level, I might be able to escape. But it too was bolted shut, and the windowpanes were too narrow for me to climb through, even were I to break the glass.

With a frustrated hiss, I turned my attention to the room. The walls were made of polished stone, glowing torches in sconces studded along their lengths. Dark, heavy frames were mounted between them, their canvases depicting landscapes and still lifes and the occasional painted portrait. I shuddered, crossing my arms. As I moved, the portraits' eyes seemed to watch me, as if they were wondering what a village girl like me was doing in such extravagant surroundings.

An enormous wardrobe sat in one corner, its doors inset

with latticed mirrors. One was slightly ajar, exposing only blackness within, and it cast a long, looming shadow across the floor. I quickly turned away, leaving it to sit in its shroud of darkness.

Against the opposite wall, in front of a smoldering fireplace, were two armchairs upholstered in gold fabric. Between them was a small round table, upon which sat a bone-white tea set: an ornate teapot, a saucer, and a dainty porcelain teacup.

I licked my lips. My mouth was dry, my throat parched. I had no idea how long I'd been unconscious for, or how much time had passed since I'd had a drink. All I knew was that I was *thirsty*. And even though the tea was probably the insipid, milky privy water the Yskians favored, it was still better than nothing.

Stumbling over to the table and chairs, I poured a full cup of tea with a shaky hand, surprised to see dark, opaque brown liquid emerge from the delicately curved spout. Tiny flecks of black flurried around the cup before settling languorously to the bottom. I swallowed thickly, suddenly desperate to take in some fluid.

But I was interrupted. A rush of air blew past my cheek—strange in this chill, fell room—and I dropped the teapot with a clatter. Tea sloshed onto the tray, spreading out in a slick, dark stain.

"Is—" I swallowed, peering into the gloom. "Is anyone there?"

There was no answer, but I sensed a presence. I threw a glance over my shoulder, my pulse thumping in my ears. In my mind flashed visions of demons, monsters, ghosts—but I hoped with my entire being that I would see nothing.

". . . Hello?" My voice was thin. Weak.

From behind me came a noise. A rustling sound. Something whispery, something beyond this world. For a moment, it almost sounded like it was saying my name. *Jia.* My wound ached, and a clammy chill settled on my skin.

Drawing a shaky breath, I snatched one of the torches from a wall sconce. Holding it in front of me, brandishing its halo of light, I edged to the half-open wardrobe and its shadowed cavity within. Cold sweat beaded on my forehead. My heart thrashed, wild in my chest.

Gathering my courage, I lunged forward and flung the door open, to find . . .

Nothing.

The light of the torch chased away the darkness. There was nothing of note inside, just a row of nightgowns hung on coat hangers. I sighed. *Don't be so ridiculous,* I scolded myself. There was nothing in this room save for me, the furniture, and the admittedly creepy portraits.

Having a drink of tea would help to calm my nerves, surely? I made my way back to the chair, sank into the plush seat, and raised the cup to my lips with two trembling hands. After taking a deep, long draft, I sighed.

It was . . . surprisingly good. Not quite hot enough, but also not the dilute tea I was expecting. This tea was strong, astringent, bitter enough to shrivel my tongue. This was decidedly *not* Yskian tea.

No . . . It tasted like tea from the Jinghu Dao empire. Its sour, fermented smell suggested that more specifically, it was tea from my own province, Fengzhi Yuan.

Suddenly homesick, I gulped the rest down, feeling instantly refreshed, my head lolling against the chair cushions.

I was so exhausted. I was obviously still affected by my

near-death experience, and jittery from being spooked by the dark. Letting my eyelids slide shut, I perched the teacup on my knee—just for a moment. I wasn't planning to fall asleep again. I couldn't allow that. I would rest, eyes closed, for a little bit . . . Then I would plot my escape.

"Do you like this sort of finery now, Jia? You never used to."

I leaped to my feet, eyes open; someone was behind me. Someone was in this room. Even worse, I knew that voice.

As I spun around, everything inside me clenched: my heart, my gut, every muscle inside my body. Everything. Because standing, in this locked room, looking completely whole, solid, visceral, and *alive* . . .

Was Lin.

Lin, who should be dead.

No, I thought, fear snaking through my gut. *No! Not him!*

It wasn't enough to have seen him when I was unconscious, almost deceased. Now he was haunting me while I was *awake*? Was this a dream? Or a nightmare, rather?

He said nothing. Just watched me. And as he stepped into the light, he appeared so tangible, so real, that my fear gave way to anger.

Maybe the rumors were wrong. Maybe he never died. Maybe he just let us think that, to get away from us. From me.

"You're meant to be dead," I spat out, my eyes narrowed. I stalked closer, advancing on him.

Lin—or Lin's form, whatever he was—spread his hands. "Jia—"

"You *died*!" My voice was shaking now, bordering on a scream. "You left me and then you *died*!"

"I can explain—"

"And then you came back . . . Not dead . . . You tried to *kill* me! With that blue knife!" Casting my eyes around for something I could use as a weapon, I found nothing. No evidence of my dagger, or a hairpin, not even any implement with which to stir my tea. *Damn Lancasters.* Despite their apparent courtesies, they still didn't trust me enough to lock me in a room with sharp objects. *Bastards.*

My voice rose even higher. "The audacity you have to show your face! After . . . after . . ." I couldn't even say it. Even now, a year later, my fury was too fresh.

Lin took a step toward me. "Jia, please—"

I held up one finger, my whole body shaking. "*Don't* come closer. Don't you *dare.*"

He raised both hands, a placating move.

"Do you deny it?" I continued. "Do you deny trying to kill me? I'll give you one chance—*one* chance—to tell me the truth, Lin." It had been so long since I'd spoken his name; it felt cumbersome in my mouth.

There was a long pause. "No. I do not deny it."

Shrieking, I lurched forward, my right arm swinging. But right when my fist was due to meet his face, it just . . . didn't. Instead, I fell right through him, ending up sprawled in a heap on the ground.

Pain shot through my body, coalescing in my chest. I took a heaving, shuddering breath, then pushed myself onto my hands and knees, trying to regroup.

From above me, Lin's voice floated from the gloom. "Careful, now." There was a smirk hidden behind those words.

I clambered to my feet, my hands trembling, barely able

to catch my breath. He was there, but he wasn't there. Which meant . . .

"What *are* you?" I backed away. My scalp contracted, my gut like ice. "Are you . . . really dead?"

There was a long, loaded pause, where silence echoed like an unsung note. He took so long to reply I opened my eyes again, half fancying he would be gone and it would all have been an illusion.

"Yes," he said, finally. "I'm dead."

"Then how?" I clutched my forehead with quivering hands. "I don't understand. Why can I see you?" Then, to myself, "I must have hit my head."

Lin ignored my question. "You should take care, Jia. You are seriously injured."

"Only because *you* tried to kill me!"

"I was not the cause of that injury," Lin said, gesturing to my torso. "Or your death."

Instinctively, my hands went to my wound, and I covered it protectively. "So Brisson was right. I *did* die." It sounded even more ridiculous out loud than it had inside my head. Momentarily, my anger toward Lin ebbed, replaced by an even hotter rage for that scumbag, Andres Brisson. I almost laughed, but it came out sounding half strangled, as though I'd choked on a bone.

"Yes, you died. And you weren't supposed to, Jia. You weren't supposed to!" Lin's voice, previously measured, was rising, like it always did when he lost his careful control of his emotions. "I only tried to kill you because . . . because . . ."

He leaned closer, studying my features. It was a sort of habit he'd had when he was alive. Leaning toward me like we were sun and planet, planet and moon. Like two celestial bodies orbiting each other. Or perhaps it was more like one of us circling the other.

Was it me orbiting him? Or him orbiting me? I'd known him for so long I could no longer tell.

I raised my chin. "Because why?"

He gave me that look. The look that he'd always reserved for me. A dark look, his amber eyes flaming. Like I was the only thing in the world worth looking at.

It had been more than a year since I'd seen that look.

"To protect you," he said, softly. "Of course."

I opened my mouth, then closed it again, my hands still clutching my wound. "Protect me? How would killing me—or my ghost, rather—*protect* me?"

He grimaced. "Because things are . . . dangerous in the death realm. I wanted to spare you."

Spare me? He'd rather I die again than continue on as a ghost?

Perhaps he was lying. Perhaps he'd just wanted to be rid of me, and since it hadn't worked, he had concocted a feeble excuse.

Narrowing my eyes, I moved closer, examining Lin's ghostly form. "So I died, and then came back to what? Life?"

"It appears that way."

"How?"

Lin shrugged. "No idea, Jia. Some latent power you didn't realize you had?"

I brushed away the suggestion, filing it to dissect later. "And if we were both still ghosts, I'd be able to touch you?" I took a shaky step toward him, one hand stretched out, and brushed his cheek. Or where it should have been. Although he still bore the marks from where I, as a ghost, had punched him, beneath my hand was empty space. Lin closed his eyes anyway, almost like he wanted to lean into my caress.

"If we were both ghosts . . ." His voice was tremulous. "Then yes, you'd be able to touch me."

"And you could touch *me*? And also . . . kill me?"

He swallowed. "Yes, but I can explain—"

I cut him off. "And I could kill you? Even as a ghost, you can die?"

A pause. He nodded, his eyes still closed, and whispered, "We ghosts have a saying: What is dead can die again."

I snatched back my hand and folded my arms. "Good," I huffed. "Because when I get out of here, I'm going to die, become a ghost, and fucking *murder* you."

Lin's eyes sprang open, and he pressed his lips together in such a way that I couldn't tell if he was trying to curb a grimace or a grin. He opened his mouth to retort but was interrupted by a loud knock at the door.

"Lady Liu?" The pounding resumed. "Lady Liu!"

Lin melted into the shadows and disappeared. My pulse stuttered; one part of me wanted him gone from me, as far away as possible.

The other part, the treacherous part, ached to see him again.

"I'm not done with you yet, Lin," I shouted into the darkness. "You hear me? NOT DONE WITH YOU YET!"

The knocking on the door paused. Then came the voice again, muffled through the keyhole. "Lady Liu? Are you . . . quite all right?"

Turning away from the dark corner where Lin's ghost had disappeared, I called out, my voice edging into mild hysteria, "Yes, of course! I'm fine. Fine. Everything is just fine."

The door opened, and I stepped back, stifling a gasp. My visitor—resplendent in a blue velvet, gold-trimmed tailcoat, which brought out the blue of his eyes—turned, towering imposingly above me.

Forcing my face into a neutral expression, I swallowed the nausea that rose in my throat.

Here I was, in my enemy's castle, wearing nothing but a sheet . . .

With the Lancaster prince himself at my door.

Six

Present day

"Good morning." Prince Essien strode in. A servant, dressed in brown robes, trotted after him like a dog.

I stared, confused. Was it morning already? A quick glance out of the window confirmed that, yes, lashings of rosy light were streaked across the sky. But it was *early*. Why would an indulged royal bother getting up at the break of dawn? I'd always pictured the prince lazing around in a four-poster bed until late morning, being waited upon by staff who'd bring him bunches of chilled grapes. Leisurely to the point of idleness.

Not that I made a habit of picturing him in bed, of course.

"What are you doing here?" I blurted out. As soon as the words escaped my mouth, I realized how absurd they were; this was *his* castle. But after my exchange with Lin, I was feeling somewhat combative.

The prince didn't respond. He just leveled a cool gaze at me, one eyebrow slightly lifted, then gestured to his attendant. "Put the food on the table," he said, his tone imperious, "then leave."

The attendant moved into the room, setting down a tray

that held a shiny silver dome before shooting me a disdainful look and scurrying out. The heavy door swung shut, the latch emitting an audible *click.*

I frowned as the servant exited, then turned my attention back to the prince. I watched, wary, as he pulled a chair from the side table and sat with his legs crossed at the ankle. He looked different without his crown on. Still regal, of course, but slightly less intimidating.

As I caught a whiff of the steam emanating from beneath that silver dome, my stomach gave a deep rumble. The food smelled intensely savory, and . . . delicious. Embarrassed, I forced myself to clamp my lips shut, trying not to inhale.

"Lady Liu," the prince said, dragging my attention away from the victuals. He clasped his hands on one knee, looking a picture of comfort. "How are you feeling?"

I clenched my jaw so hard that it hurt. "I would feel better," I muttered, through gritted teeth, "if I weren't being kept prisoner."

The prince gave what was, on a technicality, a smile—but it still sent a chill through my bones. "You are not a prisoner," he said, then spread his arms wide. "This is Throft Hall, my residence. You are my . . . guest."

My mind swam. *Guest?* With the doors locked, and all sharp implements put away, I didn't feel like a guest . . . although I guess it was true they hadn't thrown me into the dungeons.

Yet.

Taking several deep breaths, I raised my head. "And *why*, pray tell, am I still here?" I kept my voice high and haughty.

The prince gave a small shrug and leaned back, the picture of casual grace. "We Lancasters treat our guests like royalt—"

"Just answer the question, húndàn." I glowered at him, daring him to ask the meaning of the insult I'd just thrown at him.

He did not. Instead, he just smirked. "Very well, then. What do you want me to say? Yes, you are a prisoner. Yes, I'm keeping you here. And you are in this bedroom"—he gestured to our surroundings—"because you were ill. You would have died had I sent you to the dungeons."

"How very *noble* of you." I sneered, my eyes narrowing to slits. "I expect that now, since I'm well, you'll throw me down there immediately. Correct?"

His lip curled. "On the contrary, Lady Liu. I wish to interrogate you. Why would I waste two whole days of dutiful care only to squander you to the Spyrre?"

My stomach lurched. "Two days?" I turned away from him, dropping the sheet, no longer caring about my modesty—or our quarrel. The prince made a sound that was half cough, half choke, which made me look around. His cheeks were reddened; he had averted his eyes.

"Oh, please," I snapped. Grabbing the camisole of my dove-gray hànfú, which had been laundered and lay folded neatly over a dressing chair, I snatched it up, then roughly shrugged it on. "I'm sure it's nothing you haven't seen before."

As the top fell down in folds over my torso, I paused. The hole in the fabric had been repaired. It was masterfully done, to be sure, but the place where Brisson's sword had penetrated was still starkly visible. A jagged scar marring the faded cotton.

Ignoring the churning in my belly, I tugged on the overshirt before winding the skirt around my waist and knotting it. Finally, I donned my robe. It was almost threadbare and a touch too short, but at least the close-fitting sleeves afforded me some cover.

I turned to face him once more, my eyes narrowed. "Was it *you* who undressed me? Who tended my wounds?"

The prince scoffed, as though it was preposterous that he, himself, would do something so pedestrian as dressing a prisoner's wound. "Of course not. It was Larch." Still refusing to look at me, he waved vaguely in the direction of the door. "My . . . physician."

"Larch?" I frowned, my mind ticking over. "Why would you send Larch to attend *me*?" Lord Larch was renowned as the master of modern medicine, the court physician, the doctor to the Lancaster family themselves. Why would the famous *Lord Larch* treat an enemy from Fengzhi Yuan—their rival kingdom? It made no sense.

"Why not him?" the prince shot back, an obstinate set to his jaw. "Lord Larch is a most excellent physician."

I didn't have the energy to untangle the conundrum further. There were more pressing matters at hand. If I had been in and out of consciousness at Throft Hall for two days, then it went without saying that my grandmother's health would have deteriorated further. When I'd left to forage in Qian Xin Lin, she was already lingering on the cusp of death. I could still picture her gaunt, wan face and the deep grooves that lined it. Her hollowed-out cheekbones and the milk-white opacity of her eyes. Without more Shadowside to lace her tonic, the chances of her surviving much longer were . . .

Shaking my head to dispel the fear, I drew myself to my full height. "Your Highness, Prince Essien Lancaster, Sixth Son of Yske, I demand that you let me go. I passed the Spyrre test. You have no reason to keep me here." My tone was formal, stilted. I knew how these Lancasters treasured these sorts of odious pleasantries. For good measure, I sank into a curtsy—the most elegant one I could muster, which was still extremely awkward, what with my injuries and lack of social graces.

Slowly, the prince turned to look at me. The dawning light from the stained-glass window threw colored patterns across his face.

I raised my chin, watching as he uncrossed his legs, rose to his feet, and prowled closer. By the time he stopped before me, I was forced to crane my neck.

We had never addressed each other on the same level before—our previous encounters had always been in the throne room, with him perched up on a dais and me languishing down in the pit. I'd never realized he was so tall. He stood so close that his body heat radiated over me, and I fought the instinct to lean in.

Everything about him, every movement, exuded confidence, elegance, refinement. This was a person who had never had to question his place in society. Never had to experience how it felt to be permanently cast as an outsider.

A fact that only made me madder.

He narrowed his eyes. "No."

I bristled, unable to speak for a moment, outrage stealing my wits. Then, I managed to grind out, "What do you mean, no?"

Essien's eyes bored into mine: his black pupils blown wide, rimmed by blue, clear as a summer sky. "I mean no. You're not leaving. Not until I get what I need." One corner of his mouth ticked up. "From *you*."

My stomach flipped. "What could you possibly need from me?" Noticing the robe of my hànfú was gaping, I jerked it closed.

His eyes dropped to my hands, then went back up to my

face, before he raised an eyebrow. "Believe me, my lady, it isn't that."

"As if you'd have a chance!" I snapped, and he snorted. "Well, what is it, then?"

For a moment, he said nothing. He merely stared at me, seemingly weighing his words. The room was silent, the only sound a ticking clock, abnormally loud in the oppressive hush.

Then he straightened, folding his arms across his chest. "How long have you known?" His voice was careful. Purposefully light.

A shiver slid down my spine. I eyed him suspiciously. "Known what?"

He fixed his gaze on me. "About your . . . ability? That you can die, and come back to life?"

I took a faltering step backward, my gut clenching. "Wh-what?"

Yes, I had died—Lin had confirmed that. I'd entered the death realm, and then had returned from it, even though I was supposed to be an Empty. And yet somehow I'd passed the Spyrre test, which was supposed to confirm my innocence, for Mothers' sakes.

Apparently, though, passing the Spyrre test wasn't enough. Somehow, Essien knew. A Lancaster—one of my greatest enemies—knew. Which was why, I supposed, he was keeping me prisoner.

I pressed a shaking hand against my stomach. The room closed in on me, my breaths struggling to fit in my chest. What could I say to get myself out of this mess? What could I do to get back to my grandmother, who was slowly but surely dying?

What would he, the enemy prince of a kingdom that hated magic, do with the information?

And what did he need from *me*?

Desperately, I flipped through dozens of scenarios in my head. If I tried to deny what had happened, he might send me back to face the Spyrre. But then again, if I admitted it outright, he could well do the same. Or worse, kill me on the spot.

In the end, I decided to claim ignorance, hoping that was enough. "I never knew I could. Before it happened, I mean."

"I see." Essien tilted his head, scrutinizing me. "Can you do it again?"

"Do what? Come back to life?"

Some curious look had stolen into Essien Lancaster's expression. Something that looked oddly like . . . *hunger.* A shudder rolled right through me.

"Yes," he said, simply.

"I—I don't know." My heartbeat thundered in my ears. "Why?"

He closed the distance between us, locking his eyes on mine. I glared right back, resisting the urge to retreat.

"Because I need you to fetch something for me, Lady Liu."

"Fetch something for you?" I almost laughed outright; it sounded so outlandish. "What, from the *afterlife*? You cannot be serious."

He leaned in closer, until our faces were mere inches apart. "I am *deadly* serious."

"No! Why in the ten hells would I do that?"

"Why not?" he challenged. "The afterlife is supposed to be a lovely place, is it not?"

For a moment, I could not begin to formulate a response. All I could do was stare at him, completely flummoxed. Eventually, though, vague recollections of Yskian death myths resurfaced in my mind.

Yskians believed in some sort of higher power, who presided over a place of blissful eternity where only those who were good would end up. They didn't believe in the things we believed in, such as the ghost realm . . .

My mouth twisted as I tried not to smile. How very wrong they were.

Still, it amused me to realize that Essien Lancaster thought *I*, of all people, was good enough to enter the Yskian version of the death realm.

I didn't say this out loud, however. Mirroring the prince's actions, I folded my own arms. "Well, I've been there, and I can tell you . . ." My words curdled in my throat when I remembered Lin.

I gathered myself, then huffed out a breath. "It is a horrible place."

Scowling, Essien stood staring down at me for some moments. Then—with the insouciance of someone who expects things to go his way—he ran a hand through his golden hair. "What say you we make a bargain, Lady Liu?"

I narrowed my eyes, debating whether I wanted to bother responding to such a question. Eventually, my curiosity won out. "What bargain?"

"There's something in the afterlife. Something I need," he said slowly, as though he was spelling out a simple concept to a child. "If you agree to fetch it and bring it to me, I am willing to let you go." He cocked his head slightly and gave me an appraising look. "Furthermore, I shall exonerate you from your crime of being a witch."

"I'm not a *witch*." I hurled out the words as viciously as I could manage. "And I would *never* make a bargain with *you*." Clenching my hands into fists to stop them from trembling, I raised my chin.

Notwithstanding the fact that I was instinctively opposed to negotiating with annoying, arrogant Yskians, the thought of reentering the death realm—even voluntarily—was terrifying. For one, Lin was there, the very person whom I wished to avoid.

Secondly, running errands for Essien Lancaster would waste precious time. Time that I could spend with my ailing grandmother.

And thirdly, if I died again . . . I honestly didn't know if I could come back.

"I see. That is indeed . . . disappointing." The prince gave me an ice-cold smile that leached right down to my bones. "Well, good day, Lady Liu. I shall be back this evening to see if you've had a change of heart." With that, he turned and strode out the door, slamming it behind him.

"Wait!" I tried to stumble after him, but my injuries made me slow. The lock clicked shut just as I reached the door. Falling against its wooden surface, I jiggled the door handle, turning it this way and that, increasingly violently. Then, with a cry of frustration, I gave up.

I slid to the ground, anger pricking at my eyelids. I'd messed it all up. Everything. I was supposed to have convinced Prince Essien to let me go. It was not supposed to end up . . . well, like *this*.

It was then that my tears finally fell, hot and stinging, running in tracks down my cheeks. I leaned my head against the dark mahogany and let them fall, my fingers clawing at the unyielding wood.

"You don't understand," I whispered against the closed door, my voice choked with tears. "You don't understand. My grandmother is dying."

Seven

Present day

I pummeled that wooden door for what felt like hours, to no avail. By the time I stopped, my head was spinning, my chest was burning, my body on the brink of collapse. Defeated, I slumped onto the ground, legs folded like a broken doll.

"Jia." Lin's voice, quiet, emanated from the darkness, followed by Lin himself. "Why are you on the floor? You need rest."

"Don't tell me what to do," I snapped. My head hurt from crying and—damnit!—my nose was running. Surreptitiously, I used my sleeve to wipe it.

"I'm just looking out for you."

I ignored him and closed my eyes. "Fancy hating myself so much," I muttered, leaning my pounding head against the door, "that I hallucinate my worst enemy to appear in my visions and scold me."

At this, Lin threw his head back and barked a short, sharp laugh. Lin laughing was not a common occurrence, but when it happened, he did it with his entire body. "Jia," he said, still chuckling. "Come now. A hallucination? You never had *that* good an imagination. I mean, look at me." He gestured to himself with a flourish. "As if you could imagine something so perfect, so sublime, so—"

My eyes snapped open, my eyelashes still wet with tears. "So irritating."

"I try my best."

"And you're still an ass."

His grin just grew wider. "And always will be. Dead or alive."

I glared at him as I scrambled to my feet. At least my grief had, temporarily, been superseded by annoyance. "So if you're dead, why can I see you now"—I swept my arms around the room—"and here?"

Lin prowled toward me, closing the distance. Unlike with Prince Essien, there was no warmth, or heat, emanating from his form. And when he moved, the edges of his silhouette shimmered, like the substance that made him was wavering in space.

"Because I'm a guǐ," he said. "A specter." His eyes, darkening, fixed on me. "Nothing but a ghostly apparition."

I didn't respond. My mind was still struggling to comprehend this information.

"And you . . ." He was now right in front of me, me breathing far too quickly, him not breathing at all. His voice dropped low as he leaned in, murmuring directly into my ear. "What are you, Jia? You were dead, and now you're alive. You can see ghosts. What does that make you?" His voice unfurled through my body, pooling at my core, lulling me into a sort of daze.

My breath caught in my throat, and I took a step back, breaking his trancelike hold.

"Why are you here?" I snapped. "Why start haunting me now?"

He stared at me. "I've always been here, Jia. Ever since I died. You just couldn't see me before."

"You've been haunting me this whole time?" My heart pounded erratically in my chest. "I just couldn't see you?" The world swayed to the sound of my pulse. I clutched at my face, trying to stem the queasiness. Was this what he'd meant by leaving me alone for "mere minutes," when Andres Brisson had stabbed me?

"Yes." Lin spoke that one word quietly. Simply.

My stomach churned. Lin had been haunting me this whole time. *This whole time!* And I hadn't known—I'd never even had an inkling. My mind raced as it rummaged through the vault of my memories, scrambling to remember all the moments I'd lived since the day I had heard of his death. "And the reason I can see you now is because I almost died? Or did die. Or whatever the ten hells happened to me."

He was silent for some moments, frowning as he examined my face. Then he said, "When mortals skirt as close to death as you did, Jia, the separation between the living world and the death realm weakens. So, now you can see ghosts." Raising one eyebrow, he said, in the most sardonic tone possible, "Congratulations."

My hands were shaking; I took a deep, steadying breath to regain some semblance of control. "What happened to me, Lin? In the . . . in the death realm." Even speaking it aloud sounded utterly absurd.

Ignoring my question, Lin drew his eyebrows down in disapproval, his eyes glittering below. "What were you doing so near the Yskian border?" His gaze darted around the room before alighting on me. "Why would you risk getting caught? I've seen you hunt, of course, but you *never* usually go that far east. And to be caught by *Brisson*, that incompetent oaf, no less!" He advanced upon me while I pressed myself back against the door. "Why, for demons' sake, would you do something so *foolish*, and end up dead? And then a prisoner. Here?" His voice, which had started out as a snarl, rose in pitch and register, until the last sentence became a roar, which made me quake.

But why was he attacking me? We had *always* been a little reckless whenever we hunted together. He knew I would push the boundaries of our range, little by little. That I'd always try to hunt more game, gather more food, do whatever it took to help my family. He used to come with me, in fact: the anchor to my confidence, my guiding force, my helper. We'd protected each other, had each other's back. He was always there for me.

Until one day he wasn't. If I'd gotten caught, well—he was partly to blame for deserting me so thoroughly.

"I went there to save Pópo." This was the one thing he couldn't argue with. The one thing he couldn't dispute. He had loved my grandmother, almost as much as I did. And in turn she had trusted him. "Her illness is worsening. And . . . she doesn't have much time left."

Lin stopped in his tracks, his face aghast, his arms now hanging limp by his sides. His jaw worked as he seemingly grasped for what to say.

Finally, he spoke, his voice strangled. "How long?"

I clasped the edges of my gown, which had fallen open, and drew it tighter before knotting the tie with trembling fingers.

"Not long. Every day that passes, I worry more that she'll—" I paused, the words catching in my throat. After taking a shaky breath, I continued. "The healers still have no idea why she's sick. It's like nothing they've seen before, they say. They keep trying and trying, but the only thing that helps is potion brewed with Shadowside." I raised my chin. "I was gathering more of it of when Andres Brisson slew me."

It seemed such a strange thing to say: *slew me*. My sense of logic still rebelled against the idea that I'd actually, truly, died.

"Shadowside?" Lin seemed to be capable of doing little but repeating me.

I nodded, blinking back tears. "It's getting harder to find. And if I don't get more to Pópo soon, she'll die." For a moment I couldn't speak. I was still trying to breathe around the obstruction in my chest. The heavy ache of worry, ever-present and immobile.

Suddenly an idea landed, fully formed, in my mind. Taking two steps forward, I lifted my hand, meaning to place it on Lin's chest. But where there should have been solid flesh—skin, muscle, and beneath it a beating heart—there was nothing. Only air. Air that was noticeably cooler than its surroundings, that rippled with some undercurrent of disturbance.

Lin made a movement that, had he been alive, would have been a sharp intake of breath. The pupils of his eyes dilated as his gaze flicked down to where my hand floated, seemingly in contact with his disembodied form.

"You have to help me," I whispered, surprised at how hoarse I sounded. "You can pass through walls freely, can't you? Which means you can see the entirety of Throft Hall. You could find a way out. A way for me to escape—"

"There is no escape." Lin gave me a reproachful look and stepped away. "You should not have been so foolish as to get captured to begin with."

I pressed on, undeterred by his grumpiness. "Please. You have to help me. You *must.* Otherwise Pópo will . . . She'll . . ." At this, I broke down.

Lin watched me crying, a look I couldn't quite parse flashing across his face. It was a look that seemed almost . . . *vulnerable.* For the first time in a long while I could see the boy that I'd grown up with.

But then the barriers came down again, his face settling into its usual mask. "Fine. I'll help. But I should warn you: It is likely to be difficult."

With my tears still falling freely, I gave a jerky nod. "Difficult is fine. I will do anything. *Anything.*"

Lin turned to go. By reflex, I made to grab at him, seizing nothing but empty air. My fist tightened to a clench, and both our eyes dropped down to where I'd failed to touch him.

I snatched back my hand as though burned. "Hurry." I blinked, and more tears dislodged from my lashes and slid down my cheeks. "For Pópo."

He nodded once. "For Pópo."

And then, just like that, he disappeared.

Eight

Present day

Once Lin had gone, I fell straight to meticulously searching the walls for cracks or loose stones, and running my hands across the floor in case of any weak spots. I flipped up rugs. I rattled the door handle. I even tried to pry the paintings off the wall, looking for a secret exit. But they wouldn't budge.

Eventually, after I'd combed the entire room, I was forced to stop. Fisting my hands against the locked door, I rested my forehead against them, swallowing my scream. There was no way out. Absolutely none. This "guest" room was as secure as any prison.

Following that, all I could do was pace.

In bare feet, I trod circles around the polished hardwood floor until my bones ached and the balls of my feet blistered. I picked at the food the Lancaster servant had brought: a little toasted bread as well as some sort of pink meat. The lumpy eggy thing, though, I left untouched. Yskian food—which smelled considerably better than it tasted—was seriously weird.

Even that small amount of sustenance churned nauseatingly in my gut. *What could be taking Lin so long?* I wondered. *What if he was right? What if there is no escape?*

I stopped pacing. He had always been a resourceful individual. I was sure he'd find a way.

I *had* to be sure. The alternative—I could not bear to think about.

Frowning, I rubbed at my eyes and resumed my pointless patrol.

A long-forgotten feeling lodged itself within my throat, and it had to do with Lin. Lin, who had agreed to help me find a way back to Pópo even though he didn't have to. Even though he'd abandoned me more than a year ago. Though we could no longer connect over anything else, including our relative statuses as living or dead . . . at least we still had this. Our mutual love for my grandmother.

Eventually, my feet started hurting too much to continue pacing. Sighing, I resigned myself to my helplessness, and decided I might as well rest.

I went back to the wardrobe and perused its contents to see if there was anything besides nightgowns. There was not. My stomach clenched—how long was Essien Lancaster planning to keep me here?

Quickly, I quashed those thoughts, shoving them away. Whatever the Lancasters' plans were, *I* was not about to submit to them. I'd escape somehow. Whether that was by incapacitating a guard, persuading the prince, or using Lin, I would find a way. I was resourceful, too.

Ignoring the nightgowns—it was safest to stay in my own hànfú, in case I needed a quick escape—I climbed into bed. I went slowly, breathing through the pain from my sword wound. Eventually I managed to ease myself under the covers and pull them over my shoulders.

In this foreign bed, within this foreign castle, everything felt wrong. The air was too stuffy, the bed too soft. Even my heartbeat sounded abnormally loud within my ears. It took a long time for sleep to find me; eventually, though, exhaustion crowded the edges of my vision and I succumbed to a fitful slumber.

My dreams were disjointed but featured flashing swords, bitter tea . . . Lin. Lin's face flitted through the murky depths of my mind with alarming frequency. His voice, too, crept up my spine and lodged in the base of my skull. *Jia*, dream-Lin whispered. *Jia, Jia, Jia.*

The voice was urgent, insistent, and pain began to cloud the boundaries of my dreamlike state. Wait, what? If I was feeling pain, then I was no longer asleep, I was . . .

I jolted awake to find the ghost of Lin bent over me.

"Mā de!" I cried out, bolting upright. "You frightened me!" Every muscle ached. I still felt exhausted; it seemed like no time had passed since I'd fallen asleep.

Lin gave a smirk. "That's what ghosts do, Jia. We scare people."

"Your face would be frightening dead or alive," I grumbled.

The smirk fell away, and Lin folded his arms. "Do you want to hear about what I found, or not?"

"Yes! I'm sorry. Yes." I scrambled out of bed, chagrined, my focus now entirely on our mission.

He summarized his findings quickly. According to Lin, Throft Hall had extensive security: Guards were stationed outside my door; still more manned every exit. "You could take one or two of them down," Lin explained. "Easy. But that many? I'm quite sure you'll be caught."

The hope that had flickered in my chest dwindled and died like a snuffed candle. "So there's no hope? No escape?"

Lin's mouth flattened. He looked away. "There is one way."

"Tell me."

"Through the dungeons." He still wouldn't look at me. "Where they imprison magical folk."

"But isn't that where they keep—?"

"The Spyrre." Lin turned to face me, his eyes hooded. "It is. And Jia, you didn't have magic before, but now it seems you do, and I can't risk—"

"But wait!" I cut him off. "Essien Lancaster tested me. Against the Spyrre. Right before I collapsed. And . . . I passed."

Lin rubbed his temples with both hands. "You passed? How?"

"I don't know. But I did. Maybe coming back from the dead was a . . . one-time thing." Raising a hand to my forehead, I paced away from him. "So. I need you to tell me how to get through the dungeons."

I perched on the edge of the bed as Lin explained the layout of Throft Hall and what he'd learned of the guards' schedules. When he finished, I raised my head and stared at him, weary. "Getting to the dungeons sounds easy enough. But what about the guards?"

"You only need to worry about the two stationed outside your door. The Lancasters don't use guards for the dungeons—they rely on the Spyrre."

I shuddered in spite of myself. "Okay. How do I get past the ones guarding my door?"

Lin passed a hand over his chin. He appeared to be thinking. Finally, one corner of his mouth tipped up and he fixed his gaze on me. "I know: I'll create a distraction. Give you a chance to run."

My eyes narrowed, just slightly. He had a look that I recognized, that meant he was about to do something . . . not bad, necessarily. But certainly morally questionable. "What sort of distraction?"

"I'll—" Abruptly, Lin's head jerked up. His voice took on a hardened edge. "Someone's coming!"

And he disappeared.

How long would it take for me to get used to him doing that?

My thoughts were broken by the resounding boom of loud knocking. The lock turned before the door swung, emitting a high-pitched creak.

I was already on my feet, but I froze on the spot. I'd been expecting Prince Essien, since he'd said he would come back, but instead it was . . .

"How is my patient this evening?" Larch, the court physician, strode into the room, wearing his distinctive royal blue robes. I'd never met him in person, of course, but I'd seen him in the throne room during my prior interrogations.

I remained silent, glancing out the window. The last lashings of the dying sun were tinting the shadowed sky. I must have slept for longer than I'd realized.

Hugging my arms around my body, I withdrew my stare

from the outside view and slowly swiveled to face the doctor, glowering at him.

"You look better," Larch continued, completely unperturbed by my silence. He set his bag down on a side table and began rummaging through its contents.

As much as I was loath to admit it, I did feel better. The pain from my wound ached when I moved, but when I was still, I almost forgot it altogether. How had Larch managed to do that, in mere days, without magic? I hugged my arms even tighter. I didn't trust this Yskian physician. I did not trust him one bit.

With quick, precise movements Larch placed a metal tray atop the table, before laying his instruments on the tray to form a neat line. Scissors, a small metal bowl, a neatly folded piece of cloth, tweezers, a blade . . .

Wait. A *blade*?

All the blood fled my face. "Lord Larch," I stammered. "What is—"

Larch straightened, and the way his eyes gleamed made my skin flush cold.

I began backing away, using one of the bedposts as leverage. It was a pathetic attempt at escape, really, because where would I escape to? Still, I tried to dart around the other side of the bed, when Larch caught me. There was little chance I could have outrun him, anyway. I was feeling better, but not *that* much better.

Grabbing me by the arms, as tight as a vise, the heavyset doctor wrestled me onto the plush surface of the bed. I thrashed, hurling out obscenities, but Larch held fast with his considerable strength. "*Stay still*, Lady Liu," he grunted. "I merely need to debride your wound."

Not knowing what he meant by "debride," I shrieked and struggled even harder, attempting to claw at his face. Larch held my wrists, undeterred, apparently no stranger to wrestling patients. With sweat sheening his brow, he procured ropes from some inner pocket of his robe and bound me securely to the bed.

I jerked at my restraints. "Fuck you!" I screamed. I even tried to headbutt him, but he was just beyond my reach.

Larch snatched the ropes tighter and thrust a stick between my teeth. "We can do this the easy way," he grunted as he worked, "or the hard way. Your choice."

What little strength I had was leaving me, so, trying to muster any remaining dignity, I finally went limp. He was right. There was no point fighting. The Lancasters had me locked up in a well-guarded room. And there was no one to help me except an annoying, unreliable, traitorous ghost.

Now that I was effectively restrained, Larch went to work. There was no way to see what he was doing. All I could do was stare helplessly up at the ceiling while I listened to the metallic scrape of the doctor sharpening his tools. There was a fluttering feeling as the physician cut away my bandages, then a wet thud as he discarded the sodden wrappings . . . somewhere. From where I was tied down I couldn't see.

He began to bathe my injury, and I inhaled sharply at the sting, biting down so hard, I thought my jaw might crack. Eventually, he finished cleaning the wound, and there was another sound of metal scraping as he sharpened his next tool.

I barely had time to draw breath, when the next lot of pain started. And this time, it was not just a sting.

The screaming that filled the room was so hoarse, so unearthly, it took a while to realize that it was actually coming from me. My back arched, my body almost bowing off the bed, as the physician began to carve away the necrotic edges of the wound.

I screamed again, tears in my eyes, trying unsuccessfully to thrash against the ropes that bound me. My whole body burned; sweat sprang across my forehead, my upper lip, my chest. It hurt. It *hurt.* It was like Andres Brisson was running his sword through me—but again, and again, and again.

"Be quiet," Larch snapped. "You are all right—"

"I am not all fucking"—my words were muffled by the stick, and I let out a hiss as the scalpel plunged back into my skin—"right."

At that exact moment, the door must have flown open, because I heard it bash against its hinges.

And then Essien Lancaster's voice rose above the scream of mine. "Larch! What in the devil's name are you doing?"

The pain abruptly eased, and I sagged, panting, against my bindings.

"I am treating the Fengzhian, Your Highness," the physician said, somewhat indignant. "As per your instructions."

There was a pause. "You were supposed to wait for me." The prince had schooled his voice to measured calm. "You do not have the authority to enter this room without my permission."

"Yes, Your Highness."

Footsteps approached the bed, and then the prince was

leaning over me, his marble-carved face oddly pale. With quick fingers, he untied the ropes, pulled the sodden stick from my mouth, and backed away to a safe distance as I shakily sat up.

He shot me a wary look, and I stared back, belligerent. What was he doing here? Why had he interrupted the physician? I was still trying to untangle his motives, when I was startled by a choked-off cry. This was followed by a strange gurgling noise. Something heavy landed on my legs, followed by a rush of warm fluid.

Prince Essien's eyes flared wide, and slowly, he turned. I raised my head. Only to see Larch slumped face down across my legs, blood soaking into the eiderdown, and—

Lin, standing behind him, holding that curved, bright-blue blade.

For a moment, I could only stare at the doctor's body in shock. Then, with the pulse in my ears roaring, I scrambled up and shoved the deadweight of Larch's corpse off me. It slid sideways and landed on the floor with an unceremonious thud.

"Careful, girl," growled a voice, and I startled to see Larch's ghost staring down at his body, frowning. He raised his gaze, piercing me with his disapproval. "You should respect the dead!"

Not stopping to answer him, I swung my legs off the bed and jumped to my feet. Essien Lancaster was staring, open-mouthed, at the body of the physician. His face was puce, the muscles in his neck corded with tension. He'd lost the usual easy grace of his stance and was trembling all over. I think he'd forgotten he was still holding the stick.

Lin's expression, on the other hand, was impassive. Almost smirking. I took in the entire scene within a mere fraction of a second. And then I noticed Lin, with the tiniest, most minute of movements, adjusting the grip of his knife. So subtly no one would notice.

No one except me, who knew him well. Or had known him well, once.

He drew back his arm to slash at the prince. For some reason, something within me snapped.

"NO!" I screamed, lunging forward, unthinking. Reflexively, I threw myself in front of Essien Lancaster, Lin's intended target.

The blade continued its downward trajectory. Too late, Lin realized what I'd done.

He let out an anguished cry as his blade slashed across my neck.

Nine

THE FIRST LEVEL
Present day

Screaming pain tore through my body, and I let out an ear-shattering shriek. Blood, hot and red, spurted from my throat. Essien gave a strangled cry, lunged forward, and caught me right before I hit the ground. The stick tumbled to the floor. In a fruitless attempt to stem the flow, he pressed one hand on my neck wound as consciousness swiftly left me.

And there I was again, rising out of my lifeless body and into the murky afterlife. The prince bent over me, letting out a continuous string of garbled curses. His face was deathly white, his normally pristine hands drenched in blood.

Lin and I—in my ghostly form—stood staring at one another. He was visibly shaking, still clutching his blood-sheathed blade. "Jia, what the *fuck* have you done?"

The answer was obvious: I'd died. *Again.*

Fury snapped within me, like branches cracking on a fire. "What do you *mean*, what have I done? What have *you* done? You . . . you *murdered* someone!"

Lin's expression darkened. "To save you, Jia. To help *you.*"

"I didn't realize you were going to *kill* to do it!"

He flung his hand in the direction of the door. "Well, *I* didn't expect someone was going to come in here and hurt you! I did what I had to do."

A gravelly voice spoke from behind us, causing us both to spin around. "I was doing my job," Larch's ghost said peevishly. "Debridement is a perfectly acceptable method of—"

"Oh shut up, old man," Lin snapped, then returned his attention to me. "Whatever's happened, Jia, you better take the chance. *Quickly.* That pale-faced prince is distracted. For now. But it won't be long before he calls in his guards." His eyes bored into mine. "Then there will be *no* escape."

I threw a glance in Essien's direction. He was still clinging to my lifeless body, his hand clamped over my neck, which fortunately had stopped leaking blood. I clenched and unclenched my fists, torn with indecision. "But . . . I'm dead." My voice sounded suddenly small.

"Then resurrect."

I blinked up at him. "What?"

"I don't think it was a one-off." He gesticulated with his hands, his movements becoming harried. "You have to trust me. You're not safe as a ghost. Not here. *Please,* Jia. Resurrect—and run."

This was my chance. Lin *had* agreed to provide a distraction, but I'd assumed he would just appear out of the shadows and scare a guard or something. I hadn't known he was going to stab Larch. How had he even done it? He couldn't touch me, and yet he could kill me? A living, breathing human being?

But now was not the time to wonder. Already Essien had

raised his head, his blue eyes hardening to steel. Lin was right: If the prince called his guards, then my escape plans would be completely thwarted.

"Jia," Lin's voice was in my ear. He'd moved closer. "Do it. Do it now! Resurrect!"

Closing my eyes, I forced myself to think of Pópo. With a heave, I folded into myself, focusing on my corpse, on the invisible, fragile threads that seemed to connect my spirit to it.

But it was like trying to clutch at water. For a second, I felt a tenuous connection to the living realm, only to have the string fray and snap. The rupture was excruciating; I shrieked, doubling over.

"Jia," Lin urged. "You have to resurrect. Now."

"If you'd just let me *concentrate*," I said, "then maybe I'd be able to!"

Gathering all my awareness, I once again tried to focus. How had I done it previously? I'd been in life-threatening danger, of course, and had done it without thinking. But now? Trying to intentionally do it? My head was on the verge of exploding.

It seemed as though resurrecting voluntarily was going to take a good deal of mental strength—something that I didn't possess. I hadn't ever possessed it, really, considering I'd never taken meditation classes seriously. An oversight that, in this moment, I regretted.

"Come *on*, Jia!" Lin's gaze darted to the closed door and back to me.

"I swear, if you nag me one more time I'm going to just give up and slap you." At least I could now, considering we were both ghosts.

He held up his hands, conciliatory. "Fine, I won't nag. Just be quick, they're coming—"

"Who—" I began, but then I heard it, too. The heavy trudge of armored footsteps, thundering through the door. Guards, presumably coming to see what the commotion was.

That was it. That did it. The threat of more Lancaster men accosting me made my errant thoughts converge on the one thing that could get me out of here: resurrecting.

Two guards rushed in—

And, with a huge jolt of pain, I fell back into my body, and woke with an enormous, rasping breath.

The prince gave a shout of surprise, but before he'd had a chance to react, I'd shoved him off me, rolled away, and leaped to my feet.

"Your Highness!" one of the guards shouted, brandishing his weapon, his gaze flicking between the prince and me.

I tried to bolt, but the prince grabbed me, his grip viselike. Heat from his skin seared into my arm. "Jia Yi," he choked out, his eyes wild—and completely inappropriately, I noticed that this was the first time he had actually said my name, instead of a condescending "Lady Liu." "What did you do?" His fingers tightened, almost painfully. *"Did you kill Larch?"*

"What? No!" My mouth went dry, my heart thrashing in my chest. Mothers be damned, if Essien thought I killed his physician, then there'd be no way he'd let me go.

I tried, unsuccessfully, to wrench myself away.

The prince squeezed his eyes shut, his face paling even further. "But—but he just *died*! Like that! He . . . he . . ." He seemed utterly lost for words.

Sensing this was my only chance to get away, I seized the

opportunity. I swung my free arm around, then punched Essien. Hard. My fist connected, pain jolting down my arm. The prince staggered backward, cursing and clutching his nose.

We stared at each other, shocked into silence for half a second, before he drew a deep breath. "Take her!" he bellowed at his guards, his voice muffled by his hands.

"Go!" Lin shouted. "I'll deal with them. GO!"

I didn't hesitate. I turned. I ran.

"*Guards!*" the prince hollered again. Behind me, I heard footsteps of pursuit, along with the unmistakable clang of clashing weapons. *No*, I thought, picking up my pace, even though my lungs were screaming and every step jolted my wounds. *I won't be prisoner here*, I thought desperately, ignoring the pain. *I won't!*

I turned down a dark corridor, my bare feet slapping the stone. Instinctively, my hand went to my neck, putting pressure on it—but while it still throbbed a little, the gash where Lin had cut me was barely bleeding. It made no sense. The blow had been fatal. How had it improved that quickly? Were my resurrection powers getting stronger, allowing me to heal?

At least I now knew I had the ability to come back—again.

My thoughts dissipated as I reached a stairwell. I almost tripped, teetering on the edge of the top step, only to stop myself by grabbing the polished wood banister.

"Come back, witch!" It alarmed me to hear how much distance Essien had gained on me.

I couldn't stop. Essien was slower than me—after all, I'd spent my entire life running barefoot through forests. I was more agile than this pampered, sheltered prince. But I was injured, and he, determined. He was also more familiar with the castle. Taking a deep, rattling inhale, I began running down the stairs, descending into the gloom. Down and down I ran. Essien pursued me doggedly, his footsteps echoing in the confined stone space.

It had grown cold, and I sensed we'd penetrated deep below ground, into the bowels of Throft Hall. Close to the dungeons, which Lin had said was the best exit point. At the end of each corridor, he had explained, there was a hole in the floor that was used to—*ugh*—wash the prisoners' excrement down into the sewage pits. This, apparently, was my best chance of escape. And I was willing to do it to get back to Pópo, even if it meant literally covering myself in shit.

Especially since I doubted Prince Essien—the golden boy, the boy who'd never had to work a day in his life, who'd never had to get his hands dirty, never mind completely cake himself in filth—would follow me.

Prisoners, thin and weak from hunger, moaned as I passed. They reached for me through the bars, and I ignored them, biting back tears, focusing only on reaching the end of the corridor.

But as I dashed through the dungeons, I heard a familiar rasping, shuffling sound from the shadows.

Damnit. The Spyrre were down here. I knew they would be, but I'd half hoped that the Lancasters would keep them chained up or something. I knew, though, from the noises, and how rapidly they were approaching, that probably was not the case.

Keep running, I screamed internally. In my peripheral vision, something materialized from the shadows, so black it was even emptier than the surrounding darkness. Then more forms appeared, and more, peeling away from the walls, pouring in through branching corridors, amassing behind me as I ran.

And congregating around Essien, too, who still chased me. I heard him give a shout, battering his way past the shuffling Spyrre. He seemed frantic, even though I knew he wouldn't be at risk; he was an Yskian, he wasn't magical, the Spyrre wouldn't go after him—

I'd reached the end of the corridor, and just as Lin had said, there was a hole in the ground covered by a grate. Trying not to gag, I dragged the grate off to one side, exposing the opening.

"Don't follow me," I whispered to myself, my eyes hot with spilling tears. This was it: My chance. My *only* chance.

I closed my eyes, held my breath, and jumped.

Ten

Present day

I surfaced in the putrid water, my hair slicked to my scalp. Everything stank. I gagged and held my arm to my nose but then gagged again because even *that* stunk.

There were no sounds above me, so I began to wade away, splashing through the waist-high water.

And then—

A splash. Another splash. And another, and another, and another.

Fuck. They were pursuing.

I didn't know if it was Essien or the Spyrre, or both. All I knew was that I had to keep moving. Picking up my pace and tuning out everything—the smells, the sounds, the unseen things bumping into me—I propelled myself forward. Even the pain lancing through my wounds and the knowledge they would probably fester . . . I ignored it all and focused on the moonlit grate in the distance.

After what felt like years but in reality was probably mere minutes, I reached the grate. Desperately, I pushed against it, heaving, huffing, throwing all my strength behind my movements, until finally, finally, it gave way. I fell then, spilling out into the silver night, to find myself in the castle moat.

Water, I thought, bobbing in the gentle current. *Sweet, clean, water.* Relief flooded my entire body. I'd done it. I'd actually done it. I'd managed to escape my room, breach the castle walls . . . *and* the moat was washing me free of all the blood and filth.

A noise jolted me back to the present. My pursuers were still in the sewers, wading after me. Spurred into action, I sucked in a breath and slipped beneath the surface, the cool, silent water enveloping me whole.

Down here, everything was dark. I blinked hard, attempting to see through the gloom. Far below me, deeper in the water, I thought I saw the flick of a shadow—a fish? Were there even fish in the Throft Hall moat? Through all my previous journeys into and out of this castle, it had never occurred to me to take notice.

Trying to ignore the shifting shapes, I swam the short distance to the other side before hauling myself onto shore. *I hope the Spyrre can't swim,* I thought as I bolted into the surrounding forest, wet hair and clothes clinging to my body.

"Jia!" Prince Essien's voice rang out after me. Shit. He *had* followed me. "Come back!"

"Come back?" I panted, leaping over fallen tree trunks as I pushed forward into the forest. "Not . . . fucking . . . likely." I risked a glance behind me and saw the prince, his hair, in disarray for probably the very first time, plastered to his head and darkened by damp. Behind him, a cluster of Spyrre, pursuing him, pursuing me.

But that brief look cost me, because when I swung my head

back around to face forward I smacked into a tree. A shock of pain reverberated right through me and I fell, my head spinning. I made a valiant attempt to scramble to my feet, but too late—Essien was upon me, and we both went tumbling, rolling down a small bracken-clad hill.

We landed, his warm weight pressing me down, his face hovering above mine. He braced his hands on either side of my head, caging me against the forest floor. Like before, his heat flooded into my body, making me dizzy. He was surprisingly strong for someone who, from a distance, always seemed so lithe, so graceful.

"Jia." He said my name again, but he was panting, catching his breath, so it sounded ungainly. "Please—"

"Let me *go*!" I thrashed and struggled, but it was useless. I was as trapped as a caged bird.

"Be quiet," he hissed. "Otherwise they will hear."

Violently, I tried to yank myself away. "What? Who? What in the Mothers' name are you talking about?"

"The Spyrre."

The Spyrre. Of course they'd still be pursuing, drawn by my trail of magic. Finally, I went still, straining to hear in the darkness.

Twigs snapped. The sound of the Spyrre's moth-eaten cloaks brushing against the undergrowth approached. Rattling breaths ripped through the silence. The creatures were sucking in the cool night air, tasting it for traces of . . . Of what? Me? Us? *Him?*

The shuffling drew closer. My heartbeat hammered in my ears. I whimpered, but Essien shushed me. His face was so near mine I could feel the touch of his breath fluttering against my ear.

"Do not be afraid," he whispered, his voice low. "If we are quiet, they should leave us alone."

"Wait, what?" I blurted. What did he mean, "leave *us* alone"?

Essien didn't respond. Instead, giving me a warning look, he just pressed his finger to my lips.

Involuntarily, my breath caught, my lips parting slightly under the warmth of his touch. I realized what he was doing now. He was trying to hide me.

But why?

The shuffling grew louder. I shook, somewhat grateful for the way Prince Essien's larger body was shielding mine. A complicated tangle of emotions surged in my chest: a mixture of relief, and gratefulness, and—truth be told—confusion.

The sound drew ever closer, and then, mercifully, passed us by. Both of us let out a small exhale and suddenly—

Suddenly I was very aware that Prince Essien, sixth son of Yske, was lying on top of me, pressing me into the mossy ground. And all that separated our two bodies were a few layers of flimsy fabric.

Even in the darkness I sensed him flushing. Muttering something under his breath that sounded like "Excuse me," he pushed himself up off me and stood, his posture very straight.

Rolling to my knees, I winced. Then I struggled to my feet, brushing dried leaves from my clothes and hair. It was only as I was finishing that I noticed the prince was still staring at me.

"What's wrong?" I said, suddenly suspicious.

He tore his gaze away and focused it somewhere above me. "Nothing," he said, his face flushing even harder. "Nothing at all."

I tilted my head, scrutinizing him. Pieces of his damp hair, no longer in its usual perfect coif, were hanging down over his eyes. A leaf had gotten caught in one of his locks, presumably during our tussle down the hill.

I edged closer to him, very slowly. "You have something caught . . . right there . . ." I pointed at the leaf. He uttered a low curse and swiped at it, but somehow managed to miss it altogether.

"Here, let me—" I was now right before him, and reaching out—my fingers shakier than usual—I plucked the leaf from his hair. As I did so, the tips of my fingers brushed his temple; his skin burned beneath my touch.

He flinched and ducked away, leaving me standing with the leaf in my hand.

I let out a surprised laugh and tossed away the piece of foliage. "You don't need to be scared of me, you know."

"I'm not scared," he said, too quickly. Then he admitted, "All right, perhaps I am a little scared."

I took a step toward him. He went rigid all over but made no move to back away.

"Why?" I jutted up my chin. "Is it because I'm Fengzhian? Is it because I'm a Liu?"

"No," he said, and grimaced. "After what happened in the room back there . . . What am I supposed to think?" He turned his somber gaze on me. "I just need to know. Did you kill Larch with . . . with *witchcraft*?"

Silhouetted by the moonlight, his face was in darkness, his eyes in complete shadow. He looked like a demon in this light. So unlike the golden, illuminated Yskian prince.

I understood his reasoning. From the prince's perspective,

he'd been untying me from the bed after Larch had worked on my wound. The next thing he knew, Larch was dead, lying in a pool of blood. Shortly after, I had collapsed, too, my blood spilling from my neck, before I had inexplicably come back alive again.

The prince couldn't see ghosts, couldn't see Larch's ghost frowning over his own corpse. Couldn't see me, as a ghost, bickering with the ghost of Lin. When Essien Lancaster stared at our spectral forms, he would have seen nothing, save for empty space. As far as he knew, it had only been him and me in that room when Larch died.

"Why, are you going to arrest me again?"

He clenched his jaw, but his throat rippled as he swallowed, revealing his nervousness. "Maybe."

"Well, it wasn't me." I scowled. "We Lius only have one power each. You already know my power. And it isn't inflicting death."

The prince raked his fingers through his hair, looking perplexed. "Then why—*how*—did he die?" He jabbed a finger in the direction of my neck. "And how did you get that wound?"

"I'm not sure," I said, improvising. "Everything happened so fast. All I remember is pushing him off me. I suppose he—he *was* holding a scalpel, and in the struggle, maybe he cut us both."

The prince stared at me for what seemed like an eternity, as though trying to establish if I was lying, before finally scrunching up his nose. "Gods above," he said. "I am sorry I did not reach you sooner."

I almost sagged with relief that he'd somehow believed my story. This Lancaster was either very gullible, or else . . . he *wanted* to believe me. Which, once again, was confusing. I could not understand this boy's logic, at all.

Prince Essien looked at me, running a hand across his chin. He appeared to be considering his next move. The silence between us stretched wide like a yawn, and I carefully avoided further eye contact.

Finally, he squinted at the turrets of Throft Hall silhouetted against the arching, amethyst night sky. "It is clouding over," he murmured, more to himself than me. Then, louder, he said. "Come, we should go back."

"Go back?" I retorted. "Nope. No way am I going back with you."

The prince turned to face me, slowly, his head cocked like he hadn't heard me properly. He arched one eyebrow. "Excuse me? Of course you're coming with me—"

"I'm going home."

"No, you're not."

"Why, *Your Highness*?" My tone made a mockery of his title. "Because you *need* something from me?"

"I have saved your life, twice now. The least you can do is hear me out—"

"Saved my life?" I scoffed, backing away from him. "What a joke! It was *your* man who killed me in the first place. And you have no right to keep me prisoner. I'll—" But as usual, my body betrayed me. I gasped, and a stab of pain sent me doubling over.

"Lady Liu!" As the prince darted to catch my elbow, I couldn't help noticing he had gone back to formal address. Apparently we were no longer on a first-name basis.

For some reason, this detail vexed me, and I fought to escape from his grip. "Let. Me. Go!"

He didn't let me go. Not at first. He just grasped me tighter, breathing hard, his fingers digging into my arm. "Be quiet." Even though I tried to fight it, that feeling of heat, of elation, began spreading through my body. "Or—"

"Or what?" I hissed. "You *will* arrest me?"

"No, no. It's the—" Abruptly, his eyes widened. There was a moment of profound silence, as if all the sound had been sucked away. And then, he jerked backward, enveloped by an unnatural darkness.

The Spyrre, was what he'd meant to say.

The Spyrre had returned.

Eleven

Present day

The prince was silent, frozen in shock, as the Spyrre converged on him. But his eyes, luminous in the moonlight, were locked on mine. I screamed his name, but the Spyrre ignored me. The night air filled with the bone-deep rattling of the Spyrre sucking out his life essence, his qì, and possibly . . . his magic?

I couldn't make sense of it. The prince didn't *have* magic. I apparently did. Why then, were they attacking him? *It doesn't matter,* I thought. This, here, was my perfect chance to escape. While the prince was otherwise . . . occupied . . . I could make a run for it. Back home. To Pópo.

Turning away from the shadowy towers of Throft Hall, I began to push in the opposite direction, crashing through the dense undergrowth. I had only taken a few steps when I stopped.

I hazarded one last look at the prince. He had passed out and was now lying deathly still, his eyes closed, his already-pale lips turning blue. The Spyrre leaned over him, feasting on his life force.

Guilt rolled through my body. My resolve wavered.

I still didn't understand why, but for some reason the prince had saved me, even if it was only to get whatever it was he needed.

He'd shielded me from the Spyrre as we shivered on the forest floor. He'd lifted me out of the throne room pit when I'd collapsed. He'd assigned his own physician to care for me in a misguided attempt to help.

Regardless of my feelings toward the Yskians and their ilk, I couldn't just leave Prince Essien to die, or whatever horrific fate the Spyrre brought upon hapless humans.

For some reason, I was still immune to the Spyrre, even though I clearly possessed powers—powers that I'd demonstrated after Andres Brisson's attack, and again when Lin had stabbed me. There was a chance I could save the prince with little to no risk to myself.

So I made up my mind. I wouldn't run.

I would go back.

Before I could renege, I swallowed my fear and charged at the horde. I had no plan, no idea how I was going to defeat the Spyrre. Crashing into them, I began to pull them off the prince, flinging them aside. Fear gave me inhuman strength. One by one they tumbled to the ground. Being desiccated husks of skin and bone made them relatively light, and since I seemed inexplicably resistant to their effects, they were helpless against me as I made messy work of battering through.

The prince was lying limp, sprawled across the crushed

bracken. When I touched him, he was cold as morning stone—a stark contrast to the usual fire of his skin. Struggling with his deadweight, I dragged him to his feet. I ignored the burning in my muscles as I hooked his arm around my shoulders.

Around me, the Spyrre began to stir from where they had collapsed onto the ground. Their inhales started again, and they began to taste the air, taste me, taste my essence, Essien's essence, their breaths rattling through the caverns of their empty nose holes.

"Quick." I slapped the prince's face, my whole body thrumming. "We need to get away from here!"

His eyes fluttered open. He gave a weak, stupefied smile. "Ji-a," he said. In his state, my name was even more mangled by his accent than usual, the emphasis in all the wrong places.

"Come *on*," I urged, trying to drag him away from the now-stirring Spyrre, panic edging my voice.

Suddenly, he jumped, realizing our predicament. His now-bloodshot eyes landed on the nearest Spyrre, who had risen back onto its feet and was lunging at us again. He tensed; we tore ourselves away from its grasping fingers and half stumbled, half ran toward the nearest tree. I pushed him in the direction of the lowest-hanging branch.

"Up!" I commanded. Mercifully, the prince complied immediately. We both scaled the tree until we were a good way off the ground. Taking my hand, he hauled me onto his branch, holding me steady to prevent me from falling.

We wedged ourselves onto one of the thicker branches, holding our breaths, closed in on all sides by the dense canopy. Below us, the Spyrre continued to circle the base of the tree, their cloaks swishing in the unnatural hush. I whispered a silent thank-you to the Mothers that Spyrre seemingly could not climb.

It felt like an age before they finally gave up and began to drag their way back to the castle. I watched them disappear over the crest of the hill and then let loose a sigh. And all of a sudden I was extremely aware of my proximity to the prince.

"Should we, uh . . ." He looked at me, his brow creased, and cleared his throat. "Should we get down now?"

My face grew hot. We were in such an intimate position. The branch was not big, and the prince had braced his back against the tree trunk, one hand grasping the next branch for stability, the other wrapped around my waist.

The moon had temporarily tucked itself behind the clouds, and it was almost pitch-black, so I couldn't see him. I could smell him, though: His scent reminded me of spring rain and new grass and a whiff of honeyed mead. And I could feel him, too. We were rammed so closely together, my hands clinging on to his shoulders. I could feel the steady thump of his heart beating against mine, the lines and muscles of his broad shoulders beneath my hands, his warmth, once again spreading through me.

I was thankful for the darkness that concealed the color rising in my cheeks. "Perhaps we should stay here," I whispered. "Until we're absolutely sure they're gone." I shuddered at the image of the Spyrre feasting on the moribund prince. That vision would be stamped on my memory forever; I doubted I'd ever be free of it.

"Very well," he whispered back. He didn't relax, though. Under my hands, I felt the way his body was strung taut with tension.

I fell silent for a moment, feeling the prince's gaze on me. Why was he still staring?

I needed a distraction. Desperately. Something to take my mind off the press of his torso and the heat of his skin and the way he smelled so . . . good. So I raised my face to his, heard his sharp intake of breath. Our faces were so close. Our bodies even closer.

"What happened down there?" I said, my tone demanding. "Why did they attack you and not me?"

The veil of clouds lifted, and moonlight spilled down over us. Our eyes locked.

He looked away for a moment, then back to me. "Perhaps they just . . . got confused. I was, after all, on top of you—" He clamped his mouth shut, his cheeks flushing.

I narrowed my eyes. "Oh, come on," I said, my voice acerbic. "Don't you *dare* lie to me. I saved your life tonight, from Spyrre who are *not supposed* to attack you, and if you don't tell me, I swear to the Mothers I will push you out of this tree and leave you to face them yourself—"

"I'm magical," he blurted out.

I stopped. Stared at him. The barbed words at the tip of my tongue shriveled and died; it took a while for me to recover my wits.

"You," I whispered finally, my voice tremulous. "You're *what*?"

He had the grace to look contrite. "I'm"—he visibly swallowed—"I'm magical."

"That's impossible." Everything inside me had turned ice-cold. I scrunched my eyes shut and shook my head. Internally, my world was crumbling to dust, reality as I knew it flying off on an errant breeze. "You cannot be."

It was known that Yskians lacked magic. That they *hated* magic. After all, that's why they'd banned it, why they'd made the Spyrre.

"I know what you're thinking, Jia." And there it was, my name on his tongue, his Yskian lilt tripping up the pronunciation and splitting it into two distinct syllables. This time, though, it irritated me less.

A *tiny* bit less, that is.

Pained by this realization—I'd never envisioned a situation where the prince of Yske would cease to annoy me—I muttered, "I'm quite certain you have no idea what I'm thinking."

He continued, ignoring me. "It was a random occurrence, my parents' advisers said." There was a tinge of bitterness in his tone. "One in a billion. One in a trillion. Who knows? There hasn't been a documented case like me before. Not in Yske, anyway."

"But . . . Where did it come from?"

"No one knows," he said, looking away. "Some relic from an ancestor who wedded a foreigner, perhaps? No one has ever been able to explain it. Least of all me."

"Is that why," I ventured, "they sent you out here? To Throft Hall?" The farthest outpost in the nation. Yske was such a big country that it gave the king and queen an excuse to barely see their son. Slowly, I was piecing together the puzzle of Prince Essien's existence. But there were gaps, like I was only in possession of a few disparate pieces. "Because . . . they don't like that you have magic?"

"My mother and father claim otherwise. They say it doesn't matter, that they love me anyway." There was definite bitterness in his voice now. His gaze snapped to mine, so steely I almost flinched. "But I don't believe them."

I remained silent for a moment, mulling over his words. I'd always thought of him as nothing more than a pampered prince, incapable of knowing pain. Each time I'd been dragged before him, and he'd reclined on his throne high above me on a platform, while I languished down below in the pit . . . I'd always thought he just wanted to act the lord. That his elevated position was to emphasize his power. Thinking about it now, though—he probably sat up there to avoid contact with the Spyrre.

Nausea swirled in my belly as I considered this new revelation. Eventually, I spoke again. "Okay. You have magic." I took a deep breath. "So what's your power, then?" I felt like he owed me this information, since we'd almost been killed by the Spyrre. Also, to be honest, I was simply curious.

There was another long pause. I sensed the prince was weighing up how much to tell me. Whether to trust me. "Healing," he finally said.

I gaped at him. "Healing? But you have Larch—" I stopped, then corrected myself. "*Had* Larch."

"Larch?" Prince Essien gave a most ungentlemanly snort. "With his blades and his leeches and his bottles full of poison?" Quickly, he added, as though by reflex, "Gods rest his soul, of course."

"But you said Larch was an 'excellent physician'!"

He gave a grim smile. "I lied. Haven't you learned by now? We are all acting in the royal court. We all have our parts to play."

"But he healed me." I was aware my voice sounded plaintive;

I couldn't process this new information, couldn't fathom a situation where an *Yskian* had more magic than me. Without thinking, I placed my hand on my chest wound, wincing at the brief flash of pain.

The prince's eyes darkened as they flicked down to my hand, then back up to my face.

"No, Lady Liu," he said, very quietly. "*I* healed you."

Twelve

Present day

The world tilted as my mind reeled.

"You?" I couldn't help sounding incredulous. "You healed me?"

"Partially," Prince Essien said.

Both my eyebrows shot up. "Partially?" I closed my eyes and exhaled through my nose.

"It works best with direct contact, and I didn't want to . . ." He trailed off, then swallowed.

I remembered the dreams of Essien touching my forehead. Had they been . . . *real*? I shook my head, ignoring the heat creeping across my own face. "But why? Why would you do that?"

"I needed you well," he said, sounding defensive. "Because . . ."

My eyes snapped back open. "Because you need my help. Right?" I didn't bother to hide my disdain.

His gaze, which had been lingering on some vague point above my head, dropped and fixed on me. "Exactly. You were delirious with fever. You were in no condition to speak rationally. Had I not healed you, then you would have been unfit to discuss . . . my proposal."

The prince spoke evenly, deliberately. But I didn't fail to notice his flush had deepened; warmth, like embers, radiated from his skin.

There was a long pause; we stared at each other in silence until eventually he shifted uncomfortably and looked away. I had to admit, as furious as I was that the prince had imprisoned me in Throft Hall, I was a tiny bit curious about the object that he wanted me to bring back from the afterlife. What had this Yskian royal deemed so important that he deigned to use his healing powers on me? To tell *me*, his enemy, his biggest secret?

Finally, I rolled my eyes. "All right then, out with it. What is it that you so desperately need from me?"

He did not answer immediately. Finally, he said, "There's a fabled sword: the Sword of Rechenblod. Have you heard of it?"

A fabled sword? I'd seen a sword once, in a shaman's vision. But it couldn't be the same sword . . .

Could it?

Not wanting to risk divulging too much information, I shook my head.

Essien continued. "According to Lancaster legend, it's a sword that can defeat any army. A weapon that can bestow its wielder any victory. It is . . . unconquerable."

I threw him the most skeptical look I could muster, and said, my voice flat, "You want me to fetch you an unconquerable sword."

Essien seemed unfazed by my response. "It supposedly belonged to one of my forefathers until some usurper stole it. When the usurper died, they took it with them, into the afterlife, beyond our reach. Apparently, whoever wields it gains mastery over life and death . . . It's even rumored to have the power to bring the dead back to life." He threw a glance at me. "Though whether that is true, I cannot say."

I stared at him, open-mouthed. "And you want me to die, retrieve this magic sword that may or may not raise the dead, use my powers to resurrect, and then bring it back to you?"

"Yes." His eyes looked abnormally bright, despite the meager moonlight. "It belongs in Yske. With us—its rightful owners."

I exploded. "Absolutely not!" My cheeks flamed, I was so incensed by his audacity. A pulse began to thump somewhere deep in my skull. "An *unconquerable* sword? Mothers save us! How do I know you won't use it to raze Fengzhi Yuan? Or wage another war against the empire?"

"I won't," the prince said, his voice rising to match mine. "I only want it returned to my family!"

I scrunched my eyes shut and shook my head. "But why? Why would you want it back, if not to use it—"

"Because then maybe they'll think better of me!" Essien snapped. I flinched at the force of his outburst. He clenched his jaw and let out a frustrated exhale before attempting to explain again. "You know my story now, Lady Liu. You know my secret. You know that my family sent me out here, to this Gods-forsaken region, because they are . . . they're ashamed of me."

I opened my mouth to frame a response but was unable to think of one, so I shut it again. The pulsing in my head had progressed to full-blown pounding.

"When I discovered what you are," Essien went on, softer now, "my first instinct was to throw you in the dungeons. You survived the Spyrre up until now, but what if your powers were newly acquired? What if we just needed to try again? I thought that perhaps if I finally caught one of the infamous hidden witches, then I would make my family proud."

Instinctively, I shuddered at the memory of facing the Spyrre.

The prince was rambling by now. "But then I realized that I could do better. You are the first person I've ever encountered who can potentially get the sword. *You* might be my only chance to show my parents that magical abilities aren't necessarily a bad thing. That they can be useful." His eyes locked onto mine, and the spark within them sent a shiver rippling across my skin.

"Don't you see, Lady Liu? If we use your magic to recover the *famous* Sword of Rechenblod, then perhaps . . . perhaps things will be different. Perhaps, with our family's weapon back in our possession, Yskians won't be so afraid of people like you—"

"People like *us*, you mean," I muttered, cutting him off. Essien, whether he liked it or not, was magical. He was one of us.

"Right, yes. Of course. People like us." He blew out a slow breath. "Perhaps I could even—I don't know—convince my parents to repeal the anti-magic laws."

I eyed him dubiously. "You really believe that?"

"I have to believe. What choice do I have?" Then, giving a weary shrug, he added, "At the very least it might improve my standing with them. Which would be a first step, albeit a small one."

I fell silent, turning over his words in my mind. What he said made some modicum of sense, though I still didn't know how I could ever entrust a Lancaster with an apparently invincible sword.

"How do I know you won't use it on us?" My question sounded more like an accusation, but I didn't care.

"You have my word."

I scoffed. "What use have I for words?"

Essien pressed his lips together and gave me a speculative look. "All right then. What would you like? Money? Protection? If it's within my power to give, then I will—provided you agree to get the sword."

"I would like you," I said, through gritted teeth, "to let me go."

Up until now, his hands had been around my waist, steadying me, but he immediately retracted them. Suddenly unsupported, I swayed, just managing to catch hold of a branch before I fell.

I peered into the shadows that spilled across the forest floor. The Spyrre seemed to have well and truly gone, so I swung my leg over the branch to begin the process of clambering down.

"Wait," Essien said, and his abruptness made me start. "Even if you won't hear me out, may I . . ." He swallowed. "May I at least finish healing you? Properly, this time."

I frowned at him. "Why would you even want to?"

"Consider it as something of a peace offering. A way to show you that I wish you no harm. All I want is the sword. Not to use, but to keep safe. And if this will help me get it, then . . ."

I paused, considering. The prince's expression was open, earnest; something in my gut told me he was telling the truth. And although my base instincts recoiled at the thought of being indebted to him, if he healed me, traveling would be less risky. I could almost certainly get home quicker. Back to Pópo. Surely that was worth it?

Before I could change my mind, I gave a curt nod. "Okay."

He held out his hand, palm up. "Your hand first."

My hand . . . The one with the wound I'd sustained punching Lin in the ghost realm. I raised it, trembling slightly.

Carefully, he unwound the bandage and pocketed it. Then, with a surprising amount of gentleness, he twined his long, elegant fingers through mine. His warmth seeped into my skin.

Letting out a long, slow exhale, he let his eyelids flutter closed, allowing me to study his face up close. His eyelashes were long, fanning out across his cheeks. He had high cheekbones; a long, straight nose; a delicate curve to his upper lip. From a distance I'd never noticed these details. Up close, his features were infuriatingly . . . tolerable.

When his eyes sprang open again, I tore my gaze away, my face heating. I flexed my hand, marveling at how the wounds had completely healed over. Then, he raised his palm and let it hover above my décolletage, stopping just short of touching me.

I froze. This was the wound from Lin's blue sword. "My neck next?"

He gave a perfunctory nod. Placing one hand lightly on my neck, he pushed his fingers up into my hair, and I couldn't help it: I let out a sigh. The pain was dissipating, blissful warmth sweeping across my skin. I remembered how he'd been crouched over my dying body, back in the bedchamber at Throft Hall, and I realized he must have been healing me then, too—as much as he could before I'd died. I'd wondered how the bleeding had stopped so quickly. Now I knew.

It seemed an age before he abruptly withdrew. My skin immediately chilled; I just managed to stifle my gasp.

"Now your chest wound," he said, his voice very quiet. His eyes skated over my hànfú.

"You—you need to touch my chest?" I felt faint.

He grimaced. "You can face away if you feel more comfortable."

No wonder he hadn't been able to heal me properly before—his propriety prevented him from touching my torso without consent.

I wasn't sure I wanted to cross this line. But then—this was it. My best chance to be healed, once and for all, properly. It would stand me in better stead for my journey home, which I was planning to do posthaste. So I could see my grandmother and help her.

My plans were *not* being derailed by an Yskian prince, or his tolerable eyelashes, or his unexpectedly magical hands . . . absolutely, definitely not.

He held me steady as I shuffled myself around on the branch. When I was facing away, I gripped the tree trunk, suddenly self-conscious about my bony frame. My jutting ribs.

This felt . . . far too intimate. It made my cheeks burn, but I was determined to see it out. I needed to be well again, well enough to travel home.

"Ready?" he whispered, his voice at my ear.

My pulse hammered. *No.* "Yes."

Very carefully, he placed his palm on my back, over my gown, until his hand entirely covered my wound.

Immediately, a dizzying rush of heat coursed right through my body. Behind me, the prince sucked in a breath. I hadn't expected this, hadn't ever expected him to be magical, so previously it hadn't clicked. But now I knew: the warmth I'd always felt emanating from him was unmistakably the sensation of magic.

We remained still for some time, neither of us saying a word as his healing powers flushed through my wound, knitting it back together. And then—O Mothers!—he slid one hand around my front until it rested on my stomach.

"Is this all right?" he asked as he went, voice low.

I nodded again, goose bumps erupting across my skin, despite the fact that his touch was scalding. "Yes," I said, mortified at the way my voice wavered.

His hand slowly, so torturously, traced upward, until it came to a stop. His fingers twitched, just once.

Then he went completely still. I tried to stay calm, too, but the sensation of him healing me, front and back, was overwhelming. My breaths came more shallow with each passing moment.

I had no idea how long we stayed like this, nestled amongst the branches. But eventually he broke away, and I gasped at his sudden absence. The heat rushed out of me, replaced by the bitter cold, and I almost keeled over, saved only when the prince reached out and caught me again around the waist.

Blinking rapidly, I ran the tips of my fingers over where my chest wound had been. It was now just smooth skin, all evidence of Brisson's sword wound gone.

Incredible. Not even our healers' magic worked this seamlessly.

Looking back over my shoulder, I was startled to find that the prince had tilted his head. The movement had brought our faces so close, and I caught a glimpse of his expression. His lips were parted, his breaths erratic; his eyes, shadowed once more, were unreadable.

Jerking my head back around to face forward, I cursed

inwardly, willing my heart to stop thumping. "I'd like to get down now," I said, my mouth abnormally dry.

The prince's hold on me tightened momentarily, but after a beat he did remove his arm from my waist. I slipped down the tree, dropping silently to the forest floor, the thuds swallowed by the damp dirt. My newly healed skin tightened and pulled, feeling unfamiliar, like an intrusion.

He followed shortly after, clumsily and far more noisily. I was horrified at just how much noise this Yskian prince could make. In the quiet of the forest, with the animals still hiding from the atrocities that were the Spyrre, the sound seemed amplified tenfold. I hoped that there was nothing concealed in the forest, readying itself to ambush us.

Brushing his clothes off with his hands, the prince turned to me. "Lady Liu," he said, offering me his arm. "Please, allow me to escort you back to the castle."

"No, thank you. I'm going home."

The lines of his jaw tightened. "I thought we had an agreement."

"*You* proposed a bargain," I corrected. "*I* agreed to nothing."

His eyes narrowed slightly. "Let me remind you: you are still on my lands, and therefore under my jurisdiction. I am being more than generous—"

A harsh laugh burst from my lips. "Generous? In what way? For not imprisoning me?" Who was he to tell me what I should or shouldn't do? He didn't know Pópo, didn't understand the responsibility I felt to help my grandmother. Did Yskians even understand the concept of filial duty?

"Well, go ahead. Try to arrest me again." My lip curled into a sneer. “Well, go ahead. Try to arrest me again. Do not forget, though, *Your Highness,* I cannot die. But you can.”

Something flickered in the black of his pupils. He stepped even closer, his gaze roving across my body. “An empty threat. You are unarmed.” It occurred to me that Essien Lancaster was probably unused to being challenged.

I raised my chin, and said, in the haughtiest tone I could muster, “There are plenty of rocks.”

The prince chuckled, the slightest shadow of two dimples appearing in his cheeks. “Who would triumph,” he said, leaning closer still, so his breath stirred the baby hairs at my temple, “in a battle between rock and blade? Do not forget, my lady: I can heal. But you cannot.”

His voice had dropped low, his tone almost teasing, but I couldn’t be certain. I didn’t respond, at first—I just studied his face, trying, and failing, to figure him out. Prince Essien was much larger than me. I knew that even if I attempted to pelt him with a rock I’d never best him—not physically at least.

No, fighting wouldn’t work. The only way out of this situation was to play his game. Which meant agreeing to get the sword he wanted.

Which meant lying.

Which I’d do, if it helped get me back to my grandmother.

Would it work, though? Would he see through the flimsy film of my deception?

Either way, I had to try. Everything I did—every decision I made—had to be with Pópo in mind, truly.

Lin had once told me: *The best lies are those that are formed in half-truths.* And I was about to test his theory.

"Okay, fine. I'll get your stupid sword." The lie part slipped out surprisingly easily. Now for the truth. "Just let me go home first. I need to see Pópo."

His brow creased. "I beg your pardon?"

"My grandmother."

"Oh, right," he said. "The one who is ill?"

I stared at him. "You knew?"

"You talked about her in your sleep—" He stopped short. "When I was healing you, of course," he added.

My stomach twisted. How often had Essien watched me sleep? "Right. So you know that I need to get back to her. Every day that passes, she worsens, and I'm worried that I'll be too late—"

"—to see her again." He finished the sentence for me.

The space behind my eyes grew hot, my throat closed over, and all I could do was nod.

He was silent for a long while, frowning. He appeared to be waging some sort of internal battle. Finally, he nodded. "I understand."

A spark of hope flared in my chest. I raised my eyes to his. "You'll let me go?"

His gaze caught mine. "That is how bargains work, is it not? We negotiate. You help me, I help you." He paused for a moment. "I shall even give you a means of safe passage."

I was so shocked at how magnanimous he was being that all I could do was gawp at him and stammer an awkward thanks.

As we hurried back toward the castle, my mind churned. I couldn't quite believe my luck. Prince Essien Lancaster, sixth son of Yske, had agreed to let me go—just like that. But why?

Half of me wondered if this was all a ruse to get me back to Throft Hall so he could finally throw me in the dungeons. But he kept his word—taking me directly to the stables, where he led a horse outside and began saddling it up. Soon enough it was fully bedecked in Lancaster livery, adornment that would provide me a degree of immunity—on this side of the border, at least.

As I approached the beast, my heart rate kicked up. It was massive. *This* was Essien's idea of safe passage?

I didn't have much experience around horses, and I'd certainly never ridden one. Seeing my reaction, the prince assured me he'd selected one "as placid as a doe."

Still, I cringed away, until he managed to coax me to mount the creature. I sat stiffly in the saddle, clammy hands grasping the reins, and looked down at him.

He gave me a few instructions, explaining how to steer and where to hold on, as well as a few simple commands. Once he'd finished his rudimentary lesson, he came close to the horse's side and looked up at me.

"One last thing," he said, and then paused, teetering on the last word, like he wanted to say more.

"Yes?"

He made the tiniest of movements, like he wanted to reach for me. But the next moment he seemed to think better of it, for he dropped his hand. Then he drew my dagger from his belt and held it out, hilt pointing upward. "Look after yourself."

I blinked, then took my blade from him. Had he kept it on him this whole time? "I will—"

"I am serious. Promise that you won't take the Stone Road. There are too many bandits."

Why was he so concerned about my safety? "Yes, I promise—"

He cut me off. "And go swiftly. Don't look back, don't get hurt, or . . ."

"Or what?"

Some emotion I couldn't read flashed across his face. Then his expression hardened. "Or else my healing will have been in vain."

Anger spiked through my chest, and I shoved my dagger into my sash with more force than strictly necessary. "You forget I've lived in the forest my whole life."

His gaze swiveled back toward me, so penetrating it was almost painful. Then he nodded.

"Goodbye," I said, gripping the reins so hard my now-healed knuckles were white.

"Farewell, Lady Liu," he said, and made a small bow. And as he tapped the horse on the rump, and she began to plod toward the forest, he said something under his breath that almost sounded like "Hurry home."

Thirteen

Five years ago

The tent was full of cloying incense, smoke billowing above our heads. Dust motes gleamed in the scant light of lanterns. Before us, the shaman sat, her eyes closed, her lined, leathery face a picture of serenity.

I tugged at the sleeve of my grandmother's robe. "Will she speak soon?" I whispered. We'd been sitting for what seemed like hours, me fidgeting, the shaman saying nothing at all and doing even less. The air was stifling, and I was ready to claw out of my skin. Anything to escape this close, confined space; anything to get back to the cool, tranquil forest.

"Quiet now, bǎobèi," Pópo said. "We must be patient."

It was hard to be patient. I was used to spending my days running around, learning to hunt, and setting up traps in the woods with Lin. I wanted to get back to something more fun. Less boring. But also, at twelve years of age, I definitely should have shown some sort of power by now. It was past the point of delayed-onset magic, and this was my grandmother's last-ditch effort. Visiting the shaman, a renowned fortune-teller, was her way of trying to look into my future, to see if it held any clues as to what my power might be.

"But—" I protested, but Pópo shushed me again.

I rolled my eyes, then flopped back against my chair. My gaze strayed to the space above our heads, and I squinted at it, trying to see pictures in the smoke.

My eyes began to sting as I stared. I stared and stared, for the smoke appeared to be condensing, until it formed a picture of a woman, lying on her side.

The woman looked older than me, but was also unmistakably—me.

I sat up, my spine straight, still watching the smoke. Nudging my grandmother's shoulders, I pointed. "Do you see that, Pópo?"

She, too, looked up, and sucked in a low breath. "Mothers help us," she murmured. She'd seen it, too. Knew it was me.

The shaman's eyelids suddenly snapped open. She was facing us, but not looking at us. Her focus was fixed somewhere beyond. Her pupils were unusually dilated, the blackness all-encompassing, expanding until her entire eyeballs were black. "Jia Yi," she said, and her voice sounded distant, like the whisper of wind through the bare branches of dead trees. "Death clings to you like a mantle."

"Death?" My voice sounded squeaky. It was true that my mother had died during my birth, and my father had followed her into the afterlife shortly after. And even though my grandmother had always reassured me that it was not at all my fault, a tiny, tormented voice inside me had always told me that it was.

The shaman turned her ink-black eyes on me then, and I shook, cold sweat breaking on my brow. "Yes, death. It shrouds your past. It stalks your present. It clouds your future." Her void-like gaze slid toward Pópo. "You will die before your grandmother. And the two of you will meet again. In the afterlife."

I held my breath, and Pópo did, too, though I sensed her tensing beside me.

The smoke shifted again, changing into a scene of me holding a sword. Before my smokelike form, the outline of Pópo stood, and behind us loomed a shadow—black as the darkest night—that instinctively I knew was Death.

"What is this?" Pópo's voice was trembling with repressed fury. "Why are you showing us this?"

The shaman waved her hand, and the smoke dissipated, leaving behind emptiness and a cold and ghoulish chill. The lantern lights flickered and went out, plunging us into blackness.

"It is the truth, Priestess," the shaman said, her voice looming from the dark. "I see nothing but death in this girl's future." A flat, dreary pause. "No life. Just emptiness, and death."

A small sob escaped from my lips; Pópo's fingers encircled my forearm, and she pulled me to my feet.

"You're wrong," my grandmother snapped, tugging me away. "I should have known you were a rotten yōngyī."

I stumbled behind my grandmother as she hauled me along by the hand. *Yōngyī*, I repeated to myself, in my mind, like a prayer. Charlatan. The shaman was a quack. I should just ignore what she'd said, because even my all-knowing grandmother said she was a quack, and not to be believed.

But then, why had my mother died while birthing me? Not my sister Dai Yu, not my sibling Hui Fen, but *me*. Maybe, just maybe, what the shaman had said was true.

Dai Yu was right. I was empty. And the little voice inside me was right, too. My parents' deaths had been my fault.

A sob caught in my throat. Tears leaked from the corners of my eyes. I dashed them away, following my grandmother through the flaps of the tent. Lin was there, leaning against a tree, hidden by shadows. He'd been murmuring something beneath his breath, so low I couldn't hear, almost like he'd been talking to someone. But there was no one there, only darkness and shadows. As soon as he saw me, he clamped his mouth shut and straightened.

Had he been . . . praying? For me? Perhaps somehow he also knew that I was a girl marked for death.

I went to him. He said nothing, just reached for me, his eyes finding mine. In the space between us, unanswered questions hung.

Later, I told him, in my expression. *I'll tell you later.* And his answer came in the slight squeeze of my hand.

My grandmother staggered to the tree and leaned against it, bracing herself with both hands. She wheezed, her breaths harsh, and then gave a couple of deep, rattling coughs.

"Pópo? Are you all right?" I asked, alarmed, my throat still thick with tears.

She waved my question away, continuing to cough. Lin and I both supported her, me rubbing her back, until her coughing fit had passed.

"Come, children," she said, taking her stick and peering at me. "I am fine. And so are you, Jia Yi. Do not listen to what that woman had to say. What she said is wrong."

Pópo turned and began striding away, her stick thumping

a steady rhythm against the ground. Lin and I gave each other a quick look before we followed.

As we walked, I blinked hard. *Don't cry*, I told myself sternly, willing my tears to stop. *You're not going to die.*

I was not going to die . . .

Because the shaman was just a quack.

Fourteen

Present day

Even though Throft Hall and my village were just across the border from one another, it still took me until late the following day to reach home. The first hour or so had been bearable, but after that my legs and buttocks had begun to burn. Soon enough, I was in agony. I'd had to stop even more frequently than the horse needed to rest my aching legs. Not only that, I'd been so fatigued I had almost slipped off the saddle twice, screaming, only managing to stay upright because my feet had gotten tangled in the stirrups.

The entire journey—when not preoccupied with trying to stay alive, that is—I'd mulled over what Essien had told me: about his healing powers, about his family, about the sword.

The Sword of Rechenblod.

A sword that can defeat any army, he'd said. *A weapon that can bestow its wielder any victory.*

Could it be related to the sword I'd seen in the shaman's vision?

Whether it was or not—I wasn't planning to find out. Honestly, I didn't much fancy reentering the afterlife at any point in the near future.

Maybe when I was old I would. Really, really old.

Dusk light was just tinting the curve of the horizon when we plodded up to the edge of my village. I pushed through the concealment wards, the magic that encircled us and kept my community secret.

We needed to stay hidden, not just because of the Yskians across the border but because of nonmagical people in our country, too.

The past five hundred years had been a golden age for the great Jinghu Dao Empire, with an explosion of scientific and technological advances. However, as a result, magic had fallen out of favor. Hence, members of the magical community were shunned. Attempts were even made to oust the legendary matchmaker, Mei Po—who was renowned for her magical abilities—from the Imperial court.

When even the most rich and powerful are ostracized and forced to exist in shadow, what hope is there for people like us? Like me?

So, when the famously ruthless General Hong Hao Mu had asked my ancestors to help fight the war against Yske, three hundred years ago, they saw it as a way to redeem themselves in the empire's eyes. Proof that even in this new world, there was still a place for people like us. In secret, they prepared to fight: Jinghu Dao's secret weapon, the empire's last chance to overthrow its enemies.

And overthrow them we did. Using magic, my ancestors

had decimated the Yskian army, assassinated their king, and even reclaimed some land—launching Jinghu Dao to resounding victory.

The general had offered, in return for our services, to grant our people lifelong protection. But shortly after defeating the Yskians, he himself was assassinated. And slowly, over decades, the prevailing attitudes toward people like us slipped back to their default state. At best, apathy. At worst, downright discrimination.

So, we fled, escaping to the forests in the farthest province from the capital. Here, we lived a quiet existence, moving often and keeping ourselves hidden.

In the end, there had been no real reward for our fealty. The Imperial palace, at the opposite end of the empire, was so far away. They paid no heed to our existence—our poverty meant little to them.

This was the reality I'd always known. On one side, we were ignored by our own nobility; on the other, we were equal parts feared and loathed.

Now, Essien Lancaster was asking me to fetch an enchanted sword for him—one that would allow the Yskians to achieve victory in any war. With the bloody history of our two territories . . .

Did he think I was fucking stupid?

Grinding my teeth, I dragged my thoughts back to the present, focusing on my surroundings as we proceeded farther into the village. Things felt . . . odd.

Normally, the first thing I'd see as I reached the edge of the settlements was the watchfires, which were normally kept stoked and burning day and night. But today, the fires had dwindled down to dying embers, the low seats around them empty.

Strange.

As soon as I was in the main clearing, a roughly circular opening surrounded by the innermost ring of huts, I dismounted, my knees buckling and my backside screaming in protest. My legs felt like they'd been minced with a meat cleaver. I had to support myself against a tree for several minutes, breathing heavily, to regain my strength.

Usually at this time, people would be readying themselves for night, and would nod to me from their huts as I passed. But today, no one was around to greet me; no one was beating rugs, emptying pots, or sweeping hearths. Our usually bustling community was completely empty.

Where was everyone?

I staggered toward Pópo's hut, determined to see her right away.

As I hobbled along, I resolved to tell her the bare minimum: I was just returning home after hunting and scavenging like normal. I'd only been delayed because of a rock slide that had forced me to take a longer route.

What I wouldn't tell her was how I'd been attacked, killed, resurrected, imprisoned, killed again, then healed by the sixth son of Yske. Once upon a time she might have been ecstatic to discover I had a latent magical power. But now? Not now. There was no need to add to her burdens.

Her hut was the largest one, located in the very center of the village. The door was, unexpectedly, standing ajar.

My stomach flipped and I quickened my stride. What the hells was going on?

I pushed inside. The interior of the hut was suffocatingly hot and smoky with pungent incense. The house was full of people. With my pulse thumping in my ears, I elbowed my way through the crowd.

And then I saw her. My grandmother, lying in her bed, her cheeks sunken, skin porcelain pale.

I ran. Fell to my knees. Grabbed her hand. It was cold, clammy, stiff. Her eyes were glassy, staring unseeingly up at the low ceiling.

"No," I ground out, pressure building beneath my eyelids before a sob ratcheted right through me. "Please, no. No, no, no no no no no . . ."

I'd missed her. She was dead, and I had missed her.

The world crashed down, feeling too heavy, crushing me to dust in its fist. People jostled around me, placing their hands on my shoulders.

But I barely noticed. Couldn't believe it. *I'd* died and had somehow managed to come back to life. Me. All so I could return to save my grandmother, or at least spend the last of our precious time together. And instead of bringing her back the Shadowside that she so sorely needed, I'd been caught and kept prisoner.

And all this time . . . *all this time*. While I was riding, stiff and in agony from long-forgotten muscles, she'd breathed her last breaths, and I had missed her. She'd slipped away into the next life, into the afterlife, while Essien-fucking-Lancaster had his hands on me, and Lin taunted me, and Larch the physician cut me with a knife.

Tears began to stream down my face, and I descended into silent sobs as the aunties stood around me, heads bowed, hands folded. Those *bastards*. I hadn't left Essien to die back in the forest with the Spyrre, but now I would. A thousand times over I would. In fact, if I saw him again, I would kill him myself, with my own bare hands if I had to. What good had it done, him healing me, when my grandmother had been dying herself?

My grief expanded until my bones ached, until it filled all the space within my broken body, where it would now reside, forever.

After murmuring soothing platitudes to me and smoothing my disheveled hair, the aunties left one by one. Until eventually, I was all alone, save for the ghosts of my ancestors, who clustered around me, silent witnesses to my pain. I refused to move from my position, bent over Pópo's unmoving form. I cried so much that my throat swelled and I could no longer make a sound. I could only tremble, anguish cleaving a hollow space in my chest.

Lin's ghost had stayed away, thankfully. He must have known . . . Our shared childhood here—all the times we'd spent playing in my grandmother's house—was fraught with too many memories, loaded with too much pain. His presence would have only made things worse.

By the time my sibling Hui Fen found me, darkness had fully fallen, the lengthening shadows creeping across the scuffed cork floor.

Hui Fen stood quietly by my side as I held Pópo's cold, stiff hand in both of mine, by now too spent to cry. Eventually, I raised my tear-streaked face. Their own eyes were red-rimmed and swollen.

"I was too late," I whispered, my voice raspy. Something in me broke once more, hearing the words spoken with a voice that sounded so little like my own. As though saying them aloud confirmed it as true. I would never, ever forgive myself for being late. "I should have come back sooner, I should have brought the Shadowside, I should have . . ." I stopped, unable to continue.

Hui Fen sank to their knees beside me, gathering me in their arms. "Do not blame yourself. Even if you had, it would not have made a difference." Tears streamed down their face. "See? She had enough Shadowside, and still—" My sibling gestured to the nightstand.

Wait, she'd had enough? But how? I raised my head, my gaze alighting on the small flask of Shadowside-laced elixir sitting right beside the bed. I'd been too preoccupied to notice it before.

Who had brought it to her?

I shook my head. It didn't matter. Not when Pópo was still dead. "I still should have been here. I . . . I was too late to tell her . . ." My words caught, and I let out another loud sob.

Hui's arms tightened around me. "She knew you loved her. She knew, mèimei."

Mèimei. Little sister. It had been so long since anyone had called me that. But I was not a small child anymore. I pushed myself away from Hui, rising swiftly to my feet, suddenly agitated. My legs cramped from having been in one position for too long, and my muscles still ached from riding that infernal horse. Stumbling, I felt my knees almost give way, but I managed to right myself—just.

"It doesn't make a difference," I said, clutching my throbbing head. "I wasn't here, and I couldn't help her, and . . ." A sudden thought occurred to me and I stopped, whirling around to face my sibling. "Did she speak about me? Did she ask about me? Did she notice I wasn't here?" My voice had turned demanding, laced as it was with grief.

Hui Fen raised both of their slim, pale hands. "She . . . she was rambling, mostly." My sibling spoke in a halting fashion. I could tell they were hiding something. "She seemed barely aware of anything—"

I strode toward Hui, taking both of their hands in my own. "Show me," I said. "Please."

Hui Fen began to shake their head, their eyes growing fearful. "Jia, no—"

"Please," I urged. "I have to see her alive again. Just once. I have to bear witness to what she suffered. To what *you* suffered, caring for her."

My sibling went very quiet. Very still. Then, they said in a tiny voice, "All right, then. I will show you."

They raised both hands, pausing momentarily before putting the pads of their fingers on my temples. They were very cool. I closed my eyes. An ice-cold sensation trickled down my spine, and then I was tumbling into the depths of Hui Fen's memories.

I'm standing at the edge of Pópo's bed. She's tossing and turning, sweat beading on her forehead. The room is close, humid, stiflingly hot.

My hands—Hui Fen's hands—hold a cold cloth to Pópo's forehead. But she's so restless, it is futile, so before long the cloth is abandoned.

"We must find her," Pópo says beneath her breath. "Where is Jia? Why has she not returned?"

"Hush, Pópo." My voice is Hui Fen's voice. My tears are Hui Fen's tears. My hands fiddle with the bedclothes, trying unsuccessfully to straighten them. *"She will be back soon. Just rest."*

"Rest? Rest? I cannot rest. I must find her, before—" Pópo tries to

sit up, but the breath rattles in her chest and she gives a single great heave. I reach for her, catching her before she flops back onto the bed.

The effort has exhausted her. Her eyelids slide shut, so thin and sunken, I can see all the capillaries branching. I blink back my oncoming tears. How long will she lie here for, delirious and suffering?

Beneath me, Pópo remains peaceful for a few seconds. Then her eyes spring open once more. Her irises burn; her gaze is unfocused.

"Jia!" she cries, and her voice is hollow. She jerks her head up, her expression wild and desperate, and snatches the front of my robe. "Where is she? Is she . . . ? Is she . . . ?"

"Is she what, Pópo?" My voice is gentle.

Pópo's eyes fix on mine. For the first time in days, she seems lucid. "Dead?"

I grip her hands in mine, my heart squeezing in my chest. "She's not dead, Pópo. I am certain she will return soon."

My grandmother's fingers are still clutching at me; they tighten. "She cannot follow me, Hui Fen. Never mind what the shaman said. Prophecies can be wrong, you hear? They can be wrong. I will find it myself, in the death realm, so that Jia Yi doesn't have to—"

"Find what?" I cannot keep the waver out of my voice.

Finally, Pópo's hands slacken, and I ease her back onto the pillow. Her eyes flutter shut and she sighs, suddenly looking her age. "The weapon."

A rushing sensation surged through my body as I was jolted back to the present, and once again I was in Pópo's little hut, Hui Fen standing before me. My chest hurt; I could barely breathe. Weapon? What weapon did Pópo speak of? What weapon did she plan to find? What weapon did she not want *me* to find?

Perhaps it was the same weapon that Essien Lancaster had

spoken of, which he had hoped I'd agree to find: the Sword of Rechenblod. Surely it could not be a coincidence?

The shaman's vision. Essien's sword. My grandmother's weapon.

What if they were all . . . one and the same?

I clutched at my heart, which was pounding erratically. Pópo had died thinking that I was dead, and that the shaman had been right.

And in some ways, she had been right. I *had* been dead. What my grandmother hadn't realized was that I'd clawed my way back to life. Twice.

But Pópo had died, in grief, thinking she was following *me* into the afterlife. If she had believed I was still alive—if she'd known I was trying to return home—might she have held on?

Might she have waited?

"Jia," Hui Fen said softly. At first, I didn't respond. I just stood there, fresh tears coursing down my face.

My mind was a tangle of emotions. I could barely tease out any coherent theories.

"I need to think," I muttered, barreling past them to the door.

Fifteen

Present day

I couldn't even remember how I'd gotten here—a clearing in the forest where I used to meet Lin. A place of carefree afternoons playing childhood games, skinning prey, and clumsy sparring games with sticks. Then, later, sparring of a different kind: self-conscious banter, heated glances . . . secret, whispered words, like a breath of summer breeze. And my name, the way he said my name. The pain tingeing *those* memories mingled with the fresh agony of Pópo's death created a crushing grief that threatened to swallow me.

I must have run. Sprinted through the clusters of deserted houses, with their windows like eyes and their doors shut tight. Crashed my way through the forest, tears blurring my vision, with no aim or intent or specific direction. But still, my muscle memory brought me here.

And it was muscle memory that found me on my knees, bent over, clutching my stomach and shaking.

The shaman had told us two things: One, that I would die first, before my grandmother. And two, that Pópo and I would meet in the afterlife—transcending life, and death, and beyond.

The first had come true. And it seemed that Pópo had believed it, too, despite her earlier claims otherwise. She'd always claimed the shaman was a charlatan and told me to ignore what had been said in that tent . . .

And yet.

When she was barely lucid, she spoke of me as though I'd already died. Which meant that she'd put more faith in the shaman's predictions than she had let on.

I massaged my temples, trying to remember what else the shaman had told us, the pictures she'd shown us in her smoke. Me, with a sword, standing with Pópo—overshadowed by the specter of Death. Was it actually the Lancaster relic, the Sword of Rechenblod, that Pópo spoke of on her deathbed? Was that the weapon that she swore she'd find herself as she begged Hui Fen not to let me follow? Perhaps, being dead now, she'd already embarked upon her search. It would explain why her ghost had not hung around.

If the shaman's prediction was true, then it stood to reason that Pópo and I would meet again in death . . . Yet it seemed that Pópo was trying to prevent that fate from coming to fruition.

But perhaps my destiny was not as preventable as Pópo wished. Perhaps my fate *was* to follow my grandmother into the afterlife. Perhaps that was why I suddenly had the ability to resurrect myself.

And for what? To help Pópo find this weapon? One that—according to Essien—might have the ability to restore the dead?

A weapon that might restore Pópo, a tiny voice whispered inside my head. *Bring her back.*

I hunched forward, curling into myself.

Something—a noise—jerked me from my thoughts. Well, not a noise, exactly. The forest was completely silent, save for the faint, sporadic rustle of leaves. It was more like . . . a shift in energy. Something intangible that I couldn't quite define, but my hunter's senses still detected.

My chest constricted. Someone—or something—had followed me. I jumped up, squinting into the darkness. Backing away from the tree line, I looked left, then right. I didn't want to be ambushed.

He managed to ambush me anyway.

"Jia," Lin murmured from behind me.

I spun around. How had he managed to appear so suddenly?

My voice shook as I blurted out, "She's dead, Lin. Dead!"

Lin looked at me, his face, usually as hard as granite, lined with grief. "I'm sorry, Jia."

His quiet words had an immediate effect. I doubled over again, my hands clamped over my face, tears gushing through the spaces between my fingers. I sobbed into my palms—still raw and calloused and creased with dirt from my long ride home from Throft Hall.

I felt as if my mortal body could not contain my sadness. Instead, it burst out, leaking through the cracks in my armor.

The shaman's words, uttered so many years ago, burrowed through my brain like a worm. *Jia Yi,* she had said. *Death clings to you like a mantle.* Was it true? I'd spent so many years trying—and failing—to ignore those words and forget they ever existed. But now it seemed as though what the shaman had said was coming true.

It wasn't just my parents' deaths that haunted my waking moments. It was also Lin's death, which had happened a year ago. My elder sister, Dai Yu, who'd died when I was fourteen. And now, my Pópo, my grandmother, the one person in the world whom I loved above all others.

And of course there was the horror, and the unnaturalness, of my own deaths, the thought of which still made me shudder. Honestly, one's death should never be thought about in a plural sense.

Death, so much death. Too much. And everyone who'd died had somehow been associated with . . . me.

The shaman had been right: I was the problem. It was all my fault.

Lin raised one hand, like he wanted to touch me. Obviously, he couldn't, so he withdrew. Instead he waited, crouching beside me while I cried.

My body was weak, my chest crushed, the heart within bruised to a pulp. No matter how much my grandmother wished to protect me, to disregard the shaman's predictions, to keep me away from death . . .

It was meant to be me. Me who entered the afterlife first. The shaman's vision had pictured *me* with the sword, not my grandmother.

As I cried, my resolve began to harden, petrifying like fossilized wood. Tears continued to dampen my cheeks as I clambered to my feet. My limbs felt loose, as if they were barely held together, like I might clatter to the ground as a pile of bones and flesh.

As I straightened, Lin shadowed me, his movements so fluid even in death. Pacing to the edge of the clearing, I pressed my fist against my forehead and *thought.*

Lin followed. He knew me well enough to know my postures, my expressions, the downward trajectory of my eyebrows. I was planning something, and he knew it.

"What are you thinking?" Suspicion was etched all over his face. "What is going on in that head of yours?"

My head snapped up in irritation. Why did he care? Lin just arched an eyebrow at me, his ochre eyes burning. Waiting for my response.

Finally, I spoke. "Have you seen her yet? As a ghost?"

"Pópo?" He scrunched up his face and shook his head. "No."

"Do you think you can find her?"

Lin sighed. "I'm a ghost, Jia," he said. "Not a tracking dog."

I scowled at him. How could he be so damned flippant? "I need to follow her."

Lin took a single step toward me, somehow managing to make it look ominous. Silence stretched out between us, the air prickling with unseen energy.

"You can't," he said, breaking the stillness.

I bristled. "You don't get to decide what I—"

"You. Just. Can't." He advanced on me another step.

I began backing away. Why was he being so obstructive? What was he not telling me? "I need to follow Pópo. I need to find her. To help her. It's my duty to—"

"Fuck duty." He took another step closer, his eyes glittering menacingly in the moonlight.

We'd fallen into our old dynamic. Just before he'd run away, abandoning me, he'd become increasingly overprotective. Skittish, as if he was forever guarding me from some unseen enemy.

I had to try a different approach. Raising my chin, I forced my gaze to meet his. "Do you remember the shaman? When I was twelve. She said that—"

"She was a quack." Lin's voice had dropped an octave, had become frighteningly quiet.

Unable to stare him down any longer, I tore my eyes from his and turned around. Pacing back to the tree, I shook my head.

"No." My voice hardened. "*No.* Pópo said she was a quack, but those predictions? They came true. The shaman said I'd *die first.* And I did."

Lin's next words sounded strangled. "That means nothing. A mere coincidence—"

"And Pópo herself spoke of finding a weapon. In the afterlife. She was rambling about it before she died. Hui showed me their memories." I turned to face Lin once more. His whole body was rigid. I could read his distress in the slope of his shoulders. "I think it's the sword I saw in that vision. She *lied*, Lin. Pópo lied to us. She told us the shaman's predictions meant nothing, that she didn't believe. But she lied."

My chest was tight, my lungs struggling to expand. Without moving my head, I scanned the edge of the clearing, searching for escape routes—for ways that I could slip away from Lin. I tried not to do it, but I couldn't help my gaze straying briefly to my boot, where I'd stowed the dagger Essien Lancaster had returned.

Where *Lin* knew I kept my dagger.

"Don't," Lin choked out. He knew exactly what I was planning: to escape into the forest and unsheathe my blade so I could use it . . . on myself.

There was a brief pause—less than a second; a tiny, infinitesimal moment—and then we suddenly, synchronously, dove for the knife.

Lin had forgotten, though, that he couldn't grab it. My hand passed through the cold emptiness of his, forcing a shudder to roll right through me, before my fingers wrapped around the hilt. I yanked it triumphantly out of my boot, holding it aloft, then turned to sprint away.

But Lin was fast. I'd only made it a few paces before I pulled up short. He stood in front of me, his own blade gleaming blue. I slashed out at him, my dagger finding nothing but air as it passed through his intangible form. Overbalancing, I just managed to right myself. By the time I'd regained my bearings, he'd used his own knife to knock mine from my hand.

I let forth a frustrated scream.

"Don't," he repeated, the growl in his voice evident. He loomed above me, his heavy eyebrows drawn down, his eyes flashing beneath. Ever so slowly, ever so deliberately, he brought the point of his knife to my chin. It pushed against the soft flesh beneath my jaw.

I raised my head, meeting his glare with mine, straining away from his weapon. My knife could not touch him; he could not touch me . . . but his strange blue blade—the one he'd killed both Larch and me with—could.

He trembled, every muscle in his body vibrating, his lips pale and pressed together. Had he been alive, I was sure that he'd be sweating. Several strands of hair had flopped down across his forehead, but he made no move to push them away.

"Do it," I spat, leaning into his knifepoint. I sucked in a sharp breath as his blade sliced at my skin. I braced myself against the sting until I smelled the coppery scent of my own blood.

Entering the death realm a third time will be fine, I told myself. After all, I knew I could come back.

Right?

We stayed like this for several loaded seconds, me breathing hard, him not breathing at all. His gaze traced a languid pathway down my cheek before lingering on my slightly parted lips. A muscle jumped in his jaw.

His hand shook. His pupils dilated, his irises swallowed by the black. He knew this was what I wanted. I *wanted* to see Pópo. It was my destiny, my duty. Grief had now been replaced by cold purpose: to find my grandmother and help her find the weapon she sought in turn. The only weapon that could, perhaps, bring her back to life.

That must have been what the shaman had seen. Me, entering the death realm to find the sword. Even if there was just a minuscule chance that the sword could bring Pópo back from death, I'd do it. It was the only thing I wanted more than life itself.

Could Lin, though, facilitate my passage? Could *he* be the one to kill me?

Our eyes locked, his focus sharpening to a point. Then he let out a pained exhale and wrenched the blade away. "I . . ." he said, then shook his head as if to clear it. "I cannot."

I drew myself up to my full height. "Then I must do it, Lin. You don't understand. She's dead, and I'm the only one who might be able to"—my voice cracked, like an ice-covered lake in the spring—"I just . . . I need to find her. Save her. I didn't get to see her, before . . . before . . ."

I broke down.

He sheathed his blade, his head bowed. Clasping the knife with both hands and hugging it to my chest, I lingered for a tense moment before turning away.

"Wait." Lin's voice was rough. Raw. As jagged as a mountain's edge. I looked up—his eyes were still trained on the ground.

"If you're going to enter the afterlife," he said, each word unnaturally precise. He raised his head, his gaze catching mine. "Then you need to see the Bone Smith."

Sixteen

Present day

Early morning, and Bai Ri Shi, the Hundred Sun City—the closest metropolitan center on our side of the border—was bustling with activity. It had taken the rest of the night for Lin and me to travel through the dense forest.

Now dawn had fully broken, and we loitered in the shadows, watching the main gate. Through it, a steady stream of carts, horses, and traders on foot passed. A pair of bored-looking guards flanked the gates, nodding at each passerby. Spirits, unseen by the living mortals, congregated around the walls, their bodies shimmering in the sunlight.

All the blood in my veins ran cold. "There are so many ghosts now . . ."

"They've always been there. You just never noticed them before until you, well"—Lin shot me a sideways look—"died."

I swallowed, my tongue scraping the dry roof of my mouth. I'd moved through the living realm for seventeen years without ever knowing we had company. "Can ghosts like you haunt anyone, anywhere?"

Lin gave a small smirk. "Why? Are you scared that you and I are bonded? Doomed to be together for eternity?"

Before I could open my mouth to retort, Lin was already continuing. "Yes, Jia, we can haunt anyone, anywhere. We can see any living person we like, if they're in the level above us. They can't see us, though, unless, like you, they've become specifically attuned to the death realm. And we can travel, though we tend to gravitate to places that were significant to us in life. I suppose that's why there are so many here, in the city."

"Places significant to you," I repeated, my brow creasing. "Why?"

He shrugged. "I don't know. It just feels like a draw, a pull. I cannot explain it."

"And what do you mean by 'the level above us'?"

"The afterlife isn't a single realm, like many imagine it to be," Lin replied. "In reality, there are layers to it. Almost like . . . multiple afterlives, each superimposed atop the next. If a living person dies, they become a ghost in the first level. If a ghost like myself dies, they then become a jiàn: a second-level ghost. Second-level ghosts can haunt my level, the first level. But my understanding is that ghosts in a deeper level than mine cannot haunt the living realm. It is too far above them. We can only haunt one level above that which we currently occupy—no more."

I swallowed. *What is dead can die again.* How many times could a ghost die? How deep did the afterlife go?

Folklore from different regions spoke of differing levels of the afterlife. In some legends, these represented the different courts of Dìyù—our "Hell." Some quoted ten courts, some quoted six, some even thirty-six. Was that the equivalent of what Lin was saying?

"Are the deeper levels"—I gestured vaguely at the ground—"somewhere else?"

"No. All levels of the afterlife are still overlying the living world. We're all in the same physical place, just . . . on different planes of existence. Together, but separate."

I pondered this. "Are you being haunted, right now? By a . . . second-level ghost?"

"I assume so." Lin's mouth twisted as he considered. "I can't see them, though."

I frowned. "Why not?" I'd always assumed the afterlife was the afterlife, all the ghosts of the world mixing together. But it seemed to be more complex than that.

Lin was silent for a moment while he formulated his response. "You know how you never saw ghosts until you almost died? The same goes for us. As a first-level ghost, I would have to skirt near enough to the next level of the death realm for the veil to thin; only then would the second-level spirits become visible. I cannot see them because I haven't come close enough to dying a second time."

Arching an eyebrow at him, I said, only half jesting, "Perhaps when I enter the death realm I can remedy that for you."

He snorted. "You can try. But even dead, I think I'd still win in a fight."

Rolling my eyes, I turned over this new information in my mind; it was certainly a lot to take in. I'd have to muse on it later, alone, when I had some privacy and separation from Lin.

Instead, I forced my mind back to the problem at hand: How could we get through the city gates? There was no way I, an unaccompanied teenager with no identification to speak of, would be allowed solo passage into the city. My grandmother had been with me that time I came to see the shaman; other visits had always been with one of the other aunties.

Lin, with his height and breadth of shoulders, could pass for someone older, but he was most likely invisible to the guards. And even if perchance one of them could see him, in the harsh glare of the rising sun he did not look entirely corporeal. I'd stolen looks at him as we'd hiked toward the city and was often struck by the way the early-winter sunlight refracted, prism-like, through his body.

My shoulders slumped as I considered this seemingly insurmountable conundrum.

"Follow me," Lin murmured into the curve of my ear. I jumped; being unable to sense him or his body heat, I hadn't realized he'd leaned so close. He turned and crept away, sticking close to the packed-earth city walls. I followed.

We crouched behind bushes, watching the travelers on the road. The majority were farmers or tinkers driving carts pulled by cows or donkeys. Most of them were wrapped in coarse cloaks, hunched against the biting air.

When one particularly overloaded cart trundled past, Lin's ears and eyes pricked up. The driver looked to be a farmer. They had a ruddy face, a wiry build, and permanent scowl marks on their forehead. As we watched, they raised their arm and began whipping the two beasts pulling the cart. I flinched; the donkeys hee-hawed plaintively, picking up their plodding pace, but the farmer did not relent.

So horrified was I by the scene that it took me a second to notice that Lin had left our hiding spot.

"Lin," I hissed, as he edged closer to that cursed cart. "Come back!"

He didn't answer. He just half turned, his finger raised to his slightly translucent lips and a dangerous gleam in his eyes. My heart started pounding. My breath felt tight in my chest. Lin sidled closer and closer, until he kept pace with the cart, until he was within arm's length of it, until he was within striking distance . . . Then he pulled out his knife.

I almost cried out as I watched, but managed to clap my hand over my mouth just in time. Instead, I moaned silently into my palm as Lin, invisible to the hapless farmer, slid the blue knife between their ribs.

The farmer took a gurgled breath, then keeled over sideways atop a pile of sacks. The movement caused the cart to jerk and tip slightly before righting itself.

The donkeys continued trudging along, but the jerk to the reins caused them to veer off course. They swerved off the dirt path altogether until they were obscured by the scraggly trees.

Lin beckoned to me, his movements harried. I understood why. Now that the farmer was no longer steering, the donkeys were plowing through the grass, headed straight for the city wall. A group of ghosts turned to stare.

Still numb with shock, I sprinted over. "What the hells, Lin? Why did you *do* that?"

"It was . . . necessary. Now bring the cart to a stop."

I ignored him, watching his growing frustration as the cart swerved more wildly off course. "Necessary?" My voice was rising. "You just *murdered* someone, Lin! First Larch, now this! What sort of person does that?"

"We needed a way to get into the city. I got you one. You want to save your grandmother, don't you?"

"Yes, but—"

Lin let out a sound of extreme exasperation. "Mothers, Jia! It's not like they're gone for good. They'll just become a ghost, like me." His expression darkened, his eyes glinting dangerously. "Now stop. The. Cart."

I folded my arms. "You do it."

He uttered an impatient growl. "I can't. I can't touch anything human-made." He leaned closer, his posture so menacing that I shivered. "Stop the Mothers-damned cart, Jia."

For a few measured moments, I did nothing. Just glared at him as the cart's course deviated further. I was furious—fire building in my chest, my pulse an all-consuming roar in my ears.

Lin just stared back, his body stiff, hands curled into fists at his side. In the final moment before the cart crashed into the wall, I ran to it, vaulted in, grabbed the reins, and pulled. Not to appease Lin, mind you. I did it to avoid the unwanted attention crashing the cart would bring.

The donkeys came to a stop.

"Now hide the body," Lin commanded.

My fingers twitched, wishing they could slap him. But I grudgingly acquiesced, dragging the farmer's bleeding body behind the nearby bushes before hauling a few empty sacks over the corpse. *Damn you, Lin*, I thought to myself as I worked. Bile rose in my throat and I swallowed it down. If I was to get caught by the city guards trying to hide a dead body, it would be *me* sentenced to death by slow slicing, not Lin.

I shivered. Yes, I wanted to enter the afterlife—but not like that.

There was no going back now. All I could do was shove the

knowledge deep into the depths of my mind. Lin had killed someone! He'd *killed* them!

Sure, he'd always been an accomplished hunter—shooting, trapping, and snaring animals with brutal efficiency. In life, he'd had a talent for concocting poisons, lacing his knives and arrow tips to achieve a more rapid kill. He'd never possessed magic himself, but his workaround was to become a master of potions, mixing them with as deft a hand as any Liu sorcerer would.

But he'd only ever killed when it was absolutely necessary: for food, for hides, or for protection. To kill a human? So callously? I had never, ever imagined he'd do something as monstrous as that.

But now . . . he'd stuck his blue knife right into the soft intercostal space between the farmer's ribs. He'd sliced open Larch's crepey white throat. With no fanfare, no concern, as though taking a human life was nothing. How had he changed so much in the year we'd been apart? Who had he become?

I suppose Lin's reality had shifted, his perspective altered. He was dead; he resided in the afterlife; now, in his ghostly form, he could transcend worlds. What he'd said earlier was true: Death was not the end. There was still the afterlife—and its multitude of layers. I knew that now. But still.

At least it seemed Lin tried to target humans with the most heinous personalities, though whether that was intentional I could not say. My heart clenched as I examined the poor donkeys. From where I stood, their countless wounds were visible: newer welts, some striped in red, and hundreds of thinner, paler crisscrossing lines.

Scars.

My gut clenched, painfully. If only Essien Lancaster were here to heal the donkeys' wounds.

Lin pointed at the farmer's cloak. "You'll need this, Jia," he said, irritation tingeing his voice. I could tell that being unable to touch things was annoying him, a lot.

I frowned, pondering. If ghosts couldn't touch anything made by humans, how had he held the knife? How had he stabbed it into the farmer's chest? Into Larch? Into me? *How?*

It didn't matter. The last thing I wanted was to ask more questions, to discover the true depths of Lin's depravity. Shaking my head to clear my thoughts, I dragged the cloak off the farmer's slumped body and wrapped it around myself. It was so large it made it around thrice, and I had to hitch it up to sit in the driver's seat.

"All that produce, wasted," a voice said. I jumped to find the farmer's ghost had risen from the corpse and was now standing on the furrowed ground beside the cart. They turned their eyes on me, their expression morose. "What are you doing, girl? Stealing my turnips?"

"They won't do you much good now," I said flatly, looking straight ahead. Using the reins, I spurred the donkeys into a walk, leaving the farmer's ghost behind.

We passed through the gates without trouble.

I did not use the whip.

The closer we got to the slum areas, the tighter and more convoluted the roads became. Ghosts watched us as we clopped by, turning their large, sad eyes upon us. At one point, the spirits converged, but I implored the donkeys to go faster, forcing Lin to speed up to a jog beside me. Whether the poor creatures accelerated because of the urgency of my voice or because they sensed the ghosts' presence and wanted to avoid them, I couldn't tell.

When the roads became too crowded and I couldn't ride any farther, we stopped. We were forced to leave the cart in a dark, secluded lane. After untying the donkeys and giving them each a bag of turnips to munch on, I draped the farmer's cloak over the remaining sacks and followed Lin into the main street.

Beggars with bare feet, dirty robes, and mouths full of stained teeth stretched their hands out plaintively—I shook my head, frowning, having nothing to give. Children darted around forests of legs. Hawkers tossed meat and vegetables in woks on the roadside; still others lowered strips of dough into boiling oil, transforming them into puffy golden yóutiáo, which made my mouth water. I had not eaten a proper meal since I'd left Throft Hall, and my stomach felt as hollow as it had been when I was dead.

We pushed through paved brick lanes threaded with throngs of people; it was always jarring being in the crowded city. It was such a contrast to our secluded forest life. Here, the smells of food gave way to the stench of too many humans crammed into too small a space. There were ghosts, too; once or twice, I was forced to pass right through one, causing a shiver to slip down my spine.

As we walked, I repeatedly attempted to interrogate Lin, increasingly frustrated at how cagey he was being. "Who is the

Bone Smith, Lin?" I said on more than one occasion as I huffed along, trying to match his pace. "Why are we visiting them?" He refused to answer, just kept plowing through the crowds as I hurried along behind him.

In the end, I wore him down. He stopped abruptly in a side street and half turned, letting out a long-suffering sigh. "We are visiting the Bone Smith to help you enter the afterlife, Jia Yi." He gave me an exasperating, enigmatic smile. "That's what you wanted, right?"

"Thanks, that's very helpful," I said, my tone sarcastic. "Who—or what—is the Bone Smith? Tell me, or I won't go."

"They make weapons," he explained, speaking slowly, as though I were an ignorant child. "Weapons that can be used across the worlds."

My gaze flicked to the blue blade hanging at his belt. "Like yours."

He gave a grim nod. "Like mine."

"And . . . you want me to go there . . . why? So I can have one, too?"

He shot a look at me. "If you insist on entering the death realm," he said, with an expression of extreme distaste, "then you must be armed. I cannot fathom . . ." He trailed off, his mouth flattening into a hard line.

"Can't fathom what?"

There was a long pause. We stared at each other, Lin studying my face. His eyes raked down my cheeks, across my lips, dipping to my collarbone. And everywhere his gaze landed, my skin automatically heated—much to my disgust.

Eventually, Lin shook his head, then muttered, "Never mind." He continued walking.

It took me a second of delay before I realized and began to hurry after him. "How many levels are in the death realm?"

Lin didn't seem thrown by my abrupt change in subject. "No one knows, Jia, least of all me," he said. "Ten? Six? Thirty-six? I don't know any ghosts who have delved deep enough to find out. Once they go down, they don't come back."

"So you can't return to a higher level, if you descend deeper?"

"No," he said, curt, before shooting me a look over his shoulder. "Death only brings us deeper into the afterlife." He faced forward again and continued walking. "Not all of us possess the power of resurrection."

I lapsed into thoughtful silence. We'd ventured into one of the most crowded parts of the city, the lanes so narrow it was a squeeze to fit between the buildings. Lin, of course, passed through easily—despite his broad shoulders, his lack of physical mass rendered walls irrelevant. He quickly got too far ahead of me, meaning I had to call him back.

"I can't fit," I grumbled, once he'd stopped to wait for me. He smirked as I struggled toward him, earning him one of my most spiteful scowls.

Finally we stopped in front of a low, stooped door. Something about it—apart from the way it glowed faintly blue—raised goose bumps across my arms. As Lin reached up to knock, I realized what it was: The doorframe and the lintel were lined with what looked disturbingly like human femurs. The door itself was encrusted with a thick layer of what seemed to be, to my alarm, fingerbones, knuckles, and teeth.

A shudder quaked through me. The Bone Smith indeed. The name was certainly apt.

"Wait," I said, and Lin paused, his fist raised.

I held my clammy hand up as though trying to grab his wrist, stopping about an inch away from the edges of his vacillating form. "Before you knock, how, exactly, am I supposed to pay for this 'weapon'?" I put my hands on my hips. "I have no coin, and I'm going to hazard a guess you don't either. And somehow I doubt the Bone Smith will want turnips—"

Lin cut me off. "The Smith does not take payment in coin. They take payment in secrets."

"Secrets?" I exclaimed. "I don't have secrets!"

But I did have one. A big one. Hadn't Essien Lancaster relayed to me his most closely guarded secret? It was given to me in confidence, though; it was not mine to tell.

Lin chuckled, interrupting my musing. "But you *do* have a secret, Jia. Or you did . . . once upon a time. We both did." His eyes found mine, something dark shifting in their tawny depths. A hint of a smile played about the edges of his lips. "Remember our cave?"

My pulse skittered and I looked away. "That was a long time ago." My dry mouth was clumsy as I formed the words. "It hardly counts."

If Lin noticed my unease, he didn't show it; instead, he just smirked, raised his hand, and knocked. The high-pitched sound startled me—this was the first thing in the mortal realm that I had seen him touch. "Wait," I blurted. "How did you . . . ?"

"Like I said . . ." Lin arched an eyebrow at me. "The Bone Smith makes things that exist in *both* worlds."

I swallowed my response, mollified. And waited. It seemed an age before the door swung open—who opened it I could not tell; there did not seem to be anyone within. Lin entered without hesitation. Clearly he'd been here before.

My gut churned, my mental unease turning physical. I lingered on the doorstep, peering into the shadowed house, before throwing a glance over my shoulder—to the brightness outside the door. Some vague voice inside my head told me not to go in. My breaths quickened, becoming sharp, fear grabbing me by the throat.

I almost turned to flee. But then I remembered the wan, sunken appearance of my Pópo's masklike face as she lay on her bed in deathly repose. The stench of illness that pervaded her room, both sickly sweet and sour all at the same time. The way she had looked at me the last time I'd seen her alive, when I was just about to leave to find more Shadowside. She'd examined me keenly, like she was trying to learn me by heart. As though she'd known it might be the last time she'd ever see me alive.

A single tear ran down my cheek. Running my tongue across my upper lip, I savored the tang of grief, of melancholy, of life.

Then I took a deep breath, and followed.

The inside of the house was sparse, and larger than it appeared externally. Still, the atmosphere was oppressive, as if there was some unseen force, some detectable energy, pressing in on us. Like it was probing. Like it was turning us inside out. And, in a startling contrast to the city, the Bone Smith's house was oddly free of ghosts, a deeply unsettling detail. What sort of place was this, where even the dead dared not visit?

I fisted my hands to stop them trembling.

The corridor we stood in was swathed in shadows. At the

end, a second door stood ajar, a spectral light glowing within. From behind the door came a deeply unsettling clacking noise. We crept along, the noise growing louder until it slithered beneath my skin. As though it was burrowing beneath the layers, sending prickling spasms through my body.

I hung back, swallowing my fear, as Lin pushed open the door.

Seventeen

Present day

The room was large but cluttered. Racks lined the walls, containing every type of weapon from spears to swords to giant battle-axes, all of them brittle white and clearly carved from bone. In the center of the room stood an enormous forge made out of coarse brick, the full-length chimney bisecting the room. Soot stains and burn marks were smeared all the way to the ceiling. The air was so cold it sent an ache down to my marrow.

"Lin," a voice said from the other side of the forge. A whispery voice—not of this world. It was like the swishing of cloaks, like wind through tall grass, like the sound of an undertaker digging a grave during the deep, dark night. "You have come back."

Lin gave a small bow of his head as the creature shuffled its way into view.

I suppressed a cry. The creature was small and squat—shorter, certainly, than I was. They wore a suit of bone armor, and obscuring their face was a mask, also made of bone. The mouth was a slash, crowded with spiny teeth. And through the eye holes glittered two malevolent eyes, like gemstones.

The crushing feeling intensified, so much so I could barely catch my breath. But still I straightened my back, lifted my chin, tried to don bravery like a mantle . . . Pretending as though *I was not afraid.*

The Bone Smith shuffled around the room, thrusting a curved knife into the fire of the forge. The flame was glowing a sickly sort of blue. And it didn't throw off heat but an icy, wraithlike chill. I guess it made sense—the making of weapons that could traverse worlds was not going to be done in an ordinary human fire.

The light surrounding the blade flared, then faded—until it looked almost exactly like the one Lin carried. No longer white, but gleaming blue. I knew, from my hunting days, that bone was usually brittle and made for poor weapons, but Lin's blade was *strong.* Perhaps the Bone Smith imbued their objects with some sort of maleficent magic that prevented them from shattering.

The Bone Smith plunged the blade into a barrel of brackish water. In my peripheral vision, I could sense Lin watching me. Shifting on my feet, I moved back a little so he wouldn't be able to see me quietly panicking.

"So, Lin-friend," the Bone Smith said in that raspy voice. They turned a pair of glittering eyes on Lin. "What brings you to this dwelling mine? Has your blade lost the sharpness of its edge? You have, perhaps, been killing too much and too often . . ." The Bone Smith paused to laugh—a deep, rattly sound that made my hair stand on end. Exactly how many people had Lin killed?

Lin frowned and shook his head. "It's not for me this time. It's for my . . . friend. She is in need of your services." Lin gestured at me with an almost lazy flick of his hand.

Now it was my turn to be perused by the Bone Smith's glittering eyes. "Ahhhh . . ." the Smith breathed. "A treat, this is! You brought me a new one." I caught a glimpse of the creature's hands for the first time as they clasped together. They were thin, bony, held together by sinew. *What the hells is this*, I wanted to scream. But instead I bit the inside of my cheek to keep from crying out. I tasted blood, sharp and metallic.

"Liu Jia Yi," I said, and gave a small bow. "Pleased to meet you, er . . ." I faltered.

The Bone Smith chuckled. "A delight! Such . . . manners. So very . . . human." Both the words and the mirth were disconcerting.

"I do not usually subscribe to such things," the Bone Smith continued. "Names and gender are of little consequence to me." A bony hand raised itself to the creature's chest. "People do, however, call me the Smith."

I nodded, and gulped painfully.

"And you?" The Smith sidled up to me, their masked head cocked. "What are you?"

"What do you mean, what am I?" I tried to keep the waver out of my voice.

Their black eyes bored into me, studying me intently. "You can see death. You can see ghosts. Yet you are not dead yourself. Are you friend or foe?"

"F-friend. Friend." I spoke quickly. My heart thumped in my chest.

The Bone Smith gave me a shrewd look. "What brings you to my dwelling, human girl?"

I tensed all over. "I—" I paused, giving a quick glance at Lin before focusing back on the Smith. I needed to concentrate on the task so I could get out of here as soon as possible. "I need a weapon." I might have imagined it, but from the corner of my eye I rather fancied Lin had given a barely perceptible nod.

"Certainly," the Bone Smith said. "Weapon of what sort, friend of Lin?"

"Um, a knife, I guess?" A sword was probably more lethal, but I was most handy with a knife.

The Bone Smith leaned toward me until I smelled their damp, earthy odor. "And what will you give me in payment, human? For my troubles?"

I licked my lips nervously. "Lin says . . . He says we pay in secrets."

"He would be correct," rasped the Smith. "And so, I repeat, friend of Lin: What will you give me?"

I gave Lin a helpless look, but he just shrugged. Then I cleared my throat and said to him, very slowly, "Can we please have some privacy?"

He stared at me hard for several seconds before huffing and turning away. His reluctance was obvious—perhaps he was just being overprotective again. I waited until he had slipped out the door.

"Just one secret?" I asked the Smith, turning back to face them.

"Indeed." They rubbed their skeletal hands together. "Choose wisely, though, for if it is not to my liking, I shall request another."

My mind scrambled for a response. I had so many secrets locked up in the stone cage of my heart. So many nights

I would retrieve them, reluctantly. Grudgingly. And I would dissect them, thinking and thinking until they were worn and filthy. I would often dwell on them for most of the night, only storing them back in their prison when the first cold light of day crept over the windowsill. In some ways, Lin's secrets, and mine, were always on my mind.

It was just so typical that now that I actually needed them, I could not think of a single one.

"What will you do with it?" I asked, stalling, trying to stretch for more time.

"That, human girl, is my own secret to keep." The leering mouth with its sharpened teeth stretched into a grin, and I recoiled. I'd thought the skull-like bone was just a mask, but apparently it was their actual face.

"Well . . ." I started, then trailed off, my mind spinning. "I am magical. And no one knew about it, before. I can come back from the dead."

"Ah." The Smith's glittering eyes roamed across my body. "An interesting ability indeed. Yet, I already knew this secret."

"You—you did?" I stammered.

"Resurrection magic is a rare power, human girl." The Bone Smith gave a deep, clattering inhale that sent me cold. "And it is well hidden in you. But not well hidden enough to escape *my* notice."

"The Spyrre couldn't detect my magic," I said, somewhat defensively.

"Spyrre only detect magic that exists in their own realm." The Bone Smith moved closer, their eyes locking onto mine. "Your power, human girl, manifests only in the realm of death. And even then, only when you want it to."

When I wanted it to? I frowned. It sure didn't seem that way.

"You must tell me another secret." The Bone Smith's expression twisted into one that resembled hunger.

"Prince Essien Lancaster of Yske"—I swallowed, wondering if the Smith would accept another person's secret as currency—"is magical too. He possesses healing powers." Guilt flared in my chest; perhaps I shouldn't be telling the Bone Smith about Essien's ability. But I quashed it down. If this information would help me follow Pópo into the afterlife, then I had no choice but to use it.

"Ah! A salacious secret indeed." The Bone Smith leaned in closer, overwhelming my senses. "Considering how the Yskians despise such powers."

I shivered a little as I said, "He only told me because I saved his life."

The Smith's eyes gleamed, and they shuffled away, pawing through a wall-mounted rack of weapons. As they handed me a knife, which shone with that familiar blue, ghostly glow, I said, "So this will still work once I'm dead?"

"Indeed." The Bone Smith peered at me sidelong. After a pause, they said, "It is not often a living human comes to my dwelling. Not many enter the death realm willingly. Pray tell—why does this mortal wish to?"

"My grandmother." My breath suddenly felt too shallow. I could tell I was on the verge of crying, so to distract myself, I sheathed my new blade in my belt. It sat against my skirt, emanating a painful chill that permeated my skin. "She . . . died. Yesterday. I need to find her."

It suddenly occurred to me that both Essien Lancaster and my grandmother were seeking a famous weapon, and here I was in the house of a creature who dealt entirely in weapons.

Perhaps the Bone Smith would have heard of the sword? So, I added, "She's looking for a weapon."

"Is she, now?" The Smith turned to face me fully, their sharp gaze piercing. *"Interesting."*

"I believe it's called . . ." I strained my memories for the name Essien had given. "The Sword of Rechenblod? At least I think that's what it's called . . ."

There was a long, weighty pause.

When the Bone Smith finally spoke, their voice came out in a whisper. "It has many names, both now and throughout history." They were no longer looking at me; their gleaming gaze was distant, seemingly hundreds of miles away. "Only the Yskians call it the Sword of Rechenblod."

My gut gave a lurch. So the Bone Smith *did* know of the sword.

Ignoring me, the Bone Smith continued speaking. "Here in Jinghu Dao it is known as 'the Sword of Life and Death,' hence its name, Shēngsǐ zhī jiàn. The Southlanders across the sea call it Portador da Vida—'the bringer of life.' In the tribes, it is known as Gol zevseg, 'the main weapon.' And up north, they call it Dødsdreperen."

"What does that mean?" I asked, trying to keep my voice even.

The Smith fixed their black eyes on me. "'Death Killer.'"

A shiver crawled up my neck. "I have heard it is very powerful."

"Yes." The Bone Smith sounded almost . . . wistful. "Its wielder can conquer anything, even death."

I gripped the handle of my new knife to hide the fact that my fingers were shaking. "How do you know all this?"

They smiled a smile that was all sharp teeth. "Have you not guessed, friend of Lin? It is I who forged it."

My mind reeled. If the Bone Smith had made the sword, then perhaps they would also know how to find it. "Do you know where it is?" I couldn't hide my eagerness.

The creature's grin fell away. "Alas, that I do not know." They stroked their chin with sinewy fingers. "Originally, it was owned by the Crimson Emperor, who lost it almost a thousand years ago. Later, it resurfaced in Yske, where it was kept by the Lancasters until the last war. When the Yskian army was overthrown, it was stolen by a usurper. However, the usurper was soon murdered. It was henceforth brought into the afterlife, and subsequently lost." They took a step closer to me, and I planted my feet, fighting the urge to run away.

The Bone Smith's voice dropped to a deadly whisper. "For centuries, it has been hidden in the death realm. Some say it is in the deepest layer. None have found it, though not for lack of trying."

I swallowed. *The deepest layer?* "Well, my grandmother is looking for it. A shaman predicted that she and I would be the ones to find it."

"Your grandmother? The very same one who has died?"

I nodded, my skin going ice-cold.

The Bone Smith tilted their head slightly, regarding me. "I believe I have heard tell of her, human girl. The ghosts whisper of a sorceress who recently entered our realm. She is making enquiries about the whereabouts of the sword."

My pulse skipped. Ghosts knew of Pópo. This creature knew of her, too. Which told me that she was more invested in finding this ghostly sword than she had ever admitted to me. *Why all the secrets, Pópo?* I wanted to cry.

With some effort, I schooled my face into a neutral expression, fighting back my tears. "I'm going to find her, so I can help her. But Lin insisted I come here first so I could enter the afterlife armed."

The Bone Smith's eyes gleamed bright. "Lin is helping you find your grandmother?"

"Yes. Why?"

The Bone Smith gave a sly smirk and turned away. "Perhaps you should ask that boy what secret bought *his* blade."

My attention snapped to the Smith, with their bleached-white armor and mask of bone and gaunt, skeletal hands. "What? Why? What do you mean?"

The creature half turned, a vestigial smile playing about their lips. "If you wish to hear *my* secret, human girl, you must give me something in return."

"What do you want?" I asked quickly. "I don't have any money. Unless you want my own dagger?" From my boot, I pulled the dagger that Essien Lancaster had returned to me and held it out to the Smith.

"I have no need for it," they said, using their emaciated hands to gesture at the weapon racks. "I have blades here aplenty."

"Turnips, then?" I was getting desperate. "Donkeys? A cart?"

"None of that is of any use to me. I am not alive, and hence I do not eat. A cart I have no need of. And, if you wish to bring me donkeys,"—here, they turned to fully face me—"then I have no need for anything save their bones."

Nausea rolled through my belly, and I glanced at the closed door through which Lin had disappeared.

Was this why the Bone Smith traded in secrets? So that they could manipulate people with knowledge, in order to get what they wanted?

And if so, what *did* they want? I had no idea what a purveyor of death-realm weapons could use. And no, I was not about to kill a couple of innocent donkeys to find out.

Defeated, I shook my head. "I have nothing else to offer."

"Indeed." The Bone Smith rubbed their hands together, their mouth curving into another leer. "Until you have something of use for me, I am afraid I cannot give you Lin's secret."

They turned away. Clearly, I was dismissed. Stumbling backward—desperate to put some distance between me and this creature—I groped for the door handle.

Just as my hand found it, the Bone Smith's chilling voice rang out from behind me. "Friend of Lin?"

I froze. "Yes?" My voice wobbled.

"If you wish to find your grandmother," they said, still facing away, "I have heard ghosts speak of her staying at the Jin Dan tavern. Perhaps you can start your search there." With bony fingers, they picked up another blade and their hammer.

I drew in a shaky breath. The Golden Egg tavern. The name sounded familiar. "Thank you."

The hammer swung, hitting the bone blade with a low thunk. "And in the meantime, human girl, be wary. Lin-friend is no friend of yours."

I bit my lip so hard that it hurt. Not looking back, I pushed open the door and fled.

* * *

Lin was waiting outside, leaning against the wall, his head lowered. As soon as I burst through the door, he looked up, tensing all over.

"Did you get your knife?" His voice was steady. Suspiciously casual.

"I did," I said, my jaw tightening. My hand strayed to the knife's handle before curling around the hilt. Lin's eyes followed my movements, gaze sharp as a crow's.

"What was your secret, by the way?" I asked, matching the lightness of his tone. "The one you used to buy *your* blade."

He raised one heavy eyebrow. "If I told you, then it would no longer be a secret, would it?"

My fingers tightened. "Just tell me." What could possibly be worse than all the things I already knew about?

A pause. Lin crossed his arms. "No."

I advanced on him, drawing my Bone Smith knife and raising it to his neck until it met a satisfying resistance. I fought the urge to release a maniacal laugh; I could touch him. Not with my hands, not with my body—but with the Bone Smith's gleaming blade.

Which meant, this time, I could finally kill him. Send him into the next layer down, where he could no longer haunt me.

What would happen to him if I did? Did I care?

"Tell me," I repeated, my voice dropping until my words oozed out, dripping with malice.

"Or what, you'll kill me?" He sneered. "Tell me, Jia, do you actually know what it means to take a life? To watch a human's soul leave their eyes as they gasp out one last desperate breath? If you did, perhaps you'd be less careless about threatening me."

"Oh, believe me," I said, baring my teeth. "There is *nothing* careless about me threatening you." For emphasis, I pressed the knife tip harder against his skin.

Lin smirked, sending a wave of fury coursing through my veins. When he next spoke, his voice was annoyingly calm. "If you kill me, then who will guide you through the death realm?"

My head pounded, hot with blood. "Who says I need a guide?"

"I know things you don't," he said. "About ghosts, and the afterlife."

My hand shook. I wished I could drive in the blade.

But I didn't. My head and my heart were waging a massive war. On the one hand, I so desperately wanted to slash out at him. To wipe that stupid grin off his smarmy face.

But on the other hand, what he said was true: I knew very little about the afterlife. I couldn't afford to lose his help. I couldn't afford anything that might delay me getting to the tavern the Bone Smith spoke of, anything that might prevent me from finding Pópo.

So, glowering at him, I relented, releasing the pressure on the knife. He rubbed at his neck and shot me a filthy look.

"All right then," I said, raising one eyebrow. "If you're so desperate to be a guide, then be a guide. I need to find the Jin Dan tavern."

"Well you're in luck, Jia Yi." He leaned in, a smug smile fixed on his face. "Because I know *exactly* where that is."

Immediately, I perked up. "You do?" All my ire had drained away in less than an instant. Now the only thing running through my veins was hope: that I could find my grandmother, here, in death.

Lin just chuckled. Then, without responding, he pivoted and strode away.

"Come along," he called over his shoulder, in the most condescending way possible.

I sheathed the knife, staring daggers at his back. But then, like the fool I was, I followed him out of the lane.

Eighteen

Present day

We traipsed through the city, weaving through the crowds, stepping around horse shit, and trying not to walk through the ghosts congregating in the streets.

Wandering ghosts paced back and forth, seeking destinations they would never reach. The benevolent guǐpó went about their business, reenacting the errands they would've performed in life. The worst were the hungry ghosts—their bellies distended and tracked with veins, their mouths just minuscule holes. They were spirits of people who had done evil deeds in life and were therefore condemned to be forever famished, in a perpetual search for satiation. They would stop and turn ravenous eyes on me, their gazes darkening as they appraised my ghostly flesh. Sizing me up as though assessing whether *I* was good to eat.

How glad was I that they were unable to fit anything in their tiny pinprick mouths.

Every time I caught sight of a ghostly old woman, my heart would give a leap, followed by a crushing sensation when I realized it was not Pópo. Still, I stared at each ghost, committing their faces to memory, wondering if—even if not Pópo—they might be the faces of my dead parents.

It was a compulsion. I couldn't help looking, couldn't stop.

Whenever I wasn't scrutinizing the ghosts, I was wondering what Lin's secret was. What had both he and the Bone Smith refused to tell me?

Once, I'd known everything there was to know about Lin. But not anymore. In the past year, he could have accrued any number of secrets that I would not be privy to.

Part of me wished that I *had* gotten rid of him outside the Bone Smith's house. But he was right: He was proving useful, since he, unlike me, seemed to know where we were going.

Still, I spent most of the journey glaring at the back of his head. Once I found Pópo, I'd have no need of Lin. We could part ways for good so I could, once and for all, forget about the pain he'd caused me. There was no trace of the boy I'd once known remaining in the empty shell of his form. Now he was just a ghost. An arrogant, cagey, infuriating—

"We're here." Lin's declaration jerked me from my thoughts.

We had ducked down a small side street and were approaching a rowdy venue. Crowds of people spilled out onto the street, many of them stumbling. Faint strains of music and the sounds of merriment floated from the windows. Two people leaned against a wall, kissing and canoodling and whispering to one another.

As we drew closer, stepping around the occasional pool of vomit, I realized: I *knew* this place.

My palms turned clammy. My pulse raced. This tavern—I hadn't remembered its name before. But I knew it. In fact, I'd been here.

When Lin had disappeared, just over a year ago, rumors had begun to circulate that he was spending his time here, gambling and drinking and goodness knows what else. I'd done my best to ignore the gossip.

But eventually, my willpower had broken. Once, only once, I'd visited him here, in a failed attempt to confront him before he'd died. And he'd acted so heinously toward me that I . . .

No, I would never forget this tavern, not in a hundred years.

Lin caught my expression and raised an eyebrow. "You recognize it now, I gather?"

I did not bother to respond.

True to my memory, clusters of bulbous red lanterns hung, suspended, against the outer wall. A red-and-white flag bearing the tavern's name billowed above a vermillion-painted door. The only things I didn't recognize were the pale ghosts with long, dark hair who loitered around the entrance. Their eyes were onyx black, their lips bloodred, their teeth sharpened into points.

Nǚguǐ. I recognized them from childhood folktales.

Glancing sidelong at Lin, I wondered why my grandmother's ghost would come *here*, of all places. As far as I knew she wasn't the type to spend time in taverns when she'd been alive. And hadn't Lin told me that ghosts were drawn to places that had been important to them in life? It seemed more likely that the Jin Dan tavern was significant to *Lin* . . . not my grandmother.

Was this another one of Lin's tricks? Were he and the Bone Smith working together? Were they taking advantage of my cluelessness? Or something worse?

But why, then, would the Bone Smith have warned me not to trust Lin? It didn't make any sense.

I had half a mind to challenge Lin about it, to demand that he give me answers. But he'd already melted through the tavern wall.

I grimaced. Too late.

Hesitating, I loitered, wondering if I should follow Lin in. What if this was a trap?

Two of the nǚguǐ turned doleful eyes on me, their crimson lips stretching into grins. I knew they wouldn't hurt me—they usually saved their retribution for the men who'd inflicted violence on them in life—but their bleak stares were still unsettling.

I ducked my head, avoiding eye contact, and scurried past the ghosts to the front door.

Once inside, I was immediately hit by the savory scents that laced the air and made my stomach grumble. The rabble of the crowd was almost deafening. My eyes, smarting with the smoke, took a bit longer to adjust, since the only illumination was scant light filtering in through the latticed fretwork windows and a couple of dismal-looking lanterns. I blinked several times in an attempt to clear my vision.

The place was absolutely packed. Living humans were crowded around round tables, drinking millet wine out of ceramic vessels and eating small dishes of yam cakes, bird's nest soup, salted duck eggs, and pickled vegetables. Some of them were gambling, playing tiles, bellowing and banging the table when they lost. One patron, clearly inebriated, was slumped against the bar counter, snoring. The smell of liquor turned my stomach, and I fought down the bile that threatened to claw up my throat.

In the corner, a table surrounded by red chairs was occupied by a cluster of glum-looking ghosts. In every tavern there was an empty table allocated for use by spirits, but I'd never been able to see the ghosts before.

Disappointingly, none of them was Pópo. They stood quietly, unable to touch the chairs, doing nothing save staring at the other occupants. Their feet sank into the parquet floor; suddenly, I remembered what Lin had said—that ghosts could not touch things that were human-made. The ghosts, including Lin, were tethered to the earth, to the dirt and mineral and salt that bound their souls to this world.

Had I ever noticed Lin's ghost feet sinking into the floor, prior to today? I couldn't remember. Embarrassingly, I'd always been far too fixated on his face.

Shoving that thought deeper into my mind, I focused on my surroundings. Finally, I spotted Lin. Elbowing my way through to him, I waved to catch his attention, raised my voice, and shouted, "Do you see her?" It was so crowded that I wasn't worried about someone seeing me speaking to empty air.

Lin's gaze swept the room, and he shook his head. Then, leaning closer to speak into my ear, he said, "Maybe we take a look out the back." He jerked a thumb at the accommodation quarters, accessible through a beaded curtain.

Mā de. How would I get through there? I assumed that access to the accommodation quarters would require payment, and I had no money on me.

Mercifully, Lin seemed to understand. A wicked grin bloomed on his face. "I'll create a diversion. Then you can slip through."

A diversion? The last time he'd created a diversion was when he'd killed Larch. "All right," I said, shouting to be heard above the din. "No killing, though."

Lin gave an exaggerated sigh. "Fine. No killing."

He drew his blade, strode to a table crowded around with mortals, and swept its entire contents onto the floor.

The humans, all yelling, leaped to their feet as porcelain cups fell to the ground and shattered; food splattered across the floor; rivulets of tea trickled through the veins of stone. One of the patrons, apparently drunk, stared at the lost food, then turned upon their companion and began unleashing a barrage of screamed curses. Clearly, they hadn't been able to see Lin's ghost wield his Bone Smith blade, and had thought the other drunk mortal had upended the table's contents.

The other drunkard pushed back, shoving the accuser in the chest, and then their friends joined in, and before long a full-blown brawl had erupted among the tables. It wasn't ideal, but, to be perfectly honest, it was better than callously committing murder.

Lin resheathed his weapon and beckoned me to follow him as he slipped through the beaded curtain without disturbing a single strand.

Fleeing the ruckus, I pushed past the scuffling patrons and slipped through the curtain myself.

Behind it was a long, wide hallway with carved mahogany doors studded along its length. Most of them were shut tight, but as we trudged along the corridor, a few had been left open. In one, a mortal reclined in a chair, pungent smoke curling from a pipe clasped between their teeth. In another, two ghosts clutched each other in a passionate embrace. In yet another, a half-naked person sprawled across the bed, fast asleep. They'd forgotten to remove their makeup.

Lin ignored all these, only stopping when we reached the second-to-last room. This time, the door was shut.

He gestured at the handle. "Living first," he said, smirking, pretending he was being polite.

I threw him an acerbic look, then turned the knob. The door swung open with a soft whine.

The room appeared to be a storeroom, the floor packed earth instead of wood. There was a broken bed, loose furniture was stacked up in the corner, and in the center of the room was—

My grandmother.

So the Bone Smith had told the truth.

Pópo's head whipped up. Her eyes shone with silvery, unshed tears. Involuntarily, I let out a cry and rushed at her. But my attempt to touch her was futile; I tried to pull her into a hug but my arms just went right through her.

She was a ghost. I couldn't touch her.

But *Lin* could.

Before I could register what was happening, he'd already brushed by me, grabbed her around the neck, and pressed his blue blade against her throat.

I stared at him, speechless. Why was he attacking my grandmother? *What was going on?*

"What are you doing?" I shrieked.

Lin's face twisted into a grimace. He wouldn't look at me. "I'm sorry."

Reflexively, I lunged at them.

"Jia," my grandmother croaked, and stretched a thin, pale hand toward me. "Don't."

My mind went blank. All I heard was my voice, screaming. The next moment I had already drawn my Bone Smith dagger and knocked Lin's knife hand to one side. Immediately, I counterswung at Lin; startled, he parried my blow. Now free from Lin's clutches, Pópo scurried into the corner, clasping at her face with both hands.

I rushed at Lin, viciously, not holding back, putting him on the defense. My blade slashed through the air, meeting his—the only way I, as a living mortal, could touch his ghostly form. He'd always been the better fighter, but in this case, considering I could come alive again, I had less to lose . . . I fought so aggressively I pushed him backward, forcing him to duck and spin to avoid being cut.

"Jia, let me explain," he said, his words coming short and sharp.

"You don't need to," I hissed, slashing at him again. The Bone Smith had warned me not to trust him. They'd told the truth about my grandmother being at the tavern, and it seemed they'd been right about Lin, too. "You just tried to kill her, didn't you? *Why?*"

"Jia, listen—" Lin's words rasped out of him as he deflected my next blow.

"No!" I lashed out again; he ducked just in time. "Bastard!" Another slash. "Traitor!" Another slash. *"I'll kill you!"*

The two blades met with the clack of bone on bone.

Our weapons strained against one another, both our arms vibrating, neither of us gaining ground. Lin's lips curved into a sneer. "I'm already dead—"

"Then I'll kill you again," I ground out. "And again. As many times as I have to, until I'm rid of you. Forever." *What is dead can die again.*

Lin gave an exaggerated swallow, his Adam's apple rippling beneath the tan skin of his throat.

I knew what I wanted then. I knew what I had to do. I had no idea why Lin had suddenly attacked my grandmother, but what I did know was that I couldn't trust him. That Pópo wasn't safe—not with him.

If I killed him, he'd be in the next level down. The second ghost level. Unable to touch my grandmother, except with his blue blade. And then, if I managed to kill him *again*, he wouldn't be able to see us, or haunt us, or use his knife.

Fierce resolve rushed through me. Inch by excruciating inch, our two blades arced closer and closer to Lin's neck, until they were hovering just above his skin.

I'd never killed anyone before. But maybe killing a ghost didn't count?

If I never wanted to see Lin or his filthy face again . . . if I wanted to protect Pópo, then I had no other choice.

Do it, Jia, I thought. *Kill him and rescue Pópo.* I wouldn't abandon her—not in life, and certainly not here, in death.

I didn't want her to die again. The first level of the afterlife was already populated by a whole host of terrifying ghosts. Who knew what horrors lay even deeper?

I roared, throwing the full force of my effort into slicing open Lin's neck.

I didn't need to, though. At precisely the same time, Lin released the pressure on his blade. Instantly, I overbalanced, my blade slashing across his throat. Ghost blood, black as burned branches, gushed out from his wound. He staggered backward, clutching his neck with both hands. He no longer held the knife.

With growing horror, I pivoted slowly, my hand flying to my mouth, muffling my cry.

For in the moment when I had killed the ghost of Lin, he'd taken the chance to throw his blade. And it had struck true, right into his target.

My grandmother.

Nineteen

Present day

I howled, rushing over to Pópo as she bled out on the ground. Lin's knife protruded from her abdomen. In the corner, Lin's spectral body lay spread-eagled on the floor, drenched in black ghost blood.

My body flooded with ice. I could not see second-level ghosts—was Lin currently haunting me without my knowledge? I scanned the room, heart thrashing, clutching my dagger so tightly it hurt.

"Jia," my grandmother said, ripping my attention away from Lin and back onto her. She raised her eyes to me, her face drawn, the edges of her form rippling, like the light-speckled surface of a lake.

"Pópo!" I crouched beside her, about to pull out the knife, but my grandmother stopped me.

"Don't pull it out. It will only give us less time."

Tears sprang into my eyes, beading on my lower lashes. "I had to see you." I flexed my fingers, wanting more than anything to take her hands in mine. But I knew it was no use—I couldn't touch her.

Pópo gave me a feeble smile. "You're alive."

"I tried to get back." My voice came out choked, grief clogging my throat. "Before you died. But I was too late. I'm sorry. So sorry. And now I'm too late again—"

"Hush, now," she interjected, her voice becoming momentarily stronger, as though her conviction had solidified it. "Let us not dwell on what could have been. Let us enjoy these final moments together."

Final? No! "I won't let you die again. I won't . . ." I trailed off, unable to continue. If she died again, she'd move into the second level, and I would not be able to see her anymore.

Pópo lifted her hand, like she wished to stroke my cheek. "It is all right. Yes, I am in the afterlife. But I have a purpose here, Jia Yi. A duty to fulfill."

I sniffed. "The Sword of Rechenblod?"

My grandmother raised her eyebrows incrementally. The next moment, though, her surprise dissipated, and she gave me a sympathetic smile. "Yes, child. The Sword of Rechenblod. Though, in our language it is called Shēngsǐ zhī jiàn. You remember the shaman?"

I nodded, then swiped at my nose with my sleeve. "The one who told me I would die before you—"

Pópo blinked, dispersing her silvery tears. "I have a confession to make. I told you that I didn't believe that woman, but the truth is—"

"I know, Pópo," I whispered. "It's okay."

"I only wanted to protect you." Her voice was growing weaker, her words becoming less distinct.

I let out another sob. "Don't go, Pópo. Don't go. I'll follow you. It's my duty to find the sword, and . . ."

With the tiniest of movements, Pópo shook her head. "No. You must not. If you search for it, the others will hunt you."

I frowned. "The others?" My mind was getting tangled.

"There are . . . others out there trying to find the sword. Others who know that *I* am looking for it. They wish to thwart me, so they can find it first. But they are not to be trusted with such a powerful weapon."

My heart stuttered, my mind churning. Did she mean Essien Lancaster? Or perhaps she meant Lin. Perhaps that was why Lin was trying to stop me from getting to my grandmother: to prevent us from teaming up to find the sword.

"We need to find it and destroy it first," Pópo continued.

Tearing my mind away from thoughts of Lin and the Yskian prince, I focused on the present, on my grandmother. "All right then. What do we do?"

"The shaman—there was another part of her prediction. A part we didn't hear. I let my emotions get the better of me, and I . . . left too early to hear it."

"The prediction." I grimaced at the memory of that stuffy, smoke-filled tent. "There's more?"

She gave a small nod. "I went back to the shaman later, in secret, to hear the rest of it. I believe it contained information on where to find the sword. But the shaman refused to tell me without you present. She said there was only one person who was permitted to hear it . . ." She looked up at me, her eyes soft. "And that person is you. It is, after all, your fate she spoke of."

I paused. Why had my grandmother never told me this before? But then I shook myself. At this point it didn't matter. "So how can I hear it?"

"She placed it in a chest and gave it to me, imbuing it with magic that keeps it sealed to anyone but you. I buried it beneath the shrine in my hut. I know I should not have hidden it, but I did not . . ." She swallowed. "I didn't want you to believe that your future held only death."

At this, my grandmother smiled at me fondly. "And look at you now. You're here, alive, while I am dead. So perhaps the shaman *was* wrong. Though you must have come close to death to be able to see me." She was back to frowning again.

"Never mind that," I said. I didn't want to tell her that I *had* been dead. That I had died multiple times. And that I now believed, without doubt, that the shaman's predictions were true.

"Go and fetch it." Her voice had tapered off; by now it was almost inaudible. Her chest heaved with her effort to speak. "I have heard the sword is concealed in the deepest layer of the afterlife, but I do not know where. Hopefully the shaman's prediction will contain that information."

"So I'll need to go home . . ." I said slowly, thinking out loud.

"Yes, child. I will go there too. That way, even though we cannot see each other, we can each be comforted by the knowledge that we are in the same place."

If I knew my grandmother was there, two levels down, would the idea of going home not seem so bleak? Would the idea bolster me, make me feel less alone? Or would it just compound my grief?

Squaring my shoulders, I let out a shaky breath, then nodded.

"Once you have the prophecy," Pópo continued, "find

some way to get the knowledge to me. You may need to consult with the spirit mediums, or send the message through another ghost. There are those in our community who will be able to help you . . ."

She spoke reverently, but I barely processed her words. "I . . . I don't want to say goodbye again."

My grandmother's eyes softened. "I know."

I blinked, and the tears that had gathered in my eyes spilled over. A heaviness had settled inside my chest, my gut. Everything hurt. But this was Pópo's last request. A request that could prevent the Shēngsǐ Sword from falling into the wrong hands. And if she was asking this of me with her last dying words, I would do it—even though my heart was shattering at having to part with her once more.

My grandmother's eyelids fluttered closed. "Goodbye, my dear child," she whispered. "If the Mothers are kind, you will remain safe."

"Please, no," I whispered, my whole body trembling, a river of unleashed grief. The words on my lips were a prayer.

By now, she had slipped out of lucidity, her gaze becoming unfocused.

Then she gave a sigh, her ghost-body going limp.

"No," I sobbed, for the second time, over my grandmother's lifeless form. Now I was here, on my own, in a bawdy tavern, while Lin's and my grandmother's consciousnesses had descended to the second level of death.

Climbing to my feet, I braced my hands against the wall, still shuddering with the force of my grief.

If ghosts could die and become ghosts of ghosts . . . could Lin and Pópo die yet again, and become ghosts of ghosts of ghosts? Was there a limit to how many times they could die? To how deep the afterlife went? Did it go on forever—a horrific sort of purgatory? Or if it did have an end, what would be waiting for my Pópo when she'd gone as deep as she could possibly go?

And what did Lin want with her? Why had he killed her?

There were too many questions, and too few answers. I had no idea where to begin. Clearly, though, Lin was dangerous. One of the most dangerous ghosts of all. I'd thought that a year ago he'd done the most heinous thing possible. Now, though? It was . . . unbelievable, but somehow he'd actually gotten worse.

He'd demonstrated the ease with which he took others' lives when he'd so callously killed the Lancaster physician. When he'd stabbed the turnip farmer.

Then he'd tricked me into leading him to my grandmother. He'd attacked me. Killed her. And it sickened me to know that as a result of my rash actions, he was now on the same level of the death realm as Pópo.

But I would not abandon her. Not now, not ever. Not when I knew that Lin could readily kill her again.

So, steeling myself, I made the decision. Yes, I would go back to collect the rest of the shaman's prediction—as Pópo had wanted. But after that, I'd delve straight back into the afterlife and hunt down Lin. To make him suffer as I had suffered.

To wreak revenge.

Only once I was confident that my grandmother was safe would I help her seek and destroy the Shēngsǐ Sword, before anyone else who sought to wield its power could find it.

Or perhaps, if it was truly able to raise the dead, then I could also use it to bring back Pópo. She and I could resurrect together, and things could go back to the way they'd been . . . just minus the threat of Lin.

To fortify my nerves, I inhaled deeply before blowing out a long, slow breath. Then, picking up my Bone Smith blade from where I'd dropped it, I held it aloft and crept back out via the corridor.

Somehow, I managed to make it back through the beaded curtain without raising any suspicion. Maybe everyone just thought I was one of the women who patrons regularly hired as entertainment in the private rooms. Whatever the reason, no one paid me any attention as I left the accommodation quarters and exited the tavern.

I stood on the doorstep, thinking. As much as I hated to steal the dead farmer's cart—and his donkeys—driving to my village would be much faster than getting there on foot.

I set my jaw. *I'll do it. I'll take the cart.* Guilt lodged in my chest like a stone. Another bad deed added to a precariously stacked pile. How long would it be before it all came tumbling down, crushing me to a bloody pulp?

Shaking off these macabre thoughts, I hurried down the steps, strode into the street, and joined the stream of people that flowed along it like a river. Not just people, I noted, looking closer, but ghosts, too, their disembodied forms passing right through the living without them even knowing. The ghost realm and the living realm existed alongside each other, and I had never realized.

A shiver snaked its way down my spine.

I shook my head to rid myself of the portentous feeling that had gripped me, and continued walking. As I rounded a corner, I stopped short, because I'd seen—

No. It can't be.

It was the hair, at first, that I'd noticed. Waist length, black, and as smooth as a lake's surface at night.

Then the ghost turned, revealing features that were as familiar to me as my own: Translucent skin that had always looked a little wraithlike. The delicately upturned nose. High cheekbones. Dark, glittering eyes.

My heart started pounding, and the back of my neck went cold. Panic flooded me like a storm. I clutched at my chest, frozen to the spot like a hunted animal.

Spotting me, my dead sister's lips curved up in a bloodless smile. She looked even more beautiful, and terrifying, in death than she had in life.

"Hello, Jia Yi" was all Dai Yu said.

Twenty

Three years ago

It was rare to hear raised voices from Pópo's room. Tonight, though, they were so loud that I could not ignore them.

Pressing my ear against the rough wood of the door, I strained to hear the conversation.

It was Dai Yu, my elder sister, chastising my grandmother. "You cannot keep protecting her. Not if you suffer for it yourself!"

My pulse skittered. Who was the "her" they were talking about? I pressed my ear against the wood even harder. Pópo's low voice buzzed through the closed door, but she spoke so quietly I could not make out the words.

My sister was louder. She let out a frustrated sigh. "Come on, now. She's fourteen. She's old enough to know."

My heart sank. Me. I was fourteen. I was the "her" they were talking about.

What was I old enough to know? I couldn't quite grasp the thread of their conversation, but something about it sent a thrill of fear coursing through me. Placing one hand against the doorframe, I clutched it, my knuckles turning bone white.

"I *know* you're sick, Pópo!" Dai Yu said, in response to something my grandmother said. "That's no reason to—"

Wait, what? I straightened. Everything inside me clenched. What did Dai Yu mean, Pópo was sick? Sure, she'd slowed down a bit in recent years, but she was as clearheaded as always, ruling the village as Priestess as firmly as she'd ever done.

Was this what my grandmother was trying to hide from me? The fact that she was ill?

More of Pópo's words, muffled again. I went back to listening at the door.

My grandmother had raised her voice, just enough that I could finally understand her. "Do not make me regret telling you," she said to my sister. "I only did so because when I'm gone, it will be you who will need to look after her."

Gone? What did she mean, "gone"? Bile churned in my gut; I swallowed.

"When you're gone? When you're gone?" my sister ranted. "I'll be High Priestess then, and I won't have time to—"

My grandmother cut her off. "Perhaps I shouldn't make you High Priestess," she snapped. "If you cannot handle the responsibility."

My mouth dropped open. Too late, I heard footsteps approaching before the door flew open.

Dai Yu stood on the other side, her face as dark as a storm cloud. Her anger morphed into a leer, though, when she saw me cowering before her.

"Fourteen years old, and still eavesdropping at people's doors? I bet you heard everything, you sneaky, irksome little—"

"I didn't!" I countered, defensive.

Dai Yu sneered. "That's too bad. Maybe if you knew, it'd finally solve all our problems."

"Knew what?" I pushed off the wall and scurried after my sister as she strode off down the hall. "Knew *what*?"

Dai Yu tossed her hair over one shoulder. For a long moment, she didn't say anything, just stared at me, face stamped with fury. But then she rolled her eyes. "Nothing." She turned and resumed stalking away.

"You are such a bitch!" I yelled after her.

"Oh, grow up, Jia."

"I don't want to grow up," I shouted even louder, after her retreating form, "if it means becoming as awful as you!"

She didn't break her stride or look back. Flicking her hand behind her, she simply used her magic to draw moisture from the air and sent a jet of water in my direction. Dai Yu could manipulate water in any form, whether vapor, liquid, or ice.

The spray hit me; I shrieked at the cold. My sister laughed as she pushed out the door. Lin, who'd been leaning against the wall, observing, wordlessly handed me a handkerchief to mop up my now-drenched face.

"She is *insufferable*." I scrubbed angrily at my forehead. "Honestly, she'd make the worst High Priestess."

"You're not wrong there," Lin murmured. "Hui Fen would be so much better."

"They would be." I tossed the handkerchief back to Lin, who caught it neatly and shoved it back into his sleeve. "But we both know that will never happen."

It was true: Hui Fen *would* make a better leader. It was not just their temperament—they were more patient and level-headed than either Dai Yu or me—it was also their memory magic.

Pópo's power was the ability to steal magic from others, something that gave her unrivaled influence and authority over everyone in our village. With just one touch of her palm, my grandmother could completely strip someone of their gift, seizing it for herself. It was the way she governed our community, the way she meted out judgment. If someone was found guilty of breaking village law, then her punishment was to take their power. Usually she'd just do this temporarily, giving the power back when the sentence had been carried out. But occasionally—if the person's transgression was severe—it would be permanent. The offender would be stripped of magic and banished into the wider world as an Empty.

Her power was the one thing I, as a child, never had to fear, since I didn't possess magic. Our trip to the shaman two years ago had yielded no answers. Besides, according to my grandmother, the shaman was a fraud.

The rest of the villagers, though . . . they feared Pópo's ability. This allowed her to rule with a fair-but-firm fist. She could have kept all the magic for herself, hoarding it, becoming invincible, almighty, goddess-like. But she didn't. She never wanted that sort of power. She just wanted fairness. My whole life, I'd never seen Pópo act with anything less than utmost integrity, not even once.

And while Hui Fen's magic was perhaps not as powerful, their ability to show people their own memories, as well as to delve into the memories of others, would give them influence over the village people in a way no one else had. Not that they'd ever use it forcefully, or without need. But the threat would be enough.

Technically, Hui Fen *could* become the High Priester. Although leadership usually passed down female bloodlines—since the predominance of yin energies was considered ideal to lead effectively—Hui possessed perfectly balanced feminine yin and masculine yang energies, making them a fine choice for High Priester. Certainly there had been High Priesters before.

According to the laws of succession, though, Hui Fen could never be the village's leader. Not unless Dai Yu died and left Hui Fen the oldest sibling.

But Dai Yu was young, and healthy, and unlikely to die.

What a shame, a small, nasty voice said, deep within my head.

Don't think such things, I admonished myself. Lin caught my eye and I glanced away, guilty, as though he could read my mind. Perhaps he could—he knew me so well that he could usually decipher my thoughts from my expressions. I'd never been good at keeping my emotions hidden.

A spate of harsh hacking, coming from within Pópo's room, caught my attention. Lin and I shot each other a glance before simultaneously rushing to her door.

Dai Yu had left it swung open. Inside her room, Pópo was standing, holding on to the back of a chair to support herself. She was having a coughing fit, her whole body convulsing, her shoulders shaking with the effort. She'd clamped a handkerchief over her mouth.

My heart dropped. I'd seen her cough like this a few times before, but she'd always dismissed it as a "tickle in my throat." She lowered the cloth, and I gasped. It was stained a deep, dark red.

She raised her head at the noise; her eyes met mine. And the expression that I saw in them struck more fear into me than the bloodstained white silk:

Pópo was *scared.*

I'd never seen her scared.

It was my fault. All my fault. First my mother. Then my father. And now . . . my grandmother. She was sick. Was she . . . dying?

The shaman was right. There was something wrong with me. Death *did* cling to me like a mantle.

I see nothing but death in this girl's future, the shaman had said.

I'd thought she'd meant my death in that moment. But, no.

She'd meant the deaths of those around me.

My entire body started shaking. I backed away as Pópo raised a hand, reaching for me.

"Jia Yi," she said. "Wait—"

She was cut off, because from behind me—from outside, slicing through the still, dark night—came a piercing, unearthly scream.

Twenty-One

Present day

My first instinct upon seeing my sister's ghost was to run. And run I did, battering through the crowds. My sister followed.

I knew Dai Yu well enough—and had seen her expression—to know she wasn't pursuing me because she wanted a happy reunion. When I'd first glimpsed her, there had been a definite glint of bitterness in the umber depths of her eyes. I suppose it wasn't entirely unjustified. After all, it was my fault she'd died, just over three years ago.

Immediately after the argument that I'd overheard between her and Pópo, she'd stormed out of the hut, into the surrounding forest, where she'd been bitten by a snake. We'd heard her scream. Rushed to her. Found her hunched over in the dirt, trembling, two puncture marks stark on the pale skin of her ankle. She'd slapped Lin's hand away when he tried to dress the wound.

Over the course of the following three days, she had steadily deteriorated, drifting in and out of consciousness. The village healers had tried everything to counter the venom. Even Lin, with his extensive knowledge of poisons, had attempted to create an antidote. But nothing worked.

On the third day, Dai Yu had gone quiet. By then, her face was sunken, her skin pale and waxy, her lips so bloodless they appeared almost white. She closed her eyes, sighed once, and then never opened them again.

Even then, I'd known it was my fault. After all, it had been me that they'd argued about. And it further cemented my belief that the shaman was right. I was a girl cursed by death.

Was that why Dai Yu was pursuing me now? Maybe she was angry: Legends told that ghosts who had been wronged became yuànguǐ, vengeful ghosts with grievances who lingered, waiting to exact revenge.

Fear tore through me like fire, and I ducked around a corner, hoping it would throw her off. It didn't. She continued to pursue, chasing me through another street, and then another.

Desperately, I wondered how I would ever lose her. Unlike me, ghosts were not impeded by walls, buildings, or living people. Which made her faster than me, a mere mortal.

Still, I wasn't about to give up, so I kept running, barreling through the milling crowds, turning down side streets and laneways, upsetting the carts of street vendors in the process. Their shouts followed me down the streets.

I kept running, until suddenly, I was forced to stop. I'd made a wrong turn and had wound up at a dead end.

It was an alley, clearly used for dumping trash. It was strewn with discarded rubbish, stagnant puddles, and tiny bones. Rats—some alive, some dead—skittered across the ground.

My entire body flushed cold; my limbs grew heavy and numb. I was cornered.

I spun. My sister stalked toward me, clutching a Bone Smith spear in her hand. If I weren't so scared, I might have laughed. In life, my sister would have never wielded a weapon. Her water magic was enough for her, she'd always claimed. And here she was, dead, looking like some sort of immortal warrior princess.

"What do you want?" I said, trying to sound braver than I felt.

She smirked. "Just to talk."

She advanced on me, and I cringed, pressing back against the wall, the stone rough through my thin cotton dress. For the first time since I'd started seeing ghosts, I felt truly, genuinely afraid. I drew my Bone Smith knife and brandished it. "Don't come closer!"

Still several paces away, she stopped. "Oh, don't worry," she said, in a falsely casual, singsong voice. "I won't."

I froze, trying to decipher what she meant by this. And I was so shocked when she raised her palm—siphoning all the water from the ground, dragging humidity from the air, and then shooting it at me—that I didn't even have time to scream.

The sheet of water hit my chest, raising me clear off the ground and pinning me hard against the wall. Foul, putrid liquid filled my mouth until I gurgled. My lungs began to burn; I couldn't breathe. She was killing me. My dead sister was killing me. Just like I'd killed her, three years prior. And my blade couldn't help me. There was, quite literally, nothing I could do in the face of Dai Yu's magic.

I went limp. At least if I died, I'd be able to resurrect again. And she didn't know that . . . which meant I still had the slightest advantage, however marginal, over her. Still, my heart crescendoed to a deafening roar.

It was a frightening thing, to welcome death.

Everything inside me went numb, fingers of ice scraping my insides, and all of a sudden I felt oddly insubstantial. As if there was barely anything holding me together.

I scrunched my eyes shut, bracing myself for my death. For Dai Yu's water, which had pinned me against the building, to finally drown me.

And then death came—but not how I'd expected it to.

Something jolted inside me, a seismic shift. My body congealed, feeling like a cold lump of flesh. I felt my soul detaching from my physical body, shifting into a spectral form . . .

Then, inexplicably, I found myself on the other side of the wall.

It took me several seconds to understand what had happened. I was imbued with that same hazy, disorienting sensation that I recalled from the first two times I'd died. The world around me was slightly murky, imprecise at the edges, and I blinked my eyes, trying to focus them.

I was . . . dead. I'd slipped into the death realm, yes, but too soon—well before Dai Yu's water magic had had time to kill me.

Understanding snapped into place. Somehow, my power was not just coming back to life. Somehow I was also able to move, at will . . . between the land of the living and the realm of death.

Trembling, I backed away from the wall, shivering; it felt like my movements were lagging several sluggish moments behind my mind. As though I was wading underwater, or in a fugue-like state. I mentally scanned my body: My chest was hollow, resonant, with no steady drum of my heart and no expanding breaths. *How on earth did I just do that?*

I had no time to think about it. My priority was to get out of here, and fast. Hopefully, Dai Yu would believe she had killed me—my physical body had presumably collapsed on the other side of the wall—but if she realized my ghost had somehow escaped through the bricks she might materialize in front of me to finish me off.

Gripping my Bone Smith blade, which fortunately was still in my hand, I began to stumble out of the adjacent alley, aiming for the entrance, where the shadows met the light.

But—too late. Someone grabbed me from behind. And my sister said, low and deadly, her hand closing around my upper arm, "Well, well, would you look at this? Now I can touch you."

I tried to jerk away, tried to claw at her, tried hard to escape . . . but I failed.

My sister's face was a grim, expressionless mask. Without another word, she hit me on the head with the butt of her spear.

And everything—the whole world—went black.

When I came to, I was bumping along some sort of packed-earth tunnel. There was a metallic chill to the air and everything glowed a faint, sickly blue.

It took me several seconds to gain my bearings. Someone had slung me over their shoulder. I could see their feet trudging along the ground; the sparse light was from several Bone Smith weapons.

I began to struggle, but my captor hit me across the backs of my legs. I couldn't see what with—possibly the flat of their sword—but either way, it didn't matter, for it stung. I yelped, and several people guffawed. Amid the laughter I heard the unmistakable voice of my own sister. The pain of betrayal jolted through me, though in truth, I should not have been surprised.

Once we'd descended for what felt like hours, the ground leveled out. I was flung onto the floor, landing in a messy heap. With a small groan, I rolled over, coughed twice, then dragged my arm across my mouth.

We were in a cell, carved out of stone. The dirt floor was damp. The dank air smelled of mold. Bones—whether human or animal, I could not tell—littered the ground. I tore my gaze away, trying to ignore their presence.

A dungeon, then.

Two ghost guards, both holding Bone Smith swords, were already stationed at the entrance, positioned to stop me escaping.

Rubbing my eyes, I blinked and squinted into the darkness. Apart from the metal bars at the front, everything composed of stone and earth. All natural structures: nothing human-made that I could pass through. This prison was perfectly designed to hold a ghost.

Someone like me, I thought. *I* was a ghost. A sudden urge to resurrect hit me: I could escape and wake up in my physical body, back in the lane where Dai Yu had attacked me.

But as I struggled to adjust my hazy vision, and before I could do anything, my sister strolled into view.

I scuttled backward, flattening myself against the rear wall. Desperately, I groped at my hip, but my Bone Smith weapon was gone. *Mā de!* My original dagger, in my boot, would be no use to me in my ghostly state.

"Are you looking for this?" Dai Yu held up the Bone Smith blade, still in its glowing blue sheath. Clearly, she'd stripped it from me during the short time I'd been unconscious.

"Give that back!" I hissed, lunging at her and swiping for it.

But Dai Yu just angled the point of her spear at my heart, stopping me from getting closer. I pulled up short, my teeth bared.

She just gave a tinkling laugh. "Don't worry, Jia Yi. You won't be needing it in a hurry. In fact, how about we give it to Wen Bo? He'll keep it safe."

She tossed the blade to one of the guards, who caught in neatly in one hand. I gaped, because the movement had turned the ghost—presumably Wen Bo—to fully face me, revealing a huge black gash that bisected his middle, and a bruised and swollen face. Now that I was paying attention, the other guard was even more terrifying: Their right arm ended in a scraggly mess, torn flesh dangling from a ghostly limb.

My sister, on the other hand, still in the nightgown in which she'd perished, appeared perfectly normal, except for the twin puncture marks on her inner ankle.

"Why are you doing this?" I croaked. Even though my sister's attack hadn't killed me, I'd been choked by enough water to make my voice raspy.

My sister gave an irritated huff. "I already told you. To talk—"

I exploded. "Talk? You tried to *kill* me!"

Dai Yu, appearing to contemplate this statement, cocked her head to one side. "Yes, I suppose you could say I did." A slow smile bloomed on her face. "But you can see now, Jia Yi:

It is not so bad. Death is not the end of life. Nor is it the end of death, as you will no doubt soon come to realize."

What is dead can die again. So Dai Yu had meant to kill me. *Had* meant to bring me into the ghost realm. And notably, she thought that she had.

But she hadn't. What she still didn't know was that I could move into the death realm voluntarily . . . and I could also move out of it.

Once again, I thought of resurrecting and escaping immediately. I had to get back to the village and find the other half of the shaman's predictions.

However, some gut instinct told me not to risk resurrecting in front of my sister, or her guards. The fewer people who knew my secret the better. I'd wait until I was alone, after I'd gotten back my Bone Smith knife . . . the one I'd bought with Essien Lancaster's stolen secret.

Plus, I needed to know why she'd kidnapped me.

By now, Dai Yu had moved closer, the tip of her spear poking my chest. I froze, our eyes locking. She leaned forward and whispered, so softly only I could hear, "How is Pópo?"

"Dead," I blurted, before I could stop myself, then cursed at myself for being so foolish. I still didn't know why Dai Yu had attacked me, or what she wanted to talk about. And I didn't yet know whether her knowing of our grandmother's deaths was a good or bad thing.

My sister's expression shuttered, and she straightened, releasing the pressure from the spear. Perhaps I had imagined it, but I'd almost fancied a fleeting look of grief passing over her features. When I next looked, though, it had gone.

I drew myself up to my full height, my fists balling at my sides. "You said you wanted to talk. So talk."

"It's not me who wants to talk to you." Dai Yu lowered her spear and backed away several paces.

My fists squeezed even tighter. "Then who?"

My sister's gaze slid to the dungeon entrance, accessed by the sloping tunnel.

"Him," she said.

It was at that moment that the guards both stepped aside, bowing and murmuring platitudes. My sister, too, immediately sank into a bow.

"General Hong," she said, respectfully to the ground.

General Hong? I knew that name. Was it . . . ?

It couldn't be.

The tall ghost who elbowed past them ignored the greetings, instead fixing his gaze on me. He was in shadow, only half his face visible. It was a rugged face with heavy-set eyebrows, and a long, oiled beard. He was clad in full military regalia: scaled iron armor complete with a helmet, and a Bone Smith longsword strapped to his side.

With a lingering look, he eyed me speculatively, then turned to address Dai Yu.

I stifled my gasp. The left side of his face was ruined. A slash wound had flayed open his lips, exposing too many teeth. Such a horrific sight . . . and yet I found myself staring, unable to look away.

"This is the sister whom you speak of, Liu Dai Yu?" he said, his sonorous voice echoing ominously in the small space. I froze. Had my sister led me into this trap . . . for *him*?

My sister bowed again. "It is, Your Excellency."

His narrowed eyes slid back to me, the saggy pouches beneath them wobbling. He seemed oddly absorbed by my appearance.

I pressed my back harder against the wall as he prowled closer, his gaze boring into mine. But it was pointless—there was nowhere to go. No way to escape. Not unless I slipped further into the death realm or resurrected right now.

Was it worth the risk? Perhaps it was. Something about this ghost, and the way he was looking at me, was deeply disturbing. It was almost like he was at a market, visually weighing a piece of meat.

Before I had a chance to react, though, he'd already pulled out his Bone Smith sword and raised it to my neck.

"The littlest Liu," he said, his mangled lips curving upward. "Finally, we meet."

Twenty-Two

THE FIRST LEVEL

Present day

"Why have you brought me here?" My voice sounded croaky and not at all like my own.

The general chuckled, a chilling sound that reverberated right down to my very bones. The tip of his sword bit into my neck, and I resisted the urge to whimper.

He didn't answer right away. Instead, he remained silent, regarding me, his head tilted back slightly. Finally he said, ponderously, "What do you know of the Shēngsǐ Sword, Liu Jia Yi?"

The sword. The Shēngsǐ Sword—also known as the Sword of Rechenblod. The sword that could conquer life, or death—which Essien had asked me to find.

Essien. Pópo. And now this general. Everyone, it seemed, was searching for the infamous sword. Could it be a coincidence?

Somehow, I doubted it.

I clenched my jaw, refusing to answer. I didn't want to play his games. But then I realized: Perhaps this, here, was a chance to learn more about this wretched weapon. The one that the shaman had spoken of, the night she predicted my future.

I pushed my hair out of my eyes and raised my chin. "Nothing. I know nothing."

General Hong raised one eyebrow at me. "I am surprised," he said. "I would have thought your grandmother would have told you. She is, after all, looking for it, is she not?"

Alarm shot through me. Dai Yu had asked after our grandmother. Had she known about Pópo's mission and told the general about it? I recalled my grandmother's words to me, before she'd died for the second time, in the tavern—she warned me that others were looking for the sword.

And, like an idiot, I'd admitted to my sister that Pópo was in the afterlife.

I snarled. "You leave my grandmother out of this—"

"I have no wish to harm your grandmother." The general gave a smile. It seemed he was trying to appear kindly, but it was terrifying. Firstly, because half his face was missing. And secondly, because he still held me at swordpoint. "But she has no idea how dangerous the Shēngsǐ Sword is."

"And you do?"

"Indeed," he murmured. "It is a most powerful weapon. I should know, since it is mine."

A pause. I narrowed my eyes. "How can it be yours when it belongs to the Lancasters?"

"Is that the story they've told you, little Liu?" The general chuckled and shook his head. "What they fail to tell you is that they lost it when I defeated their army. That sword is rightfully mine."

My gut contracted. It *was* him. This here was General Hong

Hao Mu, who had used my people to defeat the Yskians three centuries ago. With a reputation for ruthlessness, violence, and cruelty, he'd killed the king of Yske, Brennan Lancaster, who according to rumors was a bit of a sadistic tyrant himself.

General Hong's victory had won Jinghu Dao the war. But the general was assassinated shortly thereafter . . .

And what was it that the Bone Smith had said about the sword? *When the Yskian army was overthrown, it was stolen by a usurper. However, the usurper was soon murdered. It was henceforth brought into the afterlife, and subsequently lost.*

"You!" I managed to gasp out. "*You're* the usurper!"

"Usurper." General Hong pursed the uninjured half of his lips. "Such a weak, Yskian name for it. Coined by those too proud to accept their defeat. Personally, I prefer the term *conqueror.*"

Unable to stop the accusatory tone from creeping into my voice, I said, "And you mean to conquer them again with it? This so-called Shēngsǐ Sword?"

"You must understand, little Liu. I was the one who defeated the Yskians. It was *my* actions that brought an end to the war. Yet, I was murdered before I could claim the throne that rightfully belongs to me." He gave me another smile that showed entirely too many teeth. "Fengzhi Yuan is mine. The Shēngsǐ Sword belongs with *me.*"

I swallowed. *He means to take the throne.* General Hong could use the sword to resurrect, and then retake our province. What then, after that? Would he aim for a bigger target? Would the entire empire of Jinghu Dao be at risk?

Regardless of the fact that it wasn't entirely his victory, but that of my ancestors, too . . . the idea of this vengeful ghost invading the mortal realm was terrifying.

But I also, I realized suddenly, felt something else: *hope.*

Hope that if Pópo or I found the sword first, as the shaman had indeed prophesied, then maybe—just maybe—I'd be able to keep it away from General Hong. Perhaps I could even use it to resurrect Pópo, like I wanted, before finding some way to destroy it.

All I had to do was glean information from the general about the sword's whereabouts. Beyond what the Bone Smith had suggested: that it was buried in the deepest layer of the afterlife, I had no way of knowing where, geographically, it lay.

If the general had more information, then I'd dive straight into the deeper levels; if he did not, then I'd return to my village to collect the second half of the shaman's prediction, as my grandmother had instructed.

I licked my dry lips. "All right. So you took the sword and lost it, and now what? You need it back?"

"The Shēngsǐ Sword is said to have very particular powers," General Hong said. "It is the ultimate weapon. It can conquer everything, even death. Naturally, that aligns perfectly with my objectives."

I said nothing.

He tilted his head to one side, eyeing me sharply. "And that is where you come in, Liu Jia Yi. The truth is, I have been searching for the sword for quite some time. It was only through this loyal servant here"—with his chin, he gestured at Dai Yu—"that I discovered I am not the one foretold to find it. You are. According to your sister, a shaman saw a vision of you with the sword."

"*A* sword," I said, everything inside me clenching tight. "A sword. Not necessarily the sword you are looking for."

"If it wasn't the Shēngsǐ Sword, Little Liu, do you think your grandmother would be so desperately trying to find it? Do you think she would have gone to such great lengths to protect you, if she wasn't worried I would find you first?" He chuckled and shook his head. "No. The very fact that she tried to keep your existence hidden from me all this time is a testament to how fervently she believes the prophecy: that you will be the one to find the sword."

Something deep in my chest twisted. I understood now. This must have been what Pópo and Dai Yu were quarrelling about, right before my sister died. Pópo wanted to protect me from my fate.

Dai Yu, on the other hand, wanted me to fulfill it.

The general turned to face me squarely, so I could see the two sides of his face equally. The uninjured half, illuminated by his Bone Smith sword, and the flayed half, swathed in shadows.

Dark and light.

"I need you to fetch the sword, Little Liu. I can even give you some soldiers to accompany you on your quest."

I scoffed. "And where am I supposed to start?"

The general gave me an empty, bone-chilling smile. "If I knew where it was, then I would not be asking you to find it, would I?"

My chest tightened painfully, my insides clenching ice-cold. "What if I refuse?"

The general twisted his sword, still lying against my throat, just slightly, and I winced. He'd nicked my neck. A shallow cut. A warning. Just enough for me to feel a thin stream of ghost blood trickling down my skin.

I bit my tongue and swallowed my scream, refusing to react, refusing to play his games.

"I forgot to say, Littlest Liu . . ." he said, his voice deceptively calm. "This is *not* a request. If you refuse, I can assure you: We will find other ways to . . . *convince* you."

I couldn't help it; I let out a whimper.

"Do not worry," he said, feigning gentleness, though his eyes were still as hard as stone. "We have time; I am a patient man. After all, here in the death realm, time is meaningless." He paused for effect, the weight of his silence crushing me.

I gritted my teeth, ignoring the sting of the new wound on my throat. My ghost blood continued to dribble in cold tracks down my neck.

"Here, in the death realm," he continued, fleshy lips stretching into a grin, "we have all of eternity to find it."

Twenty-Three

THE FIRST LEVEL
Present day

As soon as General Hong left, I crumpled against the wall.

The general obviously believed the shaman that *I* was the key to finding the Shēngsǐ Sword. To helping him ascend back to power. He was clearly expecting me to aid his cause, under threat of torture. And if I refused, he would use force to *make* me compliant.

And he wouldn't stop. Here, in the afterlife, there was no end to my torture if I did not comply.

A shudder snaked its way through me.

I had one advantage, though. There was one thing General Hong didn't know: that unlike other ghosts, for me, delving into death was *not* just a one-way journey. And whatever happened—whether he tried to keep me captive or kill me—I could come back from it.

With a sudden sickening realization, I noticed I wasn't alone; the broken ghost bodies of other prisoners were also heaped in one corner of the cell. The sight made me shiver, and not from the cold: How many ghosts, exactly, had General Hong slaughtered in this very dungeon?

Was I being haunted, right now, by second-level spirits I couldn't see?

I shook my head. At least, unlike these poor trapped souls, I had a chance of getting out.

But first I needed my dagger back.

The guard with the torn-off arm had left the dungeon alongside Dai Yu and the general, leaving only the ghost with the gashed stomach, Wen Bo, to guard me. Now that we were alone, I could get a better look at him. He was tall and lean but appeared to have died at a young age, for his bruised face had evidence of teenage acne and was slightly rounded, as though retaining a remnant of childish cheeks. His glossy black hair was slicked back, like a soldier's would be.

He was also taking the general's command very seriously. I stared at him, and he barely blinked as he stared back.

"What are you looking at, girl?" he asked suddenly. He was acting tough, but the slight crack in his voice gave him away. Was he . . . afraid of me? All the talk about the shaman's prophecies, and swords, and burrowing deeper into death—perhaps he considered me dangerous. Or perhaps the deeper layers of the death realm scared him, a ghost, as much as death itself seemed to frighten the living.

"Nothing," I replied. Before I turned away, I took note of where he'd sheathed my dagger, as well as his own Bone Smith sword that was strapped to his right hip. *He must be left-handed*, my mind whispered, though what I could do with that information I did not know.

In the darkness, I groped my way to the back corner of the cell, then sank onto the ground with a sigh. So much had happened, and I was feeling weary. I sat, huddled among the bones, and drew my knees up to my chest, winding my arms around them.

Lowering my head, I rested my forehead on my knees and shut my eyes.

If I had been smarter, I would've made Lin teach me how to disappear before he'd had a chance to betray me—and Pópo. Unfortunately, it was too late for that. Now, the only thing I wanted Lin to do was rue the day he ever met me.

But there was, possibly, one other way I could disappear.

As Lin had explained immediately before we'd entered the city, first-level ghosts needed to come close to death again in order to see spirits in the second level—the same way I could only see ghosts after I'd been killed in the living world.

This meant that there was a chance I could escape into the second level unseen. But it would rely on two things being true: One, that my ability to move between layers of the death realm also extended to the deeper levels.

And two, that Wen Bo couldn't see second-level ghosts.

Wen Bo only had the one visible wound on him: the slit-open abdomen that had presumably cost him his life. I couldn't see any other injuries, though I couldn't rule out that he'd suffered another, nonvisible reason to have a second close brush with death.

Regardless, there was only one way I could envision getting myself out of here, intact, with my Bone Smith dagger.

Wen Bo was clearly going to keep watching me until General

Hong returned. I'd need to pretend I was resting for long enough that he became accustomed to me being still. Then, if I had the ability to, I'd slip into the second layer of the death realm, becoming a ghost of a ghost, and rise out of my body as a jiàn.

This would allow me to sneak up behind him, unseen, and steal back my Bone Smith dagger—*and* his sword . . . provided I remained invisible to him. I'd then resurrect myself, taking the weapons with me, and go back to my village to collect the second half of the shaman's prediction.

But it was risky. If he, as a ghost, *had* come close enough to death, then he'd be able to see me as a jiàn, which would derail my entire plot. Still, I was desperate. This was the only idea I had.

When I opened my eyes again, the young guard was still watching me.

My mind raced, sifting through various possibilities.

"How did you die?" I asked suddenly, breaking the profound quiet.

He startled a little, seemingly confused by my questioning, but then his mouth curved into a sneer. "Isn't it obvious?" He gestured at his stomach.

I grimaced. "Did it hurt?"

His lips pressed together in a line, his jaw muscles tightening. "Of course it hurt. Since it was a stomach wound, it took days for me to die."

A pang of pity went through me, even though he was an enemy. "That's awful. I'm sorry." I knew I wasn't supposed to feel sympathy for him, but I couldn't help it. I did.

He didn't answer. Just lapsed into silence, squinting at me

suspiciously. After several uncomfortable minutes, he suddenly spoke. "Why do you care?"

I'd been resting my forehead against my knees again, but at this, I raised my head. "I'm just . . . just scared of what General Hong might do to me." It wasn't entirely false. *The best lies are those that are formed in half-truths.*

I swallowed painfully, and elaborated. "My first death was drowning . . . and that was bad enough." Another lie.

"You think drowning's bad?" The guard gave a bitter laugh. "Believe me, that is *nothing* compared to what the general is capable of."

I bit my lip to stop it trembling. This was supposed to be a way of eking out information from the guard, but truth be told—General Hong *did* terrify me. "What might he do?"

Wen Bo seemed to hesitate for several seconds. But then, after casting a quick glance around us, he drew closer, his hand wrapping around the hilt of the sword. "You know the other guard that was with me?"

I nodded, feeling faint at the memory of the ghost's mutilated arm.

Wen Bo leveled a gaze at me. "He died from illness, not injury. He only lost his arm here, in the afterlife, because General Hong hacked it off."

I shuddered. "Why?"

Wen Bo looked at me like I was stupid. "For disobeying. Of course." He leaned closer, his voice lowering even further. "Listen, I'm not supposed to say this, but I would advise you do as the general says. He's a violent man. Cutting off a ghost's arm isn't even the worst I've seen him do. I had a friend who . . . who lied to him once. The general carved out his tongue. Here, in this very cell." It seemed impossible, since his face was bloodless, but I could almost imagine that Wen Bo's face grew paler. "Agree to it, Liu Jia Yi, and he might leave you be, like he does me. If you do not, then . . ."

He trailed off, but we both knew what he meant.

I hugged my knees tighter. "I . . . understand."

The guard took a step back, reassuming his straight posture. Once again, we both fell silent. The difference was, now I could not rest. Images of General Hong torturing his subordinates—severing arms, cutting out tongues—were burned too vividly in my mind.

After another long, protracted pause, Wen Bo noticed me staring, eyes open, at the opposite wall.

"I would advise you get some rest, girl," he said, not unkindly this time. "You'll need it for your journey. When the general comes back he will demand you start searching for the sword immediately."

"All right." I feigned acquiescence, lowering my forehead to my knees again. When the stifling silence had once again settled upon us like a blanket, I closed my eyes. Summoning all my concentration, I channeled my focus.

How had I done it before? Slipped voluntarily from the living realm into death? Dai Yu had been attempting to drown me at the time, so it was almost a reflex action—much like it had been the first few times I'd resurrected. Would it be so different doing it when not faced with extreme danger?

After I'd tried for several minutes, I realized the answer was yes. It was completely different. It seemed that when not faced with a threat, moving between the layers of the death realm took a degree of mental fortitude that I did not readily possess.

I wanted to laugh hysterically and cry all at the same time. If only I'd applied myself more during my childhood meditation classes, perhaps I would find this process easier. But I'd never bothered to concentrate, never learned how to focus—I always thought I didn't need to control my mind for magic, since I'd always believed I was magicless. As it was, my mental faculties were not cut out for this.

Still, I had to try.

And I did. For hours, I tried. My body shook with the effort, and had I been alive, I was sure I'd have been drenched in sweat.

Each time I'd get close, feeling the pull that promised to drag me deeper, the threads would snap, and I'd almost retch at the painful sting of the recoil.

By the end, I was curled up in a fetal position, my body and mind breaking. I felt hopeless. Entirely exhausted and pathetic. My thoughts drifted; my spirit sank so low it was as if I *had* actually died again.

It was only then that it happened. That I felt my power thrum to life.

Encouraged, I leaned into my emotions. Of insignificance, of being inconsequential, of being more empty space than substance. I drew my mind into the cavernous places of my body: the hollowness of my stomach; the dryness of my mouth; the still, silent chambers within my deadened heart. And after several minutes of intense concentration, I felt it.

The rupture. A splitting of my soul from this level of the death realm, as it slipped into the next.

And when I sat up, my soul detached from my ghost body, rising out of it as a jiàn.

Twenty-Four

THE SECOND LEVEL

Present day

I'd taken so long to execute my plan that by now, Wen Bo had sat down, perching on a large rock that faced the cell. He'd drawn his Bone Smith sword and laid it across his lap, his left fingers loosely curled around the hilt. My dagger was at his left hip, tucked into his belt. He was still watching my first-level body, which was slumped against the wall. It was an oddly disembodying feeling, looking at myself in such a state; I tore my gaze away.

A disturbance danced in my peripheral vision. I turned my head, peering into the corner. What appeared to be second-level ghosts prowled the cell, their faces gaunt, their eyes displaying a harrowing sort of resignation. My empty gut twisted in knots—these must be the dead ghosts whose corpses had been tossed into the corner. Now that I was in the second level, I could see them.

Every now and then one of them would notice me. They'd turn their black, void-like eyes in my direction and stare at me in abject silence.

Why hadn't they left the cell?

The outlines of their ghostly forms seemed to waver slightly. It seemed as though the further I descended into the afterlife, the murkier everything grew, and the less defined we all became.

Clenching my teeth together, I tried to quell my fear and focused on the next step of my plan, which was stealing the weapons from Wen Bo.

It was my dagger I planned to go for first, as I could draw that out without his notice. Slowly, carefully, I crept up behind him, and with the very tips of my fingers, I tugged it—sheath and all—out of his belt. Fortunately, he did not stir, and a wash of relief flowed through me as I strapped it carefully to my own waist.

His own blade would be a bigger problem. I'd realized, considering the effort it took to slip into the second level, that resurrecting voluntarily might not be so easy, either. I really needed to disarm him so that he could not attack me and I had time to make an escape.

I loitered in the shadows, chewing my lip. I could envision stealing his sword only one way:

Quickly.

Before I could talk myself out of it, I darted around his front, and—employing the element of surprise—yanked the weapon from his grip.

He leaped to his feet. "Who is it? Who's there?" His head swiveled from side to side, and he quaked all over, his fear palpable.

I backed away, clutching the weapons close, then closed my eyes to resurrect.

I'd never tried to resurrect from a deeper layer of the death realm to a shallower one, from a jiàn to a regular ghost. Both times I'd previously resurrected were from the first layer to the living realm, not the second layer to the first.

Reaching into the depths of my mind, I tried to locate the invisible threads that tied me to my first-layer body, which was still crumpled at the back of the cell.

Focus on the feeling, my mind chanted, like a mantra. *The feeling. The feeling.*

Squeezing my eyes shut even harder, I thought back to the time when Brisson had run me through with his longsword. To when I'd resurrected after Lin had accidentally killed me, back in the Lancaster guestroom. Summoning every ounce of will I possessed, I scrunched my face up, trying to lean into those memories; trying to bring calm and blankness to my fear-addled mind.

It was harder this time, bringing myself back from a deeper layer of death. Each time I descended, would it be more difficult—and take more concentration—to resurrect?

It was only when Wen Bo finally gathered his wits enough to shout for backup that I finally felt it. The shock of his roar and the fear of more ghost guards coming must have provoked it. Finally, I felt that hooking sensation in my gut, yanking me to the higher levels. With a gasp of pain, and then a lurch, I woke up in my first-level body.

Somehow, thankfully, I was still holding the Bone Smith blades. They seemed to have traveled with me. I didn't know how, but I was not about to question it.

I scrambled to my feet.

"You!" Wen Bo spat, now that he could finally see me. "What in the ten hells are you doing?"

I backed away. "I'm leaving."

"No you're not," he snarled, and tried to launch at me through the bars. I slashed at him with his own sword; he managed to duck away just in time.

"Don't come any nearer," I warned, brandishing both weapons.

He pulled up short, his palms held up placatingly. For several slow seconds, we just stared at one another. I bared my teeth.

Finally, his shoulders slumped. "I don't know how you did this, Liu Jia Yi, but think about it. Even if you escape, do you think the general will let you go so easily?"

"I'll be long gone before he returns." My words sounded more courageous than I felt.

Wen Bo's mouth twisted into something that barely resembled a smile. "Do you think he won't hunt you to the edge of the world to punish you for escaping?"

My hands, which each held a weapon, trembled. "No," I said, my voice wavering. "But you don't understand. I need to try."

"Please—"

"What?" I snapped.

"I will suffer for this. He will blame me." Wen Bo's face crumpled. "You know this."

The guilt weighed on me, another stone upon the pile. After what Wen Bo had told me, how could I not feel terrible about what I was about to do? About leaving this guard to his fate?

I almost lowered my weapons, but at the last minute, I stopped.

If I stayed, and helped the general reclaim the sword, then

things would only get worse. General Hong in possession of a sword that could not be conquered? A sword that would give him mastery over life and death? If he ascended back to the land of the living, so many more people would be in danger. Not just one single ghostly guard.

No, I wouldn't subject the living realm to that fate.

I *couldn't.*

"I'm sorry," I whispered. Letting my eyes slide shut, I mentally folded inward.

This time, the sensation came quickly, of something hooking into my soul, deep within my core, my belly.

I shook with strain, forcing my mind to focus. Trying to claw myself back to my body. I'd done it before, so I knew I could do it again. I just needed to try.

And, with the fear of General Hong fresh within my mind, I was able to recall that strange, burning feeling—despite my lack of mental discipline.

The pain expanded. From my chest, initially, then exploding outward. My internal organs started whirring, like the wings of a hummingbird taking flight. My heartbeat, feeble at first, started to pick up speed, gathering momentum.

Then: A final heave. A scream. Roaring agony. And the ghost world rushed away as I was hauled painfully back into life.

I gave a great gasp as I woke, lying in the grubby alley, surrounded by a pool of filthy water. Hanging in the air was a distinct smell of decay. Goose bumps peppered my skin, and I shivered.

The memory of Wen Bo's face flashed in my mind, and I

grimaced, my newly resumed pulse stuttering. If anything happened to him, I would blame myself entirely. Remorse roiled in my gut, but—I could not allow it to pull me under. I had a job to do.

Wrinkling my nose, I tried to sit up. My eyes were dry and tacky, and my limbs all stiff from being fixed in one position for an extended period. How long had I been dead for, up on this level? How much time had passed here in the living world?

I reached for my Bone Smith dagger, relieved to find it still with me. It seemed as though, unlike regular weapons, the Bone Smith had forged their creations in such a way that they could move between the layers of the afterlife. Wen Bo's sword, too, was clutched in my left hand. Quickly, I sheathed it.

It took me quite some time to massage out all my muscles until my joints were limber enough to bend. Even then, they felt weak and shaky, and as I rose to my feet I almost tumbled over. I tested out a small step, my legs quivering. Raising a hand to my neck, I found the spot where General Hong had nicked me with the point of his sword. It seemed that injuries I sustained in the death realm would come back to haunt me while alive, too. Fortunately, the blood had already congealed.

When I took another few steps, though, I realized I had another—possibly worse—problem. A trickle of fluid ran out of my neck wound, and the rotten smell intensified, making me gag. I moved toward the mouth of the alley, so I could use the light to inspect, and what I saw was horrifying.

My skin was no longer smooth and pale. It was mottled. My abdomen was bloated; my organs jangled inside me like they weren't properly anchored. The skin on my palms was cracked and wrinkled, as though the top layer might just slide off. Fluid seeped from the fissures, almost clear but tinged with green.

I raised my hands to my face, clutching my cheeks in horror. I'd been in the underworld for long enough that my physical body had started *rotting.*

I'd intended to go to my own village straightaway and dig up the rest of the shaman's prediction, but now I knew:

There was somewhere else I needed to go. Urgently.

Twenty-Five

Present day

The colossal towers of Throft Hall were visible, even at night, jutting up into a mass of clouds. I could see the castle, yes, but how would I gain entry? Those of us from Fengzhi Yuan were generally not welcome in Yske, even though we were neighbors. And people from my community? Even less so. I couldn't just slip into the death realm and sneak past the guards as a ghost, since I somehow needed to get my decomposing body inside the Throft Hall walls.

As I rode in the donkey-drawn cart—I'd found the pair of animals where I'd left them, having eaten through a second sack of turnips—toward the Lancaster stronghold, sweat bloomed across the back of my neck and my heart thumped, pitifully weak.

By the time I reached the gates, I'd formulated a plan. Dismounting, I drew my knife and marched right up to the entrance, where a guard in the watchtower called, "Halt!" The guard was a man, framed by the stone window, dressed in full-body mail. In the archaic culture of Yske, only men were permitted to fight or don armor.

"I'm here to see Prince Essien," I called up to the guard.

He snorted. "Oh? And who are you?"

"Liu Jia Yi," I replied.

The guard guffawed. "I should've guessed. I can smell your lowborn stink from here."

I ignored the jibe and pressed on. "I'm from just across the border—"

"I know where you're from," the guard butted in, unrestrained contempt in his voice. "What does someone like you want with His Royal Highness?"

"I'm . . . a friend."

He scoffed. "A friend? Then why are you armed?"

I didn't get a chance to respond before the guard was shoved aside by a larger man, one of formidable stature.

Ah, I thought. *Just who I wanted to see.*

"What's this?" Andres Brisson peered down from the window. When he spotted me, his mouth pulled back in a snarl. "Filthy witch! You *dare* show your face here after the stunt you pulled?" He raised a crossbow. The hinges creaked as he cranked the lever and angled it at me.

Yes, he was irate. Me passing the Spyrre test had made him look foolish in front of the prince, his respected monarch.

I had to suppress a smile. Why had I been worried? Goading a man such as Andres Brisson into anger wasn't difficult.

In fact, this was far too easy.

Pushing my hair out of my eyes, I raised my head. I probably looked fearsome, with my blanched, blotchy skin and bloated abdomen—I probably looked like a corpse. I certainly felt like one.

"Go ahead," I said, evenly. "Kill me. I'll only come back again."

Brisson let forth a snarl.

I heard the thwack of the crossbow firing a split second before the bolt hit me.

By the time I awoke as a ghost, a different guard was already dragging my body through the gates. I stood, separating from my physical form, groping around in the darkness until my dim vision cleared. Spotting the guard hauling my body up ahead, I hurried to catch up, wincing as I watched my already-decomposing corpse being dragged across the cobblestones. I tried not to think about what condition it would be in by the time I repossessed it.

"Throw her in the dungeons," Brisson commanded, "and keep her under constant watch."

The guard puffed with the effort of lugging me through a doorway. "And what should I do if she . . . wakes, sir?" The quiver in his voice betrayed his fear.

"You kill her again." Brisson's words were a growl. "And again, and again—as many times as it takes. We'll see how long this witch takes to finally die for good."

"Aye, sir," the guard said as he started bumping me down the steps. What a relief I couldn't feel it.

I followed silently, in my ghostly form, until the guard—and my body—was at the bottom of the empty stairwell. Then,

I closed my eyes, trying to summon the feeling of reviving myself.

This time, though I still needed to concentrate, the process seemed to come easier. No longer did I have to focus on each individual sensation. Instead, I pictured it as though I were lying at the bottom of a lake, swimming toward the dappled light upon the surface.

Maybe I was getting better at it. Or perhaps it was easier to resurrect from the first level, compared with resurrecting from deeper down.

Still, it was excruciating. The pain hit me just as my eyes sprang open. I gulped in air, the sweet rush filling my lungs. My back was in agony, the skin half scraped off. More foul-smelling fluid seeped from all my wounds. Fortunately, the guard had removed the crossbow bolt, but now I had a whole lot of ooze to contend with.

The guard, stunned, barely had time to reach for his sword before I'd rammed my blue knife into his throat.

He let out a horrific gurgle before collapsing to the ground. I eased him down, my fetid hand clasped over his mouth in order to muffle his cry. My stomach churned and my heart raced; my entire body felt frigid and numb.

I'd killed him. *I'd killed him!* I'd stabbed Lin's ghost in the death realm, but I'd never killed a living human before. I had judged Lin for stabbing the farmer, and before that for murdering Larch. But here I was, doing the same: taking someone else's life to secure my own.

I had little choice, though. Right? I needed to get into the castle. If I didn't, my body would fall apart and I'd be unable to hear the rest of the prediction or find the sword. And if neither I nor my grandmother found it first, then General Hong might, which would put the living world in danger of being infiltrated by a deranged, resurrected Hong Hao Mu.

What was the life of one Yskian soldier compared with the rest of the world?

At least, that was what I told myself. I swallowed, realizing I was trying to assuage my guilt. The same way I'd rationalized abandoning Wen Bo to the wrath of his master. It wasn't helped by the soldier's ghost, who by now was staring at his body, cursing colorfully, his entire spectral form visibly shaking.

"I'm sorry," I whispered. "I'm so, so sorry." With tears stinging the backs of my eyelids, I did my best to ignore the ghost's ranting—knowing he couldn't touch me—and hurriedly undressed the body.

Fortunately, the man only wore a light leather tunic and a close-fitting leather helmet, instead of full chain mail. My hands shook as I pulled the tunic on, over my hànfú, and jammed the helmet on my head. Next, I pulled on his well-worn breeches, cringing a little. The last thing I did was slip my feet into his too-large boots. They reeked, but not as much as I did.

We were in a corridor similar to the one I'd escaped via during my last visit to Throft Hall. On all fours, I groped along the floor until I found a grate, before hauling it up and to one side. With some difficulty, I rolled the guard's corpse through it, then paused to listen. A second later, I heard a splash.

I was not only a girl marked by death anymore. Now I was one who had caused it. A sob tore itself from my throat, and I doubled over, retching. Nothing, however, came up, save for a chunk of clotted blood.

You need to keep moving. With one final guilt-ridden glance at the soldier's clearly traumatized ghost, I clamped a hand against my neck wound, dashed back up the steps, and burst through the entrance door.

It was agonizing. My whole body hurt. Plus, I had to pretend I was not a half-dead, semirotted woman from Fengzhi Yuan, but an Yskian guard in full-blooded, blooming health. I walked with my back straight, my chin up, my footsteps ringing across the flagstone floor. Servants shuffled through the corridors, and ghosts glided in and out of walls.

I did not know where Prince Essien's rooms were, or even if he was at the castle . . . but he was my last and only hope.

Eventually, I stumbled into a more opulent area of the castle. I'd thought the guest room I'd been shut in had been extravagant, but this? This was something else. The same plush gold carpet that had featured in my guest room ran down the center of the corridor. There were giant murals on the walls and ceiling. Torches were lit in ornate sconces, and gold-gilt picture frames held antiquated paintings of what I presumed were long-dead Lancasters. These had eyes that followed me in the same unnerving way as the portraits had in my room—silently judging me for my sins.

I shook off my fear, summoned my courage, and turned away from the disturbing gallery. *I must be getting closer to the royal quarters,* I thought, examining my surroundings. I bit the inside of my cheek, gagging as a hunk of flesh detached—the decomposition of my body was more dire than I'd thought.

Carefully, I continued creeping along the hallway. As I passed a side corridor, I heard someone approaching, so I picked up my speed and pretended I knew where I was going.

A servant scurried up to me, avoiding eye contact. I'd struck lucky. For once, the ridiculous Yskian custom of the lower servants never looking at their superiors directly would serve me well.

"Sir, forgive me, sir," the servant said, talking to the ground. "I'm to ask you to bring a message to Prince Essien. Lieutenant General Brisson says a woman was killed at the front gates this evening. A Liu. Apparently, she is known to His Royal Highness. She is being taken to the dungeons. The Lord Lieutenant General felt that His Highness should know."

Not wanting my voice to give me away, I merely grunted. This seemed satisfactory to the servant, who retreated, bowing and wringing their hands.

If the servant had come to deliver a message to be relayed to the prince, surely that meant I was getting close to Essien's quarters. Which meant that all I had to do was find the most ludicrously lavish entrance. I was sure that the bedroom of the golden prince would not be anything less.

Roaming along the corridors, I squinted at each door, my head swiveling back and forth. It was only as I rounded a corner that I saw it—

An enormous set of double doors: elaborately carved wood inlaid with gold and marble, depicting a most accurate likeness of the prince sitting atop his throne.

I resisted the urge to roll my eyes. Typical. So very typical. Yskian arrogance at its finest.

I strode up to the doors and used the last of my waning energy to fling them both open. They flew apart, hitting the end points of the hinges simultaneously with a bang.

Prince Essien was in the far corner, sitting at a desk. His

head whipped up when I entered. "Excuse me," he said, obviously affronted. He'd half risen from his seat, a scowl distorting his features. "This is highly improper, you ought to knock first—"

I didn't respond, just hauled off the helmet, revealing the revolting state of my face.

"Lady . . . Lady Liu?" He was spluttering now. "What—What are you doing here?"

I stumbled forward, my knees buckling, fluid leaking all over his pristine carpet.

My body was crumbling, my mind shutting down. I knew that it was only a matter of minutes. This time, I really *was* dying. And if I died, and my body worsened, who knew what would happen if I tried to come back . . . again?

"I'm asking Your Highness . . ." I gasped, swaying, my breaths coming in uneven bursts. "To please . . . save my life."

Then I collapsed.

Twenty-Six

Present day

Prince Essien stood abruptly, his chair tipping until it fell to the floor with a thunk.

"What happened to you?" He strode around the desk and came to stand above me. "What is . . . all of this?" He trailed off, casting his eyes over my blemished face, my bloated belly, the bubbling of the skin on both palms.

I looked up at him. His brow was creased, his pupils so dilated I could barely see his irises. It was funny. If someone had told me just weeks ago that I'd ask a Lancaster for help . . . *voluntarily* . . . I would have laughed outright in their face.

Yet here we were.

"I was shot," I murmured, my mind going foggy. I laid a hand over my chest. "At the gates. By Andres Brisson."

He sank to a squat. "And what about this, and this?" Reaching out, he touched a finger to the back of my hand, grimacing when several flakes of skin sloughed off.

"I . . . died," I said. "For a few days, I think. And when I came back to life, my body was rotting." I made a face. My skin seemed to crack with the movement.

He eyed me. "You died? You actually went back into . . . into the afterlife?"

"Yes . . ." I took a deep breath, then gave a hacking cough. I tasted blood; blood that bubbled from my lungs.

He kept staring at me, his expression inscrutable. What was he thinking? Was he angry that I'd returned to the death realm without telling him? Was he mad that I hadn't fetched the sword?

Or was it more that I was a deceptive, deceitful murderer, with a disgustingly decayed body, and—

"Well then," he said, cutting off my errant thoughts. "Let's get you fixed up."

After propping me up like a rag doll, he helped me to remove the guard's tunic, then eased me back onto the carpet. My belly rolled with nausea, bile rising in my throat.

His forehead creased further as he assessed the alarming state of my body. After pushing his sleeves up to his elbows, he placed both hands very carefully, and very deliberately, over my crossbow wound. Then he closed his eyes, bowed his head, and gave a long, slow exhale.

The warm, languid feeling spread through my torso like syrup. It didn't take long until I began to feel better: more robust, less barely held together at the seams. I watched his face, suffused with a look of intense concentration, and basked in the pleasant heat of his touch. He shuddered a little, but then his muscles tensed and he pressed down harder on my wounds.

"It's already feeling better," I whispered.

His eyelids fluttered open, and he gazed down at me. "Good," he replied. "But there is also . . ." He seemed to be searching for words. "Some deterioration . . . of your flesh. Which I am not sure how to fix. It's not something I've had to do before."

"You'll figure it out," I murmured, luxuriating in the feeling of my wounds knitting back together. "I trust you. Which isn't something I've had to do before, either."

He gave a brief chuckle and slid his hands to a new spot.

I held my breath, tense all over, as his warm palms brushed—so slowly—over the thin cotton of my dress. Up my sides, across my chest, around my neck, along my décolletage. And wherever his touch went, the mottling on my skin cleared; the wrinkles smoothed out, and my flesh became firmer. He rolled me over gently, healing the ragged, torn cuts on my back, then rolled me face-up again. Next were my arms: Slowly, ponderously, he ran his hands up and down each of them, carefully healing all the decay.

My torso and arms fixed, he moved down to my legs. Hovering both hands above my ankles, he glanced at me. "Is it all right if I . . . ?"

"Yes. It's fine." I could barely get the words out.

He tore his gaze from mine and pulled off the dead guard's boots, one by one, before turning his attention to my feet. I squirmed and bit my lip. This felt . . . unbearably good. Slowly, he moved to my ankles, then my calves. He circled my knees, and then the skin of my thighs.

My breath hitched as his hands traveled higher, and I watched him, noticing the strain in his neck and shoulders. A fine sheen of sweat laced his perfect brow. He was concentrating hard enough that I was able to observe him unabashedly: The way the light played off his skin, highlighting the slight coppery sheen threaded through the gold of his hair. The way a single lock had escaped his neatly combed waves and fallen across his forehead.

His hands traveled up, and up, and I fidgeted. He was no longer holding his breath; instead, his breathing was coming short and sharp, his lips slightly parted, his pupils dilated.

"I think that's mostly done it." His voice was hoarse. He cleared his throat, then stood up. "Now it's just your face."

I scrambled onto my feet, too, and stood facing him, unable to hide the fact that I was now blushing furiously.

He reached up and cradled my face with both hands, smoothing his thumbs across my cheekbones. I gasped; the feeling was so intense, so . . . intimate. My nose he healed with the tips of his fingers; he did the same with my ears. Then, my forehead, my eyelids, the curve of my jaw, and then finally—my mouth.

My pulse fluttered in my neck as his thumb brushed my top lip. My heart, already pounding, sped up more, my pulse roaring in my ears. Then, with the slowest, most agonizing movement, he held my face, and ran his thumb softly across my lower lip.

Involuntarily, my lips parted, and I sighed.

He went completely still. His eyes dropped to my mouth, then back up again. A split second passed where we did nothing, said nothing, just stared at one another.

Then, simultaneously, we both broke eye contact and quickly stepped apart.

I let out a shaky breath, scrambling to retie the robe of my hànfú. "Thanks," I muttered, trying to ignore my searing cheeks.

He stepped back and bowed, back to playing the part of a gentleman. "The pleasure is all mine." But then he frowned—very slightly.

"Perhaps, though," he added, "the lady might like to take a bath?"

The prince's personal bathroom was the size of my entire house, if not bigger. The floors were a complicated pattern of black and white tiles, gold gilding bordered the enormous full-length mirror, and an ornate ceiling rose surrounded the stem of a glittering chandelier. The tub and fixtures were all shiny brass, laced with condensing steam. He'd prepared a bath for me, complete with bubbles, and I sighed when I lowered myself into the fragrant water.

By the time I emerged, all warm and sweet scented and wrapped in a fluffy robe, the prince was once again seated at his desk, scrawling something on a piece of parchment.

Inching closer, I tried to glimpse what he was so purposefully writing. But before I could read anything, he caught sight of me looking and tugged a clean piece of parchment over the top.

I frowned—though truth be told, even had he not obscured his words I probably wouldn't have been able to read them. Though Essien and I spoke in Trader's Tongue whenever we were together, from what I'd glimpsed, the loopy, cursive script was all in Yskian.

The prince leaned back in his chair, his arms folded, and looked at me.

"So," he said, eventually. "The sword."

Inwardly, I cursed. Of course we'd need to discuss it, now that I'd been forced to return to Throft Hall and have him heal my decaying body.

Pretending to scrutinize some of the small objects displayed on one of his bookshelves, I echoed him. "The sword." I kept my tone light. "What of it?"

"Do not play games with me, Lady Liu." His voice had grown stern. He leaned forward, now propping his elbows on the desk. "You said you went into the afterlife. Did you find it?"

"I . . . I searched for it. But I didn't find it. I'm sorry."

He massaged his temples. "When you say you searched for it . . . exactly how hard did you look?"

Irritation spiked through me. "Listen, I was attacked, okay?"

His eyes widened. "You were attacked? In the afterlife? I thought it was Brisson who—"

"Brisson shot me at the gates, yes. But in the afterlife, I . . ." I gulped down my fear, the memories flashing up, uncomfortably vivid. "There were some pretty nasty ghosts who tried to capture me." I left the next part unsaid: *They, too, want the sword.*

Instead, I tugged down my collar and added, "That's why I had the stab wound. On my neck. Remember?"

Essien stared at the exposed, now-healed expanse of skin. Some deep emotion—one I could not interpret—flickered briefly in his eyes, but then passed; when I released my collar, he shifted his gaze away.

For a long time, neither of us spoke. Essien appeared to be

lost in thought. Eventually, though, he sighed and rubbed at his eyes with both hands. "I suppose that is it, then."

He sounded so resigned that, perhaps foolishly, I felt a sudden need to reassure him. Maybe I simply felt indebted to him, since he'd healed my injuries with no hesitation.

So, haltingly, I said, "I did . . . learn something. Something that might help."

He raised his head. All of a sudden he looked very tired. "And what is that?"

"I found out that . . . the sword might be buried in the deepest layer of the afterlife."

The prince rose and walked around his desk. Looking every bit the graceful royal, he perched on the edge nearest to me, his arms folded. "The deepest layer?" he said. "Whatever do you mean?"

I drew in a tremulous breath before attempting to explain. "The death realm is made up of . . . layers, all superimposed atop one another. In the afterlife, ghosts can die and become ghosts of ghosts. And I presume they can then die again, and again, until . . ."

His brow furrowed. "Until?"

I raised my hands a little, then let them fall. "Who knows? Who knows how deep the afterlife goes?"

"How deep it goes . . ." Essien grimaced. "That means, to find it, you'll need to go back and . . . die. Multiple times?"

I nodded. "Something like that."

His expression was unreadable. "And you intend to do so?"

"Yes."

It was the truth. As soon as I collected the rest of the shaman's prediction, I would willingly reenter the death realm.

"But there's something I need first. Something that will help me to find the Shēngsǐ Sword." Catching sight of the confusion flashing across Essien's face, I added, "I mean, the Sword of Rechenblod. It has several names."

There was a brief pause. "Very well. What is it?"

"I—I need to go back to my village. There's information buried there that might tell us where to find the sword. That's where I was heading when I last came back alive. Before I realized"—I gestured vaguely at my body, hidden beneath the white robe—"you know."

"Right." A faint tinge of pink dusted the tops of the prince's cheeks. "Well," he said after a pause, and stood. "As soon as you've had some rest, we shall leave."

I raised my eyebrows. "We? What do you mean 'we'? There won't be any 'we.' I'm going myself."

"I insist on accompanying you, Lady Liu."

I frowned. "You can't. You know the people of my village do not take kindly to Yskians."

"When I last let you go, you assured me that you'd be safe," Essien said, advancing on me so that I was forced to take several steps back. "Only for you to come back, days later, half dead, your body decomposing—"

"That was hardly my fault!"

"Regardless." The deep blue of his eyes glinted, dangerously dark in the candlelight. "As you are no doubt aware, I've just healed you. It would be highly ill-mannered for you to squander my efforts."

By now, we stood chest to chest. I suppose I *should* have been grateful for everything he'd done. For letting me go last time, so I could go and see my sick grandmother. For healing me, just in time, when I was on the brink of decomposing. But I hated—*hated*—the idea of being even more indebted to this frankly perplexing prince.

I raised my chin, ignoring the way the movement brought my mouth closer to his. "I guess you'll try to arrest me now?" I bared my teeth in a mocking smile. "Go on, then. Try."

A muscle jumped in the prince's jaw. For a few seconds, he glared down at me. But then he dropped his head and sighed. "No. I would prefer we worked together."

I scoffed. "Your lieutenant general has killed me twice, Your Highness, probably on your orders, and you want us to work *together*?"

Essien's lips went pale, and he pressed them together. After a moment, he shook his head, and looked at the floor. "Those were not my orders, Lady Liu. My men—they do not always listen to me. You saw how Larch was. How Brisson is. Believe me, I would not have ordered anyone to kill—" He looked like he was about to say more, but he didn't.

I knitted my brows. "Why? You're their prince. Why would they defy you?"

His eyes landed back on me, his expression completely open. Almost vulnerable. "Respect is earned, Lady Liu," he said eventually, his voice quiet. "And I have done nothing to earn it."

At this I deflated, my belligerence replaced by pity. The enigma of Essien Lancaster was gradually becoming clearer. He was the youngest son of a powerful monarch. Already, according to their hierarchy, he was the least important. And not only that, he had magical powers in a society that hated magic.

He'd been ostracized by his family in the same way my community had been ostracized by society. And he saw the

Sword of Rechenblod as his way to garner respect. To reclaim his status as a Lancaster royal.

I was starting to understand why he wanted the sword so badly.

"Fine," I conceded, somewhat grudgingly. Fatigue had finally set in, heaviness stealing up my limbs. I'd died several times now, and come back to life, only to discover my body decaying. Now, after such an extreme ordeal, I was craving sleep. Intensely.

Yes, I was starting to empathize with Essien Lancaster. But more to the point: I was simply much too tired to argue.

He quirked an eyebrow. "What do you mean by 'fine'?"

"I mean you can come. As long as you promise to look after my donkeys."

"Your . . . donkeys?" The prince's brows knitted in confusion.

"It's a long story." I sighed, defeated. "A *really* long story. But first . . . I need some sleep."

Twenty-Seven

Present day

It was cold, so cold. Everything was dark. The beams of Essien's four-poster bed loomed above me, casting shadows on the ceiling.

I sat bolt upright, bedsheets puddling around my waist.

The ghost of Wen Bo stood before me, looking exactly as he had when I last saw him. The room was completely silent save for the slow, rhythmic plinks of fluid dripping onto the floor.

My heart began to pound. He'd found me. *He'd found me.* Somehow, his ghost had tracked me to Throft Hall and he was haunting me.

But why? To seek revenge for my escape? To capture me again, and drag me back to General Hong?

My entire body seized up. "I'm sorry," I tried to croak out, but I tasted metal; my mouth filled up with blood. Was it blood that was dripping from my neck wound—the one that General Hong had inflicted? I swallowed, ignoring the way my gut roiled, then tried again. "Wen Bo, I'm sorry, please—"

Wen Bo fixed his black eyes on me. He made no move. He didn't speak. All he did was stare at me, morosely, the corners of his lips tugging down. *He's not carrying any weapons*, I noted, with some relief, surreptitiously groping for my dagger.

And that was when I noticed: The dripping sound was not coming from me. It was coming from him.

Rivulets of blood streamed down his chin before pattering onto the carpet. And worse, his hands were missing, both his arms ending just below his wrists.

I tried to scrabble backward on the bed, attempting to put some distance between the ghost and me. But I was paralyzed. Trapped. Stuck to the spot, none of my limbs cooperating.

Wen Bo's ghost opened his mouth. Inside was just a black hole. His mouth kept opening, and opening, until all I could see was his tongue.

I gagged. The flesh there—it was ragged. It had been amputated. More blood gushed from his mouth.

And then, slithering out from his throat, came a full-size, white-scaled serpent.

My sister had been killed by a serpent.

I tried to scream, but no sound came. My body was still frozen, my vocal cords not working. The serpent continued to emerge from Wen Bo's open mouth, its maw wide, its fangs glinting in the moonlight. And as it uncoiled, its heavy body dropping to the floor, parts of its skin sloughed off, exposing the fine, glinting bones of its skeleton.

"Jia Yi," it hissed, but somehow it spoke in the voice of my sister. "Did you think that you would escape us?"

I sat, still unable to move. Unable to scream. The thump of my pulse grew louder until I heard roaring in my ears.

The snake unhinged its jaw wider, until it was laughing. A low, slow, lazy laugh, in Dai Yu's voice. Wen Bo laughed, too, except he wasn't Wen Bo anymore but instead the Lancaster guard I'd killed mere hours earlier. Then he morphed into the turnip farmer. Lord Larch, the court doctor. Then back to Wen Bo, his chin all wet with blood.

I stared, unable to move, unable to scream—only able to feel my fear.

And then . . . the snake was right before me.

It raised its head to strike.

I cried out as I jerked awake, screaming louder when I saw a pale face bent over my body. Without thinking, I punched it, before scrambling upright and pressing myself back against the headboard. It rattled with the force of my trembling.

"Gods!" Essien staggered backward, clutching his face. He shot me a bewildered look. "Where did you learn to hit so hard?"

My vision finally came into focus, my eyes widening as I took in the scene surrounding me.

Essien's room was flooded with light. It highlighted the elegant lines and dark wood of his furniture: The writing desk he'd sat at last night. The sofa, strewn with rumpled bedding, where he had spent the night. The floor-to-ceiling bookshelves that covered the opposite wall. A fire spat and cracked in a stone fireplace, before which were two wing-backed armchairs, upholstered footstools, and a table set with crockery and silver domes.

It was morning. Somehow, I'd made it through the night.

More importantly, there was no blood on the carpet. No half-decomposed serpent. And no ghost of Wen Bo.

It must have been a nightmare.

Aghast, I looked at Essien. "*Mothers*! I shouldn't have hit you. I'm sorry! I'm so sorry. Are you very hurt?" I scooted closer to him. "Here, let me take a look . . ."

Still clasping his cheek, Essien waved his free hand in my direction to cut off my rambling. "I'm all right. Truly, I am." Frowning, he let his face go and prodded gingerly at his jaw, which was somewhat reddened. "What were you dreaming about, anyway? You seemed . . . terrified. You kept on screaming that you were sorry." He winced as his fingers skated across a developing bruise. Fresh guilt sliced through my stomach.

I drew my knees up to my chest and hugged them, trying to settle my shivering. "I dreamed that one of the ghosts who attacked me in the death realm was standing right there." I pointed a shaky finger at the middle of the room, where Wen Bo had stood in my dream, in a puddle of his own blood. "He'd . . . been hurt."

Essien gave me a funny look. "Why would you apologize, when *he* attacked *you*?"

Tears pricked at my inner eyelids. "I don't think he had a choice. I think he'd been coerced to attack me and . . ." I blinked and looked away "I guess I feel bad for him. I feel sorry for anyone who doesn't get a choice in what they do."

The prince fell silent, studying my face as though I were a riddle he was trying to solve. Then he smiled and held out his hand. "Well, there's nothing like a hearty breakfast to chase away bad dreams."

After a moment's hesitation, I placed my palm on his,

allowing him to help me out of bed, lead me to the fireplace, and settle me into one of the armchairs. I slumped against the soft cushions and watched as he began preparing breakfast. To my surprise, it seemed as though he planned to serve it to me himself.

I can't say I didn't take perverse delight in the idea of a prince waiting on me, a village girl from across the border. I mean, surely after several days of being dead, I deserved a little pampering.

As I nibbled on what Prince Essien called a honey cake, he poured me a cup of tea. I brought it to my nose and sniffed: It was the same kind I'd drunk the first time I'd been held at Throft Hall.

I looked at him quizzically. "This tea," I said, then took a sip, giving an approving hum of pleasure. "This tea is Fengzhian."

Yskian tea was normally mild, sweet, and milky. But tea from the Jinghu Dao empire was made from loose leaves and drunk neat. In Fengzhi Yuan, my province, tea was considered even more of an art form, made from a variety of different leaves, oftentimes fermented. The preparation methods depended on the leaf variety used and involved highly complex sets of rules. And once it was brewed, the colors ranged from the palest straw to the blackest black.

He just gave a small smile and placed the teapot back on the tray.

"I didn't realize you were a tea connoisseur," I continued, taking another sip.

The prince leaned back in his chair. "Is it such a surprise?"

I lapsed into a meditative silence. I'd always thought the Lancasters and their minions hated anything and everything from across the border. Perhaps they weren't as prejudiced as I'd thought . . .

In truth, Essien as a person was confusing to me. I'd only ever known him as the arrogant, privileged brat who interrogated me and presided over his subordinates in the throne room. But then again, he'd healed me, several times, without question. He'd let me go home to see my dying grandmother. He'd run me a bath and let me sleep in his bed, and here he was serving me tea that came from my own province.

Was he just lulling me into a false sense of security? Treating me with kindness so I'd help him get the sword? It seemed that way—and certainly his words supported that notion—but every now and then I'd catch him staring, his cheeks flushing, the cold, hard shell of his exterior showing the slightest cracks.

I remembered what he'd told me, stuck up in the tree. *We are all acting in the royal court*, he'd said. *We all have our parts to play.*

Which was the true Prince Essien? Which was make-believe?

Perhaps I should be more wary.

When we'd finished breakfast, I watched the prince as he pulled a charcoal waistcoat over the crisp white shirt he was already wearing. The fine-wrought fabrics clung to his chest and shoulders. He was more well muscled than I would have expected, seeing as he rarely left Throft Hall. I supposed there was not much to do here except train in swordplay, horsemanship, and whatever else rich royal people did.

He looked up suddenly, catching me ogling, and gave a little smile. Two tiny dimples bloomed in his cheeks. I bit my lip and looked away, then took another sip of tea. If Essien noticed my hand trembling slightly, he mercifully didn't mention it.

"Why did you let me go?" I blurted out, suddenly. "In the forest."

The prince sat on the opposite side of the bed in order to tug on his boots. "If I recall correctly, you insisted, Lady Liu."

"But you agreed. After I told you about my grandmother—even though you couldn't have known for certain I'd come back. Why?"

He fell silent, pulling on his second boot rather slowly, like he was mulling over what to say.

After a protracted pause, he spoke. "I suppose I agreed because . . . I know what it's like to lose a grandparent, too."

I gripped the teacup's dainty handle so hard that it was a wonder it didn't break. "Yours died?"

A fleeting look of something—pain, if I recognized it correctly—flashed across his face. "Yes. My grandfather. My mother's father. He died four years ago." Essien raised his eyes to meet mine. "He was the only one who . . . accepted me for who I was."

"That you're magical?"

"He called it a gift. Not a curse." Essien's expression had softened; he spoke so quietly that I had to strain to hear him, even in the hush of the room. "He was my only ally. And when he died, my mother and father wasted no time in shipping me out here."

"Oh" was all I said, though that felt woefully inadequate. He would have been no more than fourteen years old. Something inside me cracked to think of a young Essien Lancaster, abandoned and alone, ordered to remain at the very edge of his kingdom.

Somehow, this Yskian and I had found common ground, not just in the way we were both outsiders among our own communities but also in our love for our respective grandparents. The fact that Essien Lancaster and I were similar in any way was truthfully disconcerting.

In this circumstance, I was unsure what to say. Should I offer my condolences? Should I try to give him a hug? What was the social etiquette in these sorts of situations?

I didn't get a chance to do anything, though, because right at that moment we were startled by a rap at the door.

Essien crossed the room and opened it a crack. "What is it?" His tone had turned imperious; he'd donned the princely persona again like a cloak. So seamlessly, and so rapidly, it made my gut flip.

"I'm sorry to bother you, Your Highness, but His Highness Prince Rowan is here. He wishes to see you."

Rowan Lancaster. Essien's eldest brother . . . and the most infamous. Rumors of his barbarity had even spread to our tiny, isolated village. Mainly because he liked to capture and brutally torture any unfortunate magical folk who strayed across his path. According to all reports, he was a true patriot who remained bitter about my community's role in Yske's defeat during the last war. He remained adamant that Yske, not Jinghu Dao, should control the trade routes that ran through my province.

Rowan Lancaster *hated* magic more than anyone.

Silently, I swore beneath my breath.

"*Rowan?* Rowan is here?" Essien straightened, his knuckles

whitening on the door handle, then threw me a look over his shoulder. "Hide," he mouthed, the color draining from his face.

I plonked the teacup on its saucer and scrambled up. Panicking, I scanned the room for somewhere to secrete myself. The only place was beneath the bed, so after gathering up my skirt, I dropped to the floor and crawled under. I guess I could have slipped into the death realm to escape. But that would leave Essien with my corpse stuffed beneath his bed, which I figured could be worse, and require more explanation.

I hid just in time, for as I wedged myself deeper into the shadows, I heard the sound of a hand clapped on a shoulder. Then, Rowan Lancaster, first son of Yske, proclaiming in a booming voice, "Brother! It's been too long."

My throat constricted. I clutched my Bone Smith weapons closer. I'd kept them on me the whole time, even slept curled around them, since I still did not completely trust the prince.

"Rowan." Essien sounded strained. "What are you doing here?"

An apt question, since it was common knowledge the rest of the royal family rarely bothered to visit Throft Hall. Too close to the border, they said, and too dangerous—they preferred to let Essien manage the region alone.

From my vantage point, crammed on the floor, I watched as a second pair of black boots strolled into the room. My breaths sounded so loud in my ears; I tried to breathe shallower.

The elder prince seemed to be poking around with little regard for Essien's privacy. "Do I need a reason to visit my dear baby brother?" he said, a false note of joviality in his tone. He chuckled. "I mean, all of us at the palace are curious as to what you do out here, in this godforsaken place. How you"—there was a pause, as if for dramatic effect—"pass the time."

I peeked out from beneath the bed. Rowan was shorter than his brother. While Essien was eighteen, from what I knew of his eldest brother, Rowan was approaching thirty. His hair was even lighter and finer than Essien's, combed back from a slightly receding hairline. Thankfully, he wasn't looking in my direction.

"As you know," Essien said through gritted teeth, "I spend my time here defending the Yskian borders. For *our* family."

Rowan dug in his pockets, procured a pipe, and lit it, blowing smoke in his brother's face. Essien waved it away with an angry flick of his hand. Then, leaning in, Rowan said conspiratorially, "The guards tell me that you have a *girl* here. And that you spent the night with her."

My heartbeat picked up pace, thundering in my ears, threatening to give me away. Was this the reason for Rowan's visit? He'd heard about *me* and had come to confront his brother about it?

Essien drew himself up to his full height. "Well, you're misinformed. I was alone." He paused, his jaw muscle ticking, before he corrected himself. "I *am* alone."

Rowan's gaze roamed the room, alighting on the breakfast table. The table, which contained two settings: two teacups, two plates, two sets of silver cutlery. My palms grew sweaty. My gut clenched. I clamped my teeth together to keep them from chattering.

It was fortunate that I'd left no other evidence of my stay, since I had brought nothing with me except the hànfú I was wearing and the weapons I'd clutched to my chest. Perhaps Rowan would think I'd already left.

"Come now, Essien," the elder Lancaster said, prowling closer to his brother. "You know as well as I do that I don't care whom you . . . *entertain*. Man, woman, whatever you wish for—I know that you prefer both. I understand more than anyone the pleasures of the flesh."

Essien gave a visible swallow, refusing to meet his brother's eyes.

Rowan began pacing around Essien, a predator circling his prey. "But, to be clear, little brother, if you're going to have playthings, then be sure you dispose of the evidence. *Discreetly.* In such a way that no one can trace the marks you leave upon their bodies."

Nausea rose in my throat; I swallowed it down, revolted. Was Rowan Lancaster really saying what I thought he meant? Rage uncoiled within me, hissing like a snake, and my fingers tightened on my Bone Smith blade. There was nothing I wanted to do more than rush out from beneath the bed and stab this disgusting man to death.

"Well, you needn't warn me, Rowan." Essien's face had turned even paler than I ever thought possible. "As I told you, I am alone—"

Rowan slammed his fist down on the table, so hard the plates jumped and the cutlery clattered to the floor. At the noise, I flinched, hitting my head on the bottom of the bed, my eyes watering from the pain. "DO NOT lie to me, boy!" Rowan shouted, spittle flying into Essien's face. "There were *witnesses*! Larch was murdered while attending her, only a week past. And just last night, she and the guard escorting her simply . . . disappeared." His mouth twisted with distinct disgust. "Brisson tells me she has died and come back to life. *Twice*. She is . . . an abomination. Do *not* forget what her people did to ours during the last war."

Rowan stopped, exhaled through his nose, then continued in a voice that was calmer but more deadly. "Who you bed is not my concern, brother, but I will *not* allow you to sully the Lancaster name."

Essien didn't respond. Instead, his eyes hardening, he drew his handkerchief from his pocket and calmly wiped the flecks of saliva from his face.

This small act of defiance seemed to enrage Rowan further. The elder Lancaster fisted his hand in his brother's collar, yanking him forward with such force that even *I* was afraid for Essien's safety. "Remember your place, *dear* Essien. If you defy me . . . if you lie to me, then I might just slip"—he shoved Essien away from him so that he stumbled back a few paces—"and my poor little brother might find himself accidentally locked in the dungeon with the Spyrre."

I stifled a cry at this unmasked threat, clamping a hand over my mouth to keep silent.

Essien and his brother stared at one another, chests heaving, each unwilling to surrender. Then Rowan spun on his heel and strode out the door, slamming it behind him.

And then Essien was hauling me out from under the bed by my elbow.

"We need to leave," he said, his breaths sharp and serrated. "We need to get you out of here."

Flustered, he pulled a book from one of his shelves. It only slid out partially; I stared, for the entire wall had swung open to reveal a hidden corridor.

He yanked a caped greatcoat from his wardrobe and hurriedly bundled me in it. It was several sizes too big, but its deep collar thankfully obscured most of my face. Then he all but pushed me into the secret passageway. The bookshelf slid closed behind us, plunging us into darkness.

We hurried along, Essien tugging me firmly by the hand, the only sound our heavy breathing. When we emerged, through what appeared to be a trapdoor, I squinted at the brightness; we'd surfaced in the stables.

"Oh no," I said, hanging back and shaking my head vigorously. "Not this again, no."

Essien tried to pull me forward. "Come, Lady Liu." When I didn't move, his voice grew more urgent. "You said you needed to go back to your village, did you not? This will get us there the fastest."

I jerked my hand out of his grip and stepped away, crossing my arms tightly. "Nope. No way. Don't make me regret letting you come with me."

He frowned. "How do you propose we go, then?"

"We walk," I said, and pouted. "I'm good at walking."

"Walk!" He looked aggrieved. "But walking would take *days*—"

"Better than braving one of these cursed creatures!" I countered. "The last time you put me on a horse, I nearly died!"

His eyes widened. "You fell?"

"Nearly," I huffed. "Twice."

"Well, then." His lips twitched. "It is lucky you can come back to life again." He took a step closer, his clear eyes shadowed by the dim dawn light. "How about we ride together? I shall hold you steady, and besides"—one corner of his mouth turned up, just slightly—"we're short one horse. You never returned my last one."

"You can have it back," I grumbled, and Essien chuckled.

Just then, the unmistakable sound of tramping armored feet rang out, cleaving the cool morning air. Essien's smile died on his lips. Grabbing my arm, he hauled me into the dark space behind the half-open door.

My blood chilled as about a dozen Lancaster men marched past. I shrank against the stable wall; Essien shifted subtly, shielding me from view. From where I was wedged into the small space behind the prince's body, I watched the soldiers pass us by.

As soon as they'd gone, Essien whispered, his face pale. "They are looking for you. We must hurry."

There was no choice, really. Either I agreed to ride Essien's horse, or else Rowan—or one of Rowan's men—would discover us. In a way, I was less concerned for myself than for Essien. At least *I* could always escape by slipping into the death realm. Essien, not so much.

So, I nodded my agreement.

Moving quickly and almost silently, Essien chose a sturdy-looking beast, helping me to mount before springing up himself. His arms encircled mine, his body nestled up behind me.

His warm breath ghosted across the back of my neck, raising goose bumps. I yanked the greatcoat's collar up, trying to create an extra barrier.

"Ready?" he whispered, right into my ear. How could he make a single word hold so much . . . *promise*?

I shivered, and nodded. "As ready as I'll ever be."

Holding both reins, the Lancaster prince spurred the horse forward, leading us back to my home.

Twenty-Eight

Present day

The journey from Throft Hall seemed to take even longer this time, not least because I was mortifyingly aware of Essien Lancaster pressed up against my back. For most of the plodding journey I was squirming, desperate to get away from his heat, his smell, the hard muscles of his chest. My only periods of sweet relief were the few times we stopped to rest and water his horse.

Eventually, on the last leg, I drifted off from exhaustion, only to wake when we abruptly changed direction. I'd slumped backward, leaning against him, one of his strong, steadying arms encircling my torso. Startling, I pulled away, mumbling an awkward apology for having fallen asleep.

He didn't answer, just directed us into a small copse of trees, before pulling the mare to a stop and sliding off the saddle. With his hands around my waist, he lifted me down. I almost tumbled over, but managed to stagger to a tree and support myself against it.

After taking several deep, shuddering breaths, I raised my

head, then fell into a silent stare. I'd been so distracted by his proximity that I hadn't even noticed how close we'd drawn to my village.

"What's wrong?" Essien said, coming over to my side.

I turned slowly to face him. "We're here. At my village."

"Yes. And?" His eyebrows bunched in confusion.

Propping my hands on my hips, I regarded him through narrowed eyes. "How did you know where to come?"

His mouth opened, then closed, then opened again, before finally he said, "I meant to tell you earlier, but . . . I've been here before."

My eyebrows shot upward. "You've been here before." A statement, not a question.

The alabaster of his cheeks had flushed pink. "When your grandmother was ill . . . I came to deliver her some Shadowside."

Essien brought the Shadowside? *Here?* For a moment, I couldn't gather my thoughts enough to answer. Instead, I strode forward, put my hands against Essien's chest, and shoved him—hard.

"You?" I hissed, then shoved him again; caught unawares, he stumbled back a few paces, then raised his arms to block my attack. "It was *you*?" My voice was rising, each word punctuated with another blow. "Why didn't you *tell* me, you pompous ass?"

Yes, I knew I should've been grateful, but the knowledge that Essien had been to my home—my *secret* home—without me knowing was a rather unwelcome shock. For as long as I could remember, we'd kept the location of our village hidden for a reason: so Yskians like him wouldn't find us in the forest and destroy us for wielding magic.

Plus, now I owed Essien Lancaster yet another debt.

"I didn't think it was important to mention!" He hurled each word at me while simultaneously fending me off. "I just heard you mumbling about it in your sleep—"

My voice was rising—it now bordered on a shriek. "Well, you shouldn't have been watching me sleep!"

By now, I'd backed him against a tree. I clenched my fists by my sides, my fury so thick I could taste it.

"You're absolutely right," he said hurriedly, raising both hands in defense. "Now will you stop hitting me? Please?"

In that moment, he looked so like a puppy cowering before its master that my anger immediately evaporated. I stopped pummeling him, took a step back, and folded my arms. "Fine. I'll stop. But next time you decide to go behind my back and uncover one of my biggest secrets, *you tell me.* Okay?"

He nodded and gave a sigh, passing a hand over his chin.

Now that my fury had ebbed, it had been replaced by curiosity. "How did you find this place to begin with, anyway?" Our village was protected by concealment wards that made it almost impossible for the average human to detect. But then—I'd forgotten Essien Lancaster was not an average human.

"If you want the truth, I . . . I have known where it was for quite some time." He gave a small and extremely irritating shrug. "I've stumbled across it before, in my travels. I can kind of . . . sense the magic."

I stared at him. I'd never known that Essien even traveled beyond his own four walls. Did he do it in secret? And even worse . . . he could *sense* magic? "You knew where we lived, this whole time?"

"Well yes."

My mouth went dry. "Have you . . . told anyone?"

"Of course not!"

"But . . ." Scrunching my eyes shut, I massaged my temples. "Why not? Why didn't you attack us? Aren't you, as a Lancaster, supposed to be rooting my people out?"

"I am not my brother, Lady Liu," he snapped. "Have you not realized that by now?" Without waiting for an answer, he turned and stormed off, his shoulders hunched.

I stayed silent for a few moments, deliberating, before rushing to catch up to him. "Your Highness?"

"Yes?" He stopped and turned to face me, his tone wary.

I bit my lip. "Thanks. For keeping it a secret."

He almost chuckled, but when he caught a glimpse of my expression his mirth dissipated. *Good*, I thought, crossing my arms and looking away. If we were to be on friendly terms, then it was best he learned how mercurial I could be.

The sound of a twig snapping nearby caused both of our heads to jerk around, and I quickly grabbed his arm and hauled him behind a bush. It was two of my cousins, foraging for wild herbs. With my pulse racing, I drew Essien and myself deeper into the undergrowth, our bodies pressed uncomfortably close.

The people in my community were not aggressive. But many of them did have quite considerable powers, and it was unlikely they'd take kindly to an Yskian in their midst. They so rarely encountered foreigners. To them, people like Essien were the enemy: dangerous and unpredictable. I'm sure most Yskians felt the same way about us.

Perhaps it had been a bad idea letting him accompany me.

"Follow me," I whispered, when my cousins had passed. "I'll have to sneak you through the back."

* * *

We circled around the far edges of the village, before I skirted through a scraggle of densely packed shrubbery and ducked beneath a fence. This was a route I'd taken many times before, when I'd returned post-hunting and did not want to be disturbed. Essien scrambled after me, and I cringed at how much noise he was making, but fortunately no one came to investigate.

We stole past a few deserted huts until we were right before my own. After looking left and right, I shoved him unceremoniously through the door and shut it fast behind us.

"This is . . . my place," I ventured, feeling suddenly shy. "You'll need to hide here."

My house was tiny, just a single room, and it smelled slightly fusty—not surprising, since it had sat so long unoccupied. The forest was not very forgiving. In such a damp environment, mold didn't take long to set in.

The prince glanced at the door and back to me. "I can't come with you?"

"No!" I cut in, too quickly. Then, I added, tempering my tone, "No. I'm sorry. But you need to stay out of sight. You must know how my people feel about yours."

He blew out a long breath, then nodded—somewhat grudgingly.

"Remove your shoes, please," I instructed, slipping my own shoes off and moving farther into the room. My floor was just a thin layer of cork tiles, but I still adhered to custom. While the prince yanked off his boots, I moved around, cracking open the windows and shaking out my single blanket. For privacy,

I kept all the curtains drawn, which left my house swathed in darkness.

Being here brought back a flood of memories. Lin, lounging on the only sitting surface—the bed. Lin, huddling over tea at my kitchen table. Lin, throwing open the door and leaning against its frame, arms crossed, smiling at me.

I shook my head, trying to clear the visions. Ghost Lin couldn't haunt me. Not now. Not since I'd killed him in the afterlife and sent him deeper down, to the second level. As he'd explained to me, ghosts could only haunt the level that was directly above them. I was safe from him. So why in Mother's name was I still letting his memories haunt me?

Prince Essien, having finally removed his shoes, edged into the room. He looked around, turning a slow, deliberate circle as he took everything in.

My pulse quickened and my cheeks began to burn. For the first time in forever, I was looking at my humble little hut through a stranger's eyes. What would the prince think of our modest village, with its makeshift buildings, thatched roofs, and communal lavatories, when the space in his bathroom alone exceeded the size of my entire dwelling?

I remained silent as he drew closer to my walls, studying them. The rough wood was plastered with the odd pressed flower, scraps of poetry written in Jinghu Daoian calligraphy, and—taking up most of the space—drawings. Charcoal drawings, hung up everywhere. There were scrappy sketches of trees, elegant depictions of the night sky, hands pushing open a curtain.

Most of the drawings, though, were of me. Me sitting at the table, my chin propped on my hand. Me from behind, raising my long hair on a hot day in an attempt to cool off my neck. Me poised in the forest, an arrow nocked into my bow, basking in the stillness of a winter's morning.

Essien touched one of the pictures with the tips of two fingers. "Did you do this?" he asked, seemingly awed. Objectively, I could appreciate that they were very good.

"No," I said. Lin had drawn them. All of them. During those lazy days we'd spent lounging in the forest, using charred sticks from the fires we'd built. Back when we were young, he'd had a special interest in drawing pictures of, well . . . me.

"It was . . ." It pained me to talk of Lin just as I was trying to forget him. But I couldn't very well allow Essien to believe I had talent that I did not possess. "An old friend. He died."

"Oh." The prince snatched his hand away from the drawing, as if it burned. "I'm sorry."

"Don't be," I said, blinking and turning away. "He was not a good person. We did not part on good terms." Now, come to think of it, I didn't know why I had kept the pictures when I'd gotten rid of everything else.

Essien continued his perusal of my small space, frowning at the folded blanket on the floor. "You sleep here?"

I gulped and nodded, not wanting to tell him about how I, in a fit of incendiary rage, had hauled my straw mattress out of my hut and burned it on the watchfire. All because I'd tried to sleep on it after Lin had left me, and discovered that it still smelled like him, from all the times we'd lain there, our limbs entwined, dreaming of a future that we would never have.

Now I was annoyed *and* embarrassed. "It's not much," I mumbled, wrapping my arms around my stomach to shield myself. "My house, I mean. It's small, and basic, and—"

"It's perfect."

I stared at him, surprised. "What do you mean?"

"It just reminds me so much of . . ." He glanced sidelong at me, then shut his mouth and looked away, seemingly unwilling to elaborate further.

We fell into an awkward, oppressive silence during which I pretended to straighten my possessions, of which I had rather few. The back of my neck prickled, feeling hot; suddenly, it seemed awfully invasive to have the Yskian prince in my space. He was too resplendent, like an ostentatious piece of jewelry displayed on an otherwise plain set of clothes.

It made my gut churn how much he was learning about me and my family. Some base instinct told me that he was honorable, that I could trust him—but the truth was, just because I *could* didn't mean I *should.*

After I'd tidied the already-neat room, I turned to him.

"I need to make a visit." I stepped back into my boots, sheathing my knife inside one. Just before I slipped out the door, I looked back, arching an eyebrow at Essien, who by now had perched against the edge of my wooden dresser. "Stay here. If anyone comes, then . . ." I meant to say *hide*, but in my tiny, single-roomed abode, there really was nowhere to conceal oneself. So I just shrugged and added, "Then you're on your own, I'm afraid."

He folded his arms across his chest, the corners of his lips tipping up. "That's all right, Lady Liu," he said. "I am, after all, quite used to being alone."

I almost laughed, but stopped myself just in time. Then, purposely avoiding eye contact, I turned and left the hut.

Twenty-Nine

Present day

As I headed into the communal areas of the village, I took everything in with a newfound appreciation. If only I could freeze this moment as indelibly as the ice-capped Northern mountains: the sounds—of laughing children, birdsong, the pitter-patter of dewdrops falling through the leaves. The brisk air. The clean forest smell . . . I'd missed all this, missed it so much.

At the same time, *everything* here reminded me of Pópo. Everything. It was as though I saw her face in every leaf on every tree. Heard her low, melodious voice with each soughing breath of wind. It felt like she could be around every corner, behind any door, silhouetted behind each papered window. As if I could just turn at precisely the right moment and she'd be standing there, her black eyes gleaming, a smile playing on her lips.

My heart lurched, thumping pitifully in my chest. *She isn't here*, I had to keep reminding myself. After I'd unearthed the second half of the shaman's prediction, I'd be plunging back into the afterlife to pursue her, and Lin, too. I couldn't allow myself to wallow in bittersweet nostalgia.

Who knew when I'd see my home again?

If I'd see it again at all?

There seemed to be no adults about, but a group of children did spot me. They milled around, crying my name in joy and jostling to get closer. To them, my return meant meat from hunting and other fun trinkets I occasionally happened across. Laughing, I greeted each of them, spinning a few of the smaller ones around as a consolation prize; they were visibly disappointed when I told them I had no food.

"Where is Hui Fen?" I asked one of the older children, a sweet girl whose name was Shay-Lin.

"They are in the longhouse," she said, blinking up at me. "The grown-ups are holding a meeting."

"Xièxie." I ruffled Shay-Lin's hair. "Thank you."

Hui Fen was presiding over a meeting when I ducked into the dark, incense-laced longhouse.

Inside, it was packed; it looked like all the adult villagers were in attendance. As per the succession rules, Hui Fen was the new High Priester, a fact the villagers had apparently accepted without dispute. It made sense, really, since everyone knew that out of the three of us, Hui was the best suited. Their combined yin and yang energies gave them a levelheadness unmatched by most others.

Still, seeing Hui Fen at the front of the room, their long hair slicked up in a High Priester's signature braided bun, made guilt punch right through my chest. I remembered the night I'd wished Dai Yu dead because Hui Fen would be a better leader.

Now Dai Yu *was* dead. She wanted me dead, too; wanted me working for General Hong. I swallowed, a thick lump lodged in my throat.

Blinking, I slipped into the back row, doing my best to stash those memories deep in my subconscious. A few of the other adults nodded at me; they weren't surprised at my prodigal return. I went out hunting so often that my random reappearance was not unusual. To them, nothing had changed, even though to me . . . everything had.

The agenda was just wrapping up with a robust discussion about who would be stationed at the watchfires for the coming week. Finally, the rota was agreed upon, and Hui Fen adjourned the meeting.

They found me immediately afterward. "I've been so worried about you, Jia Yi," they said, after we'd embraced. "It was not like you to miss Pópo's funeral." They paused and shook their head, their eyelashes studded with tears.

"I'm sorry." What else could I say?

Hui gripped my shoulders, their eyes boring into mine. "But Mothers have mercy. Where have you been?"

"I got . . . lost for a few days. My"—I grappled for a way to describe Essien—"friend helped me find my way back."

"And are you back for good now? Will you stay?"

I shook my head. "I only came back to fetch something. After that I must leave again."

Hui gave me a sympathetic look. "In any case, you must be hungry. Come now. At least have some tea, and a bite to eat."

* * *

We sat at my grandmother's small kitchen table, scarred and pockmarked from many decades of use. Hui Fen would be living here for the foreseeable future, as long as they were High Priester.

Hui pottered around the kitchen, banging things and opening and closing cupboard doors. I startled when they suddenly plonked down two teacups, then set about laying out an impressive spread of small dishes. I spied garlic eggplant, fried green vegetables tossed with water chestnuts, a spicy hotpot, and, my favorite, soy-soaked chee cheong fun. A huge bowl of steaming rice sat in the center. There was no meat—I hadn't, after all, been around to hunt, and the small amount we'd cured would need to last all winter. Still, my stomach growled as I ogled the spread; the tiny delicacies Essien had brought me before our journey had hardly been enough.

As soon as I started eating, Hui gave me an inquisitive look.

"Now," they said. "Tell me truly: Where have you *really* been?" Perhaps they thought the food might loosen my tongue.

At first, I considered lying. But then I realized if I omitted anything, Hui Fen could just use their memory magic to find out. While I didn't want to discuss the fact that I somehow suddenly had resurrection magic—it seemed prudent to keep that information to as few people as possible—I also didn't want Hui to ask too many questions.

The best lies are those that are formed in half-truths.

So, gripping my bamboo chopsticks tightly, I told them that I'd been searching for information about the Shēngsǐ Sword, because I believed Pópo was in the afterlife, trying to find and destroy it before anyone else could.

I didn't mention that I'd actually seen Pópo—or her ghost, that is—since it would only raise more questions. As far as Hui Fen knew, I did not have the ability to see ghosts. As far as they knew I had no powers at all.

As the current High Priester, my sibling was already shouldering countless burdens. They were already grieving our grandmother's first death—I did not want to add to their worries with the knowledge that Pópo had died again, this time by Lin's hand.

"The Shēngsǐ Sword." Hui Fen scrunched up their brow. "Was that the weapon Pópo spoke of before she died?"

"I think so. From what I can gather, it's very important it doesn't fall into the wrong hands."

"Who else is searching for it?" Frowning, my sibling squeezed a lump of rice between their own chopsticks before delicately transferring it to their mouth.

"The Lancasters," I said, forcing a deeper frown from Hui. "And others. Apparently the sword can . . . bring ghosts back from the dead. There are some vengeful spirits who wish us harm, and if they get the sword, then . . ."

Hui frowned. "Aunty Ai Li did say the spirits seemed restless." Ai Li, a village elder who had the power to sense ghosts, wasn't really our aunt. But it was common in Fengzhian culture for those older than us to be called Aunty, Uncle, or Auncle as appropriate, regardless of whether they were related. Hui's gaze drifted to the hut's entrance. "I will increase the concealment wards. And we will put up more fúlù."

They stood, stacked the dishes, and brought them to the sink. I half rose to help, but they waved me away. My grandmother had never abided by the usual Jinghu Daoian rules of hierarchy and rank. In our village, it was considered inhospitable to allow guests to help clean up.

And I supposed that now, in this hut, I was considered a guest.

I sat back down, frowning at the fúlù they already had in place: yellow papers hung up beside the doors used as talismans against ghosts, demons, and other evil spirits. "I don't think that's enough. We'll need additional protections. And to warn everybody, make sure they're prepared. These ghosts seem very angry." Then I added, "I'll also need the rest of the prophecy. The one Pópo buried."

Hui Fen threw me a look. A silent look that seemed to contain a multitude of questions.

"She didn't want me to hear it, did she?" I balled my hands into fists. All of a sudden I felt, once again, like a child, stamping her foot to get noticed.

With great care, Hui set the stack of plates on the bench before turning to face me. "Pópo didn't tell me much about the weapon she was seeking. But I do know she wanted to spare you from your fate." They gave a rueful smile. "She believed if she protected you well enough in the present, that she might change the course of your future."

I clenched my fists tighter, willing away my tears. "Well, she was wrong. The future . . . it is inevitable. I need the rest of the shaman's prediction. And quickly. Otherwise we're all at risk."

Hui Fen was silent for several seconds. But then, they nodded.

They strode over to the small ancestral shrine that adorned the southern wall of the hut and knelt before it. Taking a key out of the sleeves of their hànfú, they unlocked a trapdoor in the floor, before drawing out an elaborately carved box.

"This is what the shaman gave Pópo when, unbeknownst to you, she went back." They held it out to me.

I took it, hugging it to my chest. Bizarrely, it felt warm, almost body temperature, and was heavier than it looked from the outside. "Thank you."

"Open it alone, Jia. The shaman was very particular about the fact that it is your destiny. Only you can hear it."

"What will happen if I'm not alone?"

Hui gave a small shrug. "There is probably some enchantment on it. Perhaps, it may even be destroyed."

Involuntarily, my fingers tightened around the small, innocuous-looking box. "All right then." A tremor rolled through me, but I did my best to tamp down my fear and began to turn away.

But Hui Fen rose and caught my arm. "There's one more thing."

This stayed my feet, and I turned back to face my sibling.

"I don't know what the significance of this is, but when we prepared Pópo's body for the funeral . . ." Their eyes misting, Hui paused for a moment before pressing on. "We found an injury, on her abdomen. Like a knife wound. According to the healers, it was old. Maybe even more than a year old. But . . ."

I shivered, goose bumps peppering my arms. *A knife wound?*

My grandmother had never been in battle, nor any other violent conflict. Not to my knowledge, anyway. How had she gotten that? "But what?"

"But it had festered." My sibling swallowed. "And there were black lines that tracked around it, almost like—"

"—poison." I shuddered. I knew what those black lines meant.

Hui Fen bowed their head. "She hid it from us, all this time. We thought it was the sickness she'd been battling for years that resulted in her passing, but we now think what killed her was this wound."

I lapsed into silence, my mind churning. *A knife wound.* Who would have stabbed my grandmother? With . . . poison?

Bile churned in my belly. There was only one person I knew of in our village who routinely used poison. Or who *used* to use it.

Lin. He'd been our community's most proficient poison master back when he was alive. That is, until he'd fled and abandoned me, right before—

My heart stuttered. Lin had disappeared right around the time that Pópo's sickness had worsened. It was part of why his betrayal had cut me so deeply—that he'd left me just when I'd needed him the most. But what if the two events were connected? And I'd just never realized?

According to the healers, it was old. Maybe even more than a year . . .

I pressed both hands on my stomach, fighting the urge to be sick.

"Promise me you'll be careful." Hui Fen's voice pulled me out of my thoughts. They reached out to cradle my face, their big brown eyes fixed on me. "Make sure you do not put yourself in danger. Whatever she herself faced, Pópo went to great lengths to protect you. It was . . . her last wish." They dropped their hands to my shoulders and squeezed, so gently. "It is my wish too."

My chest seized, ice gripping my heart. How could I tell my beloved sibling that I was planning to reenter the death realm, where there were vengeful ghosts, and violent sisters, and the most traitorous monster of all: Lin?

I couldn't. I couldn't bring myself to do it. So, adding another lie to my collection, and more guilt to my teetering pile, I nodded.

"I will," I reassured them. This time the dishonesty tasted bitter. "I'll be careful."

Then, holding the box to my chest, my heart fracturing—

I left.

Thirty

Present day

Clutching the ornate box, I wandered out into the now-blazing sun. It had reached early afternoon, and the sparkling frost that blanketed our surroundings seemed to amplify the light.

I felt more alone than ever.

I hurried past the outer edge of the village, stopping just beyond the line of trees. Bending over, I placed the box atop a snowdrift—it seemed to shudder, as if it were alive. I frowned, sweat slicking my palms, and wiped my hands on the hem of my skirt.

Then, my entire body rigid with tension, I held my breath . . . and flipped open the box.

Inside, nestled among swathes of bloodred silk, was a single stick of incense.

I plucked it out. *Incense?* For a moment, I was confused—but then I remembered the shaman's tent, and the sickly-sweet fragrance that had surrounded me, and understood: I was supposed to read the rest of the prophecy within the smoke. But how was I to light it?

It took me the greater part of an hour to generate a spark from scraping two rocks together. Once I'd set the end of the incense stick alight, I stuck it upright in the snow and sat back on my heels to watch.

The smoke curled up into the cold, glittering sky, and as I watched, the shape of it condensed into a perfect caricature of an old woman: the shaman.

The smoke version of the shaman opened her mouth and spoke words that seemed to originate from somewhere inside my head:

Jia Yi, the voice whispered, weaving into the corners of my mind as though the smoke itself were entering. *In your future . . . I see only death.*

I'd heard this part before, so I held my breath, waiting for the rest.

You will die before your grandmother. But the two of you will meet again. In the afterlife.

It was true—that *had* happened.

The smoke wavered in an errant breeze, almost dispersing out of existence, before condensing back into the shadowy figure of the shaman. *In the deepest level of death*, it said, *at the beginning and the end of the afterlife, you will find a weapon. A weapon with complete mastery over life and death.*

So the Bone Smith's hypothesis had been right: The sword was secreted in the deepest level. But what did "the beginning and the end of the afterlife" mean?

The smoke figure began to talk again, and I shifted my attention back to it, not wanting to risk missing anything.

The weapon can be used for good or ill, the smoke said. *It can restore the dead, and wreak havoc on the living.*

There will be a choice: sacrifice, or salvation.

By now, the stick of incense was almost burned to the stub. The smoke figure vacillated, the edges of it wavering. Then, as the last bit of incense crumbled to ash, the smoke drifted away upon a sigh of wind.

"Did you find what you needed?" the prince asked as soon as I reentered my house. He was sitting on the floor, his back against the wall, his long legs crossed before him. It occurred to me that he'd been waiting patiently for me for more than an hour.

He must really want that sword.

"Kind of." I bit my lip, the images swirling through my mind: the fluttering yellow fúlù, talismans to ward off evil spirits. The pungent, flameless smoke that had assumed the shape of the shaman. Hui Fen's expression as they begged me to stay safe. "I found out where the sword is meant to be buried, but . . ."

The prince's eyebrows rose incrementally. "But?"

"I still don't fully understand where it is." I admitted. "The information was in the form of a riddle that I'm not sure how to interpret." I needed to track down and ask my grandmother. She'd always been good at deciphering such puzzles. Besides, the longer I was away, the more likely it was that Lin would attack her again.

Drawing in a shaky breath, I added, "I need to go back into the afterlife. I think there's someone there who can help me."

A faint line appeared in the smooth marble of Essien's

forehead. "The same afterlife with the ghosts who attacked you? The same afterlife you're having nightmares about?"

I threw him a sheepish look. The bruise on his jaw where I'd hit him was beginning to ripen. "Yes."

The line between his brows deepened. "And you mean to leave right away?" It had been subtle, but I hadn't missed the way his gaze had flicked to the floor and then back up.

With forced nonchalance, I gave a shrug. "I have to. We need to find the sword before the others do—" I stopped and clamped my mouth shut. I'd said too much.

The prince stood, and I was abruptly reminded of how tall he was. My back stiffened as he drew closer. Narrowing his eyes, he said, "What 'others'?"

I fisted my trembling hands behind my back. "Well, I . . ." I wasn't sure how much to tell him.

With a stern raise of his eyebrow, Essien lowered his voice. "If I am to help, Lady Liu, you must be frank with me."

At this, I snorted. "I wasn't aware you were here to help, Your Highness. I rather thought you just wanted to keep an eye on me."

I might have imagined it, but had the corners of his lips twitched?

After a pause, he spoke. "If you are indeed going into the afterlife to find the Sword of Rechenblod, then it is my duty to aid you. It is, after all, a Lancaster relic." He leaned closer, a look of determination hardening the set of his jaw. "But in order to do that, I need you to tell me the truth. The *whole* truth."

I hesitated, weighing the benefits of telling him about the general. Perhaps it *was* wise to alert him. Perhaps he *could* help me.

The Yskians had been overthrown by General Hong Hao Mu in the last war, after all. It had been the general who had stolen the sword. Perhaps if Essien knew that Yske's greatest enemy was still searching for it, that might be somewhat . . . motivating.

So, I relented. "Do you remember how I told you some ghosts attacked, and tried to imprison me?"

Essien's mouth pressed into a grim line. With an infinitesimal nod, he assented.

"What I didn't tell you is that one of the ghosts was General Hong Hao Mu."

His mouth fell open. For a moment, he said nothing. Then he blinked, and choked out, "General . . . Hong Hao Mu?"

"You know, the man who overthrew Yske—"

"I am well acquainted with my country's history, Lady Liu," the prince interjected, his tone curt. "I'm just trying to come to terms with the fact that Yske's greatest enemy is still out there."

"Well, technically, Your Highness," I said, thinking of all the ghosts I was now able to see, "everyone who's ever existed is still out there."

Essien's mouth twisted in a bitter smile. "According to our faith, he was supposed to be in Hell, suffering for eternity. For being the usurper who stole the sword." He lapsed into a brooding silence, his attention seemingly miles away.

I curbed the impulse to roll my eyes. There really wasn't time to deal with Essien's existential crisis over the fact that everything he'd ever believed was wrong. "Yes, well, he lost the sword. In the afterlife. But now he wants it back." I fidgeted with my fingers. "He's trying to search for it as we speak. So you can see why I need to hurry."

"Indeed." Essien's focus snapped back to me. "That is quite

an alarming revelation." Absently, he rubbed at the back of his neck.

When he spoke again, he'd adopted the officious tone he'd always used when sat upon his throne. "Very well. I suppose we should devise a plan. And quickly, if we're racing against the usurper to find the sword."

I pursed my lips. "What sort of plan?"

He gave me a penetrating look. Then, he said, "You go into the afterlife, and I shall look after your body. Keep it from . . ." Something shifted in the depths of his eyes. *"Deteriorating."*

An image of the most recent healing session he'd given me flashed, unbidden, in my mind. The feel of his hands as they smoothed over my skin. The warmth that had washed through me as he repaired my decaying body. The pad of his thumb brushing gently, so gently, across my lower lip.

My face flushed hot. It had been so intimate. Uncomfortably so. Was it the same for him? Maybe not, if he was offering to do it again.

By now he was standing so near that I could feel the heat from his body. I could see the subtle tints of his eyes—mostly blue, but shifting to gray, like an encroaching storm. This close, the light smattering of freckles dusted across his nose was also visible.

I blinked and looked away. "You'd do that?" I could not help but sound incredulous.

With the most fleeting touch, he brushed his thumb over the curve of my jaw as if he, too, was remembering the times he'd healed me. Gently, he turned my chin to face him. "Yes."

My pulse started racing. Unconsciously, I leaned into his hand. "That's . . . very helpful of you."

It suddenly seemed like the effort required to keep breathing had increased exponentially. Trying to quell the labored rise and fall of my chest, I licked my lips.

Immediately, Essien's eyes darkened, dropping to my mouth. I froze. For a second, we stared at one another, completely still, both of us caught up in this interminable moment. Very slowly, Essien swallowed, the muscles in his jaw rippling.

Then, at precisely the same instant, we both pulled away, rupturing the charged atmosphere that had somehow formed between us. I stepped back, letting out a shivery exhale; he straightened, raking a hand through his hair, combing it back from his forehead. It just flopped down again, landing in a flawless curl, because of course it did.

I almost scoffed. Did everything Essien Lancaster do have to look so damned . . . perfect?

"It will give you the best chance of finding the sword. You'll be better off if you aren't worried about what's happening to your body while you're gone." The formalities were back, the spell between us broken. "If what you say about the general is true . . . That man already destroyed my country once. We cannot allow such a powerful weapon to fall into his hands again."

Something inside me shriveled, mortified. Of course it was only about the sword. Of course he wouldn't be offering to help me out of the goodness of his own heart.

Or for any other reason.

Really, it was foolish—utterly foolish of me—to entertain the idea that Essien could have any other motivation. Even if only a few moments ago he'd looked at me like . . . like *that.*

Mentally, I shook myself, dusting off my injured ego.

Regardless of how Essien did or didn't feel about me—he *could* prove to be useful.

Could I trust him, though?

If we found the sword, Essien planned to return it to his family—an idea I still found reprehensible. While it was true that General Hong had been a cruel warmonger, the Yskian king at the time wasn't exactly faultless, either. According to historical records, King Brennan Lancaster had slaughtered as many enemies as the general had. Perhaps, if some sources were to be believed, even more. Letting the sword pass back into Yskian ownership was, in my view, extremely unwise.

Searching the prince's face, I tried to find another solution to what he had proposed. But I could find none.

I supposed that allowing Essien to help me find the sword didn't necessarily mean I needed to give it to him, despite what I might have promised. And if this was the only way to avoid what had happened to my body last time, then . . .

"All right, you can help me," I said finally, forcing myself to maintain eye contact. "And, in return . . . I'll bring you the sword."

With that, I turned away.

After all, every good lie begins with a half-truth.

And every good betrayal begins with a lie.

Thirty-One

Present day

We arrived back at Throft Hall in the middle of the night. I leaned heavily on Essien as he led me through a secluded back entrance. After two long journeys on horseback, my legs were burning, my backside in such agony that I would willingly welcome death. Essien's healing magic, permeating into me whenever we made contact, was probably the only reason I, as an inexperienced rider, had survived.

During our many rest stops, we had solidified our scheme. The plan was, after I died, he'd keep my corpse hidden, buried in snow to stop it decaying, and visit me frequently. If he noticed any injuries, he'd heal them straightaway. Hopefully, with this plan, I would manage to prevent the horror of my most recent resurrection.

Avoiding the main castle so as not to run into Rowan, Essien brought me to a guesthouse secreted in a corner of the grounds. Its rooms were garishly bright compared to my own modest dwelling, and I wilted in shame at the stark contrast. I knew Essien barely noticed the difference—or if he did, believed it charming—but privileged people rarely do. It's those of us who've had to live with the reality, not the sanitized, romanticized version, who see such things with painful clarity.

As I stood in the middle of a sumptuously decorated sitting room—all velvet chesterfields and ottomans and other furniture I didn't know the names of—Essien pulled back a rug, revealing a trapdoor neatly set into the polished hardwood floors. He raised it. Descending beneath the floor was a ladder. The space below was several degrees cooler than outside, and I shivered as I climbed down.

At the bottom was a corridor, entirely made of stone. The prince grabbed a torch from a sconce and led me along, the flame flaring like a beacon, shadows dancing on the walls. We seemed to be tunneling down, deep underground, and I felt suddenly claustrophobic, desperate to see the sky.

Finally, after what seemed like eons, we reached a wooden door, its iron crossbars rusted as though it was rarely used. After producing a small brass key from some inner pocket of his coat, the prince unlocked the door, which opened with a wail.

Inside was a narrow bed, a small writing desk with a single chair, a chamber pot, a cast-iron bath, and a set of shelves upon which sat a number of lidded jars. Directly across from us was another door, similar to the one we'd come in through, and when I looked up, another neat trapdoor was fitted into the ceiling. The entire room—walls, ceiling, floors—was lined in stone, apart from the three doors mentioned.

"What is this place?" I said, alarmed at how harshly my voice cleaved the silence.

The prince turned to face me, the torch illuminating his

features with an eerie glow. "It's a safe room." He pointed to the opposite door, then to the trapdoor in the roof. "That door leads to another sally port that burrows under the walls of the castle and opens into the surrounding forest. And the trapdoor leads to a remote part of the estate. My family built these secret rooms and escape passages into every Lancaster castle. In case of an attack."

I examined the two doors, contemplative. Then I said, my voice flat, "In the event of an attack, you would come here to hide out, while your soldiers fight on your behalf?"

"I said my family built this room," he replied, a brittle edge to his words. "*Not* that I would use it."

Chagrined, I clamped my mouth shut. As usual, the prince had surprised me into silence. When would I unlearn my inherent hatred of a Lancaster royal?

Essien noticed my silence. "Is something wrong?"

Breathing an exhale, I admitted, "I think I've judged you too harshly."

He cocked his head. "Judged me?"

"For being a Lancaster."

He chuckled, his dimples making a reappearance. "Judge all you like, Lady Liu. Most of us Lancasters are idiots."

I raised one eyebrow at him. "Do you exclude yourself from that assessment, Your Highness?"

Still smiling, he shook his head. "No. In fact, I am probably the biggest idiot of them all." He fell silent as his gaze caught mine, his expression morphing from humor into something far . . . softer.

My pulse began hammering harder and faster. Embarrassed,

I turned my attention to my surroundings. As I inspected the meager contents of the room, the prince busied himself lighting several tallow candles. Moving closer to the orbs of light, I ran a finger along the desk's polished wood-grain surface. It was remarkably free of dust.

"Where will you put me?" I asked, suppressing the waver of fear in my voice. "And how will you get the snow?"

The prince placed the torch in a sconce fixed to the wall. "As I said, I will come here every day, shovel some snow above"—his eyes flicked to the trapdoor—"and bring it down here. You'll be in the bathtub."

I leaned closer to the tub, seeing that it was plumbed with pipes into the floor. "And you'll come here for as long as it takes?"

"As long as it takes. I promise." I could tell his words were sincere; he meant what he said.

"Won't your servants think it strange?" I continued pushing, dragging out time, my mind trying to find a way to escape what was inevitable. "A prince, shoveling snow each day?"

"No. All of them have worked with my family for a very long time. They're used to Lancaster eccentricities." Catching sight of my scandalized expression, he added quickly, "Not mine, of course. I'm sure you're aware that some of my brothers have certain . . . proclivities . . ."

"You mean, like Rowan?"

A scowl settled across Essien's features. "Yes, like Rowan. Trust me, they won't question me simply shoveling snow." Then he muttered, more to himself, "Not that they care what I do, regardless."

My heart squeezed in my chest, but I forced the feeling down. I couldn't afford to dwell on my pity for Essien Lancaster—not when I was about to leave the living realm entirely.

For several long seconds there was an awkward silence, before my discomfort forced me to break it. "What if all the snow melts?" Lìdōng, the start of winter, was creeping ever closer. And once winter arrived, we'd have a good few months before the snow receded. But my nerves were jangling inside me, and I needed to know every potential outcome.

Prince Essien gave a small half shrug. "Let us hope it doesn't come to that. But if I must, I will go to the mountains and cart ice back from there."

Something twisted inside me, painfully. I turned to face him and straightened my shoulders. I needed to ask the question, the one that had been haunting me. "Why are you doing this?"

A look of surprise flitted across Essien's face. "Doing what?"

"Being so . . ." I wrinkled my nose. "*Kind.* I mean, you healed me, three—no, four—times now."

Had he simply been keeping me safe, and close at hand, so I could retrieve the missing Lancaster relic for him?

Or was his kindness genuine, and he'd done it simply to be . . . honorable?

The truth was, I couldn't tell. I was still unfamiliar with his moods, his expressions; to me, he was too hard to read.

"It is the right thing to do, is it not?" Essien's eyes met mine, as though challenging me. "If I were dying, and you had this power, wouldn't you save me?"

"No," I retorted. "I'd let you fucking *die.*"

Momentarily, the prince's eyes widened. But then he threw back his head and laughed, shaking with the effort of keeping quiet. I glared at him until his mirth died down and he wiped his eyes. "You see, this is why I like you. You're not afraid to speak your mind."

My stomach did a flip. *He likes me?* What sort of improbable alternate reality was this?

Maybe this wasn't reality. Maybe I was actually asleep, or dead, and this was just some sort of hyperrealistic, protracted hallucination. Because, this . . . a Liu and a Lancaster, talking civilly to one another? This couldn't be real. Couldn't be right.

"By the way," he added. "I don't believe you. I don't truly think you'd let me die."

I pressed my lips together, fuming. He was right, of course. I'd leaped in front of Lin's blade for him, hadn't I? I'd gone back to save him from the Spyrre. Even *I* didn't quite know why. Probably to pay back him back for whatever dubious debt I owed him.

"Maybe not," I grumbled, half jokingly. "But don't worry: It doesn't take much to change my mind."

He grinned and leaned against the wall, arms crossed, watching as I continued my inspection. I peered at each bottle on the shelf, ran my hand across the bedspread, slid a finger down the cool stone wall. After a few beats of silence, he spoke.

"So what is it like?" He tilted his head, a pensive expression settling on his face. "The afterlife?"

"It's just like here. But more . . . ghostly."

His eyebrows lifted. "'Ghostly'?"

"There are spirits. The world is darker. Gloomier. And sometimes things look strange . . . more . . . fuzzy around the edges."

Essien appeared to ponder this. "Hmm," he said after a beat. "That is nothing like what I've been taught."

Raising my head, I looked at him. Really looked at him.

Until only recently, I'd hated Essien Lancaster with all my heart. And he'd hated me. I'd been raised that way, born with animosity burning in my veins.

Now? I was not so sure.

"I don't think *anything* is like what we've been taught," I murmured, then resumed my pacing.

He was silent again for a few minutes. Then he said, "Before you do this, will you promise me something?"

I stilled. "What?"

"That you'll come back."

I turned to face him slowly. "With the sword?"

He pushed off the wall and drew closer, until he was standing right before me. I stood my ground, resisting the urge to flinch at his proximity.

When he spoke, it was in a low murmur. "With or without the sword."

For a second, the entire world went silent as I stared at him, gobsmacked. Then every sensation came rushing back. Warmth, flushing through my body. My pulse pounding in my temple. The sudden tightness in my chest. Perhaps I'd gotten it wrong. Perhaps . . .

No. I had to quash those thoughts. Immediately. I was about to willingly enter the death realm, not knowing what I would encounter, the things I'd have to do to defeat the general, or when I would be back—if ever. For my own peace of mind, I couldn't afford to make presumptions about Essien Lancaster's intentions.

And equally, I could not give him empty assurances. "You know I can't promise that."

"Promise something else then," he urged.

I swallowed, the movement suddenly so conspicuous given how self-conscious I'd become. Regarding him with a wary look, I said, "What's that?"

A muscle tensed in his jaw, his gaze still locked on mine. "Stay safe." He raised his hand slightly, as though reaching for me, but then dropped it again.

My voice was but a whisper. "You know I can't promise that either."

A small furrow formed between his eyebrows, and he passed a hand across his mouth and chin. "Very well then," he said eventually, shoving his hand in his pocket and fishing something out. "If you really must throw yourself headlong into danger, then at least . . . take this."

It was some sort of pendant, wrought in gold, hanging on a chain. He held it up; I plucked it from his fingers, eyeing it admiringly. It was deceptively heavy, with a pretty filigree pattern embossed on the front—the usual, ostentatious Lancaster style.

"You're giving me this?"

One corner of his mouth lifted in a smile. "It's yours."

A small latch was set on the side. I pressed it. The cover swung open to reveal a clock face: twelve numbers and three hands, one of them ticking around, marking seconds.

A pocket watch. I'd never had any jewelry before, and although part of me felt strange about accepting this gift, the other part of me exulted in holding something so . . . magnificent. Something like this could probably keep my community fed for *months*.

Essien was still watching me. "Here, I'll help you put it on."

Giving him a dubious look, I turned around. He swept my

hair aside, the tips of his fingers feathering against my neck. My heart began to hammer so loudly that I was quite sure he could hear it.

He slipped the chain around my neck and fastened the clasp. The watch settled heavily against my chest, its cold nipping at my skin. It felt villainous, wrong, and oh so delicious to be wearing it.

I stared at it for a few moments, then spun to face him, startled to find he'd moved even closer. "But I don't understand," I said, looking up at him, my brows knitting. "Why?" It made no sense that Essien Lancaster would gift me his own pocket watch.

He gazed down at me, thoughtful. "I cannot fully fathom what things are like in the afterlife, Lady Liu." He stretched his hand out and, with the most delicate of movements, traced the outer curve of the watch. My face heated at the intimacy of the gesture.

"But I figured that you might need to, you know . . . keep track of the time. So you know how long you've been there." He lifted his finger and touched my chin—so gently—raising my face to his. "So you know when it's time to come back."

He stared into my eyes, his lips so near to mine. Both of us were breathing a touch too quickly, our exhales uneven. It felt like I couldn't quite expand my chest.

"What if I change my mind?" I blurted, unable to completely hide the tremor in my voice. Now that the moment was growing closer, anticipation was being crowded out by fear. The memory of my nightmare—Wen Bo's ghost speaking with my sister's voice—flashed up in my mind. "What if I decide not to go into the death realm after all?"

A pause. "Then that would be your choice, and I would support that." His voice was so low, so soft, I had to strain to hear him. The point of his finger still grazed my chin.

"You really mean that?" This whole time, I'd just assumed he was helping me to get the sword. But the way he . . . *looked* at me . . . told a different story.

He tilted his face closer, his mouth hovering just above mine. "I do." There was something hidden behind his words, his actions—an unasked question that had no answer.

For a moment, I wanted to lean in. To close the distance. In the past few days, I'd learned more about Essien Lancaster than I'd ever known before. What if I stayed? What if I had the chance to get to know him better?

But then the reality of our situation hit me. General Hong's words, in the dungeons: *Fengzhi Yuan is mine. The Shēngsǐ Sword belongs with* me. My grandmother's poisoned knife wound. And Lin, down in the second level of the death realm with Pópo.

Lin had had no compunction about killing her in front of me. Was it actually he who had poisoned her to begin with? Was that why she had a knife wound? Was that why he'd run away?

And if it *had* been him who'd done it—what was his motive?

No. I had to proceed with my plan. Blinking back tears, I stepped away. Abruptly, the pull between me and Essien dissipated, leaving nothing but empty space.

"I have to go." I took a deep, determined breath. "It is my duty."

It was time.

Carefully, I strapped my Bone Smith blades more firmly to my side. Once I had done so, I stood in the middle of the room.

For a moment, I considered saying a final goodbye, but then I stopped myself—it was too painful.

Essien's eyes never left mine as I began to focus, gathering all the disparate threads of my mind. I let my eyelids fall closed; focused on the feeling of emptiness in my body—on the fragility of my mortal, human self. My hands curled into fists; my muscles tightened; the back of my neck turned clammy, laced with sweat.

It was becoming easier, with practice, to summon death. I felt my qì, my life force, as it flowed out of my body, evaporating into the atmosphere like gently dispersing mist. First my core became numb, and then my limbs. My arms became floppy and nonresponsive, and as my legs buckled beneath me, I fell into Prince Essien's waiting arms.

"Farewell, Lady Liu," he whispered, and used his free hand to stroke a few stray strands of hair from my face. His fingers were so hot, almost scorching . . . Or was it just my skin, now that I was dying, becoming abnormally cool? A look of fierce determination came into his eyes. "I shall see you soon."

For a brief moment, I wanted to scream to undo it. I didn't want to die. Didn't want to enter the death realm. What if I never managed to come back? Would my corpse stay enshrined in Essien's hidden room forever? Until such a time came when, through death, disease, or simply him tiring of my presence, he would no longer care for my dead body? Until I disintegrated into dust and bones?

I supposed that was as it should be. But the thought filled me with dread.

Truth be told, I was scared. Petrified. I wondered when I would next feel the deep thud of my heartbeat jolting through my chest. When I might feel the tidal flow of my breath rushing in and out of my lungs. If I would even feel those things again. This time, I was planning to dive deeper into the death realm than I'd ever ventured before. This was risky, very risky. So much could, and probably would, go wrong.

I shut down those thoughts, steeling my resolve. I had made my decision, for better or worse. Already I was succumbing to the relentless creep of paralysis; my lids were drooping heavy. I had the sensation of floating. The world was going fuzzy; my pulse was slowing; all of my extremities were becoming weak and flaccid and completely useless.

I blinked slowly and looked up into Essien's face hovering above mine, lines of worry marring his brow. My words were slurred, but I managed to choke out, "I think you should . . . call me by my first name now. I think we're on a first-name basis." I swallowed, struggling to get the words out. "It's Jia, by the way. Not Jee-yah. Jia. I never told you . . ."

The prince's arms tightened as my body slackened further. My eyelids fluttered shut. As his face faded from view, I heard his voice echoing through the dark caverns of my rapidly receding consciousness.

"Ji-a," he said, trying to twist the word on his Yskian tongue. "Ji-a. I'm Essien."

His pronunciation wasn't quite right, I thought as the blackness took over.

It wasn't quite right, but it was enough.

Thirty-Two

THE FIRST LEVEL

Present day

The prince was still cradling my body when I awoke again, as a ghost. I stood, waiting until my vision cleared, watching him watching me. Reaching out, I tried to touch him, but my hand just went through his shoulder.

I balled my fist at my side. A lead weight of regret had settled low in my abdomen. Was it regret at leaving *him*? Or was it simply regret at leaving my life behind?

Either way, I could no longer give him comfort. So I checked that my Bone Smith weapons were still in place and, after a final backward glance, exited through the wall.

I'd lost time, up in the living world. And given that each level of the afterlife seemed to be murkier and more frightening than the last, I needed to get moving. I wanted to get as close to my village as possible before slipping into the second layer of death. Then, once I'd found my grandmother, we could untangle the riddle of the shaman's prediction together, before descending deeper into the afterlife, to the very last level, where the Shēngsǐ Sword was supposedly hidden.

And if I happened across Lin again, I'd kill him.

Stealing silently across the grounds, I hurried toward the boundaries of the expansive Throft Hall estate. The entire world was cloaked in gloom. I rubbed my eyes and blinked. The crescent moon hung like a fingernail among cottony wisps of clouds. Winking stars studded the inky sky, casting everything in eerie shadow.

Thankfully, it would be easier to enter or exit the Throft Hall grounds as a ghost. I could easily move through solid barriers, and I'd be unseen by the living guards stationed at the watchtower.

When I melted through the outer wall, however, I cursed, teetering on the banks of the river that skirted the perimeter of the estate. Its surface was completely still; the night sky reflected in the water was framed by skeletal trees. Every now and then there was a small splash, followed by a series of repetitively expanding rings that gently lapped against the bank. Fish? Or something else?

I'd forgotten about the river. In the living realm, the water was easily traversed by a bridge . . . but as a ghost?

I ground my teeth. In my current state, I couldn't walk on anything human-made. Briefly, I considered resurrecting temporarily to cross the bridge, then slipping back into the first level. But that would mean moving out of Essien's safe room, exposing my body to the elements—a risk I wasn't willing to take.

Sinking into a crouch, I peered into the water, thinking

through my options. Finally, I clenched my jaw. I'd made my decision.

Since I couldn't cross the bridge in my current state, I'd have to swim.

The back of my neck prickled; this was a haunted place. My grandmother had once told me that the Yskians, if they thought the Spyrre weren't effectively detecting magic, would sometimes take a suspected witch to a body of water and try to drown them. The idea being that a witch wouldn't die but a regular person would. Of course, most of the suspects drowned—considering that few of us magical folk had the ability to breathe underwater.

Or to resurrect.

I swallowed, my throat dry. After rising to my feet, I toed the edge. With my ghostly vision, which seemed attuned to the dark, I could see right down to the riverbed. The dirt edge cut away abruptly, dropping sharply into deep water. Several lithe, shadowy figures lurked near the bottom. I knew now what they were. Shuǐguǐ: the drowned ghosts. Spirits of the poor souls who had died, innocent, in the water.

Stalling, I went to grab the pocket watch, intending to see how much time had passed since I'd left Essien in the safe room. But I was unable to touch it. It was incorporeal.

I cocked my head, listening; there was no ticking. The second hand was still, frozen, eternally arrested in time.

Of course—it seemed obvious now. Objects in the living world didn't function in the ghost world, not unless they were wrought by the Bone Smith themself. Despite Essien's intentions, here in the afterlife his watch would be useless.

I turned my focus back to my task, and before I could change my mind, jumped feetfirst into the river.

The water closed over me as I plunged into the murky depths. It felt oddly warm—being dead, I was now cooler than the river. Once fully submerged, I began swimming to the opposite side.

It was a strange sensation, not needing to breathe, not feeling the usual burn of hypoxia in my lungs. The shuǐguǐ jostled closer, their eyes black and hungry, their skin deathly pale, their fingers strangely elongated. Dark hair swirled around their heads like crowns, and their mouths were hinged open in silent, perpetual screams.

It was difficult not to shudder, to focus on stroking my arms through the tepid water, on reaching the other side. Shuǐguǐ fed on qì, the life force of living mortals, leaving their victims to drown in their place. Maybe they wouldn't attack me, a fellow ghost.

One of the shuǐguǐ floated toward me, its black mouth stretching into a distorted grin, full of mossy teeth. I pushed myself to swim faster, kicking my legs with increasing panic.

Not fast enough. *What is dead can die again*, my mind thought frantically, as several long, icy fingers wrapped around my leg.

I screamed. The fingers tightened, tugged. I sank.

Wen Bo had told me that there were worse deaths than drowning, but in this moment, I felt like he was wrong. Drowning was *awful.* Though as a ghost, I didn't need to breathe, water still flooded my nostrils, my lungs, my mouth. It was warm, like blood, and the pressure caused unbearable pain.

The entire river's worth of shuǐguǐ descended upon me, grabbing at my body with jointed fingers. Local lore claimed this river was haunted, so no living person ever swam here. As a result, these guǐ were hungry. These guǐ were *starving.*

I'd been wrong about them not attacking ghosts. So utterly and completely wrong.

They fed on me, their vacuous eyes and ravenous mouths sucking at the remnants of my qì. They ripped apart my soul, feeding on the entrails of my energy. Until mercifully, everything went black.

By the time I'd died and reawoken, the shuǐguǐ had all dispersed. I slumped in relief. Though the method wasn't ideal, I *had* made it into the second level, which was where I wanted to be. But I couldn't allow myself to revel for long. Quickly, I ascended, treading water when I broke the surface. Now that I was even more dead, the water was warmer still.

I felt frayed, weak, like I'd fragmented into an array of untethered parts . . . the discombobulating feeling of being deeper in the death realm, I supposed.

Eventually I rolled over, feeling a dull, hollow ache deep in the marrow of my bones, and clumsily swam to the opposite shore, lugging my weapons alongside me. Emerging from the water dripping wet, I wondered what I looked like: pale skin glinting in the moonlight, cavernous mouth and bloodred lips, black hair long, tangled, and soaked with water.

As I'd expected, the second level of the afterlife was even murkier than the first. The edges of everything were blurred, as though the world had been drawn with a shaky hand. I groped my way through the relative darkness, once again waiting for my vision to clear, like it usually did when

I died. Gripping the hilt of my dagger, I crept into the close-knit trees.

In life, the forest was dark. Two levels into death and it was even darker. My ghost eyes could still just make out the shapes and shadows. Spirits from the first level, identified as such by their incorporeal appearance, glided between the trees. When I turned to face them, they almost seemed to disappear, although they continued moving and fluttering at the edges of my vision.

It took me a moment to understand: *I* was the second-level ghost that was haunting *them*. It seemed the further I descended, the less solid things appeared. Even time seemed less significant, slowing and congealing as I delved deeper and deeper into death.

At least I was finally on the same level as Lin and Pópo—provided neither of them had died again. Of course, I had no idea where they were or how long it would take me to find them. I rubbed my temples, thinking hard.

Before her first-level ghost had died, Pópo had said she would travel to our village. But would she still be there? How differently did time pass in the land of the living, compared with the second layer of death?

There was only one way to find out, really. Our village, nestled at the foot of Fengzhi Yuan's tallest mountain, Gui Ku Shan—Crying Ghost Mountain—lay to the north. I'd travel there. Hopefully, my grandmother would still be there, waiting.

Usually it would take me days to cross the border from Yske to Fengzhi Yuan on foot, although perhaps I could get there faster as a ghost since I wouldn't need to sleep. Still, it irked me that it would take even more time to get home. I couldn't shake the memory of Lin with his knife held to Pópo's neck. Or the knowledge that Pópo had hidden an unhealed stab wound from all of us, for a whole year. Why had she kept it a secret?

Everything I'd thought I knew about Pópo's death was wrong, it seemed.

In the recesses of my memories, images flashed up of the time when Lin had suddenly abandoned me. It coincided with an abrupt deterioration in Pópo's condition, which began a slow decline that would plague her—and finally kill her—over the ensuing year.

Was it *Lin*? Lin who'd tried to kill my grandmother? Was that why he'd run away?

Perhaps it wasn't just the circumstances around Pópo's death I'd gotten wrong. Perhaps I'd been wrong about Lin the whole time, too. Once, I thought I'd known everything there was to know about him. But I was starting to realize that wasn't the case.

I have to get to Pópo, I thought, tamping down my desperation. The longer I tarried, the more likely Lin might attack her again. *There's no use loitering here and wondering how much time it might take.* The only thing to do was get started.

Grasping my knife handle, I began to walk. In this level, shadows swayed and shifted. Slivers of moonlight flitted across the ground, disorienting me. The edges of my vision were blurry, translucent, and ill-defined, and occasionally things seemed to move, as if the very trees were shifting. I lost my direction several times. Every now and then I'd be following a pathway, the rising moon suspended in the sky behind me, only to find that the path had looped around and suddenly the moon was in front.

Just as I was passing under a particularly dark archway formed by the thickset branches, something white flashed through the trees. My skin tightened, cold with dread. I drew my knife and held it aloft as I peered into the darkness.

When I spotted it, I gasped. A horse, one so majestic that I could barely look away. I was no friend of horses, as had become abundantly clear over the preceding weeks, and they were no friends of mine. But this one . . . this one was *magnificent.* Its pale, slightly opalescent coat shone, as if it had been fashioned from the light of stars.

A ghost horse. Perhaps one of the Yskian horses that had died, then died again, bringing it to the second level. We watched each other cautiously, neither of us moving.

How did Essien talk to these creatures? I strained to remember, though truth be told I'd always been so nervous around the beasts that I'd barely paid attention. From what I could recall, he'd murmured low words and approached them carefully, stroking their necks when he got close.

Maybe I could try to copy him? Softly, I clicked my tongue. The horse's ears pricked up, its nostrils flaring, the silver sheen of its long tail flicking.

Incredibly, the horse allowed me to sidle closer until I was standing right by its shoulder. A female, I noted, now that I was close. She even allowed me to rub the short fur between her eyes.

She gave a soft whinny, nuzzling into my palm, and I giggled. "You like that?" I whispered, stroking her velvety muzzle, marveling at the way it gleamed, spectral in the moonlight.

So focused was I on the horse that I didn't notice, at first, what was behind me. Not consciously, at least. Somehow, my body recognized its presence before my mind registered the fact.

Goose bumps sprang out across my arms. A chill trickled down the back of my neck. I shivered.

Who's there? I almost said, my hand slowing on the horse's flank. But instead of speaking, I held my tongue, and slowly turned around.

The ghost stared at me, completely silent . . . until it opened its mouth to scream.

Thirty-Three

THE SECOND LEVEL
Present day

The sound pervaded me, scraping all the way down to my bones. The shock of it forced me to stagger back.

The ghost was doused in blood, a vine tethering them to a tree. How they had ended up there I did not know, but they wailed again: a sound of deep and harrowed mourning.

My entire body froze. I knew these ghosts. Or, at least, I'd heard of them. They were ghosts of those who had died in pregnancy or childbirth. The back my throat tasted bitter, like grief—though that didn't make sense, since I was dead twice over. But as I moved closer, drawn inexorably by the ghost's palpable anguish, I couldn't help but wonder:

Would my own mother's ghost have looked like this?

My throat felt thick. Whoever this ghost was, they'd been bound here. But why? Surely the people who had loved this ghost in life wouldn't have wanted them to end up like this.

Another of their wails tore through me, making me tremble, and I crept forward. Behind me, the horse whinnied and pawed at the ground, clearly distressed by the noise. I didn't know why I felt compelled to do it, but I had to help the ensnared spirit, had to free them from this everlasting trap.

The ghost turned their eyes on me as I drew closer. Their face was hideously deformed, as though the skin around their eyes and nose was melting. Their eyes dripped dark, bloody tears; their long, black hair was tangled; bloodstains marred the white of their dress.

Trying not to get too close, I lunged, my knife aloft, and cut the vine clean through. For a moment, neither of us made a noise.

I went as still as a statue, suddenly regretting my decision. The urge to help had dissipated as soon as I had severed the vine. And in a crystalline moment I realized: The ghost hadn't been trapped by the vine.

The ghost had used my pity to trap *me*.

Their blood-rimmed eyes turned on me, and they surged forward with inhuman speed. I stumbled backward, hacking at the ghost with my still-drawn blade. It slashed through the ghost's gown, a spray of black splattering across the fabric. But that did not deter them. They lurched at me, wrapping their hand around my neck, crushing, crushing, until I couldn't scream.

All I knew was survival as I fought and scrabbled, stabbing the ghost repeatedly until finally their grip loosened. With a heave, I kicked them off me, turned, and ran.

But something clamped around my ankle. A new vine from the forest floor had uncurled and wrapped itself around my calf. Even as I watched, the creeper slithered, spiraling higher and higher up my leg. An innocuous-looking flower clamped its petals on my shin, drawing blood.

Now that I had put some distance between me and the ghost, the forest was reclaiming them. Vines had wrapped around their torso, pulling them back to the tree. But the vines were trying to take me, too.

And now the whole forest floor was writhing.

I screamed, and tried to tug my leg free, only for a second vine to snap around my other calf. "Help!" I cried, to no one in particular, just as dozens more plants around me began to unfurl their leaves.

Spurred into action, I drew the Bone Smith's knife and hacked at the sentient vines. There was a hiss, and the vines temporarily retracted, allowing me to jerk away. I stumbled over to the ghost horse, scrambled onto her back, reached for the reins, and . . .

My hand went right through.

Rising panic flooded my chest. The horse must have died while wearing its tack, and here in the afterlife the bridle didn't have form. I was no horsewoman in the living world, and I was sure that I would be equally clumsy in death. Here there was no Essien Lancaster to hold me steady, arms tight around my waist.

Instead, I clamped my thighs tighter and clung on to the horse's neck as she spurred into a gallop, bouncing me so hard my teeth clacked together.

Branch-tangled vines snaked down from above. I raised my knife, intending to hack at the creepers, but they were ready. The vines wrapped around the knife and began to wrest it from my hands. I screamed, only just managing to tear it from their grasp.

"Faster!" I bellowed. Vines whipped and lashed at my face and arms while I rode, beads of blood welling from the linear welts they caused. I fought the plants off, urging the horse to go faster, terror seizing my entire body in a painful, nightmarish grip.

We'd been fleeing for a while before we came across the open road. The Stone Road—the most dangerous thoroughfare of all. Weaving through several territories, bisecting Qian Xin Lin, in the living world it was no place for someone like me to be traveling alone on horseback. Though, judging from the attacking forest, here in the second level of the underworld, safety *anywhere* was not a given.

Having escaped the grips of the forest, the horse dropped in speed, finally slowing to a walk. This allowed me a chance to assess my situation. Things felt wrong, unsettled, as if I didn't belong here, this deep in the death realm; with my resurrection magic, perhaps I retained a vestigial spark of life that the underworld rebelled against. Perhaps this was why the ghost had attacked me, and why the forest had, too. The horse had seemed safe, so presumably it was me—the afterlife trying to expel me since I did not truly fit in.

Well, fuck you, I thought bitterly, making a rude gesture at the forest. It would take more than a ghost tied to a tree and a few creepy vines to get rid of me. I was pretty much an expert at not fitting in.

Now, though, I faced another quandary. If I'd thought normal horse riding was bad enough, then ghost riding was worse.

The mirage of a saddle and unusable reins meant I was using muscles I never knew I had. Plus, here there was no Essien, and no healing magic, to continually repair my injuries.

We plodded for some distance, but didn't make it far before I was too sore to continue. I kept pushing until we reached Xinfei He, the river that ran alongside the Stone Road as it cut its way through the forest. At least I was still heading in the right direction: My village lay directly north.

There was a point, just inside the Fengzhian border, where the river went around a sharp bend, branching off into a separate creek before plunging into a waterfall. It was here, in the fork, halfway down a rocky outcrop, that Lin and I had once built a cave shelter. A secret hideout, of sorts. We'd used it on some of our longer hunting trips, or to hide from others . . . or sometimes just to spend time together.

Without being consciously aware of it, I found myself directing the horse there. When we neared it, I slid off her back, my entire body stiff and sore, my chafed inner thighs screaming with pain. *Just for a little bit*, I thought, scrambling onto the rock ledge, before pushing apart the trailing branches that hid the entrance to the cave. I'd camp here only as long as it took to regain energy, and then continue on to my village to look for Pópo. It was the safest place to stay if I couldn't continue riding.

The location had been strategic when Lin and I had set it up. For one, it was completely hidden. The entrance was angled so that we could see out if we wished to but intruders could not see in. Its position on higher ground gave us a clear view of the Stone Road and across the river to Qian Xin Lin, giving us the advantage over any enemies long before they discovered us. Plus, being near the confluence of two water bodies gave us ample drinking water—not that it mattered in my current state, of course.

Once inside the cave I dropped to my hands and knees, crawled into the far corner of the shelter, and curled up in a ball. My core muscles were aching, my legs were in agony, I was covered in cuts and lacerations from the sentient vines of the forest . . . and to top it all off, I was really, really fucking angry. All I wanted to do was continue my journey, but my body had thwarted me, again.

If only the prince were here, I thought. He'd be able to take away this pain. I hoped Essien would keep his word, and heal my wounds, not just the decay. If he did, then perhaps my injuries down here would heal, too, and I'd be able to get back on the horse sooner.

My chest squeezed when I thought of Essien. It discomfited me to realize that I . . . actually missed him. I missed the way he looked at me, the warmth of his hands on my skin, even the clumsy way he said my name. Or maybe I was mostly missing the person I became when I was with him: more gentle, more patient, just more . . . good.

I sighed, pressing a hand to my chest. I'd always thought my heart was cold and stagnant, and not just because I was dead. My heart had hardened when Lin betrayed me. Would a friendship like Essien's be enough to soften it again, to turn it back into beating flesh?

I'd spent my whole childhood with no friends, being bullied, building up walls that no one except Pópo and Hui Fen could get through—and then, later, Lin. Until even he, the one person outside my family whom I'd grown close to, had abandoned me. Lin's treachery had been like the final shovelful of dirt upon a grave. His actions cemented, once and for all, my general wariness of others.

Never trust. Never let people in.

Really, my forced separation from Essien Lancaster could only be a good thing. I was letting him get dangerously close to the real me.

Plus, regardless of how *I* felt, or the nice things he had said . . . he was probably only using me to recover the Sword of Rechenblod. To curry favor with his despotic family.

I curled up tighter, hugging my knees to my chest, and watched as a ghost beetle moseyed its way across the floor. It was better for everyone if I tried to forget about the Lancaster prince, to quash the unfamiliar fondness that fluttered in my chest. But as soon as I forced myself to stop thinking of Essien, my traitorous mind strayed to Lin.

I suppose I could not be blamed—in this cave, the echoes of Lin were uncomfortably apparent. There were too many reminders of the times we'd spent here, together. Better times. If I searched the cave, I was sure I'd find the evidence: the charred remains of an extinguished campfire. The brittle, dried-out grass beds we'd made here when we'd camped. Our names scratched into the wall.

Stop it, Jia, I chided myself, tucking my hands beneath my armpits. My eyes squeezed shut, as though that alone could disperse my memories.

And then I sensed it. Some sort of movement outside the shelter. A vibration in the air currents, a subtle shifting of the shadows.

My eyelids sprang open. "No," I whispered, suddenly terrified. What was it? I was in the death realm. No one was supposed to know this place. No one had ever been here with me before. No one except for . . .

Mere moments later I was already up, brandishing my knife . . . when someone ducked through the cave entrance.

Thirty-Four

One year ago

My heartbeat thumped, thunderous in my ears.

Tightening my hand on my bow, I drew back the arrow. My right arm shook as I pulled my elbow back into full flexion. Through the trees, I set my sight on the boar that was nosing at the forest floor, completely unaware of my presence.

But before I could loose the arrow, another one whizzed past my head.

"Mā de!" I cursed under my breath as the arrow missed the boar by several yards. Its head whipped up, and it gave a deep grunt. Fury welled in my chest, white and incandescent.

Lin. That foolish bastard. If only he hadn't taken the shot! Not only had he missed; he'd spooked the boar, alerting it to our attack. That damned boar could have fed our village for weeks—or longer, if we were careful to preserve the meat.

"What the hells, Lin!" I hissed over my shoulder. Why had he missed? He *never* missed. Neither of us did. It was one of the reasons we'd been able to keep our community fed, how we'd managed to stave off famine.

Lin emerged from the bushes, lowering his bow, his mouth set in a stubborn line. He knew I was about to lash out at him and was ready to defend himself. He opened his mouth to speak, but instead of a sarcastic comment, he gave a yell.

"Jia!" His eyes went wide. "Watch out!"

I turned just in time to face the boar; the boar that was now charging at me. I dove to the side, flung out an arm, my hand splayed, to break my fall.

A scream tore from my lips as I landed heavily, jarring my wrist. In a move that was either extremely brave or completely stupid, Lin ran at the animal, waving his arms and bellowing.

Somehow, it worked. The boar ran off—bolting past, narrowly missing me, then crashing through the undergrowth in the opposite direction.

I let out a shaky breath as I rolled onto my knees. My hands were trembling, pain reverberating up my arm. Cradling my wrist to my chest, I bit back a sob, not wanting to show any weakness, especially in front of *him*.

Lin was by my side. He'd moved so quickly. "Are you hurt?" he said, concern etched across his features. Dropping to one knee beside me, he reached for my injured hand. I flinched away. The movement was excruciating.

"Come on." Fleetingly, he touched my shoulder. "We're close to our cave. I need to take a look."

Once we were in our secret hideout, Lin tore a strip of fabric from his shirt. By now, my wrist was swelling, the spongy flesh throbbing. Thankfully, though, I was able to move it. I poked it with one finger, promptly wincing at the pain. "I don't think it's broken. Only sprained."

Lin took my hand, his brow creasing, his hair all mussed from our hunt. Leaning closer, he began to wrap the bandage around my injury. His large hands cradled me so gently; his fingers barely brushed my skin. The only light was the faint glow from the cave opening, which lit his profile, highlighting the errant curls that crowned his head like a halo.

I swallowed. My tongue felt too big for my mouth. He was so near . . . If I leaned in just slightly, and tilted my head just so, our lips would meet. How often had I imagined this? How often had I fantasized about kissing him? We'd known each other since I was ten. Now I was sixteen. And Lin? His true age was unknown, but he couldn't have been more than a year or two older.

Over the six years we'd known each other, we'd grown up together, hunted together. And in the past year, what had begun as innocent friendship—the inside jokes, the secret looks, the occasional casual touch—had transitioned into . . . something else.

For me at least. He'd never shown any sign that he felt the same in return.

Finally, he finished wrapping my injury, and as he leaned back on his heels, I glared at him. "What happened out there?" I said, unable to hide my bitterness. "You cost us a month's worth of meat!"

I was only too aware that my fury was misplaced. While my words made it sound like I was angry at Lin, in truth I was more angry at myself. For being silly enough to develop feelings for my oldest childhood friend.

Lin turned to look at me, his eyes glittering in the dim light. "I missed, that's all—"

"But you never miss!"

Something had gone awry with Lin for him to miss. I knew him so well that I hadn't failed to notice how distracted he was of late. For weeks he'd been acting strange. Distant. Oddly jittery.

But what was it? What was wrong? Was it something to do with me? Had he figured out that I liked him—in ways not strictly platonic—and was trying to push me away?

He scrambled to his feet, crossing his arms: a defensive posture. I stood, too, matching him. Scowling, he said, "Well, I did this time, all right?"

I took a step forward, ignoring the pain in my wrist. Ignoring the way my pulse sped up at his nearness. Ignoring his smell, the heat of his body, the way he towered over me. My head had grown hot, the back of my neck clammy.

"I had it." I glowered at him, eyes narrowed. "You shouldn't have interfered."

His nostrils flared. "I was trying to *help*. I don't think you realize how dangerous boars are—"

I gave a vicious laugh. "Oh, I realize. *I* wasn't the one stupid enough to run after it!"

"I wasn't thinking straight, okay? I was scared you'd get hurt!"

What had happened to Lin lately? As he'd matured, he'd become increasingly overprotective, treating me like I was just some helpless girl who always needed saving—even if it endangered himself.

Drawing myself up to my full height, I hissed, "If you're so scared, Lin, then maybe next time you should leave the dangerous things to *me*."

He didn't back down, just glared at me. "Maybe next time, Jia, you should . . . just . . . try to be less distracting!"

"Distracting?" My voice was rising, echoing in the small space. "How am I *distracting*?"

He blew out a frustrated breath and scrunched his eyes shut, like he was in pain. "Just leave it, okay? You don't understand—"

With my unbandaged hand, I grabbed his shirt, bunching it hard in my fist. "Then *make* me understand! You're talking riddles! And acting weird! Why have you been so *weird* lately?" I realized now: All my recent frustration was bubbling to the surface.

He didn't fight back; he just closed his fingers around my wrist. "I thought it was obvious—"

"*What's* obvious?"

Lin's gaze fell on me again. There was fire burning in those amber depths. For a long, loaded moment, he didn't say anything. He just stared at me, his jaw working. When he finally spoke again, his voice shook. "That I'm in love with you."

I reeled, my eyes locking on to Lin's. He was shaking, his face flaming with repressed rage. He was not happy. He was furious. He was *fuming*.

He did not look like a boy in love.

I tugged my wrist away and took a shaky step back. "What?" It was the only word I could manage.

He grimaced. "I'm in love with you. Okay?"

"No," I spluttered, panicked, shaking my head as though trying to clear his words. "No, you're not."

He ground out, "I am."

I shook my head harder. "Don't, Lin."

"Why not?" The words were spoken quietly, but I heard the simmering anger. The veiled threat. Somehow, this was worse than rage.

"Don't . . . toy with me!" I let out a sob, which choked off my words. "You know how I feel about you. You *know.* If you're lying, Lin, if this is some sort of *game*—"

Lin reached out, grabbed my waist, pulled me to him, our bodies flush. "Does this feel like a lie?" he growled. He reached up, cupped the back of my head. Tenderly, he touched his lips to the swell of my cheek, his voice dropping to a whisper. "Xiǎo è'guǐ. Does this . . . feel like a game?"

Xiǎo è'guǐ. *Little demon.* He'd given me that moniker years ago, because of my temper, which he was fond of provoking in amusement. But the way he said it now, breathed against my skin . . . it was the same, yet somehow so, so different.

I shivered. This was excruciating. It was everything I ever wanted, and yet—

Although I tried to fight it, I couldn't help reacting as he made his way down, planting soft kisses along my jaw. I let out a small gasp; in response, Lin whispered my name longingly against my skin.

This was it. This was the moment. I tugged his face up and pressed his lips to mine.

And then we were kissing: furiously, frantically, painfully, ecstatically. He grasped my face as lips and tongues collided, his body pushed up against mine. I wrapped my arms around his shoulders, pulling him even closer.

It was like everything I'd experienced in my life had been tilted on an axis, an angle that was now righting itself. As if Lin and I had been walking beside each other, but at two different speeds, and now suddenly we'd fallen in step.

He stopped and pulled away. I would've stumbled if he hadn't been there to steady me. Everything inside me was trembling, aching, yearning with an unmet need.

I raised my head, watching Lin. He was staring at something beyond me, his whole body strung taut, the expression on his face as dark as an approaching storm.

Placing a hand on his cheek, I turned his face toward mine. "What are you looking at?"

He dropped his gaze to mine, so scorching it almost burned. At first, he didn't answer; we stayed like that, so still, just staring at one another.

"Just you," he murmured. "I'm looking at you." Then, cradling my face with both hands, he pulled me to him, our lips crashing together once more.

And everything ceased to matter: my injured wrist, the escaped boar, our quarrels, our responsibilities. Everything else faded into nonexistence as Lin and I found each other.

Two lost souls, two outsiders, united by our pain.

Thirty-Five

THE SECOND LEVEL
Present day

Of course the person who'd found me in the cave was Lin. It was always Lin.

Why did we gravitate to each other so? Was it just the ghostly way of being pulled toward something that had once been significant in life? Or were our souls somehow intertwined, bound together until both of us were as twisted and black as the bare branches of burned trees?

Lin pulled up short. I'd been close enough to push the point of my blade into the soft flesh beneath his chin. He raised both hands in defense; he appeared to be unarmed.

"You did it, didn't you?" I spat. "You killed Pópo. Hui Fen told me there was an old knife wound on her corpse." I didn't bother with a formal greeting. We had too much history, too much pain and blood between us. We knew each other too well, and simultaneously not at all.

One look at his face told me it was true.

I blinked, my eyes gritty. "Why?"

He bared his teeth; I could not tell whether he was trying

to grimace or to grin. "If I told you, xiǎo è'guǐ," he said, "I would have to kill you."

Xiǎo è'guǐ—my nickname. Those two words dropped into my belly like a stone. It had been a year since I'd heard those words together. To hear them fall from Lin's lips in such a cruel, sarcastic manner did not make me feel nostalgic.

No. It made me fucking *angry.*

I advanced menacingly, forcing him backward to escape the bite of my blade. Pushing him toward the far wall of the cave until he collided with cold stone, I hissed, "*Bastard!* You've already killed me—"

He scoffed. "*Me*, killed you? Jia, *you* did this to yourself. With your impulsiveness and lack of care over your wellbeing—"

"*My* wellbeing? As if you care for my wellbeing!" I pressed my knife harder against his neck, pushing against the muscle and sinew, feeling a sick sense of satisfaction when he visibly swallowed.

I dropped my voice low, leaning in, my next words a monstrous caress. "Yes, you killed me, Lin. Even if not directly. You took away the person I love more than anyone. The only reason I am here, the only reason I am dead, is because *you* killed her. Twice."

For several long seconds, he didn't respond. He just stared at me, his eyes as dark as an abyss, his exposed neck stretched to avoid my blade. The only indication my words had affected him was a hint of tightness in his jaw.

He blinked at me slowly, then said, his voice unnaturally even, "I had my reasons."

I let out a bitter laugh. "Reasons! What reasons?"

He didn't respond immediately. Instead, his thick black

eyebrows drew down, until eventually he broke eye contact. "I . . . cannot tell you."

"Can't?" I said. "Or *won't*?"

He snapped his gaze back to me, his lip curling into a sneer. "Does it make a difference?"

I paused for a moment, weighing his words. "No." My tone was clipped. "I guess it doesn't."

Putting even more pressure on the blade, I took savage delight in the way his whole body tensed. "All that matters is that you lied to me, Lin. And that I know better now. I don't know why you killed her, but I do know"—here, to my immense irritation, my voice cracked—"that you only pretended to love *me* as a way of getting to *her*." Inside, my heart hardened and shriveled, remembering how he'd kissed me for the first and last time, a year ago, in this very cave.

Remembering how he had told me, in words and actions, that it was not a game.

Remembering how he'd lied.

"N-no, Jia," he stammered. "That was never—"

"*Liar!* You killed her. You tried to kill me. Everything that comes out of your mouth is a lie." Teeming with vehemence, I pressed harder, twisting the knife until a single drop of black blood beaded at its tip. A muscle flexed in his jaw.

"You're right," he said, after a short silence. "That's why you should leave. Leave this place. Resurrect. Why don't you go back where you came from, Jia?"

That asshole. He was trying to get me out of the way. "And leave you alone with Pópo, so you can attack her again?" I snarled. "Never!"

"Your grandmother isn't in this realm, she's in the next one down—"

"Because you killed her again, right?" My voice broke once more, and this made me even madder. I'd missed her—*again.*

I tightened my grip around the knife handle, my fingers stiff and cold. One stab. One little stab and he'd be dead. But then he'd be in the third layer of the afterlife, free to attack Pópo again, and I'd be stuck in this level, alone. Involuntarily, I let out a sob.

In an instant, Lin's entire demeanor changed. His face crumpled; he gave a reflexive jerk. His jaw worked as his gaze traced my face, lingering on my trembling lips, skirting down my arm and landing on my shaking hand.

He raised his eyes. I quailed at how dilated his pupils were, how their blackness encroached on the strange amber of his irises. "Okay, I admit it," he whispered, finally. "I did it. I . . . killed her."

I could barely speak; my words came out strangled. "Why would you *do* that? *Why*, Lin?"

"To help her."

"What?" I shook my head, unable to make sense of his words. "What does that even mean? How does killing her help her?"

The anguish displayed on Lin's face morphed into cold determination. "She needed someone to help her delve deeper into the death realm—"

"To find the sword?"

"Yes." He looked down at me, his eyes hooded. "I was that someone."

I could only stare at him, open-mouthed. My thoughts were tangled, like a mess of vines. Lin was the enemy . . . wasn't he? He had abandoned me, killed my grandmother, betrayed my entire community. And now he was telling me that he was helping Pópo this whole time.

Was it true? Or was he lying? Perhaps this was all part of his deception to make me believe he was on our side. He'd shown himself capable of lying to my face before. What made me think he wouldn't do so again?

Perhaps it was the remnants of *my* ridiculous feelings that made me so willing to make excuses for him, to contort my mind into believing the distorted truth he so wanted me to see.

We stared at each other, our breathless chests heaving, my mind spinning with half-formed thoughts. He was too difficult to decipher now. He'd changed too much. The boy I'd fallen in love with years ago was no longer present.

Perhaps that boy had never existed.

I adjusted the grip on my knife handle, tightening my hold. "Take me to her then," I said, through gritted teeth. "You say you're helping her—let her tell me so herself."

He grimaced. "No. You're in danger here. You need to get out. You should resurrect."

"Resurrect? No! I'm not leaving Pópo!" It was as if my dead heart was fracturing all over again.

"You have to." Suddenly, he blanched, his eyes sliding to the cave entrance. "Please, Jia. Leave." Had he heard something? Something I'd missed while I was caught up in my head?

Just a trick, I thought. *He's telling me to resurrect because he wants me out of the way.*

And in that moment, I made a decision.

"No." I released the pressure on my knife and took several steps back. "I won't resurrect. Not yet. I'm going down, Lin. I'm going to find her, and you can't stop me."

I needed to help my grandmother locate the weapon before General Hong found it. It made sense: In the shaman's vision, it was *me* who carried the sword. Searching for, and hopefully finding, the Shēngsǐ Sword—what Essien called the Sword of Rechenblod—was my destiny. I had to go down into the next layer. Pópo was never meant to do this alone.

I would help her. Not Lin. Me—whose loyalty she would never need to question.

Not bothering to wait for Lin's response, I closed my eyes, summoning my concentration. Knowing he was there was distracting, but I did my best to shut him out. Before long, the familiar numbing feeling started, just a prickle in my fingertips before spreading up both my arms, the cracks inside me widening, fracturing, my grip on this level becoming loose—

And then my focus was broken, because Lin had grabbed me, spun us, and slammed me against the wall, his own blade at my neck.

Thirty-Six

THE SECOND LEVEL

Present day

My eyes sprang open. Instinctively, I swung my knife in Lin's direction. He knocked it away; it bounced across the dirt ground. Then, he pinned me harder even as I struggled, the cold stone digging into the small of my back.

"Let me go!" I spat, making another futile attempt to escape. But he didn't budge. He was stronger than me: Formidable. Immoveable.

It suddenly hit me: He'd never been at my mercy. Before, he'd been humoring me, that whole time; if he'd wanted, he could have easily overpowered me, just like he'd done now.

He hadn't before, because he'd chosen not to.

How *fucking* condescending.

"What are you doing?" He cocked his head, his mouth twisted in the mockery of a smile.

I glared at him. "Going deeper." I tried to jerk out of his grip, snarling when I couldn't escape.

"No." He leaned forward and whispered one word into my ear: "Resurrect."

Anger spiked through my chest. "I won't."

His nostrils flared. "Why?"

"You know why," I shot back. "I know you just want me out of the way." I clawed at his knife hand, trying to break his grip. "Do you think I can't help, is that it? That I'm useless?"

He ignored my efforts, even as my nails gouged skin. "No." Something flared in the depths of his pupils.

"Then why?" I cried, exasperated. "What *is* the reason? Why do you want me to resurrect so badly?"

He stared down at me, his eyes darkening, like clouds swollen with the threat of rain. And for the first time, his knife hand wavered, like he was actually trembling. "Because I want you out of here. Because I want you safe. Because . . ." He swallowed. "Because I care."

With his free hand, he reached up and slowly, so gently, caressed my face. His other hand was still clasped in both of mine, holding his knife flush against the soft skin of my throat. Then, his voice dropped to a whisper. "Xiǎo è'guǐ," he said again, but this time it sounded like a plea.

A shiver ran through me at his touch. "You care?" I spat. I didn't believe it. Couldn't believe it.

"Yes," he whispered, running his thumb along the curve of my jaw. "I care about you. Always have and always will."

Panic drenched my insides, like ice, and I began rapidly shaking my head. "No." More tears pricked my eyes, and I had to choke my next words out. "You don't. This is just another one of your games. Why Lin? Why do you lie like this? Do you *enjoy* it?"

He erupted. "You think I enjoy this? You think I *enjoy* being this—this *obsessed* with you?" His hand dropped to my waist, pulling me closer until our bodies were pressed together. His blade scraped my neck; I hissed at the sting. "So obsessed, that even *death* did not release me?"

I gave a little whimper, my grip on his hand loosening for half a second. In response, he grabbed both my wrists, knife and all. Before I could react, he had slammed his hand—and both of mine—above my head, pinning me to the wall. Pain, jarringly sweet, reverberated down my arms.

Then he leaned in until his lips hovered above mine. So close, yet so far, a whole year's worth of heartache and empty space between them. I swallowed; it would be so easy just to close the distance. It would be our second kiss in this cave. An atonement of sorts.

But I knew: This was merely my body's desire. It was *not* the will of my mind. Nothing he said or did would ever make up for what he'd done to me. I shrank further back against the cave wall.

Lin continued, his voice bitter, full of venom. "I had to watch you for a whole *year*." His lips just brushed mine, and I shivered. He tilted his head further, the pose of someone about to kiss their lover. "Being unable to touch you . . ."

If my heart had still been beating, it would have faltered by now.

"Being unable to speak to you," he continued. "You . . . never even knowing I was there."

I ground out my words. "Stop . . . torturing me . . ."

"Me? Torture you?" He pulled his head back and gave a short and mirthless laugh. "Let me tell you, Jia Yi. You"—he leaned in harder, his hips grinding into mine—"torture me. Every moment. Every day. Eternally. Because no matter how much I tried—no matter how much I drank or fought or flirted with others, I was *never* free of you. I will *never* be free of you. Ever."

He shook with strain, his fingers tightening around my wrists. I bit my lip to stop myself from letting out another sob.

Lin's stare . . . his stare was disarming. His gaze dropped to my mouth, watching intently, almost hungrily, at the way my teeth dug into flesh. "Jia?" His voice had dropped dangerously low.

My chest constricted. I released my lip from my teeth, barely able to gasp out a response. "Yes?"

"What if I were to kiss you?" he murmured, a feral gleam sparking in his eyes. "What if I were to kiss you, right now?"

I tilted my face up to his. "That would be . . . a bad idea."

"It would be." He grabbed my chin, drawing my face closer to his, his actions incongruous with his words. "The worst idea."

I quivered beneath his hands. "I hate you," I spat. But even as I said it, my traitorous lips parted.

"I hate you more," he said. I gave a little gasp as he leaned closer, my nostrils filled with his scent—the smell of cold, still air before it snows.

He let go of my wrists and ran his fingertips down my neck, in a gesture that was almost . . . tender. I could feel the faintest brush of his mouth against mine. This was it. He was going to kiss me. And I hated myself because—in that moment . . . I wanted him to.

But he didn't kiss me. Instead he said, his mouth a hair's breadth from mine, "What is that around your neck?"

I was panting. "What is what around my neck?"

"This," he said. His hand traveled farther down, until

his fingers were splayed across my chest. With the pad of his thumb, he traced the skin around the pocket watch, circling it.

He planted a soft kiss on my jawbone, and I sighed, my treacherous body tilting my head to allow him better access.

"It's . . . a watch . . ."

"A watch from where?"

I shivered as he moved his head down, his hand still caressing my chest, his lips trailing along the sensitive skin on my neck. "Essien Lancaster."

"Did you steal it?" Lin raised his head to smirk at me. "Wicked girl."

"No," I said. "He gave it to me."

Lin straightened abruptly. The loaded tension ruptured. "He gave it to you?" He glared at me. "He *gave* it to you?"

"Yes. We're friends now."

He gave a scornful laugh. "*You* are friends? With *him*?"

Rage tore through my chest, and I shoved Lin off me so hard he stumbled back a few paces. "What, like it's so far-fetched?" I hurled the words at him. "You think I'm not good enough to be friends with a prince?"

"No!" Lin pulled a face. "*He* is not good enough for *you*."

Neither of us spoke. That feeling, the string that had drawn us together, had snapped in the most brutal way. Now nothing but hostility hung between us. I crossed my arms tightly, refusing to let him get the better of me.

Suddenly, a look of alarm flashed across Lin's face. He strode to the cave entrance, scanning the valley below.

Panic rose inside my chest. Instantaneously, our fight was forgotten. "What's wrong?"

He didn't answer. Instead, in a single swift movement, he whirled and grabbed me, clutching my body against his.

"What are you doing—" I cried, struggling—in vain, for he just tightened his hold on me and clamped a hand over my mouth.

"Shhh." His lips tickled my ear, his eyes on the cave mouth. "He's here. He's here. General Hong is here."

"He's here?" My words were muffled against Lin's hand. My stomach flipped; the general wasn't supposed to be this far down in the afterlife. He was supposed to be above us, in the first layer, close enough to the living world to launch his attack. I stared, eyes wide, at the cave entrance, almost as if General Hong and his subordinates might suddenly materialize before my eyes.

All was quiet and still.

But my mind was crowded with panicked thoughts.

I was running out of time. If I wanted to descend to the next level and find Pópo, I had to do it now. If the general caught me, who knew what he would do? I doubted he would regard my escaping his dungeon kindly. Once again, my nightmare—and Wen Bo's hacked-off tongue—flooded my mind.

This was my last chance.

Lin was motionless, his body tensed, ears cocked for the approaching army. With him distracted, I was able to close my eyes again, concentrating on slipping down into the third layer.

But the limpness of my body—and my sudden silence—must have alerted his suspicions, because I'd barely started to feel the numbness before he'd pushed me away from him and spun me to face him. Breaking my concentration, again. *Fuck.*

Grabbing my arm, he glared at me, his eyes so black, a starless sky. "Don't." So much pain loaded into that single word.

I twisted out of his grip, then dove for my knife, which still lay on the ground. If he was going to try to stop me from descending to the next level, well, then . . . I'd just have to stop him first.

Immediately alert, he lunged at me, catching my wrists just as I scooped up my blade.

We grappled, me trying to force the dagger toward him, him trying to wrestle it away. I lurched forward, the momentum from our shared weight causing us to tumble painfully to the ground.

He was stronger than me, but I was faster. I pinned him onto his back before he'd had the chance to react, shoving my knee on his chest. He still held my dagger wrist, and grunting with effort, I tried to wrench my arm away.

"Jia." Lin's arms trembled with the effort of restraining me. *"Stop this."*

"Then let me go!" Unable to wrest the dagger from him, I instead attempted to drive it in his direction.

"No!" he growled, through bared teeth. "Resurrect!"

We both shook, our muscles straining. But Lin refused to give up his hold.

Shoving the blade sideways, I twisted my elbow and slammed it into the side of his face. Bone met bone with a satisfying crunch. He roared, letting me go to clutch his temple, giving me a chance to scramble to my feet.

I ran for the cave entrance, but before I could reach it Lin pounced on me, dragging me away by one leg. He twisted my arm backward to break my grip and yanked the knife away, tossing it to the ground. We tussled, rolling together, neither of us gaining an upper hand. Over and over we went, until we rolled right out of the cave mouth and down a small hill. I found myself sprawled on my back, my head dangling over the edge of the cliff. Lin loomed above me. I went to headbutt him, but froze—I'd caught sight of a small group standing on a cliff, on the opposite side of the ravine.

General Hong was there, mounted atop a large black warhorse. Another ghost horse. His thick lips were parted in a malicious smile, exposing the whole left row of his teeth. Behind and to the left sat Dai Yu, mounted on her own horse. Moonlight limned her hair, creating a halo around her head. Our eyes briefly connected but she quickly looked away.

Flanking the general's other side was Wen Bo. This was the first time I'd seen him since my nightmare. He, I noted with despair, was now missing a hand. His left hand.

General Hong's punishment.

Wen Bo stared at me from beneath bunched up eyebrows. Dolefully? Accusingly? I couldn't tell.

I swallowed, feeling sick.

"We meet again, Little Liu," the general called out, his words dissolving into a rasping laugh. How could I hear him so clearly, despite him being across the ravine? Was it another trick of the death realm, where time and distance didn't matter?

I blinked, and General Hong seemed to flash before me, unnervingly close. But then I blinked again and he was once again far away.

Lin's whole body jerked, like he was terrified. His reaction scared me even more than the general did. "Resurrect. Quick!" he urged me. "Do it now!"

Just the thought of it set my gut churning. As though my body, yearning to escape danger, might resurrect without me realizing.

Some voice of reason, deep in the pit of my mind, began whispering. Telling me that I should listen to Lin and go back to the land of the living. Reminding me that it had been harder for me to resurrect from the second layer the last time, when I escaped General Hong's dungeon, and if I didn't do it now, what sort of predicament might I find myself in? If I plunged even deeper, into the third layer or beyond, might I find it harder still—or impossible, even—to claw my way back to life?

The familiar, hooking sensation started to prick at my insides. But I willed it away, forcing my consciousness back into the present.

"No," I said through clenched teeth, still straining against Lin's hold.

Lin slid his glance over to the other ghosts and then back to me. "Jia—" he said, then stopped. His voice had taken on a pleading edge.

No. I wouldn't run. I wouldn't resurrect. Not now. Even if I had a good chance of escaping, I couldn't do so when I knew that Pópo was only one level deeper. If I wasn't around to help her, who would be?

Nor could I stay here, with Lin on top of me and a small army of ghosts across the valley.

What is dead can die again, I thought, desperation pounding through my head.

Digging my fingers into Lin's shoulders, I grasped him tightly. Then with my last ounce of strength, I threw myself over the cliff's edge, bringing Lin with me. There was only one way to go to escape this hellish situation . . .

And that was down.

Thirty-Seven

THE THIRD LEVEL

Present day

I awoke, sprawled out on some jagged rocks. Beside me was a waterfall, which emptied into a churning plunge basin carved into the base of the cliff. The crash of cascading water was deafening, the air humid, oppressive, dark. Misty condensation billowed up in plumes, obscuring my vision further.

Groaning, I clutched my head. Was I dead? Had I reached the third level? Or had I unwittingly resurrected at the last moment? Quickly, I stole a glance at Essien's pocket watch. It was silent, the second hand still frozen; an endless moment.

My eyes narrowed as I tried to remember what it sounded like when it was ticking. Bizarrely . . . I could not. The memory had completely dissipated, as though my last links to the living world were starting to break down. I swallowed, my dry tongue scraping the roof of my mouth.

So. Still dead, then. And even worse—I was increasingly losing my grip on reality the deeper into death I went.

I rolled over and away from my second-level corpse, wincing as I assessed its obvious injuries. Thankfully I couldn't feel any pain, but Essien was going to have a big job healing my battered body up top. With each passing moment I grew more and more grateful that I'd agreed to accept his help.

The world swayed as I scrambled upright. Leaning against one of the boulders as support, I checked for any signs of Lin, hoping he wasn't about to lurch from the mist and grab me. My hand went to the Bone Smith's blade, but my fingers grasped at empty space. Frantically, I patted my other hip. Wen Bo's sword, too, was gone.

Damnit! I remembered losing my dagger in the cave, during the fight with Lin. But how had I lost the sword? And more to the point: What was I to do? I was stuck, unarmed, in the third layer of the afterlife. With my grandmother, who was Mothers-know-where, and Lin. He'd already tried to force me to resurrect in the cave; I assumed he wouldn't hesitate to attack again here, to stop me from getting to her.

I thought hard. My vision was clearing, the world solidifying, though everything around me was still suffused in disorienting darkness. Did I dare risk going back to the cave to fetch my knife?

As soon as I could distinguish the shadowy outlines of my surroundings, I began to scramble up the slope, away from the thundering waterfall. After clambering over a particularly big rock, I dropped to the ground, the damp, spongy loam muffling the sound of my feet.

I turned, and collided with Lin's chest.

My alarm became amplified to a deafening roar. I flattened myself against the stone behind me, my muscles seizing up.

"Going somewhere, Jia?" Lin flashed me a sardonic smile.

Black blood streamed from a wound on his forehead. His knife he held aloft, the faint glow of the sickly blue light illuminating the surrounding gloom. And, most infuriatingly, Wen Bo's sword—which *I'd* been carrying—was slung across his back. He must have stolen it from me before I woke. I swallowed my scream.

He fixed his gaze on me.

I froze, my mind whirring. I couldn't let him keep me from finding Pópo. *The only thing I can do is run*, I thought desperately.

So I ran.

Lin chased me, springing from boulder to boulder with a frightening degree of agility. I, on the other hand, tripped and stumbled, trying to escape him.

It was no use. He'd almost caught up. I pushed harder, but my foot got caught in a crevice, and I screamed as I fell forward, smacking face down onto a rock.

Dazed, I reached up to clutch my head. Blood was seeping from a cut.

Lin, having reached me, braced his hands on the rock's surface, caging me in. "I'll repeat that. *Are you going somewhere?*"

I turned, my hair sprawled across my eyes. "As far away as I can get from *you*!"

He gave a low, demonic chuckle. "If I cannot escape you," he said, unrelenting, "then you cannot escape me, Jia Yi." He swept my hair to one side in an almost tender gesture.

"Fuck you!" I screamed, trying to bite.

He snatched his hand away and chuckled. "Feisty."

I pushed off the stone surface, elbowing him in the process.

My intention was to escape. But part of me wanted to stay. To pull him down on top of me, to kiss him, to finish what we'd almost started back in the cave.

Then the rock lurched beneath us.

"Jia?" he said, stilling. "What are you . . . what are you doing?"

"I'm not doing anything," I said, startled. Was this—the shifting scenery—another strange feature of the death realm?

"Then what—"

The rock burst to life, cutting his question off. In an instant, Lin had dragged me off the stone surface. We stumbled backward just as the rock expanded . . . into a demon.

It was gray-skinned, its arms abnormally elongated and ending in curved, cracked claws. Its hair was black and flowing, and its deep-set eyes glowed red.

My mouth sagged open in a silent scream. Not only was I losing my connection to my living self . . . It also seemed that the further into the afterlife we descended, the more perilous it became: the more grotesque the monsters, the more terrifying the ghosts.

And the more difficult it would become for me to resurrect.

Lin shoved me behind him, his own knife held aloft. More than anything I wished I still had a weapon.

I flung a hand in his direction. "Give me my sword!"

Even though he was facing a monster, he still managed to let loose a laugh. "Why, so you can use it on me? No. I don't trust you."

"It's not about trust!" Fear was exploding inside my ribs. The rock creature advanced on us; we stumbled back. "We're facing a Mothers-damned *demon*, in case you hadn't noticed—"

Lin's eyes flicked toward me and then back to the monster. Then, with a grunt, he drew Wen Bo's sword and tossed it to me.

This sudden movement triggered something. The demon lurched at Lin. He slashed out, the blade clanging off the demon's impossibly hard hide.

It wasn't deterred, pushing forward even as Lin continued to hack and slash. Its arms reached out, long fingers closing around Lin's neck. Wildly, Lin swung at the demon, but the blade only sliced air—the monster's reach was longer, and Lin's knife was too short.

The creature lifted Lin, causing his feet to scrabble pointlessly in an attempt to reach the ground.

I raised Wen Bo's sword. It was so long that it felt unwieldy; I had to grasp it with two hands. Screaming, I darted in, trying to hack the creature's arm off. But of course that didn't work—the sword just glanced off its skin.

It roared and backhanded me with its free hand. I flew through the air, landing with a crash, white pinpricks of light flashing through my vision. It took me a few seconds to regain my bearings. If I were alive, I'd almost certainly have been concussed.

Shaking off my dizziness, I staggered back to my feet. Lin's movements were slowing. As a ghost, he didn't need air, but the rock demon was squeezing so hard that soon, Lin's neck would break.

Gritting my teeth, I lunged again and, throwing my entire body weight behind it, drove the sword right through one of the demon's red eyes.

That must have been its only weak point, because the

creature let out a long, low bellow before exploding into a shower of stony debris. Lin fell. Immediately he leaped up, backed away, rubbing furiously at his neck. "Come on, let's get out of here—"

He raised his blade again, because all around us, the rocks were stirring.

I grabbed his arm. "Run!"

Casting one final look at the waterfall, Lin and I both fled. We leaped over a rock just as it unfolded itself into its massive form. It loomed above us, double our heights. Around it, more rock demons were straightening, uncurling their hellish claws, red eyes trained upon us.

We didn't stop until we'd reached the line of the forest and—in practiced synchrony—scaled a tree. This was something we'd done many times before, when we'd been hunting and gotten ourselves into compromising situations.

Lin pulled me against him, his arm clamped protectively around my shoulders. His eyes were trained on the ground, watching the demons who were congregating at the base of the trunk.

Unbeknownst to him, I scrutinized his features; the dark, disheveled hair; the thick, jet-black eyebrows, currently drawn down in worry; his strong nose and mouth; the square angles of his jaw.

Once upon a time, his face had been dearer to me than almost anything. But now? Now it just unsettled me. That such beautiful features could obscure such a hateful soul. Fury rose like a tide, engulfing every cold, dead cell in the flesh of my ghostly body, sharpening to a narrow knifepoint in my chest.

Traitor, my mind whispered as the knife turned a painful half-twist. *He's a traitor.*

Lin claimed to care about me. Yet he'd lied to me, repeatedly. He'd kissed me and then abandoned me. He had *humiliated* me. And now, in the death realm, he was insisting I resurrect, preventing me from seeing Pópo.

He'd always been a good liar. After all, it had been him who had taught me: *The best lies are those that are formed in half-truths.*

But Pópo had also lied, hadn't she? She'd lied about not believing the shaman. She'd lied about the root of her illness. And if Lin was being truthful, she'd also lied to me about working with *him*.

Why had she deceived me, her own granddaughter?

It was all so convoluted that I couldn't tell where one theory ended and the next began. Who should I—the girl who wasn't used to trusting anyone—believe?

I didn't know what Lin's intentions were, but one thing I did know was that if I didn't somehow get away from him, or get *him* away from *me*, then he would not quit in his efforts to prevent me from reaching my grandmother. He was almost—*almost*—as stubborn as me. And if I couldn't help her find the weapon, as the shaman had predicted, before General Hong did . . . well, it wasn't just me but the living world that would be at risk.

My thoughts jolted back to the present when the entire tree gave a violent shudder. I glanced down; the demons were now throwing themselves at the trunk. Each impact of their rock-hard bodies caused the tree to creak and sway. It wouldn't hold up for much longer.

I tensed in panic. I didn't want to die. This was the level my grandmother was on; this was the level on which I needed to remain. But to reach her, I had to escape, somehow. Distract the monsters and get away.

I glanced at Lin again. An idea started to form.

Lin, distracted by the demons, didn't notice me watching him. "What are they?" he muttered, more to himself than to me. It was a rhetorical question—he knew I didn't know, either. Neither of us had ever delved this deep into the afterlife.

Below us, the rock demons circled, their fiendish carved faces turned upward. Fear took root down in the depths of my mind. These monsters were not like any creature in our known world.

"I know what they are." I didn't look at Lin; I was now staring at the patch of charred earth, scorched by the first demon's death.

He turned to face me, hair falling in disarray across his forehead. "You do? What?"

Steadying my resolve, I fixed my gaze on Lin. At this point, both of us could go deeper into death . . .

But only one of us could come back.

Reaching out, I slid my hand up his torso until it rested on his sternum. I watched the way his eyes widened just a fraction, how his body tensed beneath my touch. This was far, far too easy.

Perhaps he thought I was going to kiss him.

"My backup plan," I said, and gave his chest a brutal shove.

Thirty-Eight

THE THIRD LEVEL

Present day

Lin fell, a multitude of emotions flashing across his face. Shock. Betrayal. Hatred. My heart surged in bitter triumph. His repeated treachery had turned me ruthless.

He landed with a crash, scattering the rock demons, but they converged on him in an instant. Drawing his blue blade, he slashed and hacked, pivoting and stabbing, fighting to escape the horde.

As he battled the monsters, I crept to the very far end of the branch, as far from the fight as possible, and dropped down, landing lightly on the balls of my feet. Then, forcing myself not to look back, I stole away.

The waterfall was located roughly halfway between the Fengzhian border and our community. Beyond that, in the distance and silhouetted by the murky sky, jutted the snow-capped peaks of Gui Ku Shan.

I had to hurry. Not least because I was extremely vulnerable traveling through the third-level forest, where I was unfamiliar with what ghosts and monsters lurked within. But also because before long, one of two things would happen: Lin might defeat the rock demons and come after me and Pópo. Or, he might perish on this level and descend to the fourth. In which case he'd probably still come after me, but for revenge.

I shook away these thoughts, focusing on pushing forward. As I trudged through the forest, in the direction of my village, I mulled over my plan.

If the Shēngsǐ Sword truly gave its wielder mastery over life and death, and allowed the dead to come alive again, then . . . perhaps I could convince Pópo to use it instead of destroy it, and we could both return to the land of the living. We could both return *home.*

Now that I was three levels deep in the death realm, time felt even more abstract. It appeared to warp and stretch—or maybe it didn't exist at all—so it didn't seem long before I was skirting the outer perimeter of my village. The wards, the scattered huts, the central clearing—all as familiar to me as the lines that traced my palm. But now it was empty, silent, save for the occasional cawing of a few ghostly ravens.

Blurred shapes moved through the trees, flitting like shadowy butterflies, assuming humanlike forms in my peripheral vision only to blink out of existence as soon as I turned to look. I assumed these were the ghosts of those in the second level. Apparently, no one from my community existed in the third, except for Pópo and myself.

Was my grandmother still here? She'd always been a homebody—indelibly attached to our village, our people. This, certainly, was a place that was significant to her in life. She had told me she'd come here while I searched for the second half of the shaman's prediction. But had she waited?

My anticipation grew as I crossed the clearing, as I passed by the rest of the silent, shuttered houses. I now understood what Lin had meant about the "pull" he felt to certain places. It was as if some unseen force was stringing me along, making my legs move faster and faster, a pit of longing burning in my stomach.

Just moments now, I thought. *Just moments.* If she wasn't here, I'd be gutted . . . But if she was . . . if she was . . .

"Bǎobèi." Pópo gave me a watery smile as I stumbled through the door of her low, dark hut. She extended her arms and I ran over, enveloping her in a huge, tight hug.

She felt amazing. Smelled amazing. Her soft cheek rested against mine.

"I missed you," I choked out, squeezing harder. "I missed you so much, and I love you, and I never said it enough—"

She broke away from me, holding me at arm's length and regarding me with an incisive gaze. "I know, Jia Yi. Do not worry. I always knew."

At this, I broke down again, sobbing into my grandmother's shoulder as she held me like a child. I hated this—that I was not in control of my emotions, that I was wasting precious time falling apart at the seams. We were stuck on the third level, in a forest that probably held unspeakable terrors. We needed to both evade General Hong and his mob of ghosts *and* find the sword before they did.

And all we had to protect us was Wen Bo's Bone Smith blade, our respective powers . . . and a heritable trait of stubbornness.

When I pulled away, I was startled by the lines of exhaustion drawn across my grandmother's features. "Did you find it?" she said, studying my face. "The rest of the shaman's prediction?"

"Yes." I clasped her hands more tightly. "I heard it." Closing my eyes to summon the memory, I recited the rest of the shaman's prediction:

In the deepest level of death, at the beginning and the end of the afterlife, you will find a weapon. A weapon with complete mastery over life and death.

The weapon can be used for good or ill . . . There will be a choice: sacrifice, or salvation.

"The beginning and the end of the afterlife?" Pópo was silent for a moment, the corners of her lips pulling down.

"Yes, that was what it said." My mouth twisted. "I'm not sure what it means."

"The beginning and the end of the afterlife," Pópo repeated to herself. She was silent for a moment, probably thinking.

Eventually, she said slowly, "Shuang Yue Dong. It must be."

Shuang Yue Dong. The mythical, magical, Double Moon Cave.

It made sense—so much so, I couldn't believe I hadn't thought of it already. The cave was supposed to represent the very end of life itself.

But it also represented new life. Reincarnation.

According to legend, Shuang Yue Dong was buried beneath Gui Ku Shan. The mountain itself was supposedly where ghosts went to die, the last stop for souls before they either reincarnated into a new form or departed the world for good. In fact, Gui Ku Shan was named after the crying ghosts that could be heard wailing from its peaks at nighttime. Even as a ghost, the idea was terrifying.

It was said that when the moon was fully risen, it would

be framed perfectly by a hole in Shuang Yue Dong's ceiling, reflecting onto the pool below. Hence why it was called Double Moon Cave. Even as a ghost, the idea was terrifying.

I'd only ever heard of it in stories designed to scare us as children. In fact, it was Pópo who'd often told us these stories as she tucked us into bed at night. No wonder she, who was so familiar with our culture's folklore, had deciphered the riddle.

But all throughout history, people had searched for evidence of such a cave and found none.

"You think Shuang Yue Dong is real?" I frowned. "I thought it was just a myth?"

"All myths begin in truths."

All good lies do, too, I thought.

Chewing my lip, I pondered Pópo's theory. There were all sorts of things I'd never believed in before that actually did exist: ghosts, obviously, and rock demons, and weapons that existed in both the living world and the dead. Was it so hard to believe that Shuang Yue Dong existed, too?

No—I could believe it. So, straightening my shoulders, I said, "All right, then. We need to get to Gui Ku Shan. Let's go."

Pópo gave me a searching look, her beetle-black eyes sharp. "You do not have to come, Jia Yi. Now that we've heard the rest of the prediction, your part is done. You were not even supposed to follow me this deep into the afterlife—"

I let go of her, annoyed. "Yes I was. This was supposed to happen, remember? The shaman said that you and I would meet in the afterlife to find the weapon."

Pópo's expression tightened. "Shamans can be wrong."

"But she was right about me dying. And she was right about us meeting here. She saw the future—"

"One possible version of the future. The future can change."

Reaching out, I took Pópo's hands again and clutched them in my own. "That may be so, but I'm here now. And we need to find the weapon. I . . ." I paused, steeling myself. "I met General Hong."

My grandmother's mouth dropped open. "You met him?"

I nodded. "On the way here. I know he's looking for the sword. I know he's the one we have to keep from finding it. And"—my knuckles whitened, I was gripping Pópo's hands so hard—"he's not far behind. He followed me down to the second level. He was at the waterfall. We have to leave. Now."

I didn't dare tell her about Dai Yu. It would break her heart to know that one of her own granddaughters had taken up with the opposing side.

My grandmother looked at me, her eyebrows drawn down, before she shifted her gaze to the door. For the first time since I'd seen her, she looked deeply uneasy.

"Not now," she said. "Soon. First we must wait for Lin."

"Lin?" Even his name made panic erupt in my chest. Abruptly, I let go of my grandmother and paced away, both hands buried in my hair. "No! We don't need *Lin*." I spat out his name like it was a curse.

I felt, rather than heard, Pópo come up behind me. She placed a cool hand on my shoulder. "My dear child," she said, turning me around and squinting up at my face. "I think it's time for you to know the truth about him."

Clenching my fists, I willed myself not to scream. Lin was the last person—or ghost, rather—I wanted to discuss right now.

"He says that he's helping you." My voice sounded childish,

plaintive. "But how do you know he isn't lying? Pretending to be your ally while betraying you behind your back?"

"He isn't." Pópo raised her hand to cup my cheek, then sighed and shook her head. "I know you have only learned of the Shēngsǐ Sword recently, Jia Yi. But I knew of it before. I learned of it many years ago—before the shaman, even. From a traveling sorcerer who could communicate with ghosts."

I clutched my head. It was still throbbing from the rock demon's blow, and trying to comprehend Pópo's explanation was making my headache worse. "How many years ago?"

Pópo hesitated. "Since you were a baby."

Unable to formulate a response, I just pressed trembling fingers against my closed eyelids until phosphenes flashed behind them.

"I knew, of course, from the history books that the infamous General Hong Hao Mu had stolen the sword from the Yskians," my grandmother continued. "It was the traveling sorcerer who told me that the general had lost it in the death realm after being assassinated. They told me the general had never stopped searching for it, even in death."

I shivered and raised my eyes to my grandmother's. Hers held a distant look.

"I knew of his violent reputation. That it would be a disaster if ever he managed to recover it." Pópo grimaced. "So I set about making plans to find it before he did."

My voice shook slightly when I spoke again. "Is this where Lin comes in?"

She bowed her head in assent. "When I heard of the general's plans, I knew then that I needed someone who could help spy on him and his fellow ghosts. Someone who had cheated death."

"And Lin was that someone," I said, echoing Lin's words from the cave. The fragments of knowledge I'd gleaned throughout my childhood were gradually taking shape, becoming a blurry scene.

"Yes. I found Lin. He'd been orphaned, see." Pópo's frown lines deepened. "I won't tell you what he went through, as a young and vulnerable child. That is not my story to tell. Suffice to say, he suffered greatly, and came as close to death as one can possibly come. He lived—only just—and it was like this, half dead, that I found him and cared for him, until he was healed.

"His close brush with death gave him the ability not only to see ghosts but also to interact with them. Communicate. So, once he had recovered, I brought him back to our community."

"You . . . recruited him?" I asked.

"In a way, yes," my grandmother said. "He helped me by speaking with the friendly ghosts, and by spying on those who wished us harm. He became like a messenger, carrying knowledge from the afterlife."

My mouth was open; I shut it. I'd been convinced that Lin was using *me* to get to my grandmother, when really . . .

It was my grandmother who had used Lin.

Pópo continued. "For a while, our system was going well. Lin kept me updated with General Hong's movements. From other ghosts, he learned as much as he could about the sword. That is, until . . ."

"Until what?" I stilled, not wanting to move a muscle, not wanting to miss a thing.

"Until I learned of the shaman's prediction. That the person destined to find the sword . . ." She raised her eyes to meet mine. "Was you."

My brain searched through my murky memories. "Was that why you reacted so badly that night?"

"Yes," Pópo said quietly. "I only went there to see if you had magic . . . not to find out that . . . that . . ." My grandmother sighed, and covered her face with her hands. "That *you* were going to die. Not me."

She stopped, and her shoulders shook. "I could not bear the thought. I'd already lost my daughter and my son-in-law. I couldn't bear to lose another—" Her words choked off, and a deep sob ratcheted through her body.

Was she . . . actually crying? My indomitable grandmother was *crying.*

My dead, still heart fractured. I'd always been so focused on how I had lost my mother, and how that had impacted *me*, that I'd rarely stopped to think about the fact Pópo had also lost her daughter. It's always difficult, from the perspective of a child, to understand that the adults around you have their own lives, their own troubles.

My guilt spiked again, scraping at my insides. It was me, all my fault . . . my destiny that was marked for death. Me who had inflicted such pain on my own grandmother. *Me* who had spread my curse to everyone who came close: my parents, my sister, my grandmother, my best friend . . .

And now myself.

I couldn't say all this, though—I did not want to cause Pópo more pain than she'd already suffered. So instead, I held her, rubbing slow circles on her back until her tearless sobs petered out and her shaking shoulders stilled.

"I resolved to keep you hidden. Safe." Pópo sniffed before continuing. "But then our luck ran out, and my worst fear came to pass: Lin heard that somehow, General Hong had discovered the truth about you. That he was making plans to kidnap you and use you to find the sword."

I shuddered. It had been Dai Yu who had betrayed us and told the general about my destiny. The memory of my encounter with her and General Hong made my skin tighten.

"It became imperative that we find it before he did. Lin—he offered to enter the afterlife in lieu of you. But I did not want to sacrifice either of you. You were both young and healthy, with your whole lives yet to live. But me? I was already suffering from an illness I knew I would not recover from. I would soon meet Death naturally, regardless." Her eyes shone as she shook her head. "We quarreled about it for a long time. Lin was adamant he should take your place. But I argued that with my age, and my fading health, it should be me."

I gulped down the dread that had clawed up my throat. "What changed his mind?"

Pópo frowned. "I'm afraid I used some emotional coercion on him, Jia Yi. Appealed to his ego. The shaman's prediction foretold that you would die. But I told him that fates can be rewritten. That with his strength and his youth, he'd be in a better position than I to protect you . . . to keep that vision from coming true."

My voice faltered as I whispered, "He was protecting me?"

Pópo gave a small nod.

My gut twisted. It was true—Lin had become increasingly protective of me in the lead-up to his disappearance. Annoying as it was, I'd thought it was because he cared for me. But now it seemed he had only been doing my grandmother's bidding. He'd cared about *her*, not me.

When I spoke, my voice came out small. "So . . . you both did all this to protect me." I shook my head. "It makes no sense—"

Pópo ignored me and went on. "I asked him to brew me an elixir, using his extensive knowledge of poisons. He'd poison the tip of his dagger with it, ensuring a painless death. We planned it so that when I died, he would watch over you, to ensure you didn't die yourself, as the shaman predicted."

My throat had grown thick. I swallowed. "And then what happened?"

Pópo frowned. "At the last minute, as he was supposed to stab me, he balked. He couldn't do it. We struggled, me trying to force him to fulfill our plans. In the process, the knife scratched me, imbuing me with some, but not all, of the poison. It was enough to make me ill, but not enough to kill me. Then he ran off, taking his knife with him, wasting all the careful work we'd both done over the years."

My mouth hung open in shock, and I remained speechless for several moments. Then I said, "But . . . why?"

"Why do you think, my child?" Pópo's tone was mournful. "He loved us both too much. He was ashamed of sabotaging our plans. Yet, he could not bear to see either of us die."

All of a sudden, I understood why he'd kissed me in that cave after I'd been injured by the boar, why he had seemed so distant for days prior. Why he had run away. That kiss had been his clumsy, boyish way of saying goodbye. And running away had been his way of dealing with the dishonor of what he'd both done—and not done.

I scrubbed at my eyes, my grief breaking within me. "And then he died."

"He was remorseful over his failure. As you know, he spiraled into debauchery, attempting to deal with his shame. When he got himself killed"—at this, Pópo swallowed—"he was so consumed by terror that he'd left you alone in the living realm. I believe he began to haunt you, trying to keep you safe, even from beyond death. He tried everything he could to stop the shaman's vision from coming true."

I scrunched my eyes shut, pulling my hands away and pressing them to my temples. Come to think of it, the past year had been . . . oddly easy.

Apart from my worries over Pópo's ailing health, and my anger over Lin's disappearance, I hadn't actually run into many troubles. The forests had been relatively silent and free of predators. There had been whispered rumors of increased Yskian losses, as they patrolled through the Forest of Seld. In fact, until the night I'd first died, I hadn't run into any Lancaster soldiers for months.

Had that all been *Lin*?

I guess that was why I'd become complacent about my safety.

Still . . . this was *unfathomable.* Lin, working in concert with my grandmother, this whole time? To orchestrate her timely death? And the very fact he'd run away in shame, leaving me to believe he'd just deserted us.

Lin's words to me, the first time I died, came rushing back.

What did you do, *Jia?* he'd said. *You shouldn't be here. You are not supposed to be* here.

No wonder he'd been so furious the first time I saw him in the afterlife. He hadn't expected me to die. And he sure as hells did not expect me to come back to life again. None of that had been part of his plan.

When he'd first seen me in the death realm, he'd tried to kill me. Was that to get me out of the first level, and away from General Hong?

I rubbed at my forehead. It must have been—because the moment he discovered my ability, his efforts had shifted from trying to kill me . . . to convincing me to resurrect.

I shook my head, trying to understand. "Why did he never tell me any of this?" I said, my voice accusatory. "Why didn't *you*?"

"I swore him to secrecy." She gazed at me, her black eyes oddly bright. "I wanted to protect you."

A shard of irritation sliced through me. "Well, you don't need to protect me." If there was one thing that I resented about my grandmother, it was how she had never stopped treating me like a child, just because I was the youngest. She would always keep me in the dark, withholding information from me, protecting me like I was too delicate to handle it.

"Can you honestly say that if you knew of your fate, you would have willingly let me take your place?" She smiled sadly and shook her head. "No. You would have insisted on going to find the sword yourself."

I bristled, but she was right. I wouldn't have wanted Pópo to sacrifice herself. "But that's as it should be."

She patted my hand. "Oh, my precious granddaughter. Someday, you will understand."

I tugged my hand from hers. "I'm not completely vulnerable, you know. In fact, there's something I've been meaning to tell you. About . . . about my powers—"

I was cut off, because a voice rang out from the doorway.

"Jia," the voice said, gruff. "Don't."

Thirty-Nine

THE THIRD LEVEL
Present day

I spun around. There was Lin, in his slightly lucent form, leaning against the doorjamb. His arms were crossed, his brows drawn down, his entire demeanor guarded. From where he stood, mired in the fourth level, he appeared even more insubstantial than ever before.

"Oh, good," my grandmother said to him. "You're here."

An ice-cold shiver rolled down my spine. The fact I could see him meant that, in the fight with the rock demon, I'd come closer to death than I'd thought.

And worse, the fact that my grandmother could see him meant that *she* had also come close to death in this level. I swallowed, my throat thick. What terrors had Pópo faced down here?

"Lin." My voice was acerbic. "You lied to me." I couldn't get past the betrayal of them having worked together for years, without saying anything. And, if I was being honest with myself, of Lin choosing my grandmother . . . over *me*.

Lin uncrossed his arms and, gesturing with his head, said, "Walk with me?"

I hesitated, my eyes flicking between my grandmother and Lin, not missing the silent, wordless conversation they were having. It seemed that somewhere along the line, without me having ever realized, they'd developed the ability to communicate without speaking. And I'd never noticed.

I narrowed my eyes as I watched them, pitting my hatred for Lin against my need to see him, to talk to him, to figure out where his allegiances lay.

"Fine," I agreed, finally, before storming out the door.

"Do not be too long," Pópo's voice called from inside. "You know why, Lin."

Lin trailed after me, keeping a careful distance. I stalked to the line of trees at the edge of our encampment, not stopping to check if he was following but somehow knowing that he would.

Once we were safely shrouded by the forest, I turned to face him, hugging myself with both arms. A breeze wove through the pine trees; the branches shivered, the low-pitched rustle ominous. Something in the corner of my vision caught my eye. I peered into the dark forest. Was that a wisp of something, spiraling through the air?

My lips flattened. *Probably just a ghost.*

"Jia," Lin said, yanking my attention to him. Eyes flashing, he prowled around me in a circle, coming to a stop right before me. "What the *fuck* was that about? You practically fed me to those demons!"

He towered over me. But he was a ghost. He wasn't tangible; he couldn't touch me. Yet for some reason I still reacted, fighting the urge to retreat.

Instead, I held my ground, fists clenched at my sides. "I couldn't let you stop me from finding Pópo—"

"Stop you—Pópo—" His words, disjointed, tumbled out. He buried both hands in his hair, and began to pace. Finally, he flung his arms down again and spun to face me. "Why in the Mothers' names would I stop you from finding Pópo?"

"Because . . . I thought . . . the cave . . ." My eyelids had started prickling with the promise of tears. "You refused to let me come down to this level. You pounced on me—"

"Because I wanted you to *resurrect*, damnit! It was never about stopping you getting to Pópo. It was about keeping you safe!" He gave a long, exasperated sigh. "That's why I waited for you . . . tracked you to our cave. Because I wanted you to get out."

My ire deflated. "Well, I didn't know that. And now I find out that you were working with Pópo the whole time . . . ?" I closed my eyes, shaking my head, not able to fully grasp the threads of our conversation. My entire world had unraveled. I had no idea how to stitch it back together.

"The *whole* time," I continued, my voice shaking. "So then what was . . . what was . . ."—a sob escaped my lips—"what was I? What were *we*?"

There was a long pause. Lin's amber eyes fixed on me, burning like lit torches. "You were the love of my life, Jia," he said, very quietly. Then his face folded, and he corrected himself. "You *are* the love of my life. Always, now, and forever."

I looked away, not wanting him to read my face and see that my heart was breaking. "I . . . I don't believe you."

"I know how much you love her," Lin said, quieter now.

"Jia, your grandmother might have been the one to enlist my help to begin with." He moved closer still, though I couldn't feel his ghost form with my body, couldn't feel him at all. "But I was just a child then. The reason I kept going was because you loved her. It was all for *you*. That's the only reason I stuck around all those years."

"But you didn't! You didn't stick around. Did you?" The words exploded out of me.

Lin bowed his head, staring at the ground. "No. And for that I am sorry. I ran away—like a coward. My behavior toward you was . . . indefensible." At this, he raised his gaze to mine, holding it. "I will forever regret not telling you how I truly felt until it was too late. Until I'd died. Until all that was left of me was a haunted soul. My existence, after losing you, was pure torment—"

I took a shaky step back. "Stop it, Lin. You don't need to protect me, you never did—"

"But I wanted to. I love you." He reached for me but dropped his hand when I flinched. "I was never meant to. I was supposed to stay focused on my task. But by the time I realized how I felt, I was too far gone." His voice cracked; he looked wretched. "That day, in our cave, it all became clear. My love for you transcends death. No matter what form we take, whether ghost or jiàn or living soul . . . I will never stop loving you."

I squeezed my eyes shut, unsure whether or not I wanted him to stop. "Lin . . ."

"Jia," he murmured, running his ghostly hand down my face. "My love."

My eyelids sprang open. He was just a ghost. A ghost who was haunting me. Therefore, we couldn't touch.

And yet still I gasped, because although I couldn't feel him, somehow the knowledge that his hand was there, tracing the imaginary line of my skin, was just as intense as if he *had* actually touched me.

Raising his other hand, he positioned it as if he were cradling my cheek. He wasn't, but I still tilted my face up to meet his.

He leaned forward, his absent lips ghosting along my jawbone. "Tell me to stop and I will," he whispered, his mouth up against my ear.

But I didn't tell him to stop. I didn't *want* to.

His empty touch. His absent, empty touch. He was being so deliberate, so tender that it was like I could actually feel him. Like he was truly touching me. And . . . it made me yearn for him. The real him. Or my memory of the real him.

It made me ache.

My lips parted, involuntarily. He bent his head to mine, his mouth hovering so near. We stayed like that, unmoving, for a few mesmerizing moments, before finally—*finally*—he closed the distance.

He kissed me. And I found myself kissing him back, as surely and as passionately as if we were physically together. I kissed the air, the vacant space where his lips should have been. We moved, in synchrony, ignoring the fact we were in different ghost realms. I reached up, curling my arms around his nonexistent shoulders.

He surged forward, walking me back until I was pressed

up against a tree. "Jia," he said, his words a murmured benediction, as his lips traced the outline of my skin. "I cannot tell whether I want you down here, with me. Or safe up there, alive."

He ran his hand down my side and I squirmed, not feeling his touch but fancying I could anyway. When he started to trail kisses back up my neck, I sighed, unable to stifle the evidence of my pleasure.

"I missed that sound," he groaned. And then his lips were on mine again.

All I could feel was the rough bark behind my back, the soft soil of the forest floor beneath my feet. But his kiss, though imperceptible, was filled with so much longing it seemed real. I shivered, simultaneously chilled and on fire all at once. Desire curled, sharp and hot, deep within my belly.

He pulled back, his eyes dark and unfathomable. Then, he trailed his hand down the side of my face, my throat, across my décolletage. I stilled, not wanting to break the moment. I wanted to lose myself in the intensity of his gaze. In the feeling of his absent touch.

Very carefully, very deliberately, he hovered his hand above my chest, over my heart. "I missed this too," he whispered, leaning his head down, as if to touch his forehead to mine. "Your heart. I miss feeling it beneath my hand, as though it were beating just for me."

I looked down to where his hand was, floating intangibly against me. It was right over the spot where Andres Brisson's sword had pierced through. Right where Essien Lancaster had healed me. Essien, who was up in the living realm, *still* healing me.

I went very subdued, very silent. Finally, I whispered, "It hasn't beat for you in a very long time, Lin."

Abruptly, he withdrew and turned away. "I know."

I sagged against the tree. What was I doing? This whole time, traipsing through the layers of the underworld, descending deeper and deeper into the bowels of death . . . I'd let Lin affect me too much. I was playing make-believe with a ghost who'd shown me time and time again that he would betray me. A ghost who currently I couldn't even touch.

Despite his pretty words, I knew Lin was no good for me. We didn't work together. We were the same and yet not the same. Our souls were identical; black and twisted beyond repair. And I couldn't trust him. His words were just that: words.

He'd lied to me for so long. Had never told me of the alliance between him and Pópo. He'd sullied our memories with his deception.

What did Lin know of honor? What did he know of love? I couldn't help it; I was constantly comparing him to Essien, now that I was getting to know the latter. Whilst the Yskian prince valued duty, loyalty, justice, and valor, Lin was a master of covert secrets: deceptive, underhanded, enigmatic, sly.

So why was I continually drawn to him?

Deep down, I knew why. It was because I was those things, also. We were too much alike, Lin and I, resentful, antagonistic, mostly fueled by rage. Sometimes it felt as if we were almost the same person—like we'd been fashioned from the same dead patch of dirt. Was this the culmination of my narcissistic, antisocial tendencies? That I felt most comfortable with someone who reminded me of . . . me?

I bit my cheek, waiting for the taste of blood. It never came.

In my mind, I analyzed everything Pópo had told me. Everything Lin had told me. But I only had part of the puzzle. And now that I thought of it, I'd come out here to talk to Lin for a reason. Not to have an illusory—albeit extremely sensual—sort-of-kiss with a ghost.

I turned away from Lin, bracing myself with one hand against the tree, trying to gather my wits. I couldn't look at him, not now, not when we should be focused on seeking the sword. "The weapon the general and his forces are seeking is hidden in death's deepest layer. Is that why you keep killing Pópo? To bring her down?"

Lin was silent for a long moment. Then he simply said, "Yes."

I turned to face him. "And you? You intend to travel down with her?"

Another pause. "Yes."

I frowned, considering. I'd once wondered whether the levels of the afterlife were analogous to Dìyù. From what I could gather, though, the ghost realms weren't *exactly* like hell. There were no eternal fires for one, or lakes of blood, or perpetual torture devices.

But then, as my grandmother had said: Weren't all myths rooted in half-truths? And didn't such stories morph and twist over time, until they only vaguely resembled the original? Who was to say that some ancient ancestor hadn't possessed my very same power? Perhaps they had traveled into the depths of the underworld, like me, and survived.

Certainly when I thought of the vine-filled forest and the rock demons, the vengeful ghosts, and the shuǐguǐ, I thought perhaps this *was* hell. That the horror of hell was not literal torture—but instead, monsters the likes of which our living minds could barely fathom.

The only question was: What else was down there?

All I knew was that I wasn't about to let my grandmother face it alone.

"And once you've found the weapon," I said, more belligerently than I intended. "What then? What will you do?"

Lin's expression shuttered. I knew him well enough to know he was hiding something.

"Lin!" I advanced on him, my voice rising dangerously. "Tell me what you're planning." My hand shot out to grab his collar, but I recoiled when I felt only empty air.

"Tell me," I spat again.

"Once we've found the sword, we will destroy it. Of course." He broke eye contact as he said it.

I studied his face through narrowed eyes. "You know that's not what I'm asking." He was still hiding something. And eventually I'd find out what.

Lin gave me the bleakest of smiles. "Well, then, xiǎo è'guǐ, I suppose I must be prepared to weather your disappointment."

I folded my arms and scowled at him. "I'm coming with you."

A tremor rolled through Lin's body, and he clenched his fists. "No."

"It's not your decision."

"No," he repeated, through gritted teeth. "It's not . . . *safe*."

Setting my jaw, I took a step forward, my stubbornness ready to rise to the challenge. "Still not your decision, Lin."

He closed the distance, until we were chest to chest. "Don't be ridiculous. You have a *power*, Jia. A power that will allow you to escape, unscathed. If you can just keep yourself out of trouble and stay the fuck alive—"

"But that's the issue! General Hong isn't going to just *leave me alone* because I'm up there, alive again. It's no safer there! He knows about the shaman's prediction, and he believes it. He thinks he needs me to find the sword." Anger unfurled in my stagnant veins, like flames licking through my flesh. It made me feel more alive than ever, despite the fact that I was dead. "Our only hope is for us to get that weapon, the weapon the shaman predicted *I* would find—"

"We have a plan, Jia. And it's not your place to barge in and fucking *ruin* it—"

I stamped my foot. "Then TELL me!" I shrieked. "Tell me the plan! Instead of keeping me in the dark, like I'm an ignorant child too stupid to understand what the grown-ups are saying!"

Lin just stared at me, seething.

"You cannot force me to revive myself," I said, trying to regulate my volume. "So either you bring me along with you, or I'll go myself." And reaching over, I grabbed the only part of him that I could touch—his blue blade—my hand closing on the hilt. I narrowed my eyes; he narrowed his in response. "You tried to stop me once, Lin. You failed. You'll fail again."

He almost scoffed at that. "I won't fail." His hand went to his knife handle, superimposed over my own. And for a moment, I almost fancied I could feel him through the veil that separated our worlds. As though his thumb had stroked across mine, in the most tender of lover's caresses.

How would this end? Who would win this struggle? A

struggle between two ghosts ensconced in different levels of the afterlife?

Suddenly his eyes flicked up, registering something behind me that seemed to alarm him. I made to turn around—but he put his hand up, as though to stop me.

"We've lingered too long," he said, his words containing an undercurrent of fear. "It seems you'll be joining me after all—"

"What?" I said. "Why?"

He sighed, his shoulders slumping, full of resignation. "You're going to die, Jia." His harried gaze met mine. "For better or worse . . . we're going to be reunited."

Forty

THE THIRD LEVEL

Present day

Mist stole in on the windless air, gray and fell and foul-smelling. It leached between the tree trunks, coalescing into storm clouds, tendrils of smoke unfurling like so many beckoning fingers.

"Lin . . ." I whispered, my throat choked up with fear. "What is this?"

A riot of emotions coursed across Lin's face. Torment. Regret. "I wasn't meant to keep you here this long. I was supposed to convince you to save yourself, to return to the living realm, but . . ."

My hands jerked—I'd almost reached for him, before remembering at the last moment that I couldn't. "What does it do?" My voice was rising. "Can I outrun it? Can I escape?"

Lin gave me a pained look. "It comes here, every day. Pópo was going to use it to get to the next level. You cannot outrun it . . . It moves too quickly." He drew closer. "But if you can concentrate, and move down to this layer before it touches you . . ." He trailed off, something like fear strangling his words.

Involuntarily, I threw a look at the swirling, cloudlike mist. If Lin was this scared, then it must be bad. I stood frozen; every coherent thought had fled my mind.

"Eyes on me, Jia." Lin's voice re-called my attention. His hand twitched like he wanted to touch me. "Don't look at it. Look at me, and *concentrate.*"

I forced my eyes to meet his. Stared at the blackness of his pupils and the rim of ochre surrounding them. His whole body was corded with tension, every one of his muscles trembling, his fingers flexing and unflexing helplessly.

I tried my best to block out my awareness of the slowly creeping fog. Turning my focus internally, I tensed my body, trying to summon the disintegrating feeling that would push me into the fourth level. But just as it became more and more difficult to resurrect the deeper into death I went, it also seemed like it was harder to voluntarily descend further. A symptom, I suppose, of the fact that willingly delving this deep into the underworld was against nature.

I was shaking with the strain of trying when Lin spoke again. "Hurry," he urged. "You need to—"

"I *am* hurrying!" But it was too late: The mist had caught up to me.

Now I understood why Lin was so distraught. As soon as the condensation touched my skin, the outer layers began to blister. I screamed as shards of pain began to stab me all over, as if nails were gouging furrows into the deepest layers of my flesh.

Vaguely, I registered Lin pacing and clawing at his face, distraught at being unable to help me. I turned and stumbled toward the hut, opening my mouth to scream for my grandmother, but no sound came out. The mist gushed down my throat, burning the whole way, and blood flooded my mouth until I choked. The pain was excruciating. Unbearable. I fell, my palms hitting the ground, then began to drag myself, on all fours, in my grandmother's direction. If the mist had reached me then . . . what was it doing to Pópo?

Bits of my skin began to disintegrate, vaporizing into the air, and the whole world seemed to waver and tilt as my vision began leaching away.

My grandmother was up ahead, walking out of the hut and into the mist, her hands outstretched. Her eyes were closed, her skin bubbling, her face a twisted mask of pain.

"Look at me," I heard Lin say. He sounded distant, as though he were at the bottom of a well. "Look at me. It'll be okay. Everything will be okay."

It was not okay. The mist burrowed deep, right down to my bones. I jerked and convulsed, doubling over, the viscous fog gagging my cries. Everything hurt. My ghost flesh felt like it was burning, melting, turning inside out. And I was like this—lying on the floor of the forest, jerking in agony, Lin watching me, powerless, his face full of anguish—when my mind began to fade. Slowly, the world retreated from view.

I came to, in the fourth level, cradled in Lin's arms. The shock of waking up was only matched by him being solid, present, tangible. As usual, my vision was blurry, and Lin's face, hovering over mine, stood out in a sea of darkness.

For a minuscule, reckless moment, I imagined reaching up. Pulling his face down to mine. Kissing him—properly this time, now that I actually could. But somehow I managed to drag my thoughts out of that dark place. I shoved myself away from him, scrambled to my feet, and then backed away several paces.

When we were stuck in different levels, it had seemed logical to kiss him. But now that he was here, standing before me, as corporeal as a ghost could ever be . . . it was too confronting. Kissing him for real would be like picking at an unhealed scab. No matter how much my body yearned for him, I couldn't hide the hurt that still festered beneath the surface.

"Jia, I—" he started.

I cut him off. "We'd better go and find Pópo."

He stared at me for some moments, before pressing his lips together and giving a curt nod. "I guess we'd better."

I followed him back to the ring of houses. My grandmother was standing with eyes closed, looking completely serene, beside the little table inside her hut.

It was surreal; I'd sat at that table with Hui Fen only days earlier. Was it days? Or had more time passed in the living realm? Evidently, time moved differently there.

And I could only presume that the deeper I descended into the afterlife, the more time would distort. I could have been dead for days, weeks, years, for all I knew. Here, in the permanent twilight of the death realm, the passage of time seemed irrelevant. I placed a hand on my chest, over Essien's pocket watch, wishing that it still worked. That I could tell the time.

Would I ever see the prince again? When he'd lifted my chin and looked at me, just after giving me the watch, he'd made me feel . . . valued. The thought made my heart hurt, made me ache with sweet nostalgia. How long had it been since that happened?

I tried to capture the image of that moment in my mind. But, with a lurch, I realized that four layers deep into the afterlife, I could no longer picture Prince Essien's face. Nor Hui Fen's. All I could remember were my emotions; my actual memories were like a fleeting fog, dispersing before just . . . floating away.

My life felt like someone else's life. My memories—someone else's memories.

I was losing my tether to the living realm.

With the very tips of my fingers, I traced over the scarred surface of the table, following the scratches even though I could not touch them. Was Hui here right now? Alive, up on the top level? It made my heart squeeze, thinking that Pópo and myself could be standing right here, in the afterlife, four levels down, while on the surface her grandchild—my sibling—unknowingly went about their daily business. Together, but apart; separated by worlds. Could they sense our presence, even just a little bit?

"Pópo," I murmured, and my grandmother opened her eyes.

She looked at Lin. "Is it time?"

He placed his hand on top of hers and nodded, just once. "It's time."

"What's time?" I asked, frustrated at being left out of the conversation yet again.

Lin turned to me, his expression raw. "You should leave."

I raised my chin. "No."

"Jia." His word was a warning.

"You said you're going further down, right? I'm coming with you. And if you don't take me with you, I'll follow anyway." I set my jaw. "You know I will."

He glared at me. "Why do you have to make this so difficult? What do I have to *do*, to convince you to take your own safety seriously—"

"*My* safety? What about your safety? What about *hers*?" I flung my hand in the direction of Pópo. "I'm not leaving you. Either of you. That's final."

Lin gave me a scathing look. "Fine," he snapped, though it did not seem fine at all. "Come, if you insist. But if you do, Jia, you must promise us one thing."

"And what is that?"

Pópo's soft voice cut through the dead air like a knife. "That you don't argue with us. That you do not derail our plans. This has been many years in the making, bǎobèi. We didn't tell you because—"

I cut her off. "Because why?"

Pópo leveled a look at me. "Because we knew you would never agree."

Nausea rose, cloying, bitterness coating my throat. What were Lin and my grandmother planning? Something so bad, so ghastly, that they'd chosen not to tell me. For *years*.

They knew me too well.

I swallowed down my fear. "Will you tell me now?"

Pópo turned away, headed for the door. "I think it is best we don't. Not yet, anyway."

"That's not going to stop me," I called out to her retreating back.

"Of course it won't." Rolling his eyes, Lin went to the door. "Come on, then, xiǎo è'guǐ. We're going to climb a mountain."

Forty-One

THE FOURTH LEVEL
Present day

The wind lashed at our faces, sticking strands of my hair to my lips.

After trekking for several hours, we'd reached Gui Ku Shan, the mountain where the dead went to die. Folktales talked of ghosts congregating here, and as we climbed their forms streamed past us—gossamer thin—some going the same way as us, some in the opposite direction. Many of them were shimmering with an opalescent sheen, and when I looked at my own arms, they'd taken on the same sort of luminosity.

Around me, the terrain was barren, endless, and uncompromising. This deep in the death realm, things were even darker and more confusing, the pathways oddly convoluted. The horizon seemed to morph and shift each time I looked at it, as though the earth itself was gaining an unsettling sentience . . . until I'd blink and the surrounding mountains would return to being cold, static, immobile.

My grandmother trudged ahead of me along the winding, rock-strewn path, leaning on Lin's elbow. They were talking—

at least, I could see their mouths moving—but I could not hear their conversation above the whine of the wind.

It was lucky, in the end, that I was there. For as Pópo tired, she needed to lean on us both to climb the mountain. It was a treacherous hike, with a gale that buffeted us about, and pebbles that slid beneath our feet before tumbling into the chasm below.

"How much farther?" I said, dragging myself up the incline. But neither Lin nor my grandmother answered.

Eventually, the fatigue caught up with me, and I was no longer able to talk, or badger my companions for information. I just traipsed after them, resigned. As we crested the first peak, the incline became steeper and the path more perilous, so for a while Lin had to carry my grandmother in his arms. Even with the extra load, Lin's long legs made him faster. I quickly fell behind, scrabbling over tumbled rocks, cursing the whole time.

As I made my descent, I discovered that the only thing worse than climbing up a mountain peak was climbing down one. Every now and then it would strike me how high up we were, and a woozy feeling would dip through my belly as I imagined falling. *At least it will get me down to the next level,* I thought grimly, though the idea of having to hike all the way back up again was sobering.

Ahead of me, Lin stood in the half-hidden entrance to a cave. We were not far below the peak. "Hurry," he called, beckoning to me. "We go in here." Pópo was nowhere to be seen—she must have already entered.

"How did you get here so quickly?" I muttered as I stumbled down the rocky path. At one point, I slipped, pain jarring through my tailbone. Yet another injury that Essien would have to contend with.

Lin had already disappeared, swallowed whole by the darkness. Trying to ignore my aching muscles, I finally managed to reach the cave mouth.

I'd barely made it inside when I was grabbed from behind. I tried to cry out, but my scream was stifled by someone's hand over my mouth.

"Don't make a sound," a voice said. I knew that voice.

"Dai Yu." I'd tried to say her name, but it came out muffled against her palm. I hadn't seen her since she'd trapped me in the general's dungeon. What was she doing all the way down here, so deep in death?

My sister spoke into my ear. "We meet again, Jia Yi."

I whimpered, but Dai Yu's hold on me tightened. I was completely and utterly trapped. A tremor rolled through my body—was Dai Yu really so far gone that she retained zero vestiges of familial loyalty?

"Disarm her," Dai Yu commanded, and someone yanked Wen Bo's sword off my belt. I struggled, feebly, to no avail.

Only then did Dai Yu release me. I jerked away, rubbing at my neck. Wen Bo stood before me, having reclaimed his sword. The soldier with the mangled arm was beside him. And my sister?

My sister was watching me. A hollow pit began to expand in my stomach: The look in her eyes had crystallized into pure hatred.

I tried pleading. "Jiějie." *Big sister.* Misery flooded through me—it had been so long since that name had fallen from my lips. "Please—"

I could've sworn a glimpse of remorse flashed across Dai Yu's face. But then it just . . . disappeared.

"Are they with you?" she said, her tone falsely sweet.

"Who?"

She took a few sauntering steps closer. "Pópo and Lin. Of course."

I raised my chin and glared at her. What did she want with them?

If only my power were inflicting death rather than coming back to life. I would have used it on her right then and there. "No. They're not with me."

Dai Yu sneered. "Will you tell us the truth, Jia Yi? Or will we have to force you?" She gave the slightest nod, and both of her companions stepped forward, drawing their weapons.

I should've known. Dai Yu would always take the path of least resistance, would follow whatever and whomever gave her the most power. She'd always loved to trample those she considered beneath her. What a fool I was to have thought that death would make an ounce of difference.

Red-hot fury ripped through me and I lunged at her, only stopping because Wen Bo grabbed me and held me back. "Damn you!" I screamed. "Mothers *damn* you! Where is your honor? Your sense of duty? We are *family*—"

"What a shame," Dai Yu said, a cruel smile twisting her features, "that we cannot choose our family." She raised her eyes and addressed Wen Bo. "Tie her up. His Excellency will be here soon; we'll let him decide what to do with her. When you find the others, bring them to me. And whatever you do"—she raised a delicately arched eyebrow at the guard—"do *not* let her escape again."

I heard Wen Bo swallow behind me, and he tightened his grip on me. But I barely noticed, since I was preoccupied with staring at Dai Yu. My own sister was trying to stop me from helping Pópo, from finding the Shēngsǐ Sword before they did.

My sister, who still didn't know I could resurrect.

I could try to escape, yes. Go back to the land of the living. But if I managed to do it right here, then not only would Dai Yu know my secret, but I'd also be leaving Pópo and Lin stranded in the fourth layer. And I didn't want to leave my grandmother—I still harbored a vague but secret hope that she would agree to use the sword and return to the living realm alongside me.

I struggled, but in vain. Even one-handed, Wen Bo was too strong, and he began dragging me back the way I'd come, my feet scrabbling against the stony path. I'd escaped from him once, already; I could tell that he would not make the same mistake again.

Just as we rounded the bend, I caught sight of Lin emerging from the cave entrance. He'd drawn his knife.

"Lin!" I shrieked.

Our eyes locked. His face turned ashen.

Fear ripped through my chest. How would he fight so many on his own?

But before I had another chance to scream, he'd already thrown his knife.

It whizzed closer, and I braced myself, waiting for it to hit my captor. But it didn't.

It hit me.

*   *   *

As soon as I resurfaced, now in the fifth level, fighting had broken out in earnest. The ghosts in the level above me moved like shadows, and with a lurch of my stomach I realized Lin was facing them. Not just alone, but unarmed—his knife was still stuck in me. I could barely see since my vision was still blurry, but with a grunt, I stood, severing myself from my partially disintegrated fourth-level body. It looked insubstantial, almost nonexistent. I supposed that down here we were all just different types of energy, vibrating at different frequencies, echoes of what once had been.

I yanked Lin's blue knife from my chest as I stumbled toward the skirmish. But before I could reach Lin, the most ungodly scream tore from his throat. He staggered sideways, clutching a slash in his belly, from which copious black blood gushed. After taking two more steps toward me, he collapsed.

I understood now: He'd killed me to save me from my sister's clutches, then goaded them into killing him, too. Briefly I wondered whether Pópo had already died, and whether we'd joined her in the fifth level.

I ran to him, falling painfully to my knees. For a few minutes, he was still, his eyes all flat and glassy. But as soon as he sat up, breaking way from his fourth-level body, I hauled him to his feet.

"Let's go," I hissed, tugging on his sleeve.

Dai Yu and her guards stood a few paces away. Now that they couldn't see us, they had lowered their weapons, and were conferring in low voices.

"Quick." Lin took my hand and tugged me in the opposite direction, deeper into the cave. "Before they follow."

I tripped along behind him, trying to adjust my eyesight to the all-consuming blackness.

He led me into a tunnel hewn directly into the rock. The air around us pressed in close, suffocating. As we hurried along, I glanced over my shoulder, relieved to see no one following. In fact, the cave and the tunnel were eerily quiet compared to the crowded path leading up to the peak. It was like the Bone Smith's house all over again, unsettlingly empty, and I wondered whether ghosts were as afraid of this place as I was.

Deep underground, the darkness grew even dimmer, until we were groping our way along the wall. The tunnel began to slant downward, and I realized that this entire time we'd been walking on a slight curve. It seemed we were spiraling right into the heart of the mountain.

But where was Pópo?

Dread coiled tight in my belly. Everything felt claustrophobic this far below ground. The air weighed heavier and heavier, scraping at my skin. It was as if we were being buried—not alive, but close enough. I wondered how much longer it would be before I could no longer hold in my scream.

Finally, we burst out into a wide-open cavern. It was enormous. Similar to the landscape outside, this cave was completely barren, a dry, dusty dirt floor encircled by a perimeter of lichen-stained rock.

I scanned the perimeter. The wall appeared to have collapsed in several places, leaving piles of broken boulders. There were also other entrances to the cave, their mouths dark and yawning. It was as if every single pathway in the mountain was designed to lead us here.

"This is it, Jia." Lin frowned. "It's not too late to—"

"I won't leave you," I interjected, and Lin's frown deepened.

Be unhappy, I thought, uncharitably. *I didn't come all this way just to avoid upsetting you.*

He stared at me for several seconds, seemingly weighing his options, before he sighed, resigned. "Fine. We need to go down again. Give me my knife so I can keep watch. You go first. I'll follow."

"Wait." I drew out Lin's knife, which was still stained with my black ghost blood. The blade was glinting, chasing away the encroaching shadows with its blue, unearthly glow. "How about *you* go first, I'll keep watch, then *I'll* follow."

"Jia." His eyes slid shut, and he gave a long-suffering groan. "Don't do this."

"Don't do what?" I said, stubbornly. "Why does it always have to be you protecting me? Why can't I protect you, for a change?"

He let out a harsh laugh, which bounced around the cavern. "Protect me? Protect *me*? But Jia . . ." He scowled, his expression black. "I don't need protecting."

"You're saying that *I* need protecting?" My hands curled into fists. "Because I'll have you know, I can look after myself—"

"For Mothers' sake, I didn't mean it that way!" Reaching up, Lin grabbed my face with both hands, his fingers digging into my cheekbones. "I meant that *you are worth* protecting. Not me."

He shoved himself off me and turned away. In that moment,

he looked so desolate it made my chest ache. I couldn't help it; all my anger drained away in an instant.

I took a step toward him, reaching out, just falling short of touching him. "Don't say that. Of course you're worth protecting."

He stiffened. "There isn't time to argue. Go—go now. Dai Yu and the others may already be following."

I reached for him again, and this time I did touch him. Placing my hand on his shoulder, I guided him around to face me. "How about we do it like we've always done?"

He hesitated for just a moment. "Together?"

My resolve hardened. I held out my hand for his knife. "Together."

Lin stared down at me, his eyes so dark they looked black. Finally, he gave a small nod, and passed me his blade.

I clutched it in my fist and closed my eyes, summoning the disembodied feeling that would take me to the next level.

It took a long time. Every time I tried to push my consciousness downward, it felt like the death realm was resisting, pushing back.

But eventually I felt it: the first lashings of numbness, licking at the ends of my limbs. The creeping sense of weightlessness, and insubstantiality.

Then, suddenly, it was as though I was breaking through, tipping headfirst into the next layer.

"Are you ready?" I asked as my organs began to feel more disparate. The edges of my form began to fray, my ghostly form tearing apart. The emptiness inside me grew, expanding like a heatless fire.

Lin's voice had gone very quiet. "I am ready, xiǎo è'guǐ."

I waited. And waited. And at the very last moment—just before my consciousness slipped into the sixth level—my eyes snapped open.

Lin was leaning slightly forward, his focus fixed entirely on me.

And, without a beat of hesitation, I looked into Lin's amber eyes . . . and stabbed him in the heart with his knife.

Forty-Two

One year ago

The mornings were always the hardest.

Sunlight streamed in through the paper windows of my hut, making my closed eyelids glow red. I ignored it; I didn't want to open my eyes—not yet.

If I kept my eyes closed, then I could sometimes fool my mind into believing he was still here. Lying on my side, I burrowed my face into the lumpy pillow.

It still smelled like him.

It had been three days since I'd seen him; three whole days since we'd kissed after he'd bound my injured wrist. That night, we had settled in the cave to sleep; we'd tangled our legs together and held each other under the comforting anonymity of darkness. The next morning, when I'd woken to streaming sunlight, he had gone.

Thinking he'd just stepped out to get some water or supplies, I'd waited for him . . . and waited . . . and waited . . .

But he never came back.

I curled up into a ball, bringing my knees to my chest.

Suddenly, the smell of him seemed too strong. Overpowering. Oppressive.

Everything was happening at once. It was too much. It wasn't just Lin. Soon after he left, Pópo had taken a turn for the worse. Yes, she'd been sick for a long time, seemingly unable to shake off her latest cough. But a few days ago, she'd suddenly become more frail. She could only walk short distances, and even then she needed support. And occasionally, when she thought no one was looking, she would wince in pain, though she always waved dismissively whenever we expressed concern.

Tears stung at the corners of my eyelids, and I ground the heels of my hands against my eyes. Pópo was more ill than she'd ever been before—and Lin chose *now* to abandon us?

He had kissed me once, fooled me into believing he loved me, and then vanished.

Why? I couldn't tell. Was it because he was scared? We'd finally confessed our feelings. Maybe he couldn't handle it?

Or maybe it was something else. Maybe he'd been lying about loving me, and felt guilty for his deception.

I groaned, rolling onto my back. Now, the smell of him was making me sick. My head grew hot. My pulse pounded at the base of my skull.

Don't be pathetic, I scolded myself. *Don't spend your time pining for someone who doesn't want you.*

I wrenched my eyes open and threw off my covers. If I lay here, wallowing in self-pity, then all that would mean was that Lin had *won*. He'd gotten what he wanted and then disappeared.

Bastard! He didn't need to take anything else from me. Like my dignity, for one. Or my self worth.

Grinding my teeth, I rolled up my mattress, pillow and all, and bundled it into my arms, muttering a stream of vulgar words beneath my breath. As I hauled it out my door, dragging it through the dirt, a few people called to me, asking what I was doing.

I ignored them. Just continued dragging it, muttering curses. The pounding in my head had progressed to a full-blown roar. As soon as I saw the watchfire, I sped up.

"Fucking bastard!" With a final heave, I threw my entire bed and its coverings straight on top of the fire.

It flared bright, forcing the watchwomen to lean back to avoid the surge of heat. The mattress, which was full of straw, caught quickly. Yellow flames licked and spat. With my hands propped on my hips, I watched with vindictive pleasure as the straw bed blackened and curled into ash.

"Was that your . . . bed, Jia Yi?" one of the watchwomen asked, tentatively. The others just averted their eyes. Most of them knew better than to risk provoking my temper.

"Yes." My voice was curt, but inside, my pulse was racing. What had I just done? I'd burned my only bed until it was merely charred remnants. Where the hells would I sleep tonight?

Never mind. I'd deal with it later. For now, at least I wasn't going to have to put up with Lin's scent—his memory—sullying my house.

Dusting my hands off, I turned to make my way back to my hut, only to bump face-first into Hui.

My sibling glanced at my face, then at the watchfire, then back at me. They chafed their hands. I knew them well enough to know that they were about to tell me something. Probably something bad.

My chest tightened. "What's wrong?"

Had Lin been found? Or worse, had something happened to him? What if he hadn't run away out of cowardice, as I'd assumed, but instead was injured . . . or dead?

"It's Lin, isn't it," I continued, my voice rising. "Has something happened to him? Is he . . . hurt?" I couldn't bring myself to say *dead*, even though the more I thought about it, the more it was possible. I mean, just being around me put him at risk, didn't it?

Death clings to you like a mantle, the shaman had said. My mother, my father, my sister Dai Yu—all of them had died due to their association with me.

"He's fine," Hui said, and I exhaled. "It's just that . . ."

"What?" I grabbed Hui's shoulders. "Tell me!"

A pause. "I saw him. Outside a tavern in the city."

My fingers slackened. "Did you speak to him?"

"No. But people have been talking." Hui gave me an apologetic look. "Apparently he's been spending a lot of time there."

I frowned. A *tavern*? Yes, Lin was old enough, since he was probably a few years older than my age, sixteen—but he'd never previously seemed the type. What was he doing at a tavern?

There was only one way to find out.

I wasn't very familiar with the city, but I figured I could probably convince an aunty to accompany me. All I needed was to know the way. Luckily, Hui Fen had been there. And they had memory magic.

"Show me," I said. "Please."

* * *

I pushed through the crowd, wrinkling my nose at the stench of stale wine, grimy bodies, and sour, days-old sweat. People sloshed their drinks on me as I shoved past, but I barely noticed. All I could focus on was Lin.

Like me, he loved my grandmother. He would want to know she'd gotten sicker. Wouldn't he?

Finally, I spotted him in a dark corner of the inn. He was sitting at a table, alone, a drink clutched in his hand. Above him, smoke curled through the rafters, the dust motes sparkling in the hazy air. As I approached, he brought his ceramic tumbler to his lips and took a long, throaty draft.

I frowned, my steps slowing as I approached. Why was Lin at the ghost table—the one with red chairs, that patrons were supposed to keep empty? He seemed to be muttering to himself. Folktales warned that disrupting the ghosts would bring bad luck. Did he not realize? Perhaps he just didn't care.

I paused and studied him from a distance. He looked . . . terrible. His sharp cheekbones were even more prominent than usual, the hollows below painfully gaunt. Beneath each eye were dark smudges, like he hadn't slept for days. His usually curly hair was lank, and his tunic was half unbuttoned, exposing a glimpse of tan chest.

He raised his head as I approached, his eyes oddly unfocused, until I was close enough for recognition to dawn in those amber depths.

"Jia," he slurred, smirking. "You found me."

"What are you doing?" I raised my voice in an attempt to cut through the rabble.

He cocked his head to one side and raised his tumbler. "Why, isn't it obvious, xiǎo è'guǐ? I am drinking."

"I can see that," I snapped. "I meant, why are you acting so ridiculous? Hui Fen said they saw you, passed out drunk in the streets. They *showed* me. You're acting the fool, Lin."

"It seems silly to dwell on Hui's memories of me," Lin said, frowning at the tumbler, then taking another swig of wine. "When I can't even remember them, myself."

Fuming, I tried to snatch the drink from Lin's hands. But his reflexes were good even despite his inebriation, and he managed to jerk the cup away. I let out a frustrated cry and stamped my foot. "Stop *drinking*!"

Lin stood, suddenly, forcing me to take a step back. His height was overbearing. My pulse, already racing, began hammering so fast that I could feel it in my neck.

"All right. I'll stop." His mouth curved into a grin. Then, very slowly, and very deliberately, he poured the remainder of his drink—right down the front of my dress.

"Oh look," he said, his tone mocking. "I *missed*."

I gaped at him, and he laughed. A bleak, merciless laugh. It only took me a moment of staring down at my now-soaked gown, for my rage to roil and rise and bubble right over.

I drew my hand back and—while he was still laughing—slapped him.

"You *bastard*," I screamed. "You don't even know why I *came* here! I came to tell you Pópo is worse. She can barely get out of bed." A hush had fallen over the tavern. All the patrons were staring, but at this point I didn't care.

Angrily, I snatched up a napkin and began blotting at my chest.

This seemed to snap him out of his callousness, because his face fell into a stricken expression. "She—she what?"

"She's worse. Much worse." I threw the napkin down, then straightened, my chin jutting up to face him. "I thought that you would care, but it seems not. So"—I drew myself to my full height and glared at him—"you can go to hell."

His eyes widened, and his nostrils flared. "I care, Jia. I do."

I scoffed. He was such a good liar. Even now I could tell he was lying through his teeth.

Just then, a group of young men crowded around us. Off-duty Lancaster soldiers; I could tell from their outfits.

Here, near the city ports, Yskians and Fengzhians did mingle. It was generally an unspoken rule that, if they wanted to visit these sorts of establishments, that they didn't brawl. People complied—most of the time, at least—their love for drink outweighing their hatred for political rivals.

"Hey," one said, elbowing his friend. "Who's the girl?"

I scowled. Of course they would address Lin, when I was standing there.

Lin turned slowly, his features transforming into an expressionless mask. "No one you should be concerned with." His voice was measured. But I could tell from his posture, and the set of his jaw, that he was holding back.

A second man leered at me, his eyes dropping to my chest, where my damp gown clung entirely too close to the swell of my breasts. Glancing down, I suddenly wished I'd kept my cloak on.

"You're pretty," the man said, his voice slurring slightly. "But your gown is a little wet." He shot me a debauched grin. "Perhaps it'd be better if you just . . . took it off."

Fear began to crawl up my throat. "Fuck off," I said, trying to cover myself with my arms. This only made things worse.

"Aw, come on," the first man said, reaching out to tug my hands away. My skin crawled where he touched me. "We're only looking out for you. It's for your own comfort, you know—"

Lin shouldered me aside, advancing on the group. My stomach dropped; he was outnumbered. And foolishly, I hadn't brought any weapons. I'd only come here to confront Lin. To tell him about my grandmother. I'd never expected that we'd be getting into a silly tavern brawl.

"Get out of here, Jia," Lin snapped, over his shoulder.

"No," I said, stubbornly. "I'm not leaving you—"

He half turned at that. His face had reddened, the vein on his forehead distended. "Don't you understand? I *don't want you.* You don't belong here. Get. Out."

I faltered, stumbled back a few steps, still clutching at my saturated chest. I'd thought he was trying to defend me. That maybe he still harbored some lingering loyalty. But it seemed I was wrong. Perhaps these horrid men were his new friends, and it was true—he didn't love me, never loved me. The kiss we shared was, for me, profound, but for him . . .

For him it had all been a lie.

Tears blurred my vision. I fled, pushing past the throng of people who'd gathered to watch the "fight," stumbling out into the street, where Aunty Ai Li was waiting.

It was the last time I ever saw Lin alive, because that night, according to the rumors . . .

That was the night he died.

Forty-Three

THE SIXTH LEVEL

Present day

This time, I woke up even groggier than usual. My body felt oddly light, like a cluster of parts held together by empty spaces.

With each descent, it was more and more difficult to gain my bearings. Being so deeply entrenched in the afterlife would make it even harder to resurrect, I was sure of it.

Unthinkingly, I pressed my hand over my chest, where the pocket watch hung. It was silent—no ticking, no vibrations, and of course my hand went right through.

Still dead, then. I counted inside my head: We were now in the sixth level. How many more would there be before we reached the end?

Trying to remember what the living world looked like, I found, with alarm, that I couldn't. I couldn't even remember what it felt like to be alive. I'd become so accustomed to the constant gloom, to the lack of definition that characterized the deeper layers. And while I remembered that it was Prince Essien Lancaster who had given me the watch, my last connection to the mortal realm, I couldn't remember the exact circumstances, couldn't remember why. Just as with my memory of his face, and his voice, the specifics of our conversation escaped me. A picture in the clouds, dispersed by gusting wind.

Shaking off this unhelpful thought, I sat up, trying to clear my dizziness. I clutched my forehead and swayed to my feet, blinking and trying to peer through the dense veil of darkness. My eyes were still foggy, but a halo of light filtered around the edges of my vision.

As my eyesight cleared, I turned and squinted at my surroundings.

Just one layer down, and the cave had transformed. It was no longer barren. Instead, it was majestic. In the center, a vast, shimmering lake had appeared—the water so clear I could see right to the bottom. Braziers were positioned around the periphery of the cave, and within them burned blue fire, their reflections bouncing off the water with a brilliant cobalt sheen. Dappled light danced across the cave walls, reflected from the water's surface, wavering lines of shifting shapes.

A rickety wooden bridge bisected the lake. It had no guardrails and was so narrow that only one individual could traverse it at a time. It led to the far side of the cavern, which, unlike everywhere else, was cloaked in shadows. The darkness there looked solid, almost physical—an insidious blackness that contrasted with the utter radiance of the lake.

And crouched by the shore, facing away from me and silhouetted against the turquoise water, was Lin.

For a moment, I couldn't move. I couldn't speak. Something in his posture, in the slant of his shoulders, told me that we'd reached some sort of turning point: There was no going back.

Where, then, was my grandmother? My stomach lurched. I forced my legs to move. "Lin," I croaked.

In a single fluid movement, he rose and turned to face me, his expression guarded. His bloodstained knife hung loosely in his fingers, and as I watched, he sheathed it.

"Is Pópo here?" I edged closer, and as I drew nearer to the lake, whispering sounds rose from its depths.

"She's searching for the sword." He caught sight of my reaction. "She's safe, don't worry. It's all part of the plan."

I narrowed my eyes at him. "And are you going to tell me what 'the plan' is now?"

Lin ignored my question, instead turning and gesturing at the water. "Do you recognize this place, Jia?"

I shot him a questioning look before edging closer to the water. Despite its ethereal beauty, something about it felt wrong. Like it was empty, frozen in the liminal space between life and death. And as I approached, the whispering grew louder, not one person's whisper, but many. Thousands? Millions? Billions? I couldn't tell. All the voices mingled until they reverberated painfully within my ears.

My toes reached the edge of the embankment we stood on, and I stared at the lake's surface. A circular reflection shimmered at the center.

Above us was a hole that hadn't been there before. A hole that seemed to traverse the entire height of the mountain.

I let my gaze drift back down. "We must be in—"

"Shuang Yue Dong." Lin finished my sentence for me.

Double Moon Cave. The beginning and the end of life and death.

I stared at the water, at the small patch of reflected sky; it had taken on a pink-tinged cast.

We'd made it. We were in the deepest layer of death. No wonder nobody in the living realm had ever found this place; it only manifested itself in the sixth level of the afterlife.

But then what was the darkness at the opposite end of the cavern? *That* hadn't been mentioned in the stories . . .

My gaze alighted back on the lake's surface. It was rippling despite there being no breeze, and all of a sudden . . . dawning realization unfurled in my mind.

If this was Shuang Yue Dong, then it meant the lake was . . .

Quickly, I stepped back from the edge.

The water itself was so clear—so dazzling in its beauty—but the scent it gave off was strange. Not unpleasant, necessarily, and not sulfurous like a regular mountain spring. But it was just . . . *too much.* It was like an amalgamation of all the world's smells mashed into one blend, so strong it stung my nostrils.

Yes, I knew what this lake was. Even though I'd never seen it before, a visceral part of me recognized it with the very essence of my humanity.

"The Lake of Forgetfulness," I murmured. The words tasted ominous on my tongue. It was said to be created from every single tear ever shed by a human, throughout all of history. Tears of embarrassment, tears of joy, tears of untold grief. The sounds were merely echoes of human memories, the susurrating whispers spanning the full spectrum from bliss and joy to heartrending sorrow. Legend told that the moment the water touched your skin you'd lose all your memories, forever.

"So," I started, then swallowed. "If we go in there, then—"

"We . . . reincarnate." Lin was watching me; I looked away.

If we went in there, we'd forget everything. We'd wake up in a new body, a new form . . . with no recollection of our past life whatsoever.

Suddenly, I understood. "You're planning to jump in. Once we find the sword." I swallowed around the obstruction that had lodged in my throat.

"Not just me," he said, turning his attention back to the lake. His eyes held something in their depths—some emotion I couldn't read. "We both are."

We both are. At first, my mind couldn't quite comprehend his words, but then it hit me. I pressed a hand on my chest, over the cavern housing my silent heart, as I slowly pieced things together.

"You mean you and Pópo." It was not a question.

He looked down, scuffing the toe of his boot into the ground. "Yes. After we destroy the sword, we'll reincarnate."

"Why?" I asked, though in truth . . . I already knew.

"Because we have nowhere else to go, Jia. Unlike you, we cannot go back."

I fell silent, Lin's words swirling around my head. It all made sense now: Lin was planning to reincarnate. So was Pópo. Once they touched the lake water, my grandmother would lose her powers, lose her memories. She'd forget everything.

Which meant . . .

She would even forget me.

Both of them would. They wouldn't remember I ever existed.

The knowledge hit me like a monsoon. A year ago, I'd

already gone through all the stages of grief with Lin: denial, sadness, anger. Then I'd lost my grandmother. I hadn't even been able to properly say goodbye.

I'd chased them both, delving deeper and deeper into the underworld. Racked by grief and thirsting for vengeance.

And then Lin and I had kissed—as ghosts, of course, though it had still felt real—and for a moment it was as if no time had passed. Like we were still in our cave, kissing for the very first time.

Now these memories were trickling down my spine like cold sweat, haunting me like Lin had, and continued to do. Suddenly, the thought of never seeing him again, just after we'd reunited, was heinous.

But then I had to remind myself that *I did not trust him.* He'd betrayed me so many times, convinced me beyond a doubt that his soul was tarnished, and yet . . .

I burned for him. More than I burned for anyone. It was like our souls were permanently entwined. We were forged from the same star, we were planets perpetually orbiting one another. It was as though something had gone irrevocably wrong in the world when we'd met. Like when our friendship—and later love—clicked into place, it damaged us both in ways we could not fathom.

Perhaps we'd known each other in our past lives and reincarnated repeatedly, finding each other every time. Being drawn together as inexorably as the moon draws the tides, as a flame draws the flickering wings of a moth.

Truly, it seemed like we were the only two in the world who completely understood each other. Whatever we had was forged from anger, from hatred, from discord, from loneliness. But equally, it flamed hotter and more ferociously than normal love should.

I was not foolish; I vaguely recalled there was someone I cared for, waiting up on the surface in the living realm. Although the specifics escaped me, the emotions did not.

Could I love again, though, when my heart was so blemished? When my soul, despite being scorched beyond recognition, turned toward the one who had burned me?

The truth was: I was afraid that Lin, my first love, had ruined me forever.

"You can go back," I blurted, before I could stop myself. "You both can. The sword . . . it can bring the dead back to life—"

"Jia." Lin cut me off so softly, so gently. "Even if we find it, I won't use the sword. I don't *want* to."

"But then . . . you won't be . . . *you* anymore." My voice was small.

His expression darkened, his mouth set in a grim smile. "One can only hope."

Lin's self-hatred was nothing new. Still, his words tore something open in my chest. All my wounds were reopening, gaping, raw; as though they might never heal. The thought of him ceasing to exist was unfathomable. My oldest childhood friend. He would become a new person, or a new creature, while I—

I swallowed, the movement painful. He was like a link to the life I'd once led, the last time that I'd been truly . . . happy.

Thinking about it caused me pain. Pain that crystallized into anger, heavy in my gut.

Striding to him, I shoved him—hard—in the chest. So hard that he stumbled backward. "*This* is your plan?" I hurled the words at him. Lin didn't fight back, which somehow made it both better . . . and worse.

"Jia . . ."

"Don't 'Jia' me!" I shoved him again. This time it was hard enough to throw him against the cave wall, narrowly missing a brazier. "You planned all this without ever telling me?" Yet another betrayal.

Pópo was right: If I'd known what they meant to do, I would *never* have agreed. This whole time, I'd assumed Pópo would want to go back. But now I was learning she'd never intended to survive at all.

What did this mean for *my* secret plan?

My voice shook, rising now, along with my rage. "How could you *do* that to me, Lin?" I shoved him a third time, even harder this time. "How can you throw away your entire life?"

Lin caught my flailing wrists, his fingers tightening, vise-like. "Because my life isn't mine!" he spat. "It's yours."

I stopped. Stared at him, speechless.

"It's yours. It's always been yours," he continued, his tone bitter. "You stole my life. Don't you understand? The only thing I ever think about is *you*. The only thing that I care about is *you*. The only thing I want to save"—he pushed off the wall and flipped us around, so my back was against the rock—"is *you*. It's always *you*! So take my life. Take it away. It's yours anyway."

He braced his hands against the cave wall, caging me in, his face twisted into abject rage. I began to tremble, but not from fear. It was from . . . despair.

After a moment, I reached out my hand and placed it on his cheek. He recoiled from my touch, and my heart rent in two. "My life is yours as much as yours is mine, Lin."

He leaned into my hand. Closed his eyes. "Jia." Devastatingly gently, he drew me closer. In response, I went limp, falling into his arms. Every nerve felt strung out, taut, about to snap, and my throat closed over a heaving sob. "Jia Yi." This time he said my name tenderly, each syllable traced in sorrow.

"Why?" I whispered, my resolve shattering into pieces. "You're giving up. Why?"

He clasped me against his chest, his nose buried in my hair. "I've done terrible things, Jia. I've killed people, I've lied, I've betrayed you—so many times. What I did to you the last time I saw you was unforgivable." His disgust at himself was palpable; his teeth ground so hard it was a wonder his jaw didn't crack. "It set in motion everything that happened until this point: Me, dying, no longer able to protect you. You, dying, and then being exposed to General Hong—"

I cut in. "My death wasn't your fault, Lin. *I* decided to stray close to the border, not you."

"No, but—" He stopped, paused, then continued, the dual edges of frustration and resignation hardening his voice to steel. "If I could go back in time and reverse what I did, I would, Jia. I would. But I can't. This will mean . . . I won't be able to hurt you again. I'll be forced to let you go."

Now all I felt was pity. I was only beginning to understand the depths of what Lin would do—how much he would debase himself—to protect those he loved. I could see it now: When I'd seen him for that very last time at the tavern, he'd hated himself. So thoroughly, that he'd done his best to make me hate him.

All to set me free.

The memories of that day had haunted me, every waking moment, for the entire year that followed. I'd fled the tavern because I thought Lin detested me. But when I'd heard he'd gotten into a fight with the lecherous men who'd pawed at me, it had made me wonder. Had he actually died defending my honor?

The guilt had eaten me up, like a parasitic insect devouring the young of its prey. How many times had I been ripped from sleep, covered in sweat and heart pounding, because of a nightmare I'd had about Lin being hauled to some back alley? About him being beaten to death by the group of men who'd threatened to rip off my hànfú?

He had never thought himself worthy of a better fate. Of love.

And in a way, he was right. What he'd done *was* unforgivable. I'd learned by now that good intentions don't necessarily outweigh monstrous actions.

Perhaps the pity I felt was actually for me. For everything I'd lost and was about to lose. Loving and then hating Lin had been an anchor. I'd never realized how much I clung to those feelings.

I'd never quite worked out how to exist without them.

"But we won't ever . . ." My knees buckled beneath me. "We won't ever see each other again . . ."

Lin's eyes widened as I sagged; he held me up, one arm encircling my shoulders and the other clasped around my waist. "Jia," he said for the third time, my name a tortured plea. "Save yourself. Go back to the land of the living. Forget about me."

"It'll be *you* who forgets about *me.*" I could barely choke the words out.

He gripped me harder, straining my body against his. "Forget *you?*" he ground out. Our lips were almost touching, just a hair's width between them. "I would sooner forget my own *existence* before I forgot you!"

The power behind his words punched me in the chest. I tilted my face up, and then his mouth was on mine.

Our second proper kiss.

This time, it was explosive. Like we were unleashing all our pain from more than a year of misunderstandings. It was so intense that it burned. We didn't stop, didn't need to draw breath. I swiped my tongue against his, and he groaned, pushing me up against the wall.

I clung to his shoulders like he was the only thing left in the world. His arms wound around my back, crushing me, possessing me, as he ran his lips down my neck, and then nipped me. I cried out, flexed my hips without thinking, my fingers digging into his skin until he gave a low, guttural growl.

He slid his hand up, twisted it into my hair, and tilted my head back. I yelped—not out of pain, but in surprise.

His eyes were flaming, his pupils dilated, the muscles in his neck tensed and corded. He gave me a searing gaze, and a flush of heat filled my belly. "It's selfish," he said, his voice strangled. "I want you to stay here, with me. But I shouldn't. I shouldn't."

I panted as his lips brushed down my neck, his hand still coiled in my hair. Everything was overpowering—the sensations, my emotions, his scent, his taste.

"I like you being selfish," I whispered as his lips trailed along my collarbone. I threw my head back, arching into his touch, my fingernails digging into his shoulders until I was sure that they'd leave marks. "I am . . . selfish . . . too."

He raised his head, his mouth claiming mine again. Pressing his lips against mine, he spoke, so I felt the vibration of his words. "We belong together, Jia. It doesn't matter how many fancy trinkets that pretty prince gives you, we belong to each other. You hear me?"

"I hear you," I rasped out.

"Say it," he said, his voice unraveling. "Say you're mine."

"I am yours," I whispered. Down here, this deep, I couldn't think of anything else. I could still taste Lin on my lips.

He pulled my face to his again, and kissed me—hard. And I kissed back, winding my arms around his neck, knowing that he was right. No matter what happened, no matter how many worlds or lives came between us, we'd never be truly free of each other.

But even as I kissed him, I realized that everything inside me was breaking. This kiss was passionate, yes, but even more so . . . it was *painful.* Because it was not a lover's kiss. There was no affection, no warmth, no fondness in our touch. Instead, it was more like a clash between our shattered souls as they struggled to unite. As if we'd been created from one spirit that had been torn asunder, cleaved forever into two bodies.

I knew it now, as well as I knew myself: I would never live a happy life with Lin, nor he with me. To be two halves of one whole, but in separate bodies, eternally apart—that wasn't love. It was codependency. An addiction. Torture of the sweetest, and most excruciating, kind.

And everything we'd been through had led us to this point, where the only way to reach redemption was for our paths to split. Perhaps, in another universe—or another life—things could be different. Here, though, there was only the two of us. Stumbling together, along the same broken road.

Earlier, I'd thought there was no going back in our plan. Now I realized . . . there was no going back for *us*.

When we finally broke apart, Lin rested his forehead on mine. His chest was heaving, even though he had no breath to catch.

"Go back," he whispered, each word like a twist of a knife. "Live. It's the right thing to do."

"Lin—"

He scrunched his eyes shut, as though speaking caused him pain. "I mean it. Once we've found the sword, go back to that little princeling. He can make you happy. Let him."

I flinched at the mention of Essien Lancaster, whose watch still hung around my neck. Lin's words had unlocked a trove of memories in my mind.

I choked back a sob. Essien, who'd been kind to me, even when he hadn't needed to. Who was up there on the surface, dutifully watching over my dead body. The boy who hadn't hesitated to help me, to heal me, even though he was supposed to hate me. The boy with the golden hair, who felt so distant from this cold, dark place of death that I could barely even recall his memory without prompting.

I thought about the little time we'd spent together. The rush of warmth I felt at every touch. The glances he threw me when he thought I wasn't looking. I'd assumed the feeling that pooled within me whenever Essien Lancaster drew close was just his magic calling to mine. But what if it wasn't that?

What if it was *more*?

I didn't answer Lin for the longest time. Reaching up, I caressed his face, until he opened his eyes again. With the tips of my fingers, I traced his cheek, his jaw, memorizing his granite-hewn features. His lips parted, his expression raw. Until finally—I gave the smallest nod.

He let out a sigh—one of relief—then bent his lips to mine again.

But this time, although tender, it wasn't a kiss of love.

It was a kiss of goodbye.

Forty-Four

THE SIXTH LEVEL
Present day

A noise sounded from behind us, and Lin and I sprang apart. Dread pooled at the base of my skull.

We were surrounded.

It was my sister and her guards. But this time, she'd brought more: around two dozen ghosts, their reflective eyes and blood-stained armor shimmering in the darkness. Lin and I had been so absorbed in our shared grief—in the melancholy of our final farewell—that we hadn't noticed them sneaking in.

Immediately, Lin pushed me away. "Go," he said under his breath, so only I could hear. "Resurrect. Now."

The group closed in on us, a circle of prowling predators. As if they were hunters, herding us.

A moment ago I'd agreed to resurrect after we'd found the weapon. To leave Lin here with Pópo to reincarnate. But now, facing this small army, we were already severely outnumbered. If I left, as Lin wished me to, I'd be abandoning him to face them alone.

"No," I said. A muscle flexed in his jaw, but he didn't argue. I suppose he knew me well enough to know I wouldn't leave him. Or my grandmother, since I still didn't know where she was.

"How sweet." Dai Yu strolled into a patch of moonlight, holding her spear. In a subtle but swift movement, Lin shifted in front of me.

Dai Yu smirked at the sight. "Sorry to interrupt your . . . ah . . . happy reunion."

Panicking, I cast my eyes around the dim cavern. Where was Pópo? Lin had said she was safe. But now that the other ghosts were here, was that still the case? I made an effort to catch Lin's eye, but he was staring resolutely forward, his knuckles white against his knife handle.

Trying to keep my voice steady, I called out, "Why are you here?"

She tilted her head, birdlike. "We want what you want. To find the weapon you so covet."

"But why?" I insisted, trying to buy time. "Why betray Pópo? Why side with the general?"

In my peripheral vision I could see the other ghosts tensing, closing ranks, ready to defend her. Dai Yu flipped her long hair over one shoulder and raised both eyebrows at me. "Do you know what it was like for me, having you as a sister?"

I reeled. "Me? I . . . uh . . . what?"

She angled the point of her spear at me. "Yes, you. You and your *lack of magic*." Her nose wrinkled. "Not only did you kill our mother . . . after Father died, Pópo diverted all her attention to you. She spent all her time visiting shamans, researching the history of other Empties like you, trying to figure out if there was anything she could fix."

Her hardened gaze fell onto Lin, whose shoulder was

abutting mine. Surreptitiously, he turned his hand slightly until his thumb brushed against my knuckles.

Dai Yu noticed, and scowled. "And things got worse when *he* came along. Pópo was even more absent, spending hours tutoring him. Trying to train him to become a civilized person." She sneered. "Too bad it didn't work."

"You're doing all this because you're *jealous*?" It was . . . completely ludicrous. And yet, part of me wondered if it was really true. I certainly hadn't ever noticed Pópo paying more attention to me. But then again, I hadn't noticed much beyond my own childhood grievances. Petty squabbles and trifling disappointments that had, at the time, loomed large. Had I truly been favored but too self-centered to realize?

Dai Yu gave a derisive laugh. "Jealous? Mothers, no! As if I could be jealous of two little insects like you." Her lip curled. "I'm doing this to show the two of you—*and* Pópo—that despite being neglected for almost my entire childhood . . . I will still find a way to win."

"That's completely illogical," I said. "That's—"

Dai Yu cut me off, her expression bored. "I really don't care about logic, little sister. All I care about"—her lips spread in a smile—"is victory." Then, she gave a casual wave of her hand—

And they attacked.

I ducked out of the way just as the first ghost slashed at me with a sword. They overbalanced. Desperate, I took the chance to grab an arrow from their quiver and plunge it into their chest. They keeled over, screaming, then disintegrated into dust before my eyes.

I stared, shocked. Up until now, in the ghost realm, dying meant descending to the next level. And each time, the bodies became less corporeal, but they never crumbled away to nothingness. Was it different perishing here, in the very last level of death?

Panting, I swiped the Bone Smith bow and arrows the disintegrated ghost had left behind, slinging the quiver onto my back. After scrambling up an embankment of tumbled rocks, I nocked another arrow.

Below, Lin was engaged in a knife fight with two separate ghosts, while several others tried to scrabble up the rock face to reach me. Fortunately, the space between the cave wall and the lake was narrow, and the ghosts seemed reluctant to crowd into it, for fear of falling into the lake. But they were steering us closer and closer to the far side—where the darkness fell like a curtain. An unnatural barrier to . . . what?

I didn't know.

I fought hard, trying to retain my position. Trying not to retreat defensively toward the darkness. It was lucky that none of our opponents seemed to be seasoned fighters. Their weaponwork was amateur at best.

As I shot my arrows, one by one, each ghost I hit exploded in a shower of debris. The residual dust swirled around, choking me, like smoke from a green-branch fire, before it streamed into the strange black hole at the far side of the lake.

I couldn't afford to wonder what was happening; all I could focus on was the fight.

Lin successfully dispatched his attackers by pushing them into the water, only to have two more run at him. Before they reached him, he turned to me, his hair plastered to his forehead, and shouted. "Do it! Do it now!"

"*No,*" I screamed back, then shot another arrow. I wasn't

going to resurrect now, mid-fight. One of the ghosts leaped at me, grabbing at my foot, and I slid heavily down the rock face, landing on my tailbone with a crash. The pain was jarring, but I couldn't stop. I rolled to the side to avoid the arc of an axe blade as it swung into the ground beside me. I screamed—it had just grazed my shoulder, raising a flap of skin.

Luckily the axe itself had lodged into the dirt floor. My attacker was struggling, attempting to pull it out, so I grabbed an arrow with my hand and ran it through their neck.

Jumping to my feet, I scanned once more for Lin, ignoring how much my wound hurt. When our eyes met, it was like we were back in the forest, on a hunt. Instinctively, we moved toward each other, until we were standing back-to-back. Here, we resumed fighting.

We were used to this: struggling for our survival. It had always been this way. Us, together, stronger.

The next ghost to launch himself at me was Wen Bo. He stalked forward, brandishing the sword I'd previously stolen before he'd taken it back. But this time, he held it in his right hand, because his left hand had been hacked off.

He swung out, and I ducked to avoid it. Clearly not used to wielding a weapon right-handed, he stumbled, then spun back around to face me, scowling.

We fought scrappily, his brawn making up for his clumsy sword-work. I shot arrow after arrow at him, missing narrowly. Within minutes, he'd managed to steer me toward the black hole, until I felt it pressing against my back.

It wasn't just shadows—an absence of light. No, this darkness was *palpable.* As if it might drown me, choke me, swallow me whole. There was something very wrong about it, something that burrowed beneath my skin. I teetered at its edge, an arrow aimed at Wen Bo's heart. He, on the other hand, stood at the very edge of the lake.

We both froze. Around us, the fight continued, all clashing swords and clanging steel. But neither of us moved.

This was it. Either I was going to shoot him, or he would stab me. Down here in the deepest death layer, one of us would disintegrate like all the ghosts I'd killed.

But . . . he didn't attack as I'd expected. Instead, he raised his sword and tossed it onto the ground between us. It clattered onto the rock, skidding and spinning across the ground.

Wen Bo's ghost raised his chin. "Go on," he said evenly. "Shoot me."

I shook my head, unable to tear my eyes away from his mutilated limb. "No—" I felt like I was going to cry.

"Please." He raised both arms—the one with the hand and the one without—as though surrendering. In his eyes, I read resignation. Sadness. Regret.

Suddenly, I understood. He wasn't asking me to kill him. He was asking me to give him a second chance.

An escape from this miserable existence.

I'd been drawing my bow for so long that my arm had gone numb. My hands were trembling. A sob brewed in my chest, threatening to burst out. All I could do was whisper, "You don't need me for this."

Wen Bo went completely still, eyes fixed on me.

Then he saluted, closed his eyes, and fell backward, into the Lake of Forgetfulness.

He landed with a splash. At the last moment, his eyes opened and fixed on me as he sank into the translucent water.

My sob burst out of me as I lowered the bow. "I'm sorry," I whispered to the space where he'd once been. For as soon as the waves had folded back over him, his ghostly form had disintegrated, in readiness for reincarnation.

"I'm sorry, I'm sorry . . ." Slinging the bow over my shoulder, I bent to pick up Wen Bo's sword. What had happened to him—what the general had done—was my fault. My voice shook as I repeated the words, over and over again. But there was no answer to my desperate regrets. Only the whispering lake, its surface shimmering with rapidly expanding ripples.

A shout jerked my focus back to the fight. Only Dai Yu and two of her guards remained. One of the ghosts—alongside my sister—was fighting Lin, though their technique was sloppy. The third ghost was running at me. Immediately, I spun, aiming the sword at my assailant's heart. But before I could drive it in, there was movement from another entrance, on the opposite side of the lake.

"Jia Yi!" Pópo came into view. She was being dragged by the neck, General Hong's hand around the soft, wrinkled column of her throat. "Stop!"

"Pópo!" I screamed. At exactly the same moment, the ghosts who Lin and I had been fighting pressed their swords against *our* necks.

"Shut up!" The general tightened his hold on Pópo. From the shadows beside him, the one-armed ghost emerged, a Spyrre leashed beside him.

My heart lurched. A Spyrre, here? My mind scrabbled for an explanation. I hadn't thought of Spyrre as living creatures, or that they could die and become ghosts. But thinking about it, it made sense. They weren't undead; they were unusually long-lived, monstrous beings born from Lancaster hatred. And General Hong appeared to have captured one. A ghost version.

The Spyrre raised its gaunt skull, turned the emptiness of its eyes upon my grandmother, pointed its nasal cavity at her . . . and sniffed.

An agonized cry tore from my throat. I tried to struggle, but it was useless: I was helpless to save Pópo.

General Hong tossed a careless glance in my sister's direction and grinned. "You've done well, Dai Yu."

She smirked, almost . . . preening. I felt ill. It was all becoming clearer now. Why my eldest sister—who'd suffered through both of our parents' deaths at an age when she could remember, and then had grown up feeling neglected—gravitated toward General Hong. An authority figure, who gave her the tiny slivers of praise and attention she so desired.

I'd thought she'd defected to General Hong's side for revenge. But now I was wondering . . . was it actually for acceptance? This disturbing realization sat heavy in my gut.

"And you." The general addressed me, jolting me out of my thoughts. "The littlest Liu. You've certainly made good work of my soldiers. Really, you are lucky that I asked them to go easy on you—since I do, in fact, need you for my plans."

The fleshy half of his lips twisted into the mockery of a smile. "I'd advise you to stop now, though." He gestured to both Lin and my grandmother. "If you attack us again, one of them will die." As if for emphasis, the ghost Spyrre snarled again.

For a moment, I didn't respond. I just glared at him, my teeth bared.

But there was no way around his threat. We were cornered.

So, with shaking hands, I lowered the sword.

"Disarm them," the general barked at his soldiers. They quickly complied, divesting me of the bow and sword and Lin of his knife. After tossing the weapons to the ground, they grabbed each of us by one arm.

General Hong gave an approving nod, then turned to address me. "Do you know what happens to ghosts who die down here, Liu Jia Yi?"

"They reincarnate." My eyes flicked to where Wen Bo had fallen.

"If you enter the lake and have your memories washed away, then yes. But if you *die* here? No." His tone was didactic, like he was a tutor giving a lesson rather than a vengeful ghost determined to wreak revenge upon the living.

"Then what?" I snapped. I'd had enough. Enough of his games. Of his disdainful smirks.

"If you die here, without entering the water, your soul has nowhere to go—but there." With a jerk of his head, he gestured toward the ominous black hole behind me. Its power pulsed with malevolent energy.

General Hong tightened his grip on Pópo's neck. She tensed, but remained impassive, her black eyes boring into mine. "That there is the Abyss; a kind of . . . eternal death, if you will," the general continued. "It's where souls go if they fail to reincarnate, or if they choose not to. And it's where they stay. Forever."

My insides shriveled. Total, eternal death. A wave of guilt coursed through me for all the ghosts I'd killed.

But that guilt was superseded by my fear for my grandmother, which suddenly kicked up tenfold. My mind spun, trying to figure out how to help her. I didn't want her to die. Not here. No—I wanted her to *live.* To have a chance to resurrect.

I swallowed down the panic that had snagged inside my throat. "Why are you telling me this?"

"So you know what's at stake if you don't comply." He scrutinized me. "Believe me, I do not wish to harm you, Liu Jia Yi. All you need to do is surrender. Give me the weapon. If you do, I shall spare your loved ones. If you do not, then"—he gestured at Lin with a jerk of his chin—"he dies first."

My stomach dropped. General Hong wanted what he'd come here to get: the famed Shēngsǐ Sword. The Sword of Rechenblod. Death Killer.

The weapon that would allow him to come back to life. The one thing I couldn't give him; the one thing we had yet to find.

I clenched my fists so hard that they hurt. Lin and I . . . we shouldn't have wasted our last precious moments kissing. Hurting each other with our inevitable goodbye. We should have looked for the sword.

An unuttered scream lodged in my throat. It was supposed to be down here. We should have found it.

Steeling myself, I straightened my posture and looked the man in the eye. "I'm afraid I cannot do that. We haven't found the sword." Remarkably, my voice only shook a little.

At this, General Hong threw his head back and laughed. The sound shook me, chilled my flesh, right down to my core.

"Foolish girl," he said as his laugh subsided into a sinister chuckle. "Foolish, foolish girl. The weapon we seek is not a *sword.*"

"What?" I blurted. "But you said—"

"Oh, it was once. Indeed, my search for the Shēngsǐ Sword consumed me for centuries. But that was before I realized that there was something else—some other power—that could help me invade the living realm." He nodded at the one-armed soldier beside him, who loosened the leash on the Spyrre.

This time, it didn't lunge at my grandmother. It lunged at *me*.

I shrieked, almost tripping as I scrambled backward. The Spyrre pulled up short, straining against its bindings. Its long, sinewy fingers swiped at the air mere inches from my face. Its jaws snapped and it snarled, its rotted teeth bared.

The soldier had given the leash just enough slack for the Spyrre to almost reach me. Almost, but not quite.

My gut turned to ice as I stared, horrified, at the Spyrre. The Spyrre, which wanted so badly to reach me. The Spyrre, which could smell my magic . . .

My *resurrection* magic.

Magic that could restore the dead.

Nausea unfurled through my body as everything clicked into place. With sudden clarity, it all made sense. Why General Hong had pursued me and my grandmother all the way down here—to where ghosts could finally die, or reincarnate. Even though he, himself, couldn't go back.

Not yet, anyway.

"How long have you known?" My voice tremored, the words choked.

General Hong fixed his cold eyes on me and smiled. "I had my suspicions, little Liu, when you escaped from my dungeon with nary a trace. But when you and your boyfriend were tussling on that cliff, and he yelled at you to save yourself?" His smile widened to a sneer. "Well. That was when I *knew*."

I swallowed. It seemed so obvious. Why hadn't this occurred to me before?

The weapon wasn't the Shēngsǐ Sword, the Sword of Rechenblod. The sword was just a legend, a fairy tale. I realized now that the shaman had never even mentioned a sword. The shaman had only spoken of a weapon.

And the sword in the shaman's vision was exactly like Wen Bo's Bone Smith sword—the one that, up until a few minutes ago, I had been holding. We'd visualized that very scene in the shaman's smoke: me, holding a sword, and Pópo—both of us surrounded by pervasive, pitch-black Death. We'd just interpreted the vision wrongly.

Now I knew. The sword was a false clue, something that both Pópo and I had fixated on. It was also a story, one General Hong had used to lead his soldiers down here, telling them he was searching for it, when what he really wanted was . . .

. . . *the ultimate weapon*, he'd told me, when I'd first met him in the dungeon.

The weapon that the shaman's prediction had said could *restore the dead* as well as *wreak havoc on the living.*

No, the weapon wasn't a sword, or a bow, or anything wrought by the Bone Smith.

The weapon they were seeking was *magic*. A power that—now they'd captured us both—they could force my grandmother to steal. A power that, if General Hong took it, would give him the ability to resurrect, then infiltrate and attack the living realm.

I understood now why he'd pursued me so doggedly. And also why he'd been searching for Pópo. It wasn't to use me to get the sword, and it wasn't to stop Pópo from finding it first. It was because, for what he wanted, he needed both of us.

What is dead can die again.

But what is dead can live *again.*

I dropped Wen Bo's sword; it clattered to the ground.

The weapon wasn't actually a weapon. It was something they could use to restore the dead. And at some point, General Hong had realized that . . .

It was me.

I was the weapon.

Forty-Five

THE SIXTH LEVEL
Present day

I turned my head, just slightly, to find Lin's eyes fixed on me. In those light-brown depths I read desperation. Pain. Grief. I knew in that moment he'd just reached the same conclusion. It was as if we were connected, not in physicality, but soul to soul.

And just like we'd always communicated wordlessly when faced with danger in the forest—we did so again.

With the slightest of movements, I let my eyes flick toward the lake and back again. Without breaking eye contact, he blinked once, and from this I knew he understood.

Inside my head, I counted, like I always had when we'd hunted together. *One . . . two . . .*

And as soon as I reached *three*, Lin and I simultaneously bolted. We had the element of surprise; wrenching away from our captors, we hurled ourselves at the lake.

Our plan? To jump into the water together, washing away our memories, our lives, our identities, our sense of being. Because faced with this conundrum—that I, in fact, was the weapon that could destroy the world—there was only one way to stop that happening.

And that was to destroy myself.

There is always a moment, right before dying, that feels like leaping into the great unknown. Each layer of the afterlife is slightly different from the last, and each time I jump, I never know where I will land.

This time I really, truly did not know. As soon as Lin and I hit the water, we would be washed free of anything that made us *us*. And we'd be heading into something new, different, and terrifying. Who would I be, the next time I surfaced into life?

I didn't have time to be scared. Especially since I knew that what I was doing was right. All I could hope for was that Pópo, too, would find some way to get herself to the lake. Maybe my actions would be enough to create a diversion.

As soon as we reached the lake's edge, we both leaped, our arms pinwheeling, and then landed on the water with a—

Smack.

Instead of submerging, I landed on one shoulder, then skidded painfully along the ice.

Ice. The lake had turned to ice. Struggling to get upright on the slick surface, I lifted my head.

Dai Yu, my sister, stood on the shore, both hands raised, her face blank with concentration. My sister, who wielded water magic, had frozen the entire lake.

Lin and I threw panicked looks at each other. My mind scrambled for what to do: How would we get out of this mess now?

I didn't get a chance to consider this, because the next moment there was a huge crack, followed by an explosion.

Lin and I were thrown from the lake, massive ice shards flying into the air all around us. I collided with the cave wall. Pain jolted through my entire body. I wondered if any bones were broken. I wondered if bones *could* break this deep in the afterlife. And when I touched my throbbing head, my hand came away covered in black blood.

I looked up. Dai Yu was now standing before me. In one hand she clutched a huge piece of broken ice, which had evidently come from the cracked lake surface. It curved up, bluish white and lethal, its edge sharp and forbidding.

This was no normal shard of ice. Dai Yu could manipulate water into any form she chose. And this ice had been forged into a blade.

"Dai Yu," I croaked as she raised her makeshift weapon, its honed edge gleaming in the dim light. Was she going to kill me? Down here? Cast me into the Abyss? Surely not—General Hong wanted my powers. He needed me. Didn't he?

She raised the ice, higher and higher, as I cringed, flattening myself against the rock. Then, as her arm arced downward, I closed my eyes and sent a final prayer to the Mothers.

But the shard never hit me. It took a second too long. I cracked open one eye. Dai Yu had whirled around and was flinging the ice the opposite way.

It hurtled through the air, hitting General Hong. At the same time, Pópo elbowed him in the gut, diving away from him and rolling with a degree of agility I'd never known she had.

The ice shard rammed the general back against the cave wall, piercing his midsection and pinning him to the stone.

Simultaneously, Dai Yu raised a thin column of water from the lake, lassoing it around the two other soldiers. They barely had time to react before they were both dragged, yelling, into the lake.

There was a splash. The now-thawed lake water sloshed at the edge.

Then, silence.

I stared, frozen in shock for several moments. Eventually I scrambled to my feet. Dai Yu had already stalked across to my grandmother and was helping her to stand up.

Swaying a little, I stumbled toward them, Lin following close behind. Somehow General Hong was still alive, though his head was lowered. As we watched, he gave a deep, bone-rattling wheeze.

I edged closer to the injured man, the back of my neck prickling with fear. He looked smaller pinned against the cavern wall. For some reason, I couldn't tear my eyes away from his bloated face. Or from the coalescing drops of blood that clung to his chin before dripping to the floor, pattering the sand with small wet dots.

My entire body felt numb. I could barely speak. But with some effort, I managed to say, to no one in particular, "What the *hells* is going on?"

Pópo was still struggling to stand, Dai Yu supporting her beneath the elbow. "Dai Yu," Pópo said, panting, "was working with us the whole time."

Every rational thought fled my mind in an instant, and I stood staring at them, gobsmacked. I caught Dai Yu's eye—despite the fact that she was, apparently, on our side, she gave me a scornful smile. I realized my mouth was hanging open, and I shut it, my teeth clicking together.

Pivoting slowly on my feet, I turned to face Lin. "Did you know about this?" One look at his face told me that he did. I narrowed my eyes. "For how long?"

He wouldn't look at me. "A while," was all he said.

I turned back to Dai Yu and Pópo. "You planned *this*?"

Pópo hobbled over to a rock and sank down upon it with a sigh. Then, bracing her hands on both knees, she looked up at me. "Not all of it, bǎobèi. You were never meant to be here." She shook her head, her face lined with regret. "I would not have wanted Dai Yu here either, but she was already dead."

"Dai Yu," I repeated. I turned to my sister. "So you were a spy? All this time?"

She gave an arrogant grin. "Yes, *Empty*." My gut twisted; she still called me that, even though she now knew I had a power.

Some things, I guessed, would never change.

My mind was reeling. I clasped a hand to my forehead. "But why"—I pressed my fingers against my temples, squeezing my eyes shut—"did Dai Yu have to join the general's side?" I understood why Lin was involved. He was helping Pópo descend through the layers of death. But what was Dai Yu's role in all of this?

Pópo's gaze slid to the lake, and when she spoke, she didn't look at me. "When Lin ran away, I lost my only spy." Behind me, I heard Lin shift on his feet—a sure sign of his discomfort. Residual guilt, perhaps?

My grandmother paid him no mind and continued. "I knew I had to have another source in the afterlife, someone who could keep me informed of General Hong's movements. That's where Dai Yu came in."

"You two started to communicate?" I prompted. My head was beginning to hurt.

"The one benefit of nearly dying," Pópo said, "was that I could suddenly communicate with ghosts. Dai Yu returned." My grandmother reached out and clasped my sister's hand. "She . . . haunted me."

My sister cut in. "The ghosts knew we did not get along, Jia Yi."

My grandmother gave a small nod. "We decided to capitalize on that. Make them believe she wanted revenge against you, against our community, against anyone who was once her enemy. However petty the reasons. Fortunately vengeful ghosts do not need much encouragement to believe someone is seeking retribution."

Vengeful ghosts. Like General Hong. A feeling of foreboding was beginning to roil in my gut.

I gaped at Dai Yu. "But . . . you tried to kill me! You almost drowned me! Even though you were on our side. Why?"

Dai Yu and Pópo shot each other a silent look.

Eventually, Pópo answered. "Your sister and I disagreed about how to handle the shaman's prediction." Her voice went quiet. "I felt as though I could cheat your fate; she felt otherwise."

"You were the one who was supposed to come down here, to find the sword." Dai Yu rolled her eyes. "I never understood why we couldn't just *let* you. Beat the general to it."

I was . . . speechless. Really, I should have been angrier at the way they'd all tried to make decisions for me rather than letting me make them myself. But I was still in shock.

Ripping my gaze from my sister, I threw a glance at the

general, still pinned to the wall with the ice. He was slumped over, the outline of his body becoming less defined, like a picture drawn in dry sand. Trails of dust were trickling from his form.

I couldn't help it; something—curiosity perhaps—compelled me to approach him. This one person who'd caused so much grief. Who had planned to steal my power and attack the living world.

As I drew nearer, the general raised his head. A trail of ghostly blood trickled down his chin. "You think this is over, girl?" His voice was deceptively quiet, like the inhale before a scream. He leered at me, his teeth stained black with blood. "You think this ends with me?"

And I realized, too late, that I was standing too close.

Somehow, he found the strength to pull the ice shard free and push away from the wall. And, despite the fact that blood was pouring from his mangled torso, he grabbed me around my neck with both hands.

I spluttered, flailing, clawing at my throat. Fighting for my life—and death—I grappled desperately with the general as he squeezed his fingers tighter. Tighter. Tighter still.

"There are more like me, Liu Jia Yi," he spat. "Even if you get rid of me . . . you won't defeat the others."

The others? Vaguely, I registered Pópo, Dai Yu, and Lin shouting. I ignored it. All I knew was my struggle. An instinct not to give up, not to acquiesce.

To fight back.

My vision was shutting down, a vignette of blackness. Summoning the last of my strength, I heaved us both sideways . . .

Straight into the Abyss.

Forty-Six

THE SIXTH LEVEL

Present day

We plunged into the blackness, so thick and insidious it was like being buried in pitch. Immediately, the general was ripped away from me.

I was completely and utterly alone.

Viscous air snaked up my nostrils, poured into my mouth, crawled down my esophagus until it lodged at the base of my throat. I couldn't hear anything. I couldn't see anything. Groping, I tried to get my bearings, but I could not tell which way was up or down.

Fear grabbed me in a choke hold. This, here, was death. Death, and its empty permanence, was everywhere—but somehow it was also nowhere.

Shadows swirled around me, like slow-moving mud. Clinging to me, tasting the source of my existence, until I began to fragment, disintegrate, and evaporate into the ether.

Slowly, I spun in the darkness, feeling as though the shadows were wrapping me tighter, folding me into Death's embrace.

Promising the bliss of oblivion.

But I realized that if I succumbed to the Abyss's power, where emptiness saturated everything like smoke suffocating air, then I'd be trapped. Forever. Alongside the souls of the general, of the ghosts I'd slain, of all the spirits who'd died down here before they'd had a chance to reincarnate. Instinctively, I knew that they no longer existed—not in a form I would recognize, anyway—their consciousnesses lost to eternity.

But me? Miraculously, I wasn't dead. Not yet, anyway. Somehow, the Abyss knew me. And I knew it.

A tiny flame sparked, deep inside me. A kindled power, fluttering weakly in the absent breeze. I could smell it, feel it, taste it. Not life, but something resembling it.

The last vestige of my power.

My magic, which, however tenuously, still tethered me to the living realm, was the only thing that had stopped me from dissolving into nothingness. I was the only spirit who had ever entered this place—a place of death and waylaid souls—who could resurrect. Who had any chance of getting out. The shaman had said: *Death clings to you like a mantle.*

But down here, in the Abyss, I realized what she had forgotten to say: *Life* clung to me, too.

I suppose, in the end, there is no life without death. And no death without life.

Clutching at that hope, I forced my mind still, holding on to every last thread of my humanity, my spirit . . . my existence. I was the weapon. A weapon with complete mastery over life and death.

And then I began to kick.

Up and up I kicked, thrashing against the emptiness. Toward the minuscule scents of life and death above me in the darkness. I flailed, trying to surface, trying to reach whatever lay waiting beyond the Abyss.

The shadows tugged at me, pulling me back. But I fought. Harder than I'd ever fought, pain tearing through my entire body. I imploded, exploded, turned inside out. Scrabbled for my existence.

And, just as I was on the cusp of breaking free, something glinted, a beacon in the black. A glimpse of a sword—a Sword of Death, and Life, and everything in between—buried right where the Bone Smith had said it'd be: the deepest layer of death.

But I only caught a fleeting look before I tore myself from the Abyss.

Screaming, I flew from that dark space before crashing to the ground.

Miraculously, it had worked. I was back in the sixth layer, in the Double Moon Cave.

I rolled over, coughing, trying to calm my quivering muscles. I'd done it. I'd actually done it. Gritting my teeth from the pain, I pressed my forehead against the cave floor in an attempt to settle my queasiness.

Pópo hurried over, falling onto her knees. She put her arms around me, seemingly lost for words. Finally, she managed to speak. *"How?"*

How, indeed? How did I escape the Abyss? The place of eternal death?

I passed a shaking hand across my eyes. "I . . . I resurrected."

"Resurrected?" she repeated. Her lip trembled, and she said it again, to herself this time. "Resurrected." Eyes wide, she stared at me, a grievous sort of understanding solidifying in her expression. "*You* can resurrect?"

"I only discovered it recently." I clumsily sat up. "I can move between life and death. That's what the general meant, before when he said—"

"You . . . can resurrect." She began to tremble, her mouth opening and shutting several times before she managed to grind out the words: "*You* . . . are the weapon."

I nodded, the movement weak.

Pushing me away from her, she struggled to her feet and turned to face Lin, looking lost. "Is this . . . true?"

Lin pressed his lips into a grim line and nodded. He'd already seen me do it twice before. And now, a third time, when I escaped the Abyss's clutches—a place from which no ghost should return.

How long had he suspected it was *me* that General Hong sought? Perhaps he had known, in some way, since the very first time I'd come back to life.

"Why did you not tell me, Lin?" My grandmother's voice betrayed her hurt.

"Because I was afraid of what might happen to her if you knew." He didn't look at me. His glittering eyes were fixed on Pópo. Raising his chin, he added, "I won't apologize for it, either. You know where my loyalties lie."

I stared at him. Lin had known, and he'd never told anyone, not even my grandmother. For once, he had not betrayed me.

My fingers twitched; I wished I could reach for him, but I didn't dare.

Instead, I stood, turning my focus back to Pópo. "I'm what they wanted," I said in a shaky voice. "The general meant to force you to steal my power using your own gift, and give it to him." This whole time, General Hong had been herding us. Forcing us together so he could take what he wanted. And not even Dai Yu knew.

And now the general had told us, right before he'd died for good, that this did not stop with him. That there were others. The thought filled me with terror.

"A weapon . . ." Pópo's voice had dropped to the faintest whisper. "With complete mastery over life and death."

"It can be used for good or ill," I said, echoing the shaman's words.

A haunted look stole into my grandmother's eyes. She drew close to me, her gaze piercing mine. "So *you* are what I am meant to destroy?"

"I suppose I am." I swallowed painfully. "I'm . . . the sacrifice."

She reached up to touch my face. "Or the salvation."

My eyes stung, and I blinked. "I guess that, there, is the choice."

A choice; sacrifice, or salvation.

A moment of silence, and then Pópo swayed on her feet. Right before she collapsed, I darted forward, just managing to catch her. She leaned heavily on me as I eased her down onto the rock.

I knew her conundrum, what she was grappling with. For so long, she'd had one purpose: to find the weapon. After we visited the shaman, she had focused all her efforts on finding and destroying it. Had lied to protect me, all the while making plans with Lin and Dai Yu.

And her heart—the part that loved me, her granddaughter—was warring with her head. The logic that told her that to remove the threat, one of us must die. For good.

We'd all heard the general: There were more ghosts seeking to steal my power and resurrect. They'd have no compunction about using torture to force Pópo to cooperate. My grandmother—my kind, compassionate grandmother—had to weigh the worth of our lives against the worth of all others. These were the kinds of decisions she, as the High Priestess, always had to make.

And I also knew that for my grandmother, who held such an abundance of love in her heart, having to make the decision would *ruin* her.

In that moment, seeing the distress stamped upon her face, I made up my mind. I wouldn't force my grandmother to make the decision. I would make it for her.

"What if it doesn't have to be *your* choice?" I whispered.

Pópo looked up at me, her expression hollow. "What do you mean?"

Sinking to my knees, I took Pópo's hands in my own. Her skin was papery. Her bones were fragile, birdlike, as though they'd shatter if I held her too tight. "It doesn't have to be your choice," I said. "It can be mine. Pópo, you have shouldered so many burdens throughout your life—and death. Let me take this one. Let *me* choose."

"And what would you choose?" She asked me as though she didn't want to hear the answer.

I squeezed her hands, so gently. "To be the sacrifice."

Pópo's shoulders hunched, and she shook her head. "I cannot ask you to do that, bǎobèi. You have so much life ahead of you." She raised her eyes to meet mine. "Go back to the land of the living, my child."

I didn't want to tell her that, this deep in the afterlife, I wasn't even sure that I *could* resurrect.

Dai Yu, who was keeping watch at the cave entrance, signaled to us. "We need to hurry," she called out. "More soldiers are coming."

More. The other ghosts that General Hong spoke of. How long had he been quietly gathering forces in his search for my resurrection power?

Lin drew his blade, interrupting my thoughts. "How far away are they?"

"Not far," my sister replied. "The general arranged for his troops to follow if he did not return before the moon reaches its zenith."

I glanced at the water. At the small circular moon, reflected as it climbed higher in the sky.

My chest constricted; we were running out of time. Turning back to my grandmother, I raised her hands to my lips and kissed them. "Take my power," I urged. "Take it. Save yourself."

Pópo frowned. "No. I won't. If you can resurrect, Jia Yi, you must do it now. They are coming, and they know what you are. If they got hold of you—"

"But me resurrecting won't help," I protested. "I'll be up there"—I gestured helplessly to the roof, though we both knew I meant the living realm—"and they'll continue to hunt me until they finally steal my magic. You heard the general. It won't stop with him, Pópo, it won't. They will find me, and they will take it."

"Without me, they cannot take it," Pópo said patiently. She sounded like she used to when she'd deliver lessons to me as a child. "You will be safe up there. I need you to be safe."

"I could say the same for you!" Anxiety gripped my chest, and I stood, letting go of Pópo's hands.

"I am old. You are young. Your magic is wasted on me."

"It isn't!" I began pacing, agitated. "Our people need you up there. They *need* you. You are their leader. If you take my power, and resurrect, you can rally our village's defenses. You can keep the living realm protected."

"You can do the same, Liu Jia Yi."

I waved away her words. "They don't respect me like they respect you. If the ghosts find a way to attack . . . I cannot lead them, Pópo. Putting me in that position will condemn us all—"

"Hurry!" Dai Yu hissed from the cave entrance. She was tense, her spear gripped in her hand. "I can hear them. We only have minutes."

"Quickly," I urged. "Take my power. Please."

There was a short pause while my grandmother regarded me, her eyes as black and as unfathomable as the Abyss. "If we cannot agree," she said, "then we will vote on it."

I should have expected it. This was always Pópo's solution when a disagreement occurred in our village. She'd gather everyone for a poll, and the majority vote would win, even if she did not agree with the outcome.

"All right," I said, and rose to my feet. First, I asked the person who I was most sure would agree with me. "Dai Yu?"

"Pópo should live," she said, without hesitation. Her eyes met mine, and I gave a curt nod.

I turned to my grandmother. "Pópo?"

"Jia Yi should live," she said, the lines on her face deepening.

"We already know my vote," I said. "I vote that Pópo should live. Which only leaves . . ."

We all turned to Lin, who was half lurking in the shadows, his fingers curled around the hilt of his blade. His gaze shifted to me, then to Pópo, then back to me. He looked . . . lost.

"Lin," Dai Yu snapped. "Hurry up."

Lin took two steps forward until both he and I were bathed in moonlight. He stared at me, hard, and I stared back, willing him to agree with me.

"Xiǎo è'guǐ," he said. His voice was heartbreakingly gentle.

"Please," I whispered. "Let this be the last thing you ever do for me. Let this be our final memory. Our final moment together."

He raised his hand, and with the back of it, he stroked my cheek. Almost like he was brushing away an errant tear.

"I cannot imagine a world without you in it. My little demon." His voice cracked. "I can't, I can't, I just can't—"

"I *will* be in it. We both will. If there is any justice—if the Mothers are real—then we will meet again. If not in the next life, then the one after." Raising my own hands, I grabbed his face and brought his lips to mine. A brief, hard kiss before breaking away. "Maybe then we can start over. We won't make the same mistakes."

"Be quick!" Dai Yu called, and now even I could hear more soldiers approaching.

Lin stared at me for several seconds, his gaze boring into mine, before giving the most minuscule of nods.

"I agree with Jia," he said to Pópo. "You should live."

My grandmother gave a heavy sigh, then started struggling to her feet. Both Lin and I rushed forward to help her, each of us holding her under one arm. "In that case," she said, "the decision is made."

I straightened. "It is."

My grandmother blinked at me, her face full of grief. Then, in a movement I'd seen her perform countless times, she placed her palm on my chest.

"When you go back," I said, my words running into each other in my hurry, "go and see Essien Lancaster. He has healing powers. Hopefully your body will still be in good condition, since it has been kept in the crypt. But Essien can heal you, if there is anything that needs to be healed. Just tell him I sent you."

Pópo's eyes widened briefly at this revelation, but then she nodded and closed her eyes.

Heat flooded through my cold, dead flesh, coalescing at my grandmother's hand. The feeling was so sharp, so primeval, so *painful* that my knees almost gave way, but Lin put a strong arm around me and held me steady.

My power rushed to my core and burst out of my chest, flowing into Pópo with such force that wind started to circle around us. Our hair blew wildly, waving in the air currents, and it was all I could do to remain upright.

Then, as the last of my power rushed into my grandmother, she dropped her hand, and I fell, half collapsing into Lin's embrace.

My grandmother put her arms around me, and I hugged her back, burying my face into the crook of her neck.

"Farewell, Granddaughter," she said, her voice muffled by my shoulder.

"Goodbye," I whispered. *I love you.* It felt like my heart was fragmenting into a million pieces.

The sound of rushing footsteps rose to a crescendo, and then the General's soldiers were pouring into the cave. Immediately, Dai Yu leaped into action, her spear whirling and clashing nonstop.

But there were too many. This group wasn't dozens of soldiers. From the look of it, this group was more like *hundreds.*

I pushed away from Pópo and snatched Wen Bo's sword off the ground. Trying to stem my sudden sobs, I said, "Quickly. Resurrect. Do it now."

The attacking ghosts split and began streaming around the lake, looking like a swarm of insects. Only seconds and they'd be upon us.

"I'm going to flood the cave," Dai Yu screamed. In moments, we'd all be drenched in water from the Lake of Forgetfulness, reincarnating us. "Pópo! You have to GO!"

Pópo looked at me, then at Lin. They didn't speak. But I saw the subtle flicker of understanding that passed between the two. The same sort of unspoken conversation I'd witnessed on the third level, before the mist. Before the kiss.

And then I understood.

"No!" I said, trying to back away. But Lin grabbed hold of my arms and pinned me in place, my back flush against his chest. I tried to jerk away, but he held me fast, keeping my sword hand angled uselessly toward the ground.

Pópo advanced on me, her palm held up, the surface of it glowing white.

"NO!" I struggled, but in vain. Across the lake, Dai Yu had clambered up to the top of a boulder, buying her just enough time to raise her hands. The surface of the lake began to bubble.

"I'm sorry," Lin said, his voice low in my ear, even as he restrained me. This was *his* doing. His last request to my grandmother. A repayment for a lifetime of service.

"You're not sorry," I spat, but it was too late.

Pópo slammed her hand against my chest, and the power rushed back into me, a torrent of agony entering all at once. My back arched; my sobs morphed into a hysterical scream.

And just as Dai Yu's tidal wave crested—just before it engulfed my family, Lin, and the melee of fighting soldiers—I felt that familiar hooking sensation in my gut. Pain, worse than anything I'd ever experienced, sliced through my body. It felt like all my organs were being carved right from my flesh. As if my skin was tearing, disintegrating, being stripped from muscle and bone.

I screamed again, a scream of agony. And then—

The scene shriveled away to ash . . . like straw burning, curled by fire.

Forty-Seven

Present day

It was a long, excruciating journey dragging myself back to life. Just as I'd been jerked out of the sixth layer, I'd seen the lake water engulf Dai Yu, the ghost army, and . . .

Pópo. Lin. Two of the people I treasured most.

So I sobbed, and sobbed, as I bumped back in to my fifth- and fourth-level bodies. And then, agonizingly, into my third-level body. It took every ounce of concentration to rip myself away and resurrect into my second-level body, paralyzed with panic and lying at the bottom of the cliff. And then, again, into my still-screaming first-level body, submerged in the Throft Hall river. And finally, finally, as my entire body burned with pain, I burst back into my mortal form, feeling as though every part of me—body and soul—had been eviscerated.

I gave a huge gasp as I awoke. Everything was dark. "Essien," I tried to croak out, but my mouth was muffled, jammed full of something. And as I shifted, my surroundings crackled, and I realized I was packed in snow.

It was fresh, not melted. Essien must have just visited.

Thrashing around, I began to flail, clawing my way out of the ice.

When I finally punched through, the light was blinding, even though a quick glance told me there was no daylight—only some lit candles. Scrunching my eyes against the sting, I took several shaky breaths. My chest felt unyielding, my lungs stiff with disuse.

My knees buckled as I hauled myself out of the tub. My body was still numb, but evidently weak, as I only took two steps before I tumbled over. Wen Bo's sword fell from my grasp. My palms scraped the stone floor, and when I held them up, the skin was intact but alarmingly blue.

Just the cold, I thought, trying to reassure myself.

As my flesh adjusted to the ambient temperature, though, the pain hit. Hard. Essien must have kept his promise to heal me, because most of the injuries I'd sustained in the death realm—from drowning, from the mist, from falling from the cliff—weren't evident. But the gash on my shoulder from the ghost soldier's axe was there. My neck ached from where General Hong had grabbed me. And my entire right side was bruised from when I'd jumped onto the frozen lake. Every breath that sawed in and out of me scraped painfully, my body unused to being alive.

Wincing, I levered myself up to standing. My head spun. I retched, bringing nothing up from my shrunken stomach.

Tied neatly on the tabletop was a bunch of Shadowside. Essien must have left me the herbs, which he had presumably gathered, in an attempt to help me should I revive without him present.

Normally they'd need to be stewed into potion to maximize their restorative powers, but Essien was not to know that. So, heedless of the usual protocol, I crammed the purple flowers into my mouth—neat. They were caustically bitter, but I chewed and swallowed, hoping they would help with the pain, if only temporarily.

I have to get out of here, I thought. The Shadowside wouldn't help me for long; all it did was give one's body a trace of healing energy. But it paled in comparison to real magic, like Essien's.

With agonizing slowness, I strapped the sword to my waist and hauled myself up the ladder. Thankfully it didn't take too much effort to push the trapdoor open. I crawled up and out and flopped onto the melting snow.

Wait. *Melting* snow? When I'd last entered the death realm, winter had just started. How much time had actually passed?

I cast a desperate look at my surroundings. There was enough snow cover to hold some vague, nebulous footprints, and I followed them with my gaze until I saw a speck up ahead.

"Essien," I cried out, though my words were slurred, my voice all croaky. "Essien!" I clambered to my feet and began stumbling in his direction, hoping with every fiber of my being that he would hear me.

I made slow progress. My arms and legs jerked, uncontrolled and uncoordinated. My heartbeat thumped against my chest wall, harder than ever, as if making up for lost time.

It was all I could do to keep struggling, inching along. To keep screaming Essien Lancaster's name as he trudged in the opposite direction. I willed him to stop. To turn around. To catch sight of me.

But he just kept walking.

I'd only managed to clear a few yards before I could no longer support my weight. I collapsed face-first, into the sludge, and started to sink as the snow slowly reclaimed me. As it melted and re-formed around me, it almost felt warm, welcoming; an icy embrace. I stopped shivering, my body reacclimatizing to the frigid temperature.

Everything went silent as I turned my face, resting my cheek against a sheet of ice. Warmth was beginning to steal through my body, taking hold of every limb, every digit, every inch of skin. My eyelids fluttered closed, and I sighed. Maybe this was it. Maybe fighting it was futile. Maybe I should just . . . lie down. Accept death. Accept defeat.

And then—the Mothers must have taken mercy—for there were footsteps. Heavy, crunching footsteps, and then gentle hands, flipping me over, brushing the snow from my face.

"Jia!" Essien's concerned face floated above me, looking pale and unusually drawn. "You're back!"

For a second, I just lay there, stunned, my pulse flickering weakly in my veins. Then, I rasped out one word, the only word I could manage: "Help."

His brow creased, and he put both his palms on me. Immediately, the warm, safe feeling I'd come to associate with him poured into me, ten times stronger than anything I'd ever experienced. He shook with the effort of it, sweat beading on his forehead.

I felt the gash on my shoulder sealing over, until the stinging disappeared. I felt the bruises on my hip and torso heal as he worked on them, too. And when he reached my throat, which was bruised and swollen, he let out a ragged exhale. I sighed as he brushed the skin of my neck, the pain ebbing like a receding tide.

The feeling was so nurturing, so wholesome, that it didn't even register that he'd run his hands over my entire body, over the damp dress that was clinging to my every curve. If I hadn't been so focused on survival, I might have found the experience mortifying.

As it stood, though, I was just relieved, and grateful, and also immeasurably tired. To stay lucid, I concentrated on watching Essien as he worked. On the way the muted sunlight glinted off his golden hair; on the focus and concentration that suffused his eyes; on his full lips as they murmured my name over and over again, like a prayer. On the way his hands shook, the way he seemingly had to force them to stay still.

Now, back in the land of the living, I couldn't believe I'd ever forgotten his face.

"Jia," he murmured as he healed one part, and then another. "Jia, Jia."

He was pronouncing my name correctly for the very first time. Had he been practicing it while I was dead?

My distraction was being overtaken by new sensations gripping my body. The warmth was becoming hot, too hot; I was sweltering—even though my skin was frozen and I was lying in a bank of snow. My dress weighed heavily on my fragile, fresh-mended skin, and I felt clammy and sticky and feverish. My breathing shallowed, the pain of it consuming my flesh like fire.

I felt like I might die of heat.

My mind clouded, and I gave Essien Lancaster, sixth son of Yske, a weak smile.

"Take my clothes off," I whispered, half to Essien and half to the sky. "Please?"

And then I promptly fainted.

Forty-Eight

Present day

When I came to, Essien had me bundled up in his arms, his thick woolen greatcoat wrapped around the both of us. Now I felt like an icicle, despite the fact that his body heat was seeping through the many layers of fabric that separated us. The pocket watch around my neck dug into my sternum, its chain chafing my skin as we walked. An unnerving sensation, after so long without.

Thankfully, most of the pain had gone, except for the sharp sting of cold.

"Wh-what's going on?" I chattered, clinging to the Yskian prince's shoulders.

"You are suffering from frost sickness," he said, tightening his hold around me. "You've been rather severely affected. But at least you're shivering now. That's a good sign. It means you are warming up." Despite his words, he began striding even faster.

"S-so you're taking me in-inside?"

His blue eyes slid to mine, our gazes locking. "Yes, Jia. I can heal the effects of frost damage, but I cannot warm you up by magic. Only a fire and warm bath can do that."

I gave a weak nod before burrowing closer to his body, soaking up his heat. From my position I could see that his hair had grown longer in the time I'd been away, fine locks curling against his collar. Snow melting, hair growing—I must have been dead for a good few months, though with the way time lost its meaning down below, it hadn't seemed that long.

He burst into Throft Hall, striding through the passageways with little regard for the servants who stopped what they were doing to stare. Perhaps Rowan had departed and left Essien to his own devices. Perhaps his winter of quiet solitude had lulled the Lancasters into a false sense of security, and they were unaware that Essien had spent months making daily visits to a dead girl's corpse. In my delirious state, I couldn't help it—a small giggle escaped from my stiff, frozen lips.

Essien gave me a concerned look. He must have thought I was losing my mind.

Eventually, the familiar double doors of his chambers came into view—life-size portrait and all—and he pushed them open with his back before setting me gently on the carpet.

I stood in front of the fire, warming myself by the dying embers, while he ran me a bath for the second time ever. My body shivered so violently it clacked my teeth together. Was it just the cold? Or was it something else? Was it my body trying to forget everything that I had lost?

Once the tub was prepared, he called me over, gesturing to the slightly steaming water. A thick layer of sweet-scented bubbles glistened on the surface.

Casting a glance at it, my gut flipped as I remembered what I'd said to him before I passed out.

"D-did I really ask you to take my clothes off?" Still trembling, I frowned, my lips all cracked and numb.

"Well, I—" He carefully avoided eye contact as he rubbed the back of his neck, his face flushing. "It's a symptom of severe frost sickness. Feeling hot."

"I see." How utterly embarrassing. All I wanted to do was crawl into a hole and hide. Since that wasn't an option, I merely said, "I think I'd like to be alone now."

"Oh. Of course. I beg your pardon." Looking flustered, Essien disappeared into the bedroom to allow me to undress.

With aching fingers, I took off Wen Bo's sword and propped it against a chair. Would I need to explain to Essien that this wasn't the one he'd been seeking? Or would he know immediately from its appearance that it wasn't the Sword of Rechenblod?

Frowning, I turned away. I'd figure that part out later. Right now, I needed to get into the damned bath. I stripped out of my damp hànfú and took off the pocket watch. It was jarring to be able to touch it again, after being unable to for so long.

Reluctantly, I placed it carefully on a side table, not wanting to let it go. It was, after all, a talisman of sorts. Not only did it signify that I was alive, but also . . . it was evidence that Essien Lancaster had, once upon a time, deemed me worthy enough to receive it.

Turning away from the watch, I clambered into the bath. The water sloshed as I lowered myself beneath its surface.

"It's not too hot just yet," the prince called from the next room. I heard the unmistakable sounds of him stacking more logs on the fire. "So as not to shock your system."

Even though the water was fairly tepid, the contrast needled me all over. I sucked in a sharp inhale, then marveled at the feeling of my lungs expanding, a sensation I hadn't felt in some time.

For several minutes, I had to grip the sides of the tub, breathing through the pain, resisting the urge to jump out again. Finally, though, I managed to acclimatize. As heat stole through my limbs, I let out a sigh, relaxing into the bath, then picked up a bar of soap to begin the process of scrubbing down. After so long, I really was obscenely filthy.

I was still so . . . *furious* that Lin and my grandmother had betrayed me. Yes, it was out of love, but it was still the height of treachery. I ground my teeth together, clenching the soap so hard in my fist that the outer layer turned to mush.

I was unable to change my situation now. All I could do was make the best of it. Heal, return to my village, and then try to equip them against a possible onslaught. Fortunately, with me back in the land of the living, General Hong dead, and my grandmother gone, with no more powers, the ghost army would have to start over with their nefarious plans. No longer would they be able to use Pópo's magic in order to harvest my own.

But it was likely only a matter of time until they found another solution. I still couldn't ignore the threat. I could not afford to become complacent.

After I'd finished scrubbing myself, I moved on to the gargantuan task of washing my hair. After several months of being dead and buried in a tub of ice, it was hideously tangled. "Mā de!" I muttered, trying to drag my fingers through the snarled knots.

There was a pause. Essien appeared in the doorway. "Are you all right?"

"No," I snapped, then cursed again.

"Can I"—he cleared his throat—"can I help in any way?"

I hesitated. I hated asking for help. But getting clean, rested, and then going back to my village was my number one priority.

"My hair . . . it's a mess." As he edged into the bathroom, I attempted one last tug at a knot before abandoning my efforts.

"Let me," he said, catching my hand gently. Momentarily, I was shocked. But then I gave him a brisk nod, slipping further below the soapsuds in order to preserve my modesty.

He moved closer and scooted a chair up behind me. I yielded to him easily as he began lathering my hair—roots to ends. His deft fingers ran along my scalp, sending tingles across my skin. I shivered. It was probably his healing touch that was making me react so; otherwise I would definitely not be sighing with pleasure, nor leaning into his hands.

I let my whole body relax. Finally, my journey was beginning to catch up to me, the cumulative effects of repetitive deaths a millstone around my neck. I allowed myself to sink further into the water, soaking up the warmth and the fragrance and the feeling of the prince's strong hands dutifully washing my hair.

He spent considerable time carefully combing out my tangles, before leaning forward to grab a jug of fresh water he'd placed on a stool by the bath. The linen of his shirt brushed my ear, and without thinking I turned my face into it. I breathed in, inhaling his scent—that woodsy smell that was so clean, so masculine, so *alive.* Unthinkingly, I nuzzled into him closer.

Essien froze. Then, almost immediately, he leaped to his feet, his posture straight, his face tinged pink. I flushed too, and sat bolt upright, covering my chest with my arms. I hadn't intended to act so familiarly.

"I shall leave you to get dressed. There is a clean gown draped over that chair." He bowed and added, very formally, "Lady Liu." Then he retreated to his bedroom, as though he couldn't escape my company fast enough.

Mortified, I rinsed my hair, then clambered out of the bath, the cold air nipping at my skin and causing it to pebble. Despite the chill, my face was scorching. Why had I done such a thing? Inadvertently made Essien Lancaster uncomfortable?

Chewing my lip, I thought hard as I reached for the satin nightgown—pale pink and empire-waisted, in the traditional Yskian style—and slipped it on, along with the matching robe. Then, picking up the pocket watch, I frowned at it, before sidling into the bedroom. Essien was standing at the window, one hand resting on the sill. His posture was rigid, like he was waiting for something.

My stomach churned. I had barely noticed when I'd arrived, so affected was I by the frost sickness. Seeing it now, though, drove it home: Everything in this room was the same. Exactly the same as the last time I'd been here. Life had continued on, unchanged, apart from the turn of the seasons and a few inches of hair. It was I who had changed irrevocably.

Essien startled slightly when he caught sight of me. Realizing the robe was fairly revealing, I drew it closer around my wasted frame. It appeared that my sojourn into the afterlife had left my body even bonier than usual.

"Do you want this back?" I said, holding out the pocket watch so it spun on its chain, back and forth like a compass arrow.

His shoulders relaxed, and he smiled, his cheeks dimpling.

It was the first genuine smile I'd seen on him since I'd come back to life.

"No," he said, moving closer to me. "I meant what I said. It's yours to keep."

"Thank you," I said, then stared at my feet, for it was hard to accept such a gift. Before I could display more awkwardness, I slipped it back over my neck, the watch dangling against the neckline of the robe. I swung open the cover. The second hand was moving, ticking its way around the clock face.

All this time. All this time it had been frozen while I wore it in the death realm. And now it was working again, as though I'd never died at all. How many people could say the same? How many others could have this: a second chance?

I stole a look at Essien, surprised to find him staring. We both tore our gazes away simultaneously. Heat rose in my cheeks. Then, just for something to do, I slammed shut the watch and let it fall against my chest, where it hung—the metal cold and heavy against my skin. I could almost fancy I felt it vibrating, as if it too were alive.

Now that I was here again, back in the living realm, I realized how much I'd missed all this. Flesh and blood, my beating heart, the rushing feeling that poured through me whenever I was in Essien's presence. It was like a drug, heady and sweet, the tension in the air so thick I could almost taste it. My fingers tensed, wanting to reach for him, but I forced myself to remain still.

"Are you feeling better?" Essien asked gently.

Turning my thoughts inward, I checked each part of my body. "Yes," I said eventually.

"Do you want to talk about what happened?"

I shook my head. "Not yet."

There was a heavy pause, during which we did nothing but stare at one another. We were close enough that the heat of his body enveloped me—one more step and I'd be in his arms.

Being in the afterlife had made me yearn for this. The visceral warmth of a fellow human. Someone so vigorously *alive.* Sure, I'd had physical contact with ghosts down below. The fights, my grandmother's hugs, the intense kisses I'd shared with Lin . . . But the touch of a spirit in the death realm was something else. Cold, ghostly, intangible in an endless, immortal way.

It lacked a sort of vivacity, the very essence of life.

I stepped forward. Reached for the prince who had been my enemy, once upon a time.

Why did I do it? I wasn't entirely sure. But at the last minute, something cracked in me. Grief. Thinking about the death realm had dragged my anguish back up from the depths of my mind.

A strangled sob burst from my lips. And, without thinking, I threw myself into his arms and started crying. The first time I'd properly wept in months.

Essien drew me closer, his warmth and quiet strength surrounding me. I shook; he rested his cheek on my head. One of his hands went to my hair, his breath fluttering past my temple.

I wept for my grandmother—that I'd never see her again. I wept for Lin, for the lives—and deaths—we'd had, and lost. I wept for the bone-rending fatigue that weighed down my mind and body. I desperately needed to sleep but didn't know if I even could. My sojourn through the afterlife had gifted me a brand-new fear: a fear of dreams.

In the land of the dead, I hadn't slept. And in that time I'd seen some of the worst horrors imaginable to a mortal mind. What sort of nightmares would I encounter in my slumber? I shuddered, worried that if I was to close my eyes again, I might just slip into the death realm accidentally.

Hot tears streamed down my face, dampening Essien's expensively tailored shirt. If he cared, he was generous enough not to show it.

"Can I stay with you?" I whispered, burying my face against his shoulder. "I—I don't want to be alone."

With a soft swipe of his knuckle, Essien brushed a tear away. "Of course." He pressed his lips into my hair, just once, and my heart stuttered.

"Just for tonight." My voice sounded so small.

There was a brief pause. "Just tonight."

We climbed into bed. Abandoning all pretenses, I snuggled into him, my legs intertwined with his. He relaxed into me, too, winding one arm around my shoulders. I suddenly realized that the usual rush of his healing powers that I normally gleaned from his touch was this time oddly absent. Probably because I no longer need his healing. He'd healed me already—physically at least, if not psychologically. Inside my head I was still grappling with everything that I had witnessed. Everything that I had faced.

"Rest easy, Jia," he murmured. "You're alive. You're safe."

I burrowed closer, tightening my hold on him. In this moment, I had no idea how to feel about Essien Lancaster. He'd kept my body safe all this time. He'd healed all the injuries I'd sustained in the death realm. He was even gracious enough not to push for information about the Sword of Rechenblod before I was ready to share.

But what would tomorrow morning bring? Would the tentative alliance we'd formed come crashing down the moment he realized I hadn't brought him the sword?

I couldn't be sure. But what I did know was that, after my journey through the multiple layers of death, and the passion and chaos of Lin . . .

After dealing with grief that had cracked me apart the way that an axe splits wood . . .

Settling into this foreign prince's arms felt a lot like coming home.

Forty-Nine

Present day

I wasn't sure exactly how long I slept, but by the time my eyelids blinked open, pale, watery light was filtering through the window. It looked like we were on the cusp of dawn.

I was still tangled up with Essien, my head resting on his chest, which was rising and falling gently with each slow breath he took. He'd wrapped his arms around me so my body was pressed up against his.

As the haze of sleep dissipated, my pulse quickened. Had I really spent the entire night in Essien Lancaster's arms?

Tilting my head back, I scrutinized him; he was still asleep, his long lashes curled on his cheek, his forehead relaxed and perfectly smooth. He looked so peaceful, asleep like this. A pink flush had crept across his cheeks from his slumber. The cotton of his shirt was crinkled. It was a different shirt—he'd changed out of the tear-stained one he'd been wearing earlier. The whole scene was suffused with a sort of sweet serenity.

It surprised me, really. Not that he had left the bed at some point, necessarily . . . more that he'd come back.

For a while, I allowed myself to be cradled by the silence. As I watched him sleep, though, the reality of my situation hit me.

Before long, he'd wake, and I'd have to tell him what had happened.

I didn't want to, though. I didn't want to admit that *I* was the weapon that everyone had been seeking, nor the fact that I'd nearly erased my entire existence and reincarnated myself to save the world. Or that although I might have glimpsed the Shēngsǐ Sword—the Sword of Rechenblod—in the Abyss, I had not, as promised, brought it back. Perhaps I'd even have to explain that *had* I brought it back, I wouldn't have wanted to give it to him anyway, since I still didn't trust his family.

I wanted to avoid his disappointment, it was true. But equally, I was trying to dodge the stark reality: That Essien had probably only kept me around because he wanted the sword. His apparent kindness had stirred a sort of deep longing within me, a feeling I'd kept caged and buried within my heart. I had been lonely for so, so long. But I was scared that the moment I made it clear I didn't have what he'd been seeking, Essien would discard and abandon me like yesterday's trash.

And even if he didn't—even if by some miracle Essien actually still wished to be my friend—I would only bring him trouble. His family hated me. My family *loathed* him. And on top of all that, I was a girl marked by death, pursued by an army of ghosts. There was no place for me beside the golden prince.

My mood steadily soured as I contemplated all this. And it wasn't helped by the crushing grief that still weighed on my chest. So, when he murmured and stirred and shifted positions, I eased out of his arms. After retrieving Wen Bo's Bone Smith sword, which was still where I'd left it in the bathroom, I deliberated for a moment. Should I bring the pocket watch? It was the only relic of my time with Essien.

In the end, I did take it. I couldn't bear to leave it behind. And, after slinging it around my neck, I went to the bookshelf, pulled out the book that opened the secret passageway, and escaped.

For two things I was grateful: One, that the Lancasters had built a sally port leading directly out of the castle. And two, that when we were ensconced in Throft Hall's secret room, Essien had told me the way.

The sun had fully risen by the time I stumbled, blinking, into the Yskian forest. As I trudged through the thickets of trees, sweat gathering at my nape, I spent my time wondering if anything—or, truthfully, *everything*—was a reincarnated version of Pópo. Of Lin. Or of my sister, Dai Yu.

Every fledgling bird that tweeted. Every dragonfly that flittered past. Every snake that slithered away before disappearing into the undergrowth.

I was jumpy, startling whenever I saw sudden movement. Whenever I did see a creature, I'd stare at them, blinking back tears, straining fruitlessly for signs of recognition. Something, anything, that would suggest we were connected.

But I knew that reincarnation didn't work like that. There was no way for me to tell what they had become, whether human or beast, reptile or insect. And while some people believed that there was a hierarchy of creatures: People who were good in life would reincarnate into humans, while people who did evil would reincarnate into beasts. . . . I had never subscribed to such theories. Yes, I'd hunt for food when necessary—of course

I would. But to me, all animals were of equal value, and I refused to believe anything but.

Except for horses, of course, who were downright scary.

And as for my loved ones? The lake water would have erased their memories completely. I could encounter any of them at any point from now until forever, and we'd all be none the wiser.

It didn't stop me thinking about it, though. Would I ever reach a point when I didn't look at things and *wonder*?

Honestly? Probably not. I was experienced enough with death by now to know that grief has no expiry.

Apart from my sadness, the day was oddly tranquil. Incongruously so. Stippled light laced the ground. The soft drone of bees sounded all around. Sparrows hopped and twittered among the branches. The air hummed with the sweet scents of spring. Of life. But I could barely appreciate it. I kept my head down, picking at some berries I'd scavenged, lost in a cloud of grief.

I had barely cleared the Yskian border when a twig snapped.

Bandits? My heart started thumping. Immediately, I dropped the berries and drew my Bone Smith sword. Whirling around, my breaths turned to pants as I peered into a copse of trees.

"Who's there?" I called out, but my voice wavered.

There was a brief lull, as if the entire forest was holding its breath. Then I heard it. Distant crashing. Shouts. And the unmistakable rumble of hooves striking ground.

My scalp tightened; my insides froze to ice as, in a clamor of dust and noise, I was surrounded. They were humans: armed, and all on horses.

Trembling, I braced myself. What was this? Had the ghost soldiers managed to resurrect?

Quickly, I scanned their armor. No, these were not ghosts.

They were mortals. Each wore the Lancaster sigil, the tree from their coat of arms. My vision blurred. My heart pounded so hard I could feel it in my toes.

Had Essien betrayed me? I couldn't make sense of anything, couldn't comprehend what was happening—

Heavy bootsteps sounded behind me less than a second before I was grabbed. I shrieked as someone twisted my arms backward, breaking my grip on my sword. It fell to the forest floor with a soft thud.

I barely had time to register how thoroughly *fucked* I was before I was thrown to my knees, the tip of a blade pressed into the hollow beneath my chin. My blood went cold.

"So. *This* is the girl you'd betray your family for?" Rowan Lancaster held me in place as his gaze raked me up and down. He was looking at me, but speaking over his shoulder. "Surely, Essien, you could have chosen someone who looks less like a half-starved cat."

Essien? He was *here*?

I was pinned to the spot, but in my peripheral vision, I saw him being dragged into the circle. He was resisting but was outnumbered: Andres Brisson and two other soldiers were restraining him, Brisson's sword held at his throat.

I'd been on the verge of crying before; now I was really crying. Tears leaked from the corners of my eyes, streaming down my cheeks. *No*, I wanted to scream. *This wasn't supposed to happen!*

Me leaving was supposed to sever any remaining connection between me and Essien Lancaster. Not bring his family, and their army, against us.

I gritted my teeth, furious at myself for weeping but refusing to be cowed by Rowan's words. "Better to be half starved," I said, forcing my voice to remain steady, "than a colossal waste of space."

Rowan cocked his head, his lips curved into a grin. "She's gutsy, Essien. I'll give you that." He chuckled. "But that is no way for a lady to speak, is it now? And only a lady deserves to wear a Lancaster heirloom."

With a quick flick of his wrist, the tip of Rowan's sword hooked beneath Essien's pocket watch. He yanked. The chain cut into my neck, dragging me forward. At the last moment, it snapped.

The clock hit the ground, hard, the lid springing open. The jolting must have damaged some internal mechanism, because the second hand—which had been ticking constantly around the watch face—got stuck, bouncing in place as it tried, and failed, to keep moving.

Seeing it like that made my chest tighten. It brought back all the memories of my long descent into death and all the horrors I had witnessed. I forced myself to look away, instead raising my chin to glare at Rowan.

The Yskian heir tilted his head and squinted at me. "Much better, don't you think? Now our darling, useless mother won't need to wonder what became of her papa's watch." A slow smile spread on his lips. "Well, the time has come, Essien, my boy. Come here. You know what to do."

I tensed all over. A trickle of sweat ran down my forehead, mingling with my tears.

The soldiers hauled a struggling Essien forward, shoving him at me so hard that he stumbled. He only managed to right himself when his brother caught him.

In the harsh light of the afternoon sun I noticed, for the first time since I'd resurrected, how gaunt Essien looked. How much paler his skin had gotten during my months away. How dark the smudges were beneath his deep blue eyes. I hadn't noticed before because I hadn't been properly looking.

The elder Lancaster gripped Essien's shoulder and whispered in his ear. "Kill her. Kill her now. Show us that you're loyal to the Lancaster name."

Essien's whole body jerked in his brother's grip. "What? No."

My pulse kicked up even faster, my blood skittering through my veins.

"You heard me. Take my sword, and stab her." He smirked. "Listen, I'll even be kind. Once you've killed her, *I* will hack her to pieces afterward. I won't even make you do it."

Turning his mocking smile toward me, Rowan spat on the ground. "We'll see how well you resurrect, *witch*, when your corpse is burned and scattered in pieces across the valley."

Essien's expression hardened. "No. I won't do it."

My heart stuttered, then quickened, drumming erratically against my ribs. Would Essien truly defy his family—his brother—for *me*?

Rowan tilted his head to one side, his eyes narrowed. "What do you mean, you 'won't'? Are you not a Lancaster? Are you not an Yskian, defender against illicit magic? Dear brother—be serious. You've had your fun with her . . . now you can get rid of the evidence." He looked at me and sneered. "If you can do this act of loyalty, then we'll know you deserve to be called a Lancaster."

"I won't do it." A muscle flexed in Essien's jaw, and he jerked, trying to escape. But the three soldiers who had dragged him here earlier stepped forward to restrain him again.

The elder Lancaster forcibly curled his brother's fingers

around the handle of his sword, which was still, by the way, pointed at my neck.

I blinked, tears sheening in my vision. Watching Essien's face, I tried to read him. What was he thinking? Was he regretting having ever known me? Was he regretting having helped me? Was he regretting trying to rope me into his schemes now that things had ended up . . . like this?

"Do it," Rowan urged. "Do it, and I promise you. You'll be welcomed back to the capital. You'll be lauded as a *hero*. Hell, we'll even give you your own room back. What do you say, brother? Just like old times, eh?"

Something painful twisted deep inside me. I knew how much Essien wanted to make amends with his distant, estranged family. How hurt he'd been by their indifference. Now, even without the famed Sword of Rechenblod, his brother was offering everything Essien wanted—all in exchange for the life of a single lowborn girl.

Would he do it?

Essien dropped his deadened gaze to the sword handle, then raised his head to face me.

Our eyes locked. The moment seemed to stretch, unending.

Then, abruptly, Essien shoved his body backward. "NO!" he bellowed. He threw his brother off him, then sank into a defensive stance, Rowan's sword held before him.

Rowan stumbled a few steps but quickly regained his footing. The elder Lancaster snatched a sword off the ground, and—before anyone could react—pressed it against *Essien's* neck.

Wen Bo's sword. He was wielding *my* sword: the one the Bone Smith had made.

"I forgot to say, Little Brother," Rowan said, his lips twisting in a malicious grin. "This is *not* a request."

I almost whimpered. Rowan sounded so similar to General Hong when he'd threatened me in the death realm dungeon that immediately my body seized with fear.

Essien didn't move, or speak. He didn't acknowledge his brother. Instead, his eyes stayed fixed on mine. He stared at me, chest heaving, strands of damp hair stuck to his forehead. And I stared back, unable to look away.

"Kill her now," Rowan snarled at Essien. "If you don't, then *you* will be the first to die. And after that"—he jerked his chin at me—"I shall kill her anyway."

The forest went still. Everything around us was abnormally quiet. Everything except my pulse, thunderous in my ears.

"Please, Rowan," Essien finally choked out. Tears glinted in the inner corners of his eyes. "Kill me, if you wish. But not her. Not her." He blinked, and a single tear spilled over, flashing silver down his face.

And the way he looked at me, the tenderness that ached in those few uttered words, made me realize:

Yes, he cared about the sword. Wanted it so badly he could probably taste it. But . . .

But.

Somehow, for some unknown reason . . . he also cared about *me.*

And then it hit me. An idea. I strained my mind toward him, attempting to communicate without words. Would he understand what I was trying to say?

I couldn't be certain. He wasn't Lin, the boy who'd known me so well he could read my countenance as easily as perusing a book.

So I took the risk, murmuring beneath my breath, so that only Essien could hear.

"Do it," I whispered. "Trust me." If Essien killed me, he would convince his brother of his loyalty, and therefore save his own neck. Meanwhile, I could resurrect . . .

A burning sensation began to flow from my core. Magic was gathering in my body, limning every muscle, every vessel, every organ encased in flesh. It hollowed out my insides, making me feel weightless. It tingled at the ends of my fingers; it shot across my skin like sparks. Like pain.

Like power.

Understanding dawned in Essien's eyes.

In one swift movement, he plunged Rowan's sword into my chest. And as he stabbed me, more of his tears spilled over.

"Jia—" he started, but he never got to finish. His sentence was choked off, because at the exact same time, Rowan impaled Essien, driving in my sword to the hilt.

I screamed. Rowan had never intended to let his brother go. Even with my sacrifice, he'd always planned to slaughter us both.

I screamed, torment cleaving my chest.

I screamed, and screamed, and screamed some more, until . . .

Finally, my power exploded.

The three of us—Essien, Rowan, and myself, were thrown backward, flung by the force of my magic. It pulsed outward, making the ground tremor, an earthquake of massive proportions.

And, as I landed painfully on my back, my vision went black. My ears rang, deafening me.

Until all I could hear were the distant echoes of Essien's unsaid words.

Fifty

Present day

As soon as I recovered consciousness, I climbed unsteadily to my feet. Pain lanced through my chest. Reflexively, I clutched at it, and when I removed my hand, it was sticky with congealed blood.

I clenched my jaw, forcing myself to focus. Essien . . . I needed Essien. With blurry vision, I squinted through the smoky shadows. Around me, the ground was a crater, all the trees in the immediate vicinity flattened.

But not just flattened. The trees . . . were *dead.*

By my estimations, it was sometime around Yǔshuǐ, the season of Rain Water, and the trees had begun to blossom, green leaves uncurling. But now? Now they were withered, the branches completely bare, the trunks brittle, gnarled, and whitened. Like they'd been exposed to the elements and bleached by the merciless sun.

Littered around the tree bases were the corpses of dead birds. And not just birds. Spiders too, with their legs curled up.

Beetles, dead, their carapaces iridescent. A tree snake hung, limp, over a branch.

Human corpses were strewn around, pale and still, their eyes flat, fixed, unmoving. The Lancaster soldiers who had ambushed me.

I turned a slow circle, terror pooling in my stomach. Everywhere I looked, there were no signs of life.

Everywhere I looked, there was only death.

I understood now: When Pópo had given me back my magic, down in the last layer of death, she'd also bestowed *her* gift upon me. The ability to steal other powers.

Truth be told, I'd realized almost immediately. In that moment, I knew how it felt to have complete mastery over magic. It had thrummed through my ghostly veins until I was giddy with it—this potent ability to steal *anybody's* power.

And just before I'd erupted painfully back into life, Pópo's power had desperately, indiscriminately sucked the magic from everything else in the cave. Incapable yet of controlling it, I'd absorbed not only Pópo's magic but also Dai Yu's magic. The Spyrre's magic. And lastly . . . that of the Abyss, and the death contained within.

Yes, I had regained my power: the power to come back to life.

But I'd also been gifted the power of death.

I stumbled forward a few paces, doubling over and retching. My gut was empty, but still I gagged until the compulsion stopped. Was that what the shaman had meant? About me, the weapon, having the power to wreak havoc on the living?

Raising my head, I scanned the clearing. Was it my

imagination, or were some of the bodies still twitching? I tried to make sense of it. If they *were* moving, was it because they were still alive? Did my death power—newly acquired, diluted, and undirected as it was—fail to kill absolutely everyone in its path?

Or did they still seem alive because we were all . . . actually dead?

No—it couldn't be, because where then were the ghosts? I didn't have time to puzzle it out. My priority was finding Essien. Rowan had slaughtered him, had slit his belly like a sacrificial pig. And I had no idea if Essien had the ability to heal himself as seamlessly as he healed others.

I was so disoriented, so injured, that I could barely maintain my balance. But I ignored my pain, wading through the piles of corpses and still-jerking bodies. Frantically, I scrutinized each face . . . until I spotted him.

Essien was at the opposite end of the clearing, lying slumped near the base of a tree.

Both of his hands were clutching his abdomen, pressing on the wound. He was trying to stanch his blood, which had stained his navy doublet even darker. Rowan Lancaster lay crumpled beside him, his skin gray, his eyes glassy. Dead.

At the sight of Essien, anguish tore through me, hewing my heart in two. It felled me. I collapsed to my hands and knees, crawling to him, inch by torturous inch. Death was everywhere—on the ground beneath me, in the corpses all around, even in the iron tang of blood that lingered in the air—yet still I crawled. Pain stabbed through my rib cage with every move I made, and the whole time my chest wound dripped.

By the time I reached the Yskian prince, I could barely talk for the agony, and he had lost an alarming amount of blood. It had seeped into the ground below, darkening the dirt.

His eyes found mine. Pleading. Desperate. He was trying to heal himself, to undo the damage his brother had inflicted, but he couldn't. He couldn't heal himself—not quickly enough. He could only heal others.

Essien had cured me, so many times, without hesitation. I'd always thought it was just because he wanted me well enough to get the sword. But now I was wondering whether he would have done it anyway. Would he have done it to be good, and loyal, and honorable? And because it was the right thing to do?

After all, when I'd returned last night, after months in the death realm, he had been nothing but kind. He'd let me grieve, and wash, and rest; he'd held me all night to stave off any nightmares. And he hadn't even asked me about the sword—not once.

As I dragged myself closer to him, my mind cast back to the question I'd asked right before he'd helped me reenter the death realm to find my grandmother. I'd asked him why he'd done it. Why he'd healed me.

And he had said: *It is the right thing to do, is it not? If I were dying, and you had this power, wouldn't you save me?*

My eyelids prickled, and I blinked several times. Now, in retrospect, I understood: That was the first time I'd looked at Essien Lancaster and seen him for who he truly was.

Yes, I wanted to tell him, though he was surely suffering too much to hear. *I would.*

He couldn't heal himself, no.

But I could.

Our eyes met. Mine, full of grief; his, frantic, the whites all showing. Gathering all my courage, I placed my palms on his chest and began to draw out his power, like a leech sucking blood from a wound. It was difficult at first, but as I eased into my newfound ability, it began to flow more readily. And as his magic streamed into me, I started to feel the pain he felt, just as keenly as if it were my own.

It was . . . excruciating.

I sucked in a breath, trying to stem the agony. And my heart twisted at the realization that every time Essien had cured my injuries, *he had felt them, too.*

His magic started to whisper, deep in the hollows of my mind. Telling me everything that was wrong with his body. The bruises. The lacerations. The slash wound in his gut. I felt all of it as I shook with effort, my muscles tense and rigid.

Fortunately, his injuries had missed his major arteries. Without intervention, though, the blood loss would soon have been too great. Essien's life force—his qì—was slipping through my fingers as I watched.

Shuddering to suppress the agony, I moved his hands away from his abdomen, replacing them with my own. Then, I gathered his power. Held it close. Felt it rushing right through me, surging through my hands until it concentrated in my palms. It was warm, that same warmth that I'd come to associate with Essien's touch.

Then, once I'd fully harnessed his power, I started to give him back his qì, allowing it to wash over his skin, across his stomach, across the gaping red gash in his flesh.

I had to grit my teeth to do it. My hands quivered; my body trembled; sweat sprang across my brow.

Immediately, he stilled. Slackened beneath my hands, into the comfort of my contact. His tension unwound, his brow relaxed, and his back arched as I shouldered the weight of his pain. I held his gaze and he held mine as his magic flowed between us, his wounds knitting back together.

Finally, the sensations receded, fading to a dull ache, and then disappeared altogether.

And once it was finished, and Essien was whole again, I gave him back his power, before taking one of his hands and placing it on my chest. On my own injury, which Essien himself had inflicted. I knew he'd stabbed me to get me away from his brother, assuming that I would resurrect. He hadn't known about my newfound mastery over death.

Until I'd had to use it, I hadn't known the full extent of it, either.

I covered both of Essien's hands with my own, not wanting to let go. The warmth that was returning to his digits radiated from him, seeping into my skin.

We stayed like this, holding each other, being together. Locked in an embrace to heal from our wounds. To heal from our pain.

But most of all—so we could heal each other from this cruel and traitorous world.

Fifty-One

Present day

I didn't regret giving Essien's power back to him. It was rightfully his, and besides, I didn't want the burden. The overwhelming amount of magic I'd inherited—from Pópo, from Dai Yu, from the Abyss—was already threatening to burst through my skin, to spontaneously ignite me until I was nothing more than charred fragments.

Tentatively, Essien and I climbed to our feet. Neither of us spoke—not at first. Night had fallen. Stars were blinking into existence overhead, one by one, and the pocket watch, half buried, glinted dully in the dirt.

And the corpses. Corpses *everywhere.* I felt . . . numb. And hollow.

Ignoring my queasiness, I turned and stumbled out of the clearing and into a thicket, until the dense trees had closed behind me. Bracing one hand against a tree trunk, I pressed my other hand to my chest, trying not to throw up.

"Jia." I felt the weight of Essien's stare behind me. When

I finally raised my head and looked over my shoulder, he was watching me.

"I—I'm sorry," I said. "For everything."

"Whatever do you mean?" He drew closer, his voice so soft, so gentle, that I almost started weeping.

I turned to face him fully then. "You've done so much for me. You've more than held up your end of the bargain. But I didn't hold up mine. I . . . never brought back the sword." Wrapping my arms around my abdomen, I shook my head. "I'd understand if you never wanted to see me again."

He frowned. "Why in the world would I think that?"

"Because . . . you wanted that stupid sword. So badly." I choked back a sob and, in a faltering voice, whispered, "To—to win your family's favor."

Everything was starting to hit me now: The realization of what we'd been through. Of what I'd lost. Of what Essien had lost.

Of how close we'd come to losing one another.

And I began to shake.

A shadow flitted across Essien's face, darkening his features. And then he was striding toward me, pulling me into a tight embrace.

"Jia," he murmured. He held me, my cheek against his shoulder. He smelled like blood, and salt, and something that was comfortingly familiar. Something indescribable, something that was purely him. "Never mind the sword. It's not important. What's important is that you are safe. When I woke this morning and you weren't there, I—" He cut himself off abruptly, and simply squeezed me tighter.

His words made me shiver, sending a low thrill right through me. I clung to him. Everything inside me felt cavernous. My power—it hadn't just destroyed life around me. It had ruined me on the inside, too, as though my chest had been cracked open and all my vital organs dug out.

Essien held me until my shaking settled, stroking my hair from my face. "It's all right," he murmured as he did so. "You're all right."

"Thank you," I said thickly, after we'd stayed like that for a while. "For saving my life."

"Thank you for saving mine."

"I never knew it hurt you—" I stopped short. I'd felt every pang of pain when I'd healed him of his wounds. And in the past, when he had healed me, I'd never stopped to think that perhaps . . . perhaps it hurt him, too.

He pulled back to look at me. "The pain is nothing if it means saving you."

Our eyes met. The rising moonlight edged the outline of his shadow, reflecting off his hair with a liquid glow.

And suddenly, in that loaded moment, I realized that I'd had enough. Enough of pushing away my feelings, of gravitating to what was safe. In some ways, Lin had been safe, volatile as he was. We knew each other so well, could predict each other's thoughts and movements. Being with him was never a challenge.

Not like this: This was new, and different. It was . . . terrifying. But facing death—accepting it, defeating it, even wielding it—has a way of making one brave, because it means abandoning fear. And besides, my grief was spent; I had nothing left to lose.

So I decided I needed to grab this—this *life*—with both hands.

I reached up and, with the tips of my fingers, brushed a strand of hair back from Essien's face. He stilled, his eyelids sliding shut momentarily. In that quiet, quivering second, when the space between us seemed infinitesimal yet also indefinably large, I paused.

A leap into the great unknown.

Sliding my hand around the back of his head, I pulled him in and brought his mouth to mine.

He was shocked, at first, I think. His lips were gentle to begin with; warm and soft. So warm, compared with Lin's cold, ghostly kisses in the afterlife. Essien tensed up further, his hands hovering inches above my skin, still unwilling to act ungentlemanly, or to cross the careful boundaries we'd set.

But then he gave a low groan and brought his hands up to my face. He backed me up against the tree, kissing me the whole time.

His kisses were soft. Slow. Deliberate. Like the touch of the first snowflake upon the frost-laced grass. His hands cradled my face like it was something precious, like it was a treasure that he'd lost, and now found.

And even as his lips dropped to my neck, even as he feathered kisses along my jaw, he whispered my name. Tenderly, almost reverently. "Jia," he breathed between kisses. "You are so, *so* beautiful."

I felt dizzy but somehow managed to say, "Never thought you'd say that to a Liu."

He gave a low laugh that thrummed through my chest. "Do you have any idea how long I've *wanted* to say it?"

My eyebrows shot up. "What do you mean?"

"I . . ." He swallowed, pausing to run his fingers idly down my cheek. "I've wanted you for a long time, you know. Even before the first time I healed you."

I stared at him. "But you *hated* me."

He shook his head. "I was supposed to hate you. I *tried* to. But . . . I could not."

I didn't respond—this revelation had rendered me speechless.

"I cannot tell you how much it pained me," he continued, looking so wretched that I thought my heart might break. "To see you dragged into the throne room time and time again, fighting like a trapped bird, just radiating . . . utter hatred for me."

He grimaced as he went on. "And . . . I couldn't do anything. Couldn't say anything." His hands slid down my shoulders until he was gripping my upper arms. "Well, I can say it now: I have wanted you for so long, Jia. So very long."

I was speechless. What could I say that would suffice? *I used to hate you, but you turned out to be less of a bastard than I'd thought, so I don't hate you anymore?*

No. I couldn't. Instead, I placed my hand on his chest and said the only thing I could say with sincerity. "Must you go back? To Throft Hall?"

Essien fixed his gaze on me. His face was cast in shadow, the dim light making his eyes glint silver. "It depends. Do you want me to go back?" His words were careful, measured.

"I . . ." I lowered my head, looking at the ground. "I killed your brother."

"He would have killed you."

I couldn't meet his eyes. "Your family *hates* me."

"That doesn't matter. Jia, listen. Look at me." He touched my chin with the tips of his fingers, tilting it up until my gaze found his. In his expression was a depth, an energy, I had never seen before. "I care for you. A lot. I would dearly love to give us a chance. But if you don't want me like I want you, then you must say so—"

"It's not that," I interrupted. "I care for you, too. It's just . . . surprising to hear you say it."

Neither of us said what we both were thinking: that none of this was simple. Us, being together. We were from opposite sides of the border—Fengzhi Yuan and Yske. But we might as well have been from two different worlds. Not just because he was a royal and I a commoner. But also because I was a girl who harnessed the power of Death. And he was a healer, who gifted life.

Regardless, he brought my face closer to his, then paused. It was as though he was asking my permission. A question, without words, that would change the trajectory of our futures.

I trembled in his arms, gripped by indecision. Was this the right thing to do? Not for me, necessarily—but for him. The stakes felt so high.

But then, I made a decision. I answered.

Our lips crashed together. And this time, it wasn't tentative. This time, it was all passion, agitation, an overflow of pent-up emotion. He pulled me closer, clasping me with something that almost felt like desperation. And I kissed him back. All my grief, all my hope, all my desire surged inside me, concentrating to a point, channeling into this single kiss.

The press of our bodies, his hands on my hips, the feeling of his lips against mine . . . It was so solid, so grounding, so . . .

real. In Essien's arms, I felt a different kind of healing, stronger than ever before, like he was no longer just fixing me from the outside, but from the inside, too.

I knew part of it was his power. I felt his magic, probing, penetrating, burrowing beneath my skin. But the other part of it was this undeniable fact: I was starting to fall, against my every instinct, for a *Lancaster.* Ugh.

Was it even possible? A Liu and a Lancaster, together?

I twined my fingers into his golden hair, deepening the kiss, trying to dispel the questions that floated in my mind. All we had was here. Now. A few sheltered moments, a desperate embrace, a hànfú that still bore the stains of my lowborn blood.

Blood that was suspiciously—

I pulled away, abruptly breaking contact, and looked down. Essien's grip tightened on my waist, but otherwise he made no protest.

Frowning at the bodice of my gown, my mind raced. I hadn't noticed before, but in the dimness the blood looked suspiciously . . . black.

Maybe it was just the light?

"Essien . . ." I whispered. My voice was tiny. The prince arched a quizzical brow at me.

Untangling myself from Essien's arms, I strode back to the clearing, where the pocket watch still lay broken in the dirt. From this angle, I could see it was bathed in moonlight, which glimmered off its golden casing.

Something lurched inside me, and I was gripped by a sudden urge to go to it. To pick it up. I itched to feel the weight of it in my hand, to once again slip its long chain around my neck.

I wanted—no, *needed*—to hear the ticking that would tell me I was here, I was real, that I was still alive.

"Just . . . give me a second," I said to Essien, who had followed me. My legs shook as I edged closer to where the watch lay, half covered by debris. Then I sank to a squat, staring down at it, trying to tame the storm of emotions warring within my body.

It was exactly as we had left it: its lid flayed open, its hands frozen and still. But then again—hadn't it broken when Rowan Lancaster had ripped it from me? Perhaps it was just broken now.

I scrunched my eyes shut, my mind churning, and cast my thoughts back to that moment: the moment my power had exploded.

My magic had killed everything in the immediate vicinity. That much, at least, was obvious. But had it also killed *us*? Were we now in the first level? Perhaps everything around us was so quiet because . . . the two of us were actually dead.

We'd both sustained near-fatal wounds. It was only through Essien's magic, temporarily co-opted by me, that we were able to heal ourselves. But what if we'd sustained those injuries not in the living realm as I'd assumed, but as we were crossing between life and death? Me, in the liminal space between two worlds, stabbed with Essien's sword. And him, dead by the Bone Smith's blade.

On the other hand, perhaps Essien and I had been spared from my death magic because we were at the center. What if, like standing at the eye of a storm, it had somehow not touched *us*?

Slowly, I opened my eyes. Fixed them back on the watch.

Should I try to pick it up? Was it worth it?

Was it worth finding out if we were dead or alive?

Essien had come up beside me. He caught sight of my face, concern flashing across his features. "Jia? What's the matter?"

I didn't answer. Chewing my lip, I thought hard.

We'd find out soon enough, of course. It was inevitable. It was only so long before we'd discover what we could or couldn't touch. Before we'd figure out if we could pass through walls. And if I turned my attention inward, instead of avoiding thinking too hard about it, I'd be able to tell if my heart was beating.

But did we need to know *tonight*?

I only vaguely registered Essien kneeling down beside me. "Essien . . ." I began, turning to face him.

Reaching out, he fingered a loose lock of my hair, then, with exceeding tenderness, tucked it behind my ear. "I know what you're thinking," he murmured, his touch lingering at my neck. "But either way, it's all right."

Distraught, I stood, pacing away several steps. Then I spun to face the prince, who by now had risen to his feet, too. "*How* can it be all right?" I threw my hands up, then let them fall. "What if we're dead, Essien? I don't even care about me. But what if you—" My words choked off. Scrunching my eyes shut, I clenched my hands, trying not to fall to pieces.

After steadying myself, I resumed. "Don't you want to *live*?"

"I want to live, Jia. Of course I do. But I also want something to live *for*." Essien stepped closer, taking both of my hands in his. Gently, his thumbs stroked my knuckles until finally my fists uncurled.

Then he laced his fingers through mine. "I would rather be in the afterlife with you than face the living realm alone."

Gently, he drew me closer. "No matter what the future holds, Jia Yi, we will face it. Together. Have faith—all will be well."

Bowing my head, I stared at our intertwined hands. My entire body ached. Everything felt so raw, broken, as if I'd been shattered into a million pieces. But in a way, it also felt like Essien was gathering me up and learning how to put me back together.

I lifted my eyes to meet his. "Do you . . . really think that?"

"I do." He gave a wistful smile, his dimples shadowing his cheeks. "And I'm not naive. I know that either way, things won't be easy. That there will be difficulties I can only begin to fathom. But let us not worry about that. Not now. Let us have this one night, together."

A small sob escaped my lips. "Just one night?"

His fingertips ghosted—so lightly—along the curve of my cheek. His voice dropped low. "Just tonight."

Chewing my lip, I paced back to the watch. I stared at it, my mind churning.

Essien was good. He was a *hero*. Whether dead or alive, he deserved to have one night of unspoiled ignorance, no matter how temporary.

What is dead can die again.

But what is dead can live *again.*

Tonight was one night. Just one night. I could give him that, at least.

And tomorrow? Tomorrow was the start of forever.

I could live with forever.

"All right," I said, squaring my shoulders. "Just tonight."

Tearing my gaze from the watch, I turned back to Essien Lancaster . . . and to his waiting arms.

Acknowledgments

When I set out to write a story that comped to *Inception* and *Wuthering Heights,* I had no idea the book was going to break me (in the best way possible). I've been chipping away at it since 2021, and it's been more difficult than anything I've ever written. It wasn't just the sheer logistical challenge of tackling multiple different death realms, or the technical aspects of writing interior emotions for ghosts who don't have beating hearts and cannot breathe, sweat, or cry . . . It was also the emotional work of writing a book about grief—and about losing one's grandmother—only a few years after losing my own.

I say all this to preface just how many people helped me bring this book to life.

First, I'd like to thank the Traditional Owners of the unceded land on which I live and work, the Wurundjeri people of the Kulin nation, and pay tribute to Elders past, present, and emerging.

I would also like to thank my first literary agent, Tricia Lawrence, and everyone at Erin Murphy Literary Agency. It has truly been a wild few years, and I am glad to have had you in my corner as I embarked on my author career. Thank you also to my current agent, Lauren Spieller, for your ongoing and unwavering support.

Humongous and unending gratitude to my editor, Lydia Gregovic, who is unfailingly patient, empathic, and insightful. I feel as though you slogged it out in this book's trenches for almost as long as I did. I am forever grateful for the work you've done in helping me to make it shine.

To everyone else at Delacorte Press: Casey Moses and Iris Lei, who created the most stunning, on-brand cover for this book; Michelle Canoni for the beautiful interiors; Virginia Allyn for the stunning map; Colleen Fellingham and the copyediting department; the entirety of the RHCB publicity, marketing, and sales teams; and Wendy Loggia, Judith Haut, Gillian Levinson, and Barbara Marcus. Also, to authenticity reader Zhui Ning Chang, for their thoughtful and considered feedback on the text.

And to my team at Penguin Australia, both past and present: Zoe Walton, Lisa Riley, Jessica De Caria, Rebecca Diep, Alexa Stevens, Georgie Martin, and others! Thank you for all your support during the launch of my debut novel—I am so thrilled to work with you again.

Thank you to my beta readers, Kate Murray, Al Hess, Frances White, and Tzeyi Koay. Some of you read early versions of this book and some of you read late ones, but all of you had incredible feedback that helped me find my way when I was lost in the proverbial wilderness. I know you're all super busy with your own projects, so I am truly, truly grateful.

There are so many other writer friends I am thankful for:

the Vestry, the Mouse Jigglers (don't even ask, lol), the Submission Slog discord, the Aussie "not just YA writers" group, the APIary, as well as the multiple other online writing groups I frequent. I'm also extremely grateful to *The Girl with No Reflection*'s wonderful street team—thank you so much for your support!

I'm a cat person through and through, so I will always acknowledge my cats for their ability to cheer me up and keep my lap warm when I am writing. Sadly, I started writing this book with two cats and ended it with only one. My older cat passed away the week I was at a writing retreat attempting to write this book. I am thankful that I snuck him into the house with me (if you're one of the retreat organizers, then . . . er . . . no I didn't) so we were able to spend that final week together. Losing a loved one when you're writing a book about death and grief just hits different. RIP, Achtung; you were the most dapper cat I ever met, and I can tell you now that you've been immortalized as the inspiration for a character in my next book.

To my family, as always, especially my children, Ada and Callan. Without you, this book probably would have been finished sooner, but life would be a lot less fun. And to my husband, Lachie, for all the times when you made me cups of tea, brought me food, made me laugh, took the kids on day trips so I could meet my deadlines, and supported me in a million other ways . . . Thank you. Thank you. I love you—in this life and beyond.

And of course, to you, the reader. Just as there is no life without death, and no death without life . . . there are no writers without readers, and no readers without writers. Thank you for trusting me and letting me take you on this journey.

About the Author

Keshe Chow is a multi-award-winning Chinese Australian author of fantasy, romance, and speculative fiction. Born in Malaysia, Keshe moved to Australia when she was two years old. She lives in Naarm (Melbourne) with her partner, two kids, one cat, and way too many houseplants.

keshechow.com

About the Author

Keshe Chow is a multi-award-winning Chinese Australian author of fantasy, romance, and speculative fiction. Born in Malaysia, Keshe moved to Australia when she was two years old. She lives in Naarm (Melbourne) with her partner, two kids, one cat, and way too many houseplants.

keshechow.com